By Elle E. Ire

Vicious Circle

NEARLY DEPARTED
Dead Woman's Pond

STORM FRONTS
Threadbare
Patchwork
Woven

Published by DSP Publications
www.dsppublications.com

DEAD WOMAN'S POND

ELLE E. IRE

DSP PUBLICATIONS

Published by
DSP PUBLICATIONS

5032 Capital Circle SW, Suite 2, PMB# 279, Tallahassee, FL 32305-
7886 USA
www.dsppublications.com

Dead Woman's Pond
© 2021 Elle E. Ire

Cover Art
© 2021 Tiferet Design
http://www.tiferetdesign.com
Cover content is for illustrative purposes only and any person depicted
on the cover is a model.

Mass Market Paperback ISBN: 978-1-64108-259-4
Trade Paperback ISBN: 978-1-64405-977-7
Digital ISBN: 978-1-64405-976-0
Mass Market Paperback published May 2022
v. 1.0

Printed in the United States of America
∞
This paper meets the requirements of
ANSI/NISO Z39.48-1992 (Permanence of Paper).

To J.A. (John) Pitts (1965-2019) author of the Sarah
Beauhall series:
I cannot adequately express my gratitude for your
encouragement, support, guidance, and the wonderful
characters you shared with your readers. Though we
never got a chance to meet in person, I considered you
a friend. You are deeply missed. I hope you've found
your place in Valhalla.

Acknowledgments

FIRST ALWAYS in my heart and my thanks comes my spouse who is forever my best support, most honest critic, and biggest fan. I absolutely could not have done this without you. And thank you for your suggestion of the series name. Nearly Departed is a much better one than what we originally had.

Next, thanks to my amazing agent, Naomi Davis, ready with her own special combination of cheerleading and advice, market knowledge and management.

Much gratitude to my incredible team of editors: Gus Li, Yv, and Brian. Your eye for detail (and catching my comma and hyphen mistakes) is much appreciated. All remaining errors are my own.

Thank you to everyone else at DSP who has played a role in the creation of this series: Elizabeth North for continuing to support my ideas, Ginnifer Eastwick for your first read thoughts and blurb and series title contributions, Naomi Grant for your promotional knowledge, my cover artist, Anna Sikorska, for the incredible art, and everyone else working behind the scenes to make this happen.

Thank you to my previous writing group: Jan, Mark, Jennye, Amy, Ann, Evergreen, Gary, and Joe for your feedback and encouragement. Some of you critiqued this; some of you offered support while I was working through the sequels. Regardless of what role you played, it is all appreciated. Also thanks to Marlana and Vivi for beta reading bits, pieces, and full drafts of one or more manuscripts in this series. If I've forgotten anyone else, I offer my sincerest apologies. This one has been a long time in the making.

And finally, a huge thank you to my readers, in particular those who have contacted me via Twitter or Facebook to offer insights and praise. Arielle, I hope you enjoy the character I named after you. I'm so glad you entered my contest!

Forward

WRITING A novel set in the real world is a little different from writing my earlier works of science fiction. Dead (Wo)man's Pond and Festivity, Florida, are fictitious names for real places, as well as the In the Dough pizza place, the Pampered Pup festival, the Village Pub, and more. I've taken some liberties with the details, but the generalities are the same.

It's a bit surreal, writing about actual places and events. I live in "Festivity." And the deeper into this manuscript I got, the more the characters felt like human beings I might encounter on the street or at work or while having dinner at one of the many restaurants. Since my spouse and daughters had read the early drafts, they all got into the act. We'd drive past Dead Man's Pond and joke about how we felt drawn toward the lake or how we wanted to hit the gas pedal instead of the brake. One of us might point toward the barstool Flynn prefers and ask when we thought she'd show up. I even got in the habit of glancing up toward Genesis's apartment window and wishing her and Flynn a quiet "good morning" while grabbing my coffee at the Starbucks across the street from "their" place above the Village Pub.

Sadly, the events surrounding Dead Man's Pond are also based on true events, though the local chamber of commerce might not care for it when the lake is referred to as such. The story Flynn hears from Genesis is fairly accurate. Tourists went missing. Tire tracks were eventually spotted. Multiple cars (and bodies) were found. People *still* keep ending up in the lake. I hope those who did not make it out have found peace.

As to whether or not the pond is really cursed, well, I guess that's up to you to decide.

DEAD WOMAN'S POND

ELLE E. IRE

Chapter 1
Expect the Unexpected

FEMALE BOWLERS HAVE BALLS.

I smooth down the peeling sticker on my bag and set the double-sized bowling ball carrier on the floor beside one of the bar's lower tables. I plop myself on the metal chair with the torn vinyl seat and tug off first one mud-encrusted work boot, then the other. The neon signs on the walls flicker through the haze of cigarette smoke, making my eyes water. Spilled beer puddles on the table's surface.

Reaching to the side, I bang the heels of the boots against the inner rim of the garbage can, knocking off the day's dried muck. Could've just used the black-and-gray-checkered linoleum floor, but the waitress and the bartender are friends of mine. No need to make more work for them.

Out of my bag I pull bowling shoes, a used pair bought from this very alley the year they upgraded to new ones. Hey, when you find a set that fits, you hang on to them. They slide onto my feet like my most comfortable bedroom slippers—if I owned bedroom slippers.

"How about a beer, Flynn? We've got a couple of new microbrews on tap."

I glance up from tying the laces, pulling my dirty-blonde ponytail out of my face and throwing it over my shoulder to hang halfway down my back. Allie stands beside the table, order pad in one hand and pen in the other. Not like she needs either one, but she says they're her version of a security blanket. My eyes trail up her long, shapely legs in the way-too-short miniskirt the manager makes her wear. A white button-down blouse hangs open almost to her belly button, where she has the tails tied in a knot.

Strictly look but don't touch. Steve, the bartender, is her boyfriend, and they make a great couple.

"Hey, Allie," I return. She prefers Allison, but everyone calls her Allie because, hey, she works in a bowling alley, and she's certainly never heard that one before. She gave up fighting it long ago. My thoughts shift to the handful of change and a few crumpled singles in my pocket—enough money for the lunch truck at the construction site tomorrow and one game. "Um, gonna have to pass on the beer. I'd love some water, if you don't mind me hogging up a table." I gesture toward the bar's exit opening out to the lanes.

Allie pops her gum. The faint scent of peppermint carries across the space between us. She makes a show of scanning the bar. Two old guys on stools at the counter. Four ladies in matching team shirts around a table on the far side, a half-dozen empty Bud Lites between them. Dave and Charlie, a couple of guys in their forties, guys I've seen before and occasionally bowled against, take up two other seats, doing exactly what I'm doing: putting on shoes, strapping on wrist support bands, wiping their sweaty fingers with rosin bags out of habit rather than current need, or applying New-Skin to old cuts and scrapes.

Lots of empty tables.

I pull out my own New-Skin bottle, almost empty, and open it. The pungent antiseptic odor rocks me back in my seat until a hand wave clears the air. A couple of dabs seal over a cut on my thumb I got when my saw slipped this morning.

"Oh yeah, I'm really swamped," Allie says. "Don't know how I'll manage all the orders." She holds out her empty notepad for me to see, then flips the chair opposite me around and straddles it, her twirly miniskirt draping to either side and barely covering the tops of her thighs. I swallow and focus on tightening my wrist support band. She leans her arms across the seat back. "Tapped out again?"

I work up a lopsided grin for her. "It'll be okay. New job—that apartment complex going up in Festivity. Steady work for over a month now, but I'm still living paycheck to paycheck. We went a long time before the company got this contract, none of the others were hiring temps, and I don't get paid again until day after tomorrow." I glance around at the pitiful prospects Kissimmee Lanes has to offer tonight. "That's why I'm here, actually." When I'd much, much rather be in a hot shower. I worked the site all day in Florida's famous ninety-plus heat and stayed three extra hours off the clock to help my foreman and friend, Tom, with the paperwork. Every muscle in my body aches, and my head hurts from dehydration.

Allie follows my thoughts. "Doesn't look good. Everyone here knows you, even if you've been avoiding us lately."

I pout at her.

She tucks the pen behind her ear and reaches across to pat my shoulder. I suppress a wince. Took a loose board to that shoulder this afternoon, and the bruise will be a beaut. "I know you aren't really hiding from us," she says. "Believe me, I understand 'broke.' Maybe you'll get lucky. We've had some newbies over the past few weeks." Allie pulls the bar rag from her waistband and wipes down the table, then stands. "Hang in there. I'll grab you some water." She flounces off, her skirt flipping up a little when she turns, revealing black boy-shorts underneath.

Oh yeah, I'll look plenty.

In the lanes area, it's all family friendly. If Allie goes out there to take orders, she buttons a few more shirt buttons and is careful not to bend over. In the bar, it's all about the guys and the tips.

"You hoping to pick up a game?"

The shadow that falls across my table is wide, the voice a rich baritone, but the grin on the sunburned, freckled face seems genuine enough. I gesture at the chair Allie abandoned. "Maybe. What's the bet?"

He's a little older, this big hulk of a man who takes a cautious seat as if he's worried it might collapse beneath him. Given the way the metal squeaks in protest, it just might. Late twenties, shaggy brown hair, all muscle, no fat on his body. His biceps strain the fabric of the white cotton T-shirt he wears. He drops a double-ball bag beside him; the equipment rattles inside, and the polyurethane balls clonk against each other with a familiar resonance.

Lots of strength in his arms. Two bowling balls. Personal gear. He takes the game seriously. Invests money in it. Doesn't mean he averages high, but....

My mind screams *bad bet*, but I need the cash. My truck's gas gauge arrow teeters on empty. Can't collect a paycheck if I can't drive to work the next two days. I'm lucky today happens to be Wednesday—the night Kissimmee Lanes hosts unofficial pickup games and bets quietly change hands to the winners.

If my girlfriend, Genesis, were here, she could ask the spirit world about the guy's skills. My lips curl upward. Gen works as a psychic, gets paid well for it, and probably wouldn't appreciate me asking her for something so trivial. She takes her job seriously, even if I don't necessarily believe everything she thinks she does. She believes in it, and I believe in her.

"Lady's choice," the guy says, scanning me as well and bringing my thoughts back to the current decision—the bet and how much. Right. He glosses over my face, eyes lingering on my upper arms and the muscles there. I'm not ripped or anything, not defined like a bodybuilder or weightlifter, but hauling tools, cinder blocks, and bags of cement mix around keeps me in good shape. His once-over ends on my open bag and the solitary blue bowling ball beside the boots I carefully tucked inside it.

That ball cost me a hundred and sixty bucks, custom-drilled to fit my hand and the odd double-jointedness of my right thumb, and worth every penny. I've had her since college. She's gotten some nicks and scratches, had a couple of repairs, but she's served me well.

"Let's say, twenty?" I offer, biting my lower lip. I don't have twenty dollars, not on me and not in the bank. If I lose, I'll have to borrow from Steve and Allie. That will suck, but it won't be the first time, and I always pay them back.

God, once upon a time I made a good annual salary, owned a condo, drove a decent car. Now… I shake off the pity party and focus.

Normally I'd go for fifty, but I don't know this guy. The other scattered players watch our interaction. Charlie grins at me from his table. Dave snickers into his rum and Diet Coke.

I can't tell if they're laughing at me or at my would-be opponent. They certainly won't drop me any hints about his skill level, considering how many times I've kicked their asses over the years.

My companion's eyebrows rise. "Twenty, huh? You sure about that, honey?"

Honey? "On second thought, let's make it thirty."

He holds out his hand, a wide smile spreading across his face. "Thirty it is."

Shit, I just got played. I roll my eyes ceiling-ward and smile back so he knows I'm aware of it. And willing to accept the consequences of my egotistical stupidity.

"I'm Kevin. Kevin Taylor."

Taylor. Taylor. Why do I know that name?

Then it hits me. The trophy case next to the shoe rental desk. First Place Team Captain, 2008. Perfect 300 Game, 2007.

"Flynn Dalton." I accept the handshake. His swallows mine in a firm, self-assured grip.

Oh, I'm so screwed.

Chapter 2
Car Magnet

I LEAVE Kissimmee Lanes after 11:00 p.m., clouds obscuring the moon to make a dark night darker and the cracked and broken parking lot lights doing little to dispel the gloom. I carry my bag hanging at my side rather than swung over my sore shoulder. My right hand fingers the crisp twenty and ten in my jeans pocket, fresh from the alley's ATM.

I have to be at the site by 6:00 a.m., and I'm gonna hate life when I wake up, but for now, things are good.

Kevin Taylor *Jr.* turned out to be a decent guy and a more than decent bowler, but he wasn't his father—the guy who won all the trophies in the case. Better still, he wasn't a sore loser, didn't mind getting beaten by a girl, and even asked a couple of questions about my approach and release. Probably hoping to get laid after the loss. He totally missed the Gay Pride sticker on my bowling bag and flirted shamelessly all night, but he took it well when I said I had to work in a few hours.

The passenger door has a tendency to stick, and I'm not going far, so I toss my gear in the bed of my battered pickup truck. I think it used to be gray once. Now it's a mottling of mud, paint splatters, and varying shades of rust. But it runs.

Not without gas, though.

The cheap Hess station closed an hour ago, and I can't bring myself to pay Disney tourist prices at the Citgo, so I plan the shortest route to my weekly rate hotel complex, through Festivity, and hope to hell the needle pointing at the *E* will stay put until I can reach a pump in the morning.

I'm doing forty-five down the empty four-lane highway with the ridiculous thirty-five mile per hour speed limit, keeping an eye out for cops, CD player blasting my mix of Alanis, Pink, and Etheridge. (Yeah, I'm a musical cliche. So shoot me.) The traffic light signifying the boundaries of Festivity come into view, along with the massive planter and a spotlit sign displaying the planned community's name in tasteful block lettering—just in case you miss everything else.

The light glows green, so I tap the brakes to make the left turn toward the town's center and the toll road access.

Nothing happens.

The truck fails to slow. I press down on the brakes again, harder this time, grimacing at the grinding, screeching wail that results. At that same moment, the engine dies, sputtering and coughing, out of gas. The planter looms in front of me. I haul on the wheel, power steering gone with the engine, pulling hand over hand and knowing there is no way I'm gonna avoid a collision with the flowers, shrubs, and low brick wall.

I squeeze my eyes shut and brace myself as best I can.

When I hit, I do it sideways, tires squealing as I bounce over the curb. The jolt knocks my hands off the wheel, and the truck slams, right panel first, into the planter. Metal shrieks as the rough bricks scrape off whatever remains of the truck's paint job. The right passenger window shatters, showering me with glass fragments, one of them cutting through the bare skin of my right forearm.

Movement stops.

Pink's "Sober" pours from the speakers, now tinny and distorted. The impact must have cracked the damn things, along with all the other damage. I snap off the stereo with a trembling hand and fall back against the headrest. My harsh breathing echoes in my ears.

"Oh… fuck."

Hearing my own voice reassures me I'm still alive.

For a long minute, I sit there, waiting for my heart to quit pounding against my rib cage. A trickle of blood runs down my arm from where the piece of glass protrudes. I grab the jagged bit with my left hand and yank it free, throwing it with more force than necessary to clatter against the dashboard. More blood wells in the wound, then flows over my elbow.

I fumble in my back pocket for my cell phone and dial the police. Funny how they don't seem surprised at all by my location, but tell me they'll be here shortly. I cut the connection and toss the phone on the passenger seat.

It takes two shoves and a kick to open my door, and I groan. Bent frame. That means the truck is pretty much totaled. I stagger out to examine the damage firsthand.

What a mess. Two flat tires on the right side. Door crunched in. Bits of plant life and brick caught in the grooves and cracks. And then there are the failed brakes. I'm not driving this piece of junk anytime soon, if ever again.

I have insurance on the truck, shit minimum coverage. It should take care of the damage to the town's property, but not much else.

The spotlights pick out my bowling bag lying in the planter, half sunk in a muddy hollow between two rows of petunias. I haul it out and shove it through the broken window to lie with my cell phone on the seat, then climb onto the bed of the pickup and wait.

It crosses my mind to call my girlfriend, but I discard that idea. Gen lives in Festivity, in a quaint little high-rent place over the pub downtown, which puts her only about a mile or two away, but I'm not seriously hurt, and she tends toward the overprotective. Besides, at 11:34 p.m., I don't want to wake her with my problems.

I grab my first aid kit, stored in a latched compartment in the cargo box, and fix up my wound with tweezers, rubbing alcohol, and gauze. On the bright side, I won't have medical bills to add to my car troubles.

I choke down a half laugh, half sob. Yeah. Bright side.

The engine makes a sound like a whimper, a puff of steam escaping from beneath the dented hood, then settles into silence. Nothing's saving it. With luck, I can sell off the parts and get a moped or something.

In the distance, I can discern the dark outlines of the building site, the framework of the new apartments, skeletal against the black sky. Out here, on the edge of town, the construction displaces a lot of the local wildlife, and several somethings skitter in the brush and trees on either side of the planter. I appreciate the spotlights. Not a single other car has come by since my accident.

A splash jerks my attention to the right, the sound coming from whatever lies behind the big Festivity sign/wall. After hopping off the back of the truck, I skirt the planter and push myself between the concrete barrier and the big trees beside it. Maybe not my smartest move, but I don't want something sneaking up on me out here.

Ah, right, the lake. I've spotted it from the rooftops when I work at the site, though exact positioning seems different at ground level. More of a pond, really. Its inky black surface ripples from whatever made the splash. Tendrils of white fog curl over the water, undulating into almost humanlike forms and stretching toward the banks—toward me—with wispy, translucent fingers.

I take an involuntary step back, then plant my feet, chuckling softly at my own foolishness. Something glows at the lake's center, a semicircular pool of light in the dark depths.

Must be the moon's reflection.

Except there is no moon.

One of the spotlights, maybe….

Gen would love this. She's totally into ghosts and spirits and what lies beyond. It's her passion, as well as her livelihood, running a fortune-telling service out of her apartment. The National Psychic Registry lists her on the internet as "highly recommended."

Gen says I have a shadowed aura, whatever that means, and she's offered to read for me, but I keep turning her down. I've had my cards read at fairs and such, on a lark, usually after a couple of beers. In fact, we sort of met through a tarot reading. But really, I'm not into anything parapsychological, not since my grandmother died and….

Well, not since she died.

Gen and I have a deal. She doesn't pressure me, and I don't let her freak me out… much.

One of the fog-ghosts drifts closer, the edge of the mist brushing across my cheek, sending chills like icy fingers skittering down my spine. I take another step back. My boot heel catches on a protruding root, and I stumble, then yelp as a pair of iron fists grab my upper arms and haul me upright.

Chapter 3
Town Tales

"WAIT. YOU'RE telling me you hit a cop?"

Genesis stares at me from across our regular table in the Village Pub. I shift in my seat, studying the symbolic glass mugs decorating the walls, honoring patrons who've drunk a hundred different beers. I have one hung up in here somewhere. Gen has two. Her brother, Chris, glances over and smiles at me from the open section of the kitchen where he prepares food. He owns the place—inherited it and a crap-ton of money when their parents died in a boating accident some years back.

The siblings make an attractive but unusual pair. Irish father, Colombian mother. Chris got the bronze tanned skin and dark hair. Genesis got the pale skin, red hair, and a Latina first name that everyone unfamiliar with her family lineage wonders about. She thinks it's exotic and suits her profession perfectly.

I return Chris's smile and unroll my silverware from my napkin, wincing at the pain from the glass puncture on my arm. Gen spots the bandaging and pulls my hand to her lips, kissing it gently before releasing me. I tuck it quickly in my lap, willing my blush to go no farther than my collar and failing as it suffuses my cheeks. I'm plenty comfortable with our relationship, but I'm not a big fan of public displays of affection.

A huge yawn sends cracks and pops through my jaw. I'm not even sure what day it is. Thursday, I think. And the clock on the wall says 5:30 p.m. Last night I begged the cop not to have the truck towed. If he did, I wouldn't get it back for parts. Then I hung out in the vehicle until sunrise, worked my full shift on zero sleep, and asked Gen to pick me up at the site. A plate of fries, Boston baked beans, and a barbeque chicken sandwich lie untouched on the table. It's on the house, but I'm too damn tired to eat.

"Flynn, hello? The cop, remember?"

"Yeah." I swallow another yawn and focus on her concerned expression. "Solid elbow to the jaw."

Her green eyes go wider, if that's possible. She rests her arms on the smooth wooden surface, bangle bracelets jingling on her wrists, one hand toying with a wayward curl of red hair. Moon-and-star earrings twinkle in the pub's soft incandescent lighting. "And he didn't arrest you?"

I shrug. "Don't think he wanted to haul me in and admit to his buddies he got hit by a girl. Besides, it was his fault, really. He should have announced himself instead of sneaking up on me. Even with all those spotlights, it's dark around that damn lake."

Gen pauses with her water glass halfway to her full red lips. "Spotlights? Oh, do you mean the lake by your job?"

Like my "job" is someplace permanent, like a store or a restaurant, instead of moving around every couple of months with housing market shifts and urban expansion.

I nod. "I'm surprised you didn't see the wreck when you picked me up. It's only a block or so down the road from the site, and not exactly the kind of garden ornament I think the town is going for. Which reminds me." I snag a fry and give it all my attention, dunking it in ketchup and shoving it in my mouth so it muffles my next words. "Think I could borrow tow money? I spoke to Town Hall, and they cut me some slack, but they'll impound the truck if I don't haul it out of there by tomorrow, and I can't afford the fees *and* buy a new junker on what I'll pull in from selling the parts." I force out the request. I hate asking for money, and Gen knows what it costs my pride.

Her fingers tilt my chin up so I have no choice but to meet her eyes. "Of course you can borrow the money. You know it's not a big deal."

"It is to me." I resist the urge to jerk away. It would hurt her feelings. "I get paid tomorrow. Then I'm paying you back."

She opens her mouth to argue, but I wave her off.

"How are you planning to get to work?" she asks instead.

"Hmm?" I take a large bite of the sandwich and swallow it with a swig of my Sam Adams. Alcohol is the last thing I need. As exhausted as I am, it will knock me flat. But I want it after the day I've had.

"In the morning," she clarifies. "If I drive you home, how are you getting to work?"

Shit. I figured I could catch a ride with one of the crew, but I forgot to ask at the site, and I haven't called anyone. It totally slipped my mind. My panic must show on my face, because she bursts out giggling—a very pleasant sound.

"Don't worry. You can crash at my place. Then you can walk, or I can drop you off." She steals a fry off my plate and pops it into her mouth, then winks. "And maybe I can take your mind off your close brush with death."

Oh boy. I know that tone, the one that often precedes a night of very hot, very intense sex, which I have no energy for at the moment. "It wasn't *that* bad," I say.

"Are you kidding? You almost became the next victim of Dead Man's Pond."

I choke on a fry and take another swallow of my beer. "Excuse me?"

"Dead Man's Pond." She leans into the table and lowers her voice, warming to an obviously popular local story. "They found over a half-dozen bodies when they dredged it about a year ago, folks who'd gone missing, and no one knew they were there. Still sitting in their cars, trapped. According to the news reports, over the last two years, at least six cars have ended up in that pond. That's why the low speed limit, the traffic light, planter, and spots. Nothing works. They still keep getting pulled into the water. Tourists, locals... nothing keeps them out. They crash right through the wall and the town keeps putting it back up."

Gen has her fortune-teller voice going, and I can't suppress a shiver at the gloom-and-doom expression on her face.

"People think it's haunted, that something evil is drawing the drivers in, pushing down gas pedals, cutting brake lines. Didn't you just have your brakes checked last month?"

I had, along with the rest of the Chevy. A working vehicle is vital to my continued employment. Doesn't mean anything. It's an old truck.

"Flynn Dalton," she says, forcing me to meet her intense green eyes, "you have no idea how lucky you were."

Chapter 4
In the Family

GENESIS JOINED her brother at the open kitchen counter and watched Flynn disappear up the back stairs to the apartment above the pub, admiring the way her jeans clung to her muscular backside and thighs. She stumbled a little on the top step, and Gen resisted the urge to call out and make sure she was okay. A night without sleep wouldn't kill Flynn, and she wouldn't appreciate the doting in a public place.

"Try not to drool on the counter," her brother said from the kitchen. "I just wiped it down."

Gen laughed and tossed one of the silverware-napkin rolls at him. He caught it neatly and returned it to the stack waiting to be put on tables. "You two still hot and heavy?"

She traced the counter with her fingers while he stirred a pot of clam chowder on the stove. Two other cooks worked with him, slicing vegetables and grilling fish. The place was hopping, waiters and waitresses hurrying around them.

"You know, it's a little weird for me to discuss my sex life with my brother."

Chris pouted. "Aw, let me live vicariously. With me spending every waking moment running this place, your stories are the closest I'm getting to laid."

Of the two of them, he had the business skills. It made sense for their parents to leave the bar and restaurant to him, and Gen didn't resent it. He even handled the taxes and expense accounts for her fortune-telling job. Managed the investments of their dual inheritance too. Numbers and profit margins had never been her strong suit.

"Nothing to report tonight, I'm betting. Flynn's had a rough day." She gave him the short version of her girlfriend's money troubles and the accident.

Chris paused in his food prep, elbows leaning on the counter. It paid to be the boss. "You know, she could give up that construction gig. We could always use more help around here. She's smart and strong, so carrying the heavy trays won't be an issue. And you've said you wouldn't mind an assistant to handle your appointments."

Gen laughed. "Food service and secretarial work? You have *met* Flynn, haven't you? I'd love it if she took something safer, but she'd see any offers from us as a handout. Besides, she loves working outside. And those muscles she's developed, so strong…." She trailed off as she thought of what those powerful hands and arms could do to her.

"Earth to Genesis." Chris waved a hand in front of her face, bringing her back to the here and now. "Well, at least she didn't end up in the lake. Maybe they'll be able to salvage her truck."

"From what she said, it's totaled. I have to drive her out there tomorrow and get it towed. And I want to take a look at the lake. All those stories, and I've never seen the source." She shivered in the pub's overpowering air-conditioning. "With the bodies now removed and buried properly, I'd think the accidents would stop. Burial usually calms angry spirits, and that's the only cause I can think of for all the bizarre accidents."

"Might be a coincidence," Chris said, returning to his work.

"There is no coincidence. Just forces we can't explain." She twirled one of her earrings, the stars and moon clinking together beneath her earlobe.

"Speaking of forces… you tell her yet?" He had his big-brother face on.

"No," Gen said, not meeting his eyes. "She's freaked enough by what I do. I don't need to add my stupid teenager mistakes to the mix."

"You're not going to scare her off. She's serious about you. She has a right to know what happened, and the potential for a relapse."

Gen's fist landed on the counter with a slam louder than she intended, earning her a couple of wary glances from the waitstaff. Her glare sent them hurrying about their business. "I won't relapse, no matter how addictive the darker power is. Haven't tapped that kind in years. And you of all people should be damn happy I *did* use it."

Chris's face softened. "I'm not ungrateful. But I never wanted you to trade part of your soul for my life."

And that, dear brother, is too damn bad.

Memories of his car accident, only a year after their parents died, attacked her in a mad rush. She couldn't lose Chris, no matter the cost, and she'd called on forces no psychic should touch. It came so easily. Without guidance or instruction, it just came. And even used once, it seduced her, always beneath the surface, so easy, so wrong. One more reason why she so desperately wanted Flynn to take a less dangerous job.

To remove the potential for temptation.

She shook her head, hard. "Flynn doesn't need to know." She pointed an unsteady finger at Chris's chest. "And don't you dare tell her."

He held up both hands in surrender. "Not my secret to tell. But I know how hard it was for you to break the desire for the dark stuff, that it still calls to you sometimes. And any potential long-term partner of yours should know it too. Anyway," he said, changing the subject with the smoothness of the bartender he'd been before taking on the pub's management, "you be careful if you do go out to that lake. If the ghosts don't get you, the alligators and snakes might."

The lake. Right. Dead Man's Pond. One more reason to worry about Flynn.

Chapter 5
Daily Grind

"DALTON, I need you to do me a favor."

It's late. Quitting time in another couple of hours. This can't wait until tomorrow?

I close my eyes and count to five before facing Tom Bowers, my foreman. Instead of the stereotypical clipboard, he has an iPad with each day's assignments, blueprints, delivery schedules—everything he needs to run the site. His interior straps must not be tight enough, because his hard hat rattles on his bald head. He comes to a halt in front of me, an unfamiliar worker in overalls and a tank top in tow.

"Take our new guy, Paul, on a tour of building three and get him started on the drywall."

I toss him a mock salute and tighten the tool belt at my waist. Pulling a handkerchief, I mop the dripping sweat from my brow. It's a hot one, even for Florida, and it's been a long day.

Paul strikes an all-too-familiar pose, arms crossed over a broad chest, scowl dipping his mustache at the corners. "You told me Flynn was showin' me the ropes. Who's the chick?"

"This 'chick' *is* Flynn," I inform him.

"And she knows the site, the crew, and the proce-dures better than anyone I've got on staff," Tom says. "She's also the best damn bowler on the company team and has a mean right hook. Don't get on her bad side. I'm not just talking about bowling."

I turn away to hide the redness creeping into my cheeks.

Tom's a good guy, though I get really tired of breaking in the new hires for him. I understand it. Tom has a gay sister, more butch than me, and deter-mined to graduate from college and make a mark in the male-dominated business world. He's cool with who she is and who I am and judges me on my work, not my sex or sexual preference. Anyone who can't deal with me doesn't keep a job with him. Besides, Tom's grooming me for a foreman job of my own, and this is good practice.

If the look on Paul's face is any indication, he isn't lasting long.

Tom pulls me to the side, lowering his voice. "The company had him over in St. Cloud, working on that hotel going up out there. He couldn't get along with his team, so their foreman asked me to try him with us. Hoped it was just a personality thing. See what you can get out of him and let me know if he's salvageable."

Wonderful.

Tom winks and mouths "I'm sorry" before walking back to his trailer. I take off for building three without checking to see if Paul follows.

When I hear his boots on the gravel behind me, I have to admit, he's surprised me. Time for another test, then. "If you're working building three, I'm your team leader."

He mumbles a curse, followed by a halfhearted clearing of the throat to hide it.

I point out the different half-constructed apartment buildings, ending with number three. I show him where we store tools, equipment, and materials, indicate his work area, and end with the Port-o-Pots in a neat row behind the building.

"What? You don't get your own powder room?"

One, two, three, four— Oh, fuck it. "You know, instead of working drywall, how about you haul in some two-by-fours. I think there's a hand truck behind Tom's trailer, but if not, I'm sure a big, strong guy like you can carry them without one."

Back to the crossed-arms stance. "That's not my assignment."

"Your assignment is whatever I say it is." And if he keeps pissing me off, it'll become less and less desirable. Though there isn't much worse than hauling two-by-fours, except maybe lugging cinder block around. No one wants that job, but we're past that point in the construction process.

"You're welcome to complain to Tom," I add, "but given the state of your boots, you need this job."

He glances down, staring in silence at the extensive scuff marks, the worn-away laces, the thinning leather. Construction workers depend on good footgear. If it looks that bad, you haven't worked in a while.

"Two-by-fours," he says, heading for where the hand truck should be. Then, under his breath, "Fucking dyke bitch."

Yep. Fucking dyke bitch… *boss*. Get used to it, asshole.

I warn a couple of the other guys to keep an eye on Paul and climb up a ladder to the top crossbeams where

I've been working for the day. Sunburn central but an amazing view, especially now with the sun dipping in the western sky. The entire town of Festivity spreads out to the north, today sporting white-tented booths along the main streets for one of the many festivals they hold each year. Dead Man's Pond sits to the east, Kissimmee out west, and highways behind me.

I shift my stance, placing my feet with care, checking the tools on my belt to make sure they're secure. Crouching, I take one last look around… and spot Gen down in our parking area, perched on the trunk of her black Charger.

Hot car. I would love to own one of those.

And the driver does things to me I never would have imagined.

Gen wears that ankle-length tiered skirt, tie-dyed in a dozen colors, and an off-the-shoulder white blouse that almost, *almost,* dips below her strapless bra line.

I drink in the sight of her, knowing she wears it just for me.

A picnic basket rests beside her, what looks like a loaf of french bread sticking out the open top.

Huh. Impromptu date. I like it, but I'm suspicious.

Gen rarely tries to surprise me. Early in our relationship, a couple of surprises caught me off guard and almost ended up disasters. So why is she doing this today? It isn't a holiday, or my birthday, or… shit.

It hits me. A year. Genesis and I have been together a whole year. Damn, I hope she didn't get me a gift. I have nothing to give her.

Knowing she's watching, I make a point of tucking the shirttail up under my sports bra, revealing my abs while I work. I earn the attention of several members of the male crew, even if they know they aren't my type. Most importantly, Gen stares at me and only me.

I glance away, to the northwest and downtown Festivity, the white tents bright in the sunlight. Of course. The Pampered Pup festival, always held at this time of year. Should have remembered that sooner. Should have remembered our one-year anniversary.

That's where we met.

Chapter 6
Bitchy Beginnings

PAMPERED PUP is one of Festivity's quirkier street festivals.

Wealthy people like to keep pets, so the residents include a huge number of dog and cat owners—mostly dogs, and mostly exotic purebreds. The restaurants offer outdoor seating so dogs can accompany the patrons. The shops include a dog bakery, of all things, specializing in canine treats and organic pet foods, even dog clothing and costumes—at exorbitant prices, of course.

So it makes sense for them to have a cheesy, overblown fair celebrating the bow-wows and their owners.

Now, don't get me wrong. I like dogs. Can't afford to keep one, but I like animals of all kinds. Still, Pampered Pup pushes a lot of my snark buttons.

Back when I met Genesis, I'd been between construction jobs, so I'd been working the festival....

I'D HAD a booth set up, building and selling custom dog houses. Cost me an arm and a leg to rent the ten-by-twelve square of pavement, but I'd already sold three doggie abodes, and at a couple hundred a pop, I made back my investment within the first two hours.

The organizers had me stuck between a pet rescue organization, complete with cute, adoptable kittens and puppies, and a table from the pet bakery, treats laid out and so delectable, I wanted to try a few myself.

But the open blue tent covered in gold stars set up across from me had my attention. Or rather, the young woman seated within it.

Fire-engine-red hair, obviously dyed, but given the freckles and green eyes, she was probably a natural redhead anyway, and the brighter shade suited her. Turquoise veils hanging from a silver circlet around her forehead framed the sides of her face. The candles caught the glitter of dangly earrings and a ring on each of the fingers folded neatly on the table before her. Tarot cards rested in a pile on the black velvet tablecloth. The sign out front advertised "Genesis McTalish—Psychic Readings for You and Your Pets."

While I dripped sweat despite my white canvas awning blocking most of the sun, she had at least a couple of fans in her tent, aimed so as not to put the candles out. She showed no signs of discomfort as she beckoned her next customer—an elderly woman with her pink-toenailed poodle—into the folding chair opposite her. Still fanning the dog's wet nails, the woman sat and cut off my view.

I focused on my work, sanding the edges of a log-cabin-themed doghouse a man and his pudgy beagle had admired earlier. I'd just started building it that morning, right there at the festival, and I wanted it to be perfect. The man had asked when it would be done and indicated he'd buy it if I could complete it before

Pampered Pup ended on Sunday, meaning I'd make my rent on schedule. By the time I next looked up, I'd finished smoothing the rough spots, my T-shirt was soaked, and she was watching me with those fathomless eyes.

Then she smiled.

Oh… hell.

I did not like psychics. I did not like anything connected with them, or spirits, or whatever lay beyond. No, I didn't.

Peeling a loose strand of sweat-damp hair off my face and tucking it behind my ear, I smiled back.

At noon I took a lunch break, carefully hanging my "Will Return In An Hour" sign on the weather vane of a barn-themed dog house with cute little swinging doors leading into a cozy interior I'd cushioned with weatherproof padding. The rescue group agreed to look after my booth, and I patted a Doberman pup on the head before setting off down Main Street to In The Dough, a pizza takeout place around the corner. Cheapest food in Festivity, and generous slices and toppings.

On my return trip, I stopped off in one of the restaurant bathrooms to splash cold water on my face and straighten my ponytail, then returned to my rented space. Genesis waved to me from across the street, beckoning me into her tent. An apple and a salad sat beside the tarot cards, along with a cardboard clock stating when she'd begin telling fortunes again. A couple of teens with their pit bulls waited outside.

"How about a reading?" she said, gesturing at the empty folding chair.

I glanced at the pricing sign and shook my head. Attracted to her or not, I wasn't paying fifty bucks for fifteen minutes. Besides, what were the odds she preferred women?

Okay, about one in twenty-five. But I'd seen a handsome guy bringing her beverages in Styrofoam cups with the Village Pub logo printed on them, so I wasn't getting my hopes up. And she had money. Lots of money, judging from the continuous line of customers she'd had all day and the Festivity address on the stack of business cards on the table's corner.

I had nothing to offer a woman like her.

She followed my gaze and flipped the price sign over. "On the house," she amended, flashing me another brilliant smile.

As if an ass magnet pulled me down, I sat.

She rolled her shoulders, set her half-eaten apple aside, and picked up the deck of tarot cards. With careful precision, she laid them on the table, creating a long line down one side and a cross in the center with several cards placed atop the others.

In the movies, I thought the person getting the reading always shuffled and cut the deck, but hey, what did I know?

I found myself drawn to her hands, the way her fingers moved in delicate waves and patterns, like they were performing an elaborate dance. The gaudy gemstones in her rings flashed green, red, and blue in the candlelight from the standing sconces behind her. The scent of incense and her lavender perfume dizzied me, and I blinked to clear my head.

"You've been touched by the occult, and you don't like it. It bothers you," she said, "yet you are here."

My eyebrows rose. While I'd shown an issue with her prices, I'd given no indication of my discomfort with her profession, at least not on purpose. A trickle of ice water ran between my shoulder blades.

Or maybe it was just sweat that had turned cold. Shaking it off, I shrugged. "You invited me. And it's cooler in here." I grinned and tilted my face toward one of her fans for a few wonderful seconds.

"An opportunist, then," she said, the corners of her eyes crinkling. "That's good. Because you're about to be offered a rare opportunity. But first, your reading." She turned over the cards one at a time. "I see strength and intelligence, a fierce desire to protect, and... loneliness. Are you seeing anyone?"

I glanced at the card she indicated. Single woman standing alone in a desert landscape, a vicious tiger by her side. It didn't look like a traditional tarot deck, but they were pretty pictures.

I focused on her question. Lonely. Okay, yeah. "I haven't dated in a while," I admitted. Okay, not in a long, long while. I'd had a couple of girlfriends when I attended the University of Florida, shortly after I'd come to terms with being gay. Nothing serious. Then I'd moved to Kissimmee. My one long-term partner, for all of six months, had decided I was a nice experiment and gone back to her ex-boyfriend. Last I heard, they were married. She didn't invite me to the wedding. Not like I would have gone.

Since then, there'd been no one. A whole year of celibacy. The Orlando area sported a heavy gay and lesbian population, but the local bars and clubs charged hefty covers. And if I was being truly honest with myself, it wasn't just the money. I was scared.

She flipped a few more cards, one with a grim reaper. Lovely.

"Change," Genesis explained at my grunt of concern. "It just means change. And facing this way, it means a positive one." Another card. The Lovers. Crossed by the Queen of Pentacles, depicted as an attractive redhead.

A redhead who looked an awful lot like Genesis.

Huh. The "lonely" card, followed by her pointed question about my current dating status, followed by change, lovers, and a girl who resembled her.

I smelled a setup.

And now I knew why she hadn't let me shuffle the cards.

Schooling my expression into something unreadable, I waited. Gen studied me across the table, searching my face for my reaction to the cards she'd shown me. But I wanted to see where she'd go if I gave her nothing.

"This is interesting," she said. "The Lovers would suggest a new romance in your life, but the Queen, obviously, is a woman, so, maybe a platonic love? A visiting female relative?" Her voice faltered. All the earlier bravado evaporated. She took a steadying sip from her Village Pub cup. She'd stepped outside her comfort zone, faking the reading, stacking the deck, testing my waters. Her boat floundered. Two bright red spots appeared high on her cheeks.

"Yeah," I said, perking up. "My cousin's coming into town for the Fourth of July. Gonna show her around Disney. Should be fun."

Her face fell. My heart broke.

I placed my palms flat on the table, leaned forward, and looked her straight in the eyes. "I don't have a cousin," I said, low and sultry. "Maybe I just like girls."

Gen swallowed hard. Her tongue darted out to lick her lips. The blush spread further, suffusing her face and creeping down her neck. Fucking adorable. She had to clear her throat twice before she could speak. "Which, um, brings me to that opportunity you've got coming."

"Mmm-hmm?" I leaned back in my seat, stretching my legs beneath the table, my T-shirt taut across my chest. One of my jean-clad knees brushed hers through the fabric of her skirt.

Her confidence shattered. Gone was the in-control professional, replaced by a twentysomething woman afraid of being shot down.

Been there.

I took pity on her.

"Go on, just ask," I said softly. "I'm an opportunist, remember?"

I'm not going to reject you.

Hell, I'm going to make you mine.

She parted her full red lips to speak. Something loud as a gunshot popped in the street outside the tent.

"Hercules! Hercules, come back here! Bad dog! Bad!"

Growls and sharp barks followed the frantic shouting. Next thing we knew, the left side of Gen's tent caved in, the blue fabric crashing down atop us both, entangling our arms and legs. Genesis shrieked. In my haste to escape the poorly constructed shelter, I caught my leg in the rung of the folding chair and knocked over the table. Navy blue and stars shrouded the world. I grabbed at the material to pull myself up, only succeeding in yanking over the fan it had caught on, which toppled that and pulled down the other two sides of

starry blue. Thank God the candles didn't catch. At
least I hoped they didn't. I didn't smell any smoke or
see flames. The tent must have snuffed them out.

Something muscular and heavy landed on the
tent's exterior, and under it, me, the thing squirming
and thrashing as I tried to crawl from beneath the bil-
lowing fabric. Massive jaws snapped on the other side
of the too thin material, one incisor cutting through and
tearing a hole. Gasping, I twisted to the right. A fold in
the fallen tent showed daylight, and I headed for it. Fingers closed around my ankle, and I resisted the urge to
jerk away. I spit out a mouthful of velvet. "Keep holding on to me!" I called to Gen over my shoulder.

Okay. Maybe that was extreme, but even if she
could have found her own way out eventually, if she
was letting me play her hero, I was happy to oblige.

Other shapes outlined themselves against the fabric—human legs and feet, reaching hands. The jaws
snapped again, closing around my forearm, teeth driving deep even with the tent in the way.

"Shit!" I yelled, yanking and tearing my skin further before I got free. Damn, I hoped that dog had all
his shots.

I tucked my arm to my side, blood welling up in
the wound, crawling on three limbs instead of four. Gen
clinging to my ankle didn't make things easier. And the
bite hurt like a sonofabitch. No pun intended.

We made it outside just as the owner, one of the
teenagers who'd been waiting for a reading, got hold of
the pit bull's leash.

One thing I'd say for Festivity, their first respond-
ers were fast.

In ten minutes, we had the paramedics, the festival
organizers, and the teenager's father surrounding us,

making sure we were okay. It seemed like they doted on Genesis a lot more than me, and I was the one bleeding all over the concrete. Then again, pain and blood loss had made me kinda woozy.

My attacker sat panting on the sidewalk, huge tongue lolling out of his grinning dog mouth, unaware of the damage he'd done. And the consequences. His owner, a skateboarder type with bad acne, had his arms wrapped around the dog's neck, tears streaming down his face despite the un-macho appearance.

Yeah, he knew what happened to dogs who bit people.

So did I, and I wasn't letting it happen to Hercules.

I got the story from one of the passersby. Some idiot tossed a firecracker. The dog startled and jumped against the tent, which collapsed. In his panic, he'd bitten down on anything within reach. Which happened to be my arm beneath the velvet.

"Don't worry," I told the kid's dad when he knelt to ask after my injuries. "I'm not filing a report."

I thought the man might cry along with his son.

"I would, however, appreciate it if you'd cover the medical expenses?" Opportunist. Yeah, that was me. No insurance. Also me.

He passed me a hundred-dollar bill along with his card, David Chellings, Attorney at Law printed in nice gold leaf across it. Perfect.

"Send me the bills. They'll be taken care of," he assured me, laying a hand on my shoulder. "And thank you."

Genesis sat on the curb beside me while the medics cleaned and bandaged my arm and the town volunteers set her tent to rights. "That was really nice of you," she said.

I shrugged, wincing at the pain the movement caused me. "Not the dog's fault."

"I knew you were the kind of person to do something like that."

My chuckle escaped before I could stop it. "Your psychic senses tell you?"

"Yes, they did," she said with all seriousness.

I shut up.

"So." Gen stared out at the lake beyond the tents. Festivity boasted a dozen or more lakes with most scattered between its various housing development phases and one in the center of town. The rest of her question came out in a rush, words stumbling over each other, but I got it. "Would you like to have drinks with me at the pub tonight?"

I cocked my head at her. The veils had come loose, her red hair spilling across her face in unruly curls and her mascara smudged. She looked like she'd just rolled out of bed after a night of great sex—an image I hoped to see for real sometime in the near future.

"Yeah," I said. Drinks at the pub would be pricey. But I had a hundred dollars in my pocket, and there was no way I was saying no.

To that or anything else she asked of me.

Chapter 7
Evil Attraction

MY FOREARM itches, and it takes me a second to remember it isn't the healing dog bite from a year ago, but rather the glass cuts from my truck accident the day before yesterday. I rub at the bandages, resisting the urge to peel them back and scratch underneath.

Focus, Flynn, focus.

I'm finishing up reinforcing the crossbeams atop the future apartment complex when I happen to glance east toward Dead Man's Pond. My truck's gone, towed that morning by the cheapest company I could find to the nearest legal chop shop. They'll call me later and give me a number on what they'll pay me for the parts. Goody.

Not far from where my truck gave its last gasp sits another vehicle. Can't make it out too well from this distance, but at a guess, I'd have to say it's an exotic sports car… in bright neon orange.

Holy mother of fuck, if you're going to spend a hundred grand on a car, you shouldn't paint it that color. Don't give it gold rims or add undercarriage lights or do anything else to mar the perfect beauty of a well-crafted vehicle.

Then again, you probably won't have to worry about theft.

I don't spot the driver. He might be in the car, or maybe he's visiting the lake. But I'm very curious about the guy who treats a thoroughbred like a donkey. And yeah, it's sexist, but I bet the owner is a guy. Shaking my head, I scan the area around the water, noting the few picnic tables and the porch-style swing hanging from a thick branch of a large tree, all empty.

Maybe it's the heat. Maybe the sun reflecting off the water distorts my vision. Whatever the cause, my eyesight blurs for a moment. It lasts just long enough for me to experience the construction worker's worst nightmare, the one thing you never want to do when you're walking a beam across the roof of a three-story unfinished building.

I lose my balance.

For half a second, I flash back on a worker we lost over a year ago falling from a half-finished balcony. I didn't know him—he belonged to a different team—but images of his death haunted my nightmares for weeks.

My arms pinwheel, but with a hammer in my right fist (that I don't dare drop for fear of conking someone below me) I'm weighted wrong on that side. I impact wood right away, which is a good thing. It means I've hit something close and not thirty feet below me.

My knee slams into the beam where I previously stood. Hitting a crossbar knocks the wind from my lungs. I lose the hammer anyway, and my grip closes on wood. I balance at an odd angle, my right hip, thigh, and lower torso hanging over empty space.

Well, shit.

Breathing hard from the hit and barely contained panic, I lever myself up until I kneel on two beams, both hands clutching them, the knuckles white with stress. Only then do I become aware of the shouting—my crew beneath me, those scrambling up ladders to my position. Farther away, Gen screams my name. Of all the days for her to decide to bring a picnic dinner.

I pry one of my hands free and manage a weak wave, telling her I'm okay, even if I'm not sure of that yet. My knee hurts like a sonofabitch, the ribs on my left side not faring much better. Gen stops screaming, but she doesn't head back to her car either. I know she'll stand right there until I get down to her.

"Dalton! You all right?"

Diego's head pokes up from the closest ladder to my position. His wrinkled forehead wrinkles further in concern. Diego's the oldest member of my team, kind of a father figure to us, and I adore him.

"I'm good," I tell him, though the breathiness of my voice betrays me. "Got a little dizzy."

"Wrong time of the month, Flynn?" Boots cross the beam beside me until they enter my field of vision.

I crane my neck to glare at the speaker, Alex, a guy I trained up from nothing two years earlier. His grin and the chuckle accompanying his comment help me dial down my irritation. It's a running gag. If I bitch more than usual, or screw up, rare as that might be, my period is the cliche excuse, and I let them tease me with it. Besides, half the time it's true.

Alex's work glove closes around my hand and helps pull me to a more comfortable seated position. "First thing you ever taught me was to watch myself in this heat." He passes me a bottle of water, and I take a long swig. While I drink, I check myself over: jeans torn at the knee, bruised ribs, still alive, didn't go splat.

I give Diego and the handful of other heads popping up around me the okay sign with my free hand, and my teammates disappear back to their jobs like the critters in a Whack-A-Mole game. Alex plunks himself down on the nearest beam and passes over my hammer.

Holding two fingers a couple of inches apart, he quips, "Missed me by this much." His grin disappears. "Seriously, though. *Are* you all right? I don't think I've ever seen you place a foot wrong."

Yeah. Six years of gymnastics from middle school through my junior year will do that. I'm not dehydrated either—downed a bottle of water right before meeting up with the boss and that new hire. And, of course, I had to take my nosedive with Gen watching. The heat creeps into my cheeks at that thought. So much for showing off for the girlfriend.

"I'm fine. Caught a glare off the lake and moved when I should have stayed put. Consider it a refresher course for you and the other guys—what *not* to do when you're temporarily blinded." I laugh it off and he joins me, but my hands shake, and he sees it.

"Come on," Alex says. "You're done for the day. Follow me down."

He talks to me the way I would have talked to him if our positions were reversed, so I can't hate him for it. Instead I count to ten, exhale a long breath, and position myself above him on the nearest ladder, letting him lead. Safety move. If something's really wrong with me and I fall again, he'll have a chance of catching me.

Either that or I'll take him down with me, but we don't think in those terms. He's bigger and stronger than I am, with his bodybuilder biceps and broad chest.

Hell, if I were into guys, he'd be my first choice.

Our boots hit the dirt, one set after the other, my damaged knee buckling a little before I steady myself. Turning, I face both Gen and the boss man. Behind them stands Paul, the new guy, smirking at me. If it weren't for the foreman being there, I'd knock that smirk right off his dumbass mouth, along with a few teeth. I'm worried and embarrassed, and my mood is shit, but being aware of it all helps me control the impulse. Kind of.

"Our insurance can't afford a slip like that," Tom jokes, though I hear the note of truth beneath his words.

Too much. All of it. And I snap. "I fell, all right? Shit happens. I'm not gonna claim worker's comp, if that's what you're worried about, so everyone just back the hell off." I turn my glare on Genesis, who's reaching to wrap me in a concerned and all-too-public hug. "Everyone."

It halts her midmotion. She drops her arms to her sides.

I prepare to stomp—or rather limp—away, when the crushed expression on her face stops me cold. I glance from one to the other. Tom rolls his eyes, used to me after our years working together, but I still feel guilty for biting his head off. He isn't upset about the insurance. He's worried I've hurt myself and wants to make sure of my safety. And Gen....

Her eyes shine with unshed tears, and she blinks too rapidly. Then she walks away, headed for her car.

She knows me too. But today…. Today she planned something special for us.

I close my eyes. Sometimes I'm a real bitch.

"Sorry," I say to the men surrounding me. "Not used to fucking up so bad."

Alex's hand falls on my shoulder. "Happens to the best of us."

"Yeah," New Guy mutters. "And we all know *you're* supposed to be the best, right? Maybe you'd be safer hauling some two-by-fours on the nice solid ground."

Tom hears it and steps between us so I can't take a swing at the asshole, but with Gen's departure, all the fire has gone out of me. Instead I whisper, "Maybe I would," and leave it at that.

Their gazes follow me as I limp to the row of portable lockers to grab my things, store my hard hat and tool belt, clock out, and head for the parking area. At least I don't have to pick up my check. Thank God for direct deposit.

To my utter amazement, Gen's car still sits there, and she's still perched on the back, though her elbows rest on her knees and her hands hide her face. From the shaking of her shoulders, I guess those unshed tears are falling now.

Happy fucking anniversary, Gen.

I take a deep breath and walk over, then nudge her to the side of the open trunk with my hip and sit my dumb ass down. My ribs ache, and I suppress a groan as I settle into the small space. "Hey," I say, as always the master of brilliant conversation.

She drops her hands but doesn't look at me. "H-hey." Hiccups.

A soft smile curls my lips. Gen gets hiccups when she cries. Though knowing I caused it dampens my humor pretty fast.

"I'm sorry."

It takes me a second to realize we've both said the same thing at the same time.

"Wait. What?" I stare at her while she focuses on nothing in particular.

"I shouldn't have done that," she says miserably. "Shouldn't have tried to hug you. Not in public. Not when you were already embarrassed. I know how much you hate that." Now she does look at me. Her hand reaches up to brush my sweaty hair from my forehead. "It's just… when I saw you fall, I thought— I thought—" The hiccups cut her off, followed by a fresh flood of tears.

She thought I was going to die.

"I don't want a seance to be the only way I can reach you," she sobs.

She worries about me a lot, and we've discussed it a lot. Gen would much rather I have a nice, safe office job, one that doesn't involve sharp things, nail guns, and heights. When I first told her about my truck accident, she freaked. That is, until I made her look at me, *really* look, and she saw I wasn't seriously injured.

I catch her fingers and close mine around them. Calluses cover mine, and the nails need cleaning, but she doesn't seem to mind. "I'm sorry I scared you. And I'm sorry I bit your head off." A quick scan shows the impromptu parking lot to be otherwise empty of workmen. I lean in and kiss her, the next hiccup jarring us both and making her giggle. Good. "I'm not going anywhere. Really, I'm not a klutz. That kind of thing never happens."

Well, not to me, anyway. I don't mention the guy we lost on another site before I started dating her.

Instead I pull back and wait until she looks me in the eyes. "I don't like public displays, but I should have been more understanding. And if it hadn't been for that damn lake—"

"What about the lake?"

From ground level, trees hide the water, but my head turns in that direction, almost like the lake pulls it. "Nothing. Sun glare."

"So you won't mind if we check it out?"

I blink at her. "Huh?"

Eagerness flashes in her eyes as she gestures at the forgotten basket behind her. "I thought we'd eat at one of the picnic tables. Sunset over the water might be pretty, and romantic, since, well, it's our—"

"Anniversary. One year. And before you get too excited that I remembered, I have to admit I only put it together when I saw you from up there." I wave in the direction of the building I nearly fell from.

Gen giggles again, the tension between us broken. I heave an inward sigh of relief. She has her insecurities, and I have mine. I don't worry about losing her to death, but I do worry about losing her.

"Sometimes," she says, punching me lightly in the arm, "you are *such* a butch."

I take that as a compliment.

We climb out, shut the trunk, and head up front. Gen drives us the couple of blocks to the lake. When she spots the orange sports car—a McLaren for crying out loud—she frowns.

"Someone you know?"

"Leopold VanDean." Gen spits the name. She pulls the Charger onto a dirt service road and drives down almost to the lake's edge, where she parks on the grass alongside the narrow strip of sandy "beach."

"Ah," I say, like that means anything.

She catches the sarcasm and continues, "Huckster, con man, with a modicum of psychic talent. The only other one living in Festivity. Undercuts my rates, steals my business. Fakes his readings."

"You faked *my* reading," I remind her.

She punches me again, in the chest this time. It hurts my damaged ribs, but I hide it. "It was free. Besides, you *knew* I was faking. And you haven't complained," she adds with a wink.

We grab the basket of food, pick our way through a few shrubs and trees to the sand, and settle at one of the four picnic tables. We have our pick of them. They all sit empty, giving us plenty of privacy.

She lowers her voice, eyeing the foliage. "VanDean makes promises to his customers that no respectable psychic can keep: guarantees spirit contact, pretends his predictions of the future are definitive. Even throwing in some rumored black magic, he can't be sure of those sorts of things."

I fumble the basket I carry, dropping it to the table instead of setting it down. I've never really heard her talk about magic before. Up until now, it's always been about the psychic gift, something some have and others don't. Magic seems a lot more far-fetched. A fine line, but I have a hard time crossing it, and my skepticism must show in my face.

Her gaze stays focused on me, and I get the uneasy feeling of being judged by my reaction to her statement. After a few seconds, she looks away. Whatever test she was giving, I failed.

Gen places the food items on the table, slamming plastic cups and a pack of paper plates on the wood surface with a lot more force than necessary. I really hope that's about Leopold and not me. Gen tells all her clients that her readings reveal one possible future, depending upon what actions they take from that moment forward. Some would call that hedging, but it makes sense to me.

"He's applied for membership in the Registry four times. We keep turning him down."

"Huh." I grab the bottle of wine before she smashes that down too, and use the corkscrew I find in the basket to uncork the white zinfandel. We both need a drink.

Through Gen, I'd learned about the National Psychic Registry. She's on it and had served on its board of directors for a year. Not sure why she gave that up. From what she says, it paid well. She has a gold plaque hanging in the entry hall of her apartment, notifying all potential clients of her general membership. To get listed, you have to abide by a strict set of guidelines—ethical rules for the psychic community.

"Look, forget about him," I say, passing her a generous red Solo cup of wine. "We're supposed to be celebrating, remember?" I raise my drink in a toast. "To many more years."

She taps her cup against mine, but I can tell she's still distracted. "More years," she echoes, taking a long swallow. "I just wonder what he's doing out here at the lake and where he's skulking about."

"Maybe the lake got him," I joke. The wine is cheap but good, by my standards, anyway. I know she prefers a better vintage and variety, but she defers to my taste, and I appreciate it more than she knows. I'm a bit of a beer snob, but good wine is wasted on me.

"We should only be so lucky," Gen mutters, earning a raise of my eyebrows.

Wow. She really hates this guy. In the year I've dated her (God, a whole year) I've never heard her wish harm on anyone.

A sudden rustling in the bushes beside us makes us both jump. We turn in unison, me shifting my body to place it between Gen and whatever emerges from the trees. Festivity has some native wildlife. It could be a gator or a boar.

Gen puts her hands on my shoulders, leaning over one to look but letting me protect her. I like that. I like that a lot.

The man who steps out looks anything but threatening, and I let my muscles relax. Gen's grip on my shoulders tightens, however, so I reevaluate.

Shorter than me by a couple of inches and slight of build, with neat brown hair and brown eyes. A deep green Polo shirt tucked into cuffed tan trousers, though grass stains and dirt mark up the knees. Leopold, I assume, doesn't look like a psychic, but then I only know a sample size of one.

"Genesis!" He beams at us—well, at Gen—spreading his arms wide in greeting. "Nice to know you're still hoping for my early demise. No worries there, though. The lake isn't after someone like me." Leopold glances from her to me and back again. "You do know the recent history of the lake, correct?"

"VanDean," Gen growls. "You're fishing. What do you want, and what are you talking about?"

Without waiting for an invitation, he approaches, grabs a third cup, and pours a drink for himself. His hand trembles as he does so—interesting, that—but instead of chugging the wine, he takes a delicate sip, with his pinky extended of all things. Leopold swings a leg over the bench seat and sits opposite us. "Not important. Silly superstition. What are you two celebrating?"

Genesis fixes him with a hard stare. "Quit backpedaling. Say what you started to say."

"Very well," he says, looking like he's already said more than he intended to. "The lake prefers women. Or didn't you know almost all the poor souls who've ended up at the bottom of Dead Man's Pond have actually been women?" He stares out across the lake, scanning the trees on the far side. "Dead Man's Pond," he muses. "Really a misnomer."

Gen's curls tickle the back of my neck as she shakes her head. "I know there've been men. I've seen their pictures in the obituaries."

Leopold tsks at her. "I'd think you'd do better research, being 'official' and all." He grabs one of Gen's homemade chocolate chip cookies and takes a bite, hmming appreciatively. "Psychic *and* she bakes." Leo inclines his head to me. "Good catch," he says with a wide smile, attempting once again to change the subject.

I pull the basket out of his reach. "Fuck you," I return, my smile equally wide. "Get on with it or get lost."

"Oh, if you insist." He folds his hands around his cup. "No individual males have ever gone down in this lovely lake. Every car to wind up beneath the surface has contained at least one woman. Every. Single. One."

Chapter 8
Lesser Evil

HAVING LOST the opportunity to purloin more wine, cheap swill though it was, Leopold VanDean took his leave of the no-longer-so-happy couple. He stepped into the cover of the trees, negotiating his way through thigh-high bushes and pointy-leafed plants, muttering at the picked places they left on his designer slacks, not to mention the grass stains. Ah well, he'd simply add the cleaning or replacement bill to his client's running tab.

And quite the tab it was becoming.

Contracting the continuous extended services of a high-profile psychic/warlock such as himself would run well beyond most individuals' means. It was one of the things Leo appreciated about working in Festivity—if you could afford to live here, you could afford him.

A deer path led between the trees and foliage, not as wide as he needed, but better than bushwhacking. He used it to circumnavigate the lake until he reached the side opposite the picnic tables.

"You were supposed to chase them off," came a stern voice from behind the next pair of palms.

Really, if the man weren't paying him so well, Leo would cut his current client loose.

Max Harris stepped into view, well-dressed and perfectly coiffed as always, the spitting image of a young Robert Redford but with brown hair instead of red. A few leaves caught in his hair and on the lapel of his expensive suit. He plucked them off and tossed them to the ground. Young, fit, and successful, but not the outdoorsy type.

"Chase them off?" Leo crossed his arms over his chest. "Did you see Miss McTalish's girlfriend? Practically an Amazon. Maybe *you* should try chasing them off."

"I saw her." It came out as a growl. Max strode to the tree line, pulling apart a pair of branches to get another view of the lake and the women on the other side. "I told you they were onto us."

"What are you talking about?" Leo asked, joining him. The scent of pricey cigars and European cologne wafted off his client. Not unpleasant, but a bit cloying. They stood shoulder to shoulder, watching the girls talk and drink, Genesis gesticulating wildly as she spoke.

"That Amazon," Max said, pointing at the taller woman, "is the pond's most recent victim."

Leo peered at her. "Looks pretty healthy to me."

"Near victim," Max clarified. "Flynn Dalton. The police report went up a couple of days ago. Brakes went out on her truck, and she hit the planter. It's lucky for her she wasn't speeding like the others. Probably saved her life." He pointed toward the construction site down the street, the skeletal frameworks dark bones against the evening sky. "She works there. Volunteers at some place in Kissimmee that builds shit for poor kids. Likes to spend a lot of time at the Village Pub with that female psychic."

That seemed like a lot of information to have on a stranger, police report or no police report. Then again, anything to do with the lake was currently of interest to both his client and himself. "You sound like you know her."

"I'm… aware of her."

In Leo's experience, it didn't pay to be someone Max Harris was aware of. With his contacts, Max would soon know all there was to know about Flynn Dalton. "She's dating Genesis," Leo clarified.

He watched, fascinated, as Genesis snuggled in close to her partner. The two shared a long and intimate kiss, completely losing themselves in each other, though a minute later Dalton sat up straight and scanned the shoreline. Paranoid chick, that was for sure.

"Dangerous," Max went on. "The lake will continue to want her. It's tried once to get her. It will try again. Personally, I wouldn't care if it took her to the bottom, but we don't need another victim drawing attention."

"Especially when that victim's girlfriend might connect me to the scene," Leo muttered.

Max whirled on him, causing the leaves to shake. One branch snapped back into Leo's face, and he stumbled before Max grabbed him by the shoulders. "You invoked the curse, imbued the charm with it. You took the payment. It's your responsibility to protect *me*. Now you're supposed to be putting a stop to this," Max growled.

Brushing off some invisible leaves, Leo disentangled himself and put a couple of feet of distance between them. Max Harris had height and bulk, two things Leo preferred to avoid. "*You* purchased the curse," he reminded his client. "*You* placed it on your pretty little wife's car, knowing full well what it could do. *You* were supposed to retrieve it afterward. If you'd just put it in her purse or something, she would have had some bad luck. I didn't plan for anyone to die. That was all you. And now you've got a lot more victims." Max Harris *had* planned his wife's death. Leo hadn't, but Max had. Leo just hadn't figured it out until it was too late.

"How the hell was I supposed to know the charm would end up at the bottom of a fucking lake!"

Leo waved his hands for Max to keep his voice down.

"A simple car accident," Max continued in a low growl. "On a road. Not dumping the car into a lake so deep at its center, you can't get to it without scuba gear."

Picking at his fingernails, Leo ignored Max's threatening tone. "Again, no one told you to put it on her car."

His butt hit the dirt before he realized Max had shoved him. Leo rubbed at his chest. That would leave a mark.

Red-faced and sweating in his suit, the business-man towered above, ready to hit him again. "You never told me anything. For the price I paid, some specific instructions should have been in order. It's no wonder your own kind view you as a screwup."

My own kind washed their hands of me a long time ago. And for a "screwup," the curse certainly worked well enough. Too well, Leo thought, glancing in the direction of Dead Man's Pond.

The lake had claimed too many lives. Leo's fault or not, soon it would draw the attention of the Registry, who didn't approve of making cursed charms, despite what should have been his right to free enterprise. It already had Genesis poking around. Oh, it might have looked like the two women were just having a picnic, but Leo knew Genesis. She didn't select this location by chance. Maybe the majority of the world didn't believe in curses, but she would, and if she reported it, he'd be out of business, permanently.

When the Registry decided something should be permanent, it used disturbing creativity in its methods of punishment.

Leo backed away from his client. "I'll come up with some way to counteract it," he assured Max. And himself. To assuage his own conscience, not just for the money. Curses were one thing. Deaths were quite another. Coincidence, he'd told himself when cars kept going down. Not his concern. Then yesterday, Max called. Said another vehicle almost went in. Said people would start investigating again, and here they were. He'd insisted Leo deal with the situation once and for all.

And of course that most recent vehicle's owner had to be Genesis's new girlfriend. Could Leo's luck possibly get worse?

"I can already tell you I can't see it in the daytime. Possibly not at night either." They'd met out here this evening so he could scout the lake, and while he could sense the charm's power, he couldn't pinpoint its location. Active but invisible wasn't a good combination. The damn thing shouldn't even still be working. One curse, one victim. The purchaser embedded his sense of whom he wanted cursed on the charm, and voila, that person ended up with some bad luck. That's how it was supposed to operate. "Give me some more time to study the effects and I'll figure something out."

"Don't take too long. It may have been a year and a half since the divers recovered the body and the car, but now there's new interest. The charm was no longer on the car's bumper, so it must still be down there somewhere. I don't need that other psychic or anyone else finding that thing and tracing it to me."

Or me, Leo thought.

"My high school medallion, of all damn things! 'Has to be something personal' my ass. If you had half the skills you claim to have, you should have been able to use anything."

That's not how it works, Leo thought, though he didn't bother trying to convince Max. Again.

"Even if no one believes in magic or curses, I can't afford for the world to view me as a man who puts faith in the arcane. It would ruin me as an investment banker."

It would ruin a lot more than that, Leo thought. He had to find a way to reclaim or nullify that curse. And get Genesis off the trail.

For her own safety as well as his.

Chapter 9
Spooked

THOUGH GEN keeps trying to distract me with kisses, I don't fully relax until I hear the McLaren's engine roaring into the distance. I close my eyes with a deep sigh of relief. My back rests against the table, with my legs extended along the bench and Genesis in my lap. The light breeze blows her hair across her face, the setting sun glinting off the red-and-gold strands. So freaking beautiful.

Yeah, life is good.

"I wonder what he was up to," Gen says. She pops a grape in her mouth and feeds me one.

"Who knows? Forget about him." I chew, then swallow the grape. She has a point, though. No one comes out here. In the weeks I've worked the construction site, gazing at the lake from the top of the apartment building, I haven't seen anyone. Once we complete the complex, families and romantic couples will flock to this place, but for now, it's the untouched side of Festivity. Just a couple of office buildings down the road leading toward town, and the high school in the opposite direction.

I scan the ground, spotting a couple of empty beer bottles at the water's edge, along with a number of cigarette butts. So someone hangs out here, probably teens after dark, but not a man like Leopold VanDean. The prissy psychic hesitated to sit on the bench in his nice clothes. He wouldn't enjoy nature walks around the lake.

Yet he'd been here. And he had grass stains on his pants.

Gen's hand snakes its way beneath my shirt, and I let Leo fade from my mind. The sun sinks behind the tops of the surrounding trees. She traces my ribs with her fingertips, careful around the bruised ones I'm favoring on my left side. Cooler air raises goose bumps on Gen's arms, so I take her in mine and pull her close.

Nice, sitting here, listening to the crickets and night birds and frogs coming out in the dusk, Gen's head tucked under my chin. I'm not stupid. Leo isn't the only one with ulterior motives. Gen didn't pick this place at random. Nice spot, but she's ghost hunting, following up on that whole Dead Man's Pond story. I'll worry about that later. I take a deep breath and let it out. Her hand finds my breast, stroking the underside of it through my bra, then teasing the nipple through the thick cotton.

She senses my desire, stretching the elastic and slipping her fingers under. I can't suppress a soft moan.

We've both had a lot of wine. The second bottle lies empty next to the first. When she lifts my tank top for better access, however, I stiffen and sit up, almost dumping her on the ground beside the table.

"There's no one around," she grumbles, letting my shirt fall back into place. "And besides, it's almost dark."

I blink into the twilight, surprised by how long we've been out here. We took our time eating, drinking, talking, and waiting for VanDean to leave, and she's been stirring my fires for a while now too. The Festivity sign's spotlights come on, casting mist-filled beams across the lake, but none of them touch us.

"Lighten up, Flynn," she says, putting the remains of our dinner into the basket and setting it aside. She hops up on the table's surface and pulls me to sit beside her. Pushing steadily on my shoulders, she leans me back until I lie across the rough wood planking. Gonna get splinters if this keeps up, but I don't much care.

Gen's a wild one, always encouraging me to lose my inhibitions. Me, I cling to them with both hands. But after refusing her at the site, I don't want to hurt her now.

I'm still nervous, thinking about high school students coming upon us, but I don't resist when she undoes my belt buckle and zipper and slides her fingers into my jeans.

It's been a while, what with me working all the time and her heavy appointment schedule. I pull her on top of me, rubbing her back and her soft bottom through her long skirt. Her off-the-shoulder blouse drops lower with a tug of my free hand. No lace bra this time—just beautiful bare skin. I'm surprised none of the guys at the site noticed that little detail. Then again, everyone was focused on my screwup, and they know better than to ogle my girlfriend. I close my mouth around an already erect nipple and revel in her groan.

Something splashes in the water, and I flinch.

"Fish, Flynn. Or a frog. Forget it." She works her fingers lower, teasing and stroking, and I can't help writhing beneath her. "That's it," Gen whispers. "Forget it all. Forget the world."

My hips buck upward. A hiss escapes between my clenched teeth.

"It's just us, just the two of us. Don't hold anything back."

Her free hand finds my hair, brushing aside the escaped strands from my ponytail, running her fingertips over my scalp. An erogenous zone for me, and she uses it to her advantage. Her lips find the pulse point at the side of my neck and she nuzzles me, then licks, then bites, hard. I try not to think about the all-too-visible marks she'll leave.

God, I'm on fire. Between the night air, the smell of her perfume, the feel of her hands and mouth, and the sheer thrill of doing this *outside* where anyone might happen by, I'm utterly lost. Never thought I'd find exhibitionism arousing, but it works wonders for me tonight.

My hips find the rhythm, matching the strokes of her fingers. I clamp my jaw on a groan.

"I want to hear you," she whispers.

"Someone else might… too," I force between ragged breaths.

"Baby, my apartment neighbors are more likely to hear you than anyone way out here. Come on. Don't fight it."

Her brother, Chris, lives right next door to her, and I blush furiously at that thought, but the motion of her fingers drives it from my mind.

The next moan breaks free, wrenched from my throat like something animal, not human. The sound of my own arousal in my ears pushes me harder and faster, and Gen keeps up with me, relentless, never easing off for a second.

"Lose control. You don't have to control everything. Let go."

I do as she commands, gasping and crying out with my release. Money problems, car wreck, embarrassment, our fight, they all go. Sparks flash behind my squeezed-shut eyelids, and I drown in fathoms of undeniable pleasure.

"Happy anniversary, baby," she whispers. Her words hit home with mind-numbing force.

A year. A full year. She's put up with my bullshit for a whole fucking year.

I BIT my lip to keep from screaming as Gen brought me to my fourth mind-blowing orgasm of the night. We lay in her king-sized bed, stretched out on top of the comforter, our bodies too hot and sweaty for blankets.

It'd been wonderful—hours of exploring each other for the first time, finding what worked and what didn't, getting past those little embarrassments that couples had to overcome.

My energy surprised me. After fourteen months of abstinence, I thought I might be rusty from disuse, but she'd pulled more pleasure out of me than I could have imagined. And in the two weeks since I met her, I'd imagined quite a bit.

She ran her fingers up and down my bare hip, facing me, eyes closed while she caught her own breath. Yeah, it'd been good for her too. Three times good. I owed her.

"Been a while for you, huh?" she teased.

I tried not to flinch, thoughts of Kat flooding back to me in an unwelcome rush, but something in my body language must have given me away.

She opened her eyes and looked into mine. "What happened," she asked softly, "between the two of you?"

"Nothing I want to talk about." That came out sharper than I meant it to, but I couldn't take it back.

"Okay."

She was so damn accepting, willing to let things lie until I was ready to tell her. "It's been over a year," I gave her, wanting to offer some reassurance. "At least you aren't catching me right after the breakup." Which had been bad. Really bad. Like didn't eat or sleep well for weeks, didn't talk to anyone, didn't work, didn't go out kind of bad.

"I think you're still feeling the effects," Gen said, "but I'm taking my chances anyway."

Yeah, maybe a little. But I was ready to move on. "What about you? I'm damn well not the first girl you've been with. You're way too good at this."

Gen smirked with pride. "No, you're not my first." Her grin faltered a little. "My first was a confusing, awkward teenage thing. She walked out when it got too intense. Another girl comforted me, but in the end, she left too."

That was a story I hoped she'd share with me someday. Not right then. We were still too new to each other, too vulnerable, but someday.

"I've had a few relationships," she continued, rushing past what were clearly upsetting teenage memories. "Last one ended six months ago."

"What happened?" It was hypocritical of me to ask, I knew, but this wouldn't be a "first time" story, and Gen tended to be more open by nature than I was.

Lying down, she still managed a one-armed shrug. "We had philosophical differences. I broke up with him."

Her simple statement hit like a punch to the chest. I couldn't bear to lose another one that way. "Him?"

"Yes…." Gen drew the word out, confused by my reaction. "I'm bi. Is that a problem?"

The pleasant warmth of the bedroom had dropped to an icy chill. I was still trying to process, to catch up. "No, no. No problem, it's just that, well…."

"You're lesbian. I know." Now she sat up and looked down at me, frowning. "Is this some sort of weird prejudice? I wouldn't have pegged you for that type." She crossed her arms over her chest.

"No! No…. It's just that, well, Kat was bi."

Gen let that sit for a while. Her face worked through a number of emotions: irritation, anger… fear? "I'm not Kat," she said finally.

"I know," I said in a small voice. Swinging my legs off the bed, I started grabbing and pulling on my clothes. "I need to go." Before I did or said something else completely stupid. Before I hurt her again.

She watched me dress. I felt her eyes on me, though I couldn't look at her. When I was halfway to the bedroom door, she jumped up and grabbed me by the arms. "Don't do this."

"Do what?"

She gave me a little shake. "Those first two lovers I mentioned? They walked out on me, remember? Disappeared from my life. That second one… she meant a lot to me, even if I barely knew her. Changed me forever. I never saw her again, but you remind me of...."

Gen broke off, and I stood there, dumbfounded by my own stupidity and my callous disregard for her feelings.

"Put yourself in my place, Flynn. We just made love. Now you're leaving. What the hell am I supposed to think?"

I took a deep breath, let it out. "That I'm an idiot," I said, staring at my work boots.

Gen pulled me in to her, holding me close. "Whatever she did to you, it hurt you so much you aren't thinking straight. I get that. But if we're going to make a go of this, you need to judge me for me. I can't win against that kind of pain."

I nodded, but the knot in my throat kept me from speaking.

Gen released me. "When you're ready to give me a fighting chance, call me."

I called her the very next night.

GEN KNOWS Kat left me, not the other way around. She doesn't know why. Because I never told her. Because it's too humiliating to share.

Because it could happen again.

Gen says she's more into girls than guys, but Festivity has more than its share of wealthy, good-looking, eligible men (and women for that matter) who could, potentially, turn her head.

Yet she chooses me, day after day, for reasons I cannot comprehend.

I can't handle it, as uptight as I am. Tears suddenly stream down my cheeks, stunning me.

"Flynn?" The smug satisfaction at bringing me to orgasm in a public place turns to dismay. Genesis pulls me to her, kissing away the tears while I fight to regain my emotional balance. I'm still shaking from sexual aftershocks and the intensity of the moment.

"S-sorry." I clear my throat and try again. "Sorry, Gen."

"Did I hurt you? Was it the fall? We should have gotten some ice for the bruising…."

"I'm not hurt. I'm okay. Really."

Gen studies me in the dim light cast by the spots, skepticism making her frown. "I don't think I've ever seen you cry before."

Nope, almost no one has. On the rare occasions I fall apart, I do it in private. I have no idea what's gotten into me.

"Don't get me wrong. Vulnerable you is incredibly endearing. But I wish you'd talk to—"

"You like that, huh?" No, I don't want to talk about it. I want to change the subject. "How about another cup of—"

Before I finish my question, Gen stiffens in my arms. Her head snaps up, eyes wide and focused behind me. I rise slowly, pulling her hand from my jeans as I do so, and twist my neck around to see what she sees.

A woman stands on the shore on the far side of the lake, staring across the water. Staring right at us.

As I feared, we aren't alone.

Chapter 10
Remains To Be Seen

"SHIT." I scramble up, zipping my jeans with one hand before I turn to get a better look at the stranger. She stands far enough away that I can't make out any details beyond her femininity and possibly red hair, or reddish-brown, but I have no doubt that she's been able to figure out what we've been up to.

"Flynn...."

"You said there was no one out here." Pushing Gen onto the bench, I pull the shoulders of her shirt up to cover her breasts, since she's made no move to do so. Then I buckle my belt into place.

The spotlights wash all the color out of Gen's cheeks. "There isn't," she whispers, but I must have misheard her.

Heat floods my face. How long has that woman been standing there? How much did she see? I was flat on my back on top of a picnic table. She wouldn't have been able to place Gen's hands from across the lake, but she would have seen the movement—my movement—even if we were only shadows to her. And water carries sound really, really well.

I close my eyes and take a deep breath.

When I open them, she's still watching, so I stare back. Light-colored slacks, what looks like maybe a sweater, which seems weird for summer, but who am I to judge fashion? Long hair blowing in the light breeze. The unnerving sense of familiarity niggles at my brain, but I can't make out facial details, can't even figure her age at this distance.

Not Gen's fault. She would have warned me if she'd known.

Then Gen's words register. She didn't say the woman *wasn't* there, as in wasn't there before. She said she *isn't*. And the ephemeral glow around the figure registers too.

"Flynn?" Genesis whispers, and I realize she isn't pale from the spotlights. She's just pale. And trembling. But it isn't the strange woman she's staring at.

It's me.

"Can you see her?" Gen asks, pointing a wavering finger across the lake.

A pit of ice forms in my stomach. I know where this conversation ends, and I don't want to get there, but I answer her anyway. "Yeah."

"You can see ghosts."

"No. No, I can't. It's not possible...." Memories I long ago classified as dreams or hallucinations rush to the forefront of my mind. I think I'm going to throw up.

I STOOD at the front of the funeral parlor viewing room, my grandmother's casket resting on a polished wooden slab before me. My grandmother stared at me from the head of the coffin, her frown deepening as she glanced into it. "Always despised that dress," she said.

I looked at the hideous navy suit dress covering her dead body, then nervously watched the friends and relatives revolving around, pausing to pay their respects, moving on. "I told them," I whispered, knowing I was seeing something no one else could.

Knowing I should keep it a secret.

I was dreaming or having one of those nervous breakdowns adults talked about. The thought terrified me, that I might have been losing my mind, or worse, that I was really seeing a dead person's spirit, but I didn't move, didn't run screaming from the funeral home. My imagination or not, I wasn't passing up one last chance to be with my grandmother.

Grandma smiled and brushed a hand across my cheek. I recoiled at the chill, but she didn't mind. She laughed.

"It's all right, honey. Don't worry about the dress. No one believes nine-year-olds." She peered into my face. "They won't believe this either. So don't you tell them, you hear me? You keep this to yourself. You've got enough trouble coming as it is."

"What do you mean?" I looked down at the body as I spoke, making it appear I was saying goodbye or a prayer or something, not talking to a ghost. Not going crazy, though inside, my stomach churned. I wiped sweaty palms on my black dress pants. It took everything I had not to shriek or faint or find my mother, sequestered away in the funeral parlor office after an emotional collapse of her own.

No, I couldn't go to her. Even at nine, I understood my mother's fragility and knew I couldn't add to the breakage or risk losing her too.

"People will judge you, Flynn, though they have no right to. Don't give them more ammunition."

Did she know? Could she tell even then, before I knew myself, that I was gay?

Whatever she meant, I never got the chance to ask, because she turned and walked through the wall of the funeral home.

That did it. My knees gave out, and I dropped like a stone beside the casket.

I didn't sleep for a week.

I never told anyone. I convinced myself it had all been in my head.

I never saw her, or any other ghost, again.

UNTIL NOW.

Unlike my grandmother's spirit all those years ago, this woman at the lake doesn't stroll through a wall. There are no walls.

Instead, she walks into the pond, moving deeper and deeper with each step, the water rising to cover her body until she disappears beneath its inky black surface, leaving no ripples in her wake.

"Flynn?" Gen reaches for me, but I move.

I hurl myself away from the picnic table, landing on the ground on all fours. My breath comes fast and shallow. My stomach heaves, and I vomit across the sand and dirt.

Nineteen years have passed since my grand-mother's death. In that time, the memory faded like a dream.

Or a nightmare.

But now?

No denying it. When I was nine, I saw a ghost. And now I've seen another one.

Chapter 11
Shockwave

"GOTTA GET outta here," I mumble, staggering to my feet. My knee buckles, sharp pain shooting up my leg and into the bruised joint. Genesis catches me midfall.

"We're going," she says softly, soothingly. Her arm wraps around my waist. With my greater height and weight, I nearly take both of us down, but somehow we remain standing.

Out on the lake, that soft glow returns, the one I saw the night of my crash, at the dead center.

Oh, great choice of imagery, Flynn.

I shake my head and the world rocks. Really regretting all that wine. Gen snags the picnic basket with her free hand, and we make for the car. I keep my eyes forward, not looking at the lake or the light or anything but the path. Gen glances back, almost tripping twice in her attempts to watch for the ghost's return. Chills run up and down my arms, raising goose bumps in their wake. The shaking doesn't let up. I can't focus, can't think. The trees, the dirt road, they all blur. I tunnel on the Charger, parked and waiting.

Genesis eases me into the passenger seat, buckling my seat belt like she would a child's. Part of me wants to push her away, but I can't make my body do what I want it to. "What's... wrong with me?" I manage through chattering teeth.

"Shock, I think," she says, sliding in on the driver's side. She starts the engine, the powerful V8 roaring to life, and casts a glance sideways at me. "This has happened before?"

"Later, Gen. Just get me home."

Home meaning her place. I've never referred to it that way before, and the hint of a smile touches her lips despite my current condition. Damn, I'm really out of it. She's wanted me to move in with her for a while now, but I won't. I can't afford half her rent. I can't afford a third, and I don't feel right moving in with her at this stage when I can't pull my own weight.

I'm aware of her talking on her cell as she drives, and I want to tell her to hang it up. She didn't drink as much as I did because I was nervous about the public setting, and she seems pretty clear-headed, but I know *I* wouldn't have gotten behind the wheel, ghost or no ghost.

We make it downtown without crashing, and Gen pulls the Charger into a space behind the Village Pub. Chris waits for us out back, and I realize that's who she called on the cell. Heat creeps into my face. I'm closer to Chris than to my construction crew, but he still feels like one of the guys and generally accepts me as such in return. Seeing me like this will change the nature of a friendship I like just the way it is. "You had to tell him?"

Gen shrugs, unrepentant. "I can't get you up the stairs by myself."

"I can walk." Probably not. But I'll haul myself hand over hand along the metal banister if it means one less moment of humiliation.

"Sure you can." She pats my leg above my sore knee. "Let us help you, anyway."

I think I growl at her. I'm not sure. The door opens, and Chris crouches by my side and peers into my face. I can only imagine how I must look.

Has to have been a hallucination. All that wine, or maybe I hit my head when I fell at the site and didn't realize it.

Except Gen saw it too.

"Shit, Flynn, you look like hell."

As I figured. "With pickup lines like that, it's no wonder I'm gay."

That earns me a laugh, but it fades when he pulls me up, my injured knee buckles again, and I stumble into him. His forehead creases with worry. "How do you feel about me carrying you?"

My expression must speak for me.

"Right. I'll take one arm. Gen, take the other one."

They throw my arms over their shoulders. I'm not sure how we climb the stairs, but a couple of long, painful minutes later, we stand in Genesis's apartment. In my drunken, screwed-up state, her flowery incense makes my head spin. Chris aims me at the Laura Ashley couch, but Gen draws me toward her bedroom.

"Drop her there and I'll never get her up again. Put her in my bed," she instructs.

He does it, setting me down on the edge, removing my work boots, and lifting my legs onto the peach-colored sheet. Gen joins us with a towel wrapped around what I assume to be ice. Chris turns away while she unfastens my belt and eases my jeans over my hips and then off. She pulls the comforter, folded neatly at the foot of the bed, up to my waist.

"Let's take a look at those ribs." Gen tugs my shirt up to just beneath my breasts. Chris switches on the bedside lamp, chasing away whatever might be hiding in the shadows. Her sharp intake of breath tells me how bad it is.

Chris lets out a low whistle. "Should've iced that down sooner."

I crane my neck to get a glimpse of purpling bruises crisscrossing the right side of my rib cage. My knee is probably worse.

"It was dark," Gen says, "and of course, she downplayed everything."

"She would," Chris agrees.

"Still here," I remind them both, and wish I were anywhere else. I don't do helpless. I don't do scared. Right now, I'm the poster child for both.

"In body if not in spirit," Gen says.

I clench my muscles to suppress a shiver. "Don't say spirit." Rolling away from them, onto my good side, I let them place the towel-wrapped ice on the bruising. I almost manage not to groan. Almost.

"Yeah, about that—" Chris begins, but Genesis cuts him off.

"Thanks for the help, big brother, but I can take it from here."

I press my face further into the pillow, not looking at either of them. The bed cushions my weary muscles. The alcohol fogs my brain. If not for the shaking, I could fall asleep right now.

Their footsteps recede as they leave the room. For a panicked moment, I'm tempted to call Gen back to me. I don't want more babying, but under no circumstances do I want to be alone. I clamp my jaw shut. Their voices carry from the living room, hushed words I can't comprehend. Then the front door opens and shuts.

The side of the bed sinks as Gen sits next to me. She nudges me over with her hip and lies down, pulling my head against her shoulder and putting an arm around me. I take a deep breath of her perfume and that Ocean Breezes shampoo she uses. When I continue to tremble, she pulls the quilt higher over us both.

"It's okay, Flynn. It's going to be okay."

I nod, but I don't mean it. Nothing about this is okay. Nothing at all.

"Why didn't you tell me you had the Sight?"

"I didn't know I had it."

"But you said this happened before."

I don't want to talk about it, but she won't let it go. This is her world, her area of expertise. If I examine myself closely enough, I'm relieved to share it with someone after all this time, someone who'll believe every word.

Haltingly at first, I relate my nine-year-old self's encounter with my grandmother's spirit. Before I know it, the words pour out, tumbling over one another in their haste to get free.

She strokes my shoulder and arm while I speak, the other hand combing through the tangled strands of my ponytail. When I finish, we lie in silence for a long time.

"That must have been terrifying," she finally says.

"Didn't sleep for a week. Had nightmares for months." I wouldn't have admitted that to anyone but Gen.

She stiffens beneath me. "That's why you won't let me read for you."

"Yeah. Don't invite evil in and all that." I regret the words the minute they leave my mouth, but I can't take them back.

"It's not evil. I don't work with evil." Her tone is fierce. "It's just death."

Just death. Right. No big deal. For her. "I know. Sorry."

Her tension eases. "Better than what I thought before, though." Gen touches my cheek. "I always worried you were secretly laughing at me, that you refused because you felt what I do is silly, but you liked me, so you stuck around."

It takes effort to sit up, twist, and look at her, but I do it. The towel of ice falls onto the bed as I take her hands in mine and face her head-on. "Never. I've never believed that. I respect what you do. I just didn't... *don't*... want it for myself."

"I don't think you have a choice." Gen frowns, thinking hard. "People usually fall into three categories: the total nulls who see nothing, the psychics who see plenty—and there's a wide range of those: witches and healers, mediums and walkers, channelers, potion masters, and every combination thereof. And last come the sensitives who get touched by the spirit world on rare occasions—by loved ones or others close to them who have some last words or an important message. I think you're the last sort, which is good, because it means you shouldn't have to deal with this often, but.... Did you know the woman at the lake?"

"Actually," I say, swallowing hard, "I think I might have." I tell her about the familiarity, that odd sense I had when I saw her. "But she was so far away...."

"I didn't get a good look either," Gen admits.

"Well, I suppose we could—" A huge yawn cuts me off, stretching my jaw until it audibly cracks.

"Tomorrow." Gen pulls me back down beside her. "Sleep, Flynn. Saturday's your day off, right? Sleep in. Sleep late. I've got a couple of morning appointments, but we shouldn't bother you from the living room."

She strokes my hair again. The blurry red numbers on the nightstand alarm clock read 12:47. Weights pull at my eyelids.

"Sleep," she murmurs.

I sleep.

And wake in a cold sweat, shaking from unremembered nightmares about an hour later. And an hour after that. And an hour after that.

Wash, rinse, repeat.

Fuck.

Memories of my childhood resurface with a vengeance: worried mother, missed school, the psychologist's office. Even without admitting to ghosts, after the funeral incident, they all knew I'd suffered some kind of additional trauma and had no idea how to fix me.

Exhausted, embarrassed, and desperate, I accept one of Gen's heavy-duty sleeping pills. Fifteen minutes later, it grabs my consciousness and drags it into the abyss.

AT SOME point, the quilt has been kicked or pulled away, leaving my legs bare, my plain cotton undershorts the only thing between me and the cool air of the bedroom.

Smooth fingertips trail along the inside of my thighs, sliding up and down both of them and winding in intricate swirls. Every nerve ending responds, muscles quivering with each teasing touch. My breath leaves my lungs in a shuddering exhalation.

Warm lips follow the strokes, a tongue darting out to tickle me almost senseless. I'm wet in seconds, the fabric clinging to my center, my hips shifting in anticipation, but each time the touches move close to where I want them most, they dart away, increasing the heat of my arousal.

Just as I open my eyes, something falls across them, rough and a touch damp—the towel, ice long melted away. I chuckle at the makeshift blindfold. If Gen wants to play that game, I'll be a willing participant.

I'm at the mercy of my lover—a heady sensation. A nice switch. Our moment on the picnic table aside, I usually take the lead in our lovemaking. This is an interesting change of pace. And besides, it's just a dream, right?

I reach out with my arms, but she pulls away and I wrap them around empty space. They fall limply to my sides.

A hand cups my backside, lifting me to slip my underwear off. I hear it fall to the carpeting by the bed.

We're safe and hidden here in her apartment, here in the dream. No need to be shy, so I let her part my legs, and I wait.

I'm not kept waiting long.

Instead of fingers, I feel her mouth, teasing, tickling, tongue darting but never quite penetrating. Remembering the comment about thin walls and nosy neighbors like her brother, my dream self keeps my moans low, but they're rhythmic and constant, hips undulating, back arching to press myself harder against her lips.

The bed creaks with my urgent motion. I'm losing this battle fast. She says not a single word, but blows softly across my center until I beg her not to stop.

Part of me feels a little guilty. Even in a dream, I should do something for her in return, but the pleasure of an orgasmic wave quickly erases that guilt.

Wipes it off the fucking planet, in fact.

Neighbors or no neighbors, I scream. Loudly.

THE SHUTTING of the apartment's front door brings me back to reality. The reality of a silent room.

I reach up and remove the towel from my eyes. The brightness startles me, midmorning sunlight streaming around the edges of the magnolia-covered window curtains. And no one, absolutely *no one* else is there.

The bedroom door opens and Gen rushes in. She stares, first at me lying spread-eagle, naked from the waist down, then at my discarded underwear on the floor.

My heart rate picks up. My underwear. On the floor. Not a dream. It wasn't a dream.

And I was alone.

My eyes dart back to the closed window curtains. Second floor. No balcony. Only one door leading in or out, and Gen stands in that doorway, so no one else came through there.

"Flynn, seriously, were you just…." She trails off, a blush turning her cheeks bright red.

Oh my God, she thinks I was…. "No." I swing my legs off the bed, snatch up my undershorts, and yank them on. A hickey rises on the inside of my left thigh, purple darkening to a deep shade. I fixate on it, Gen following my gaze and sucking in a sharp breath. No way I did that to myself. I might have been a gymnast in high school, but it would have taken a circus contortionist to pull that off.

Not a dream. Not a dream. Not a dream, a panicked voice in my head echoes. I am so not dealing with this. Not right now.

My jeans and boots follow, each piece of clothing taking the brunt of my anger while I snap and button and fasten.

Gen says nothing, watching me.

I stomp my way to the living room and freeze.

Candles flicker, decorating the coffee table, the end tables. Two rest in holders on the floor, beside throw pillows and neatly laid-out tarot cards. The candles have been burning awhile, judging from the amount of liquid wax; the cushions bear indentations where two people recently sat—Genesis, and—

I drop my eyes, focusing on the scuffed tops of my shoes. "Please, *please* tell me that wasn't a client I heard leaving."

She wraps her arms around me, but I twist away, unable to deal with anyone's touch right now.

"I told her the noise was newlyweds next door. Actually, I thought it *was* the newlyweds next door or I would have been in there much faster."

She must mean her left-side neighbors, because Chris lives to the right. God, I hope he's at work.

"She bought it. She left because we were done, not because of you. Geez, Flynn, what the hell went on in there?"

"I don't know. I need to leave." I head for the entry, but she skirts around me, blocking my path.

"Dammit, talk to me. If what just happened is what I think just happened, you've got bigger problems than seeing a ghost at the lake."

My hands fist at my sides. If this were anyone but Gen in front of me, I would shove her aside. "Someone was there. In your room. In your bed. With me. She—" I pause, wondering how I know the presence was female, but it was. I'm sure of it. "I swear, I thought it was you. I never would have let… I mean… you're the only one I want to be…. Shit." Because I really let myself get caught up in it. I almost never allow myself that kind of… expressiveness, even with Genesis.

She reaches out, almost touching me, but thinks better of it. My heart sinks. How many ways can I screw up this relationship in a couple of days?

"I'm not worried about you cheating. I'm worried about invasive spirits. I'm worried about you being raped."

That word strikes like a slap in the face. I suck in a sharp breath. The walls close in; the potpourri chokes me. "Leaving. Now. Move."

She moves. "You shouldn't be alone," Gen says, but she doesn't stop me again.

Throwing open her door, I go.

Chapter 12
The Not-So-Modern World

I BORROW Chris's car, a nice, expensive sedan, and tear out of Festivity. No idea where I'm headed. I just need to drive, to move, to get away to anyplace else. It isn't the smartest thing to do right now. My mind wanders, and I run at least one stop sign and a red light before the honking and the fact I'm in someone else's vehicle forces me to take more care.

Rape. Was it?

This seemed more like sexual assault than rape, though the differences are arguable. I was plenty consenting while it went on, while I screamed my pleasure for the building to hear. I wasn't drunk or stoned, unless I counted the sleeping pill. I could have gotten up at any time if I'd known. But I thought I was consenting to someone else—to Gen. Not some stranger's ghost.

I had sex with a ghost.

I slam on the brakes, narrowly missing the rear end of the semi in front of me, and don't touch the gas pedal until I've taken a few deep breaths. Okay. Time to go somewhere and get out of the car.

Thing is, it hadn't felt like a stranger. I don't know why, exactly, but I'm pretty certain, in hindsight of course, that my spiritual lover was the woman from the lake. And I'm even more sure than before that I know her somehow. She knew how to touch me, and where, and when. She played my body like a familiar, well-rehearsed instrument.

And none of it makes sense. I haven't had many lovers, and to the best of my knowledge, they're all living, and none of them in Festivity besides Gen.

Maybe ghosts just know things.

The more I think about it, the angrier I become.

Ghost or no ghost, willing or not, she had no right. Before I sleep again, I'll need to ask Gen how to prevent her return.

I flip on the radio, using the distraction to prevent a more fatal one. Old hard rock provides me with some mood music—Def Leppard and Aerosmith. I want to throw something, and a nice, heavy bowling ball would do fine, but I can't go blowing what little cash I have on lane fees when I need a new—well, used—car.

I want to break things, but nothing comes to mind.

Then it hits me. It's Saturday. If I can't break, I can build.

Saturdays when I'm not working at the site, I like to volunteer out at Central Florida Lumber and Tile. I worked retail in their showroom for about a month before the indoor customer-friendly job drove me nuts. While there, I joined a group of installers and random community members who do charity work on weekends, and I still join them as often as I'm able.

We build all sorts of structures for underprivileged and disabled kids: playhouses, wheelchair-accessible forts, pirate ships for climbing and swinging, tree houses. We also do some large-scale stuff for low-income community playgrounds.

I make a semi-legal U-turn and then a left, heading down Poinciana Boulevard. The low-lying structures of the lumberyard come into view with the warehouse/showroom out front. As I hoped, an odd mix of battered pickups and luxury vehicles fills the parking lot.

Rich folks sure love their charity work.

Okay, that isn't fair. Half the people here are poor like me. It just seems, when the doctors and lawyers turn out to "help" they end up donating money and supplies, which is great, but not doing a lot of real work on the project, and their "supervisory" advice is often dead wrong.

I park and hop out. It's a scorcher, typical June weather, so I grab a discarded baseball cap from Chris's back seat and plop it on my head before I end up with heatstroke.

Gravel crunches under my boots as I round the showroom. Volunteers fill the central square, an open space surrounded by four rectangular buildings. Wives and daughters have several long tables set up in the shade of the workers' lunch area—an awning-covered space with a couple of benches, where the employees take their breaks, smoke cigarettes, and eat.

I stop there first, grabbing a half-melted chocolate pastry and a bottle of orange juice before joining the men sanding and sawing.

"Hey, Flynn!"

"Good to see you!"

"Hola, Chica!"

We exchange friendly waves and smiles. The distraction isn't erasing my earlier freak-out, not by a long shot, but it helps.

My personal toolbox sits under the bed in my Kissimmee hotel suite, but I know these guys, and they won't mind me sharing. I grab a hammer from the closest familiar kit, next to five canisters of pink and purple paint. "What are we building?" I call to no one in particular.

"Extra-large playhouse for the group foster home in downtown Orlando. Let him tell you where you should jump in," one of the gang says, pointing to a tall man by the food tables. "He's been asking about you, anyway."

"Me?"

He shrugs. "Went down the list of volunteers, grilled me on all the folks. I said sometimes you work a real job on Saturdays, but hey, here you are."

"Um, right." I wander over to the guy who bears a startling resemblance to a brown-haired Robert Redford, and ask where he wants me.

"The group constructing the walls could use an extra pair of hands, unless you'd prefer painting," the man answers, giving me a once-over and frowning.

I return the scrutiny. Not working class, that's for sure. New jeans and T-shirt, both designer labels, so he doesn't fit in well despite the attempt. Good-looking and the kind of fit only a gym membership can buy—evenly toned, but no defined muscles. He holds a high-end power drill with a casing so shiny the sun glints off the red plastic surface.

After looking me up and down, he extends an uncalloused hand. "Maxwell Harris, of Harris and Montgomery Financial Services." The frown doesn't leave his face.

How can this guy dislike me? He hasn't even met me.

"I'm not much of a painter," I admit. "Flynn Dalton, RPL Construction." Hey, why not? It's a company. I accept the handshake.

Ah, one of those types who likes to tout his superiority with a crushing grip. Not impressed. I'm not ordinarily a power-games player, but I'll respond in kind if you insist on testing me. I bowl and build and carry heavy shit. In an arm-wrestling match, I'd probably take him.

He drops my hand. I grin when I notice him flexing his fingers at his side. "You'll be working on my project."

His, huh? So he isn't just volunteering. He donated the materials. Guess that's why he wants to know something about the volunteers, although I don't remember any of the other project starters doing that. I should like him better for his generosity, but I don't. Something in his tone, the way his eyes narrow at me, make me want to check for food between my teeth or my fly being down.

"Problem?"

A shake of the head, but he does have a problem. A problem with me. And I have no idea why.

We get to work on the playhouse, following the provided plans and putting the finished pieces together. It's a nice design, complete with a wheelchair ramp to the front door and handrails throughout.

Over the next few hours, Harris follows me around, watching over my shoulder, making adjustments to my work that I have to unadjust the minute he turns his back, and never doing any real labor himself.

"I've never encountered a woman construction worker before." He catches me by surprise, sneaking up while I help a couple of the regulars attach the roof to the walls.

"You should get out more," I say, deadpan. I'm so not in the mood for this.

"Doesn't that long ponytail catch on things? Get in the way?" It isn't what he says. It's how he says it.

Oh. Got it. Either you have a thing about women working predominantly male jobs, or you've made the assumption I'm a lesbian but you can't quite reconcile it with your preconceived notions. In this guy's reality, lesbians have short hair, and good women are teachers or housewives or nurses. And you don't like lesbians or strong women. Not one bit.

My words drop like icicles in Alaska. "Some of us wear makeup too." Not me, but that's beside the point. "Hope you got a good deal on that toy of yours." I gesture at the shiny electric drill he still holds. "Manufacturer had a recall last month. Thing gets hot when you use it longer than a half hour. Then again, you haven't had it on long enough to tell." I walk past him.

"Hope you have another job lined up. RPL Construction closed their Festivity site yesterday." He's completely sure of himself, no doubt at all in his tone. And working for an investment company, he'd know.

Well, shit.

Chapter 13
Deeper in Debt

TWO PHONE calls confirm two things—Max Harris spoke the truth, and I'm in deep shit.

I reach my foreman, Tom, after three tries, and from the resigned, frustrated tone of his voice, I get the impression he's given his speech to a few of the other workers already today.

Yes, the financing fell through on the apartment project. Yes, we're all laid off for the foreseeable future—but hey, don't worry. He's sure they'll straighten things out with the bank, or someone will buy out the contract. Our last paychecks should have been deposited before the crap hit the fan. That helps. A little. I'll make my rent for the week, and only a couple of days behind. Hooray for having a roof over my head for the next five days.

My second call goes to the chop shop breaking my poor old truck into pieces to sell the parts. Three hundred dollars. Best they can do. I can pick up a check or have it mailed. Great. I'll have to pick it up today while I still have Chris's car. Can't have it mailed. My rent-by-the-week hotel doesn't accept mail for their transient guests. Since we got this new contract, I've been able to save up a little, and in another few months, I might have had enough to afford first and last month's rent and a security deposit to move into a cheap apartment, but the earlier housing crash wiped me out so bad it shot my credit to hell, so I'm still stuck in the ratty hotel. And now it looks like I might not be able to keep even that.

On the upside, money problems help me forget about ghost problems.

I get my check and deposit it before heading back to Festivity. In the lot behind the pub, the car slides neatly into a space between a Mercedes and a DeLorean, of all things. Terrible gas mileage, poor acceleration no matter what *Back to the Future* showed us, air-conditioning problems. I shake my head. Being rich makes some people really stupid.

Then again, it's a freaking DeLorean. If someone offered it to me, I wouldn't turn it down. Gull wing doors are *so* cool. I catch myself peering through the windshield, searching for the flux capacitor, and drag myself away.

Chris accepts his keys at the pub's rear employee entrance, the concerned expression on his face telling me he and Gen have talked. When he opens his mouth to speak, I wave him off.

"I'm fine. Don't ask."

"Right. But see Gen, okay? She's worried sick." He steps back inside and lets the kitchen door swing shut behind him.

Not like I have much choice. No car means I'm stuck staying with her until she's willing to drive me home. I can't keep Chris's forever.

She meets me outside her apartment, wrapping her arms around me in a bear hug. I know she needs my touch right now, despite my discomfort both with contact after last night and public displays, so I return the hug and press my face to the top of her head. "Sorry I took off earlier. I felt like all the air had gone out of the room."

Gen nods, her head bobbing under my chin. "I understand, but you really shouldn't be alone. Not if a spirit has… fixated on you this way."

That's an interesting way to put it.

"I've been doing some research," she continues, standing aside so I can precede her into the living room.

I hesitate on the threshold, searching the shadowed corners, the arch into the kitchen, the open powder room, before stepping inside. God, is this how I'm going to be from now on? Paranoid? Waiting for something noncorporeal to jump out at me? Taking a deep breath, I stomp to the nearest couch and drop into the cushions. I rest my face in my hands.

"What sort of research?" It comes out muffled, with my palms in the way, but she understands me.

She pretty much always understands me.

"Obituaries," Gen says.

I look up at the sound of paper rustling. She's spread some printouts on the coffee table—death reports of all the bodies found in the lake, most complete with pictures. There are a lot of them, maybe seven or eight. Some of the pages overlap. Thank goodness the photos are before shots, not after. I'm not the squeamish type, but I don't need to see blue-tinged bloated faces from drowning, or worse, alligator-nibbled corpses. I have enough nightmares.

And I'm so not ready for this. "Got any beer?"

She cocks her head to the side and smiles. "My brother owns a pub."

Oh, right.

"What kind do you want?" she asks.

"Breckenridge?"

"Duh." Gen disappears into the kitchen, and I experience an unfamiliar knot of nerves in my stomach until she reappears with my favorite brew in hand. I let out an audible sigh at the sight of the chilled bottle sweating with moisture.

No glasses or mugs for me. I'm a straight-out-of-the-bottle kind of gal. A long swig eases the dryness of my throat and the tension in my back and shoulders. It's expensive stuff, shipped from Colorado, and I feel a little guilty chugging it, but I need to take the edge off.

"Let's do this," I say after emptying half the bottle.

She raises her eyebrows but doesn't comment, instead spreading the papers farther across the table.

It doesn't take long to find what we're looking for. At my sharp intake of breath, her hands cease moving, and she takes a seat beside me. "I'm guessing you recognize someone."

"Yeah. Shit." I pass her the bottle, not trusting myself to hang on to it, and reach with a shaking hand for one of the pictures. It's a wedding photo, one of those solo bridal shots. She wears a full-length white gown with a fitted bodice and long lacy sleeves. Long hair I know to be red, despite the black-and-white print, flows across her shoulders, held back at the top with a glittering rhinestone headpiece and veil. The caption reads, "Katherine O'Reilly Harris."

I have a thing for Irish and Scottish girls.

"That one?" Gen says, studying the photo. "But she's—"

"Married. I know. That's Kat."

She stares at me in obvious shock. "Did you know she had a husband?"

My mouth twists in a grimace. "She didn't, not when we were together. I'm not that kind of person." I don't break up relationships.

They break up with me.

"I'm sorry. I know better. That's not what I meant. I just wondered if she'd hidden it from you, if she was cheating." Gen's palm moves in soothing circles over my back as she looks at the woman in the photograph. "She's pretty."

And familiar. Gen has to have noticed the similarities between Kat and herself, but if she has, she doesn't mention it.

"I'm sure her husband thought so." I can't stop the bitterness. "I had no idea she'd moved to Festivity." I'm stunned and sorry Kat died. One of our mutual friends should have contacted me. Then again, we didn't have a lot of friends in common. I wonder if she hid me from hers, knowing all along she planned to go back to her ex-boyfriend. Regardless, I resent her for leaving me. For using me. I shouldn't. She's dead. I shouldn't resent the dead. But with her, I always will.

Of course, if she hadn't left, I never would have found Genesis. I try to cling to that while Gen reads the accompanying article over my shoulder.

"They married in December, two years ago." She pauses, one hand flying to her mouth. "Wait, is this why you two—?"

I nod miserably, retrieve my bottle, and drink the other half of my beer in one go. "She left me to go back to him, yeah." Hell, might as well tell her everything. Steeling my resolve, I add, "Said I was a nice change of pace, a 'fun fling.'" I don't need the air quotes to give voice to my sarcasm, but I make them anyway. "I didn't even know she was bisexual."

"And you play for keeps." Gen's fingers curl around mine.

I do now. More than anything, I want to keep Gen.

"I can't imagine how that must have felt as an adult," she says, squeezing my hand. "I had something similar happen in high school, but, you know, high school, lots of kids mess around, try things out, and we weren't together very long."

I nod. I've heard what happened to me was pretty common in high school and college. But Kat and I spent more than half a year together. I'd been so sure. And judging from the pain Gen tries to hide in her voice, her experience hurt too, even if it wasn't as serious. I open my mouth to ask her about it, but she waves it away like she's shooing a fly.

Gen pulls out another, more official-looking print-out. "Forensic evidence indicates her car was the first one to end up at the bottom of the pond, and it was down there over a month before they figured out what happened to her. No stoplight or planter or wall back then, so no definitive indicators her car had gone in along with several others after hers. Hmm, let me make sure I have the timeline straight. You dated Kat for about six months. Then she . . ."

"Went back to her ex-boyfriend," I put in, filling the awkward silence.

Gen nods but avoids eye contact. "Right. They got married almost immediately after that. She went missing shortly after their wedding. Eventually her car and body are found, but you didn't know anything about any of this. About a year goes by. Then we start seeing each other." She gives me a smile. "Much better decision on your part. And now another year has passed." Gen frowns. "Your connection to her might explain why she's so interested in you, and maybe why she's still here. Most spirits go to rest once their bodies are properly buried, but I think she has a message for you."

If by message, Gen means bringing me to a screaming orgasm, then yeah, message received, loud and clear. I flush deeply at the thought. Sometimes having fair skin can be a real bitch.

"Not that kind of message," Gen says, watching me. "I don't know. Maybe she regrets how she treated you, wants to apologize or make amends, and this is the only way she knows how."

I set the paper and my bottle carefully on the coffee table and stand, pacing from one side of the living room to the other. Gen makes sense. Kat and I didn't have a great relationship even when we were together, and looking back, I should have seen the end coming long before it arrived. I sometimes wonder what I saw in her at all. But I'd been younger and lonely, just a few years out of college, estranged from family, and desperate to share my life with someone, anyone, who accepted me and my lifestyle, and Kat gave me that much, if little else. Whenever we fought, she'd never talk things out with me. Half my fault, I know. I'm not much of a talker, but with Gen's help, I'm learning.

No, Kat and I didn't talk. But she would make things up to me with sex. Wild, crazy sex. But meaningless and empty of real affection.

Like this morning.

No words. She didn't even let me touch her. As I consider it, I figure she was incapable in her ghostly state, but the more I analyze it, the more I realize it was typical of our lovemaking.

At least my assaulter wasn't a complete stranger.

"So how do I get rid of her?" Ah, irony. A little more than two years ago I would have done anything to have Kat stay. Now I'd move heaven and earth to get her to leave.

"You sure you want to?" Gen asks in a small voice.

Whoa. Where did that come from?

No, I know where that came from. When I talk about Kat, the pain comes through no matter how hard I try to hide it. Gen knows what that woman meant to me, once.

I cross back to her, kneeling on the floor beside where she sits on the couch. It hurts like hell, my bruised and swollen knee screaming in protest, but I ignore the pain. I wait, looking up at her, until she meets my eyes and I'm certain she's listening. "Yes, I'm sure. I want her gone, as fast as possible. I don't have room for her."

Because I'm full of you.

I don't have to say it. She hears me. Sometimes I wonder if her psychic gifts include a touch of telepathy. Her mouth comes down to meet mine in a lingering kiss. When we part, I'm breathless.

"Problem is," she says, and it takes me a moment to remember what we were talking about, "I tried contacting 'the ghost from the lake' while you were gone today. Now that we know whom we're dealing with, I understand why she won't respond to me." She picks up the photo and shakes her head.

Ex-girlfriend and current girlfriend. Bad combination.

"Maybe her husband knows what she wants to tell you."

Gen has a point. I should try to contact him. Not that I intend to discuss ghost sightings, but her husband might— I jerk upright, then flop back on my ass. Husband.

I snatch the paper from Genesis, ignoring her squeak of surprise, and scan the obituary until I find the husband's full name.

Maxwell Harris. Maxwell Harris of Harris and Montgomery Financial Services.

Oh.

Does he know about my history with Kat? I can't imagine her telling him. Maybe he found out after the accident somehow.

Or maybe he just has an issue with lesbians, and Kat is a major coincidence.

Gen doesn't believe in coincidence. Right now, neither do I.

I stare at the photo in my hands. Kat stares back at me. Why can't she leave me the hell alone? She had no trouble doing that once. I can't imagine what she wants from me now. To make amends? But she was so sure of herself when she broke things off between us. One thing I do know, though—I won't get any answers from Maxwell Harris.

Chapter 14
Hints and Allegations

"I'M SORRY, sir, but Mr. Harris won't see you without an appointment," the woman said in heavily accented English.

The short, chubby Latina housekeeper kept herself firmly planted in the doorway, blocking Leo VanDean's view of the Harris household interior. Over her head he could make out the entry hall chandelier, expensive but a bit gaudy for his taste, and winding stairs leading to a second floor. An ornate banister in red wood flanked the steps on either side.

Leo slipped a hand into his blazer pocket, brushing his fingertips across his "all access" charm. "Oh, he'll see me. I'm doing some research for him. He asked that I present him with any and all results immediately upon their finding."

The woman blinked as if dazed, her pupils dilating for a few seconds before returning to normal. Her scowl turned to a smile of welcome. "Yes, of course. If you'll please come in."

A second later, Leo found himself walking over Italian tile between two marble statues of unidentifiable origins, one a naked man, the other a woman, both tacky.

And Genesis made fun of his orange McLaren.

To be honest, he'd been surprised not to find shrub animals on the front lawn and gargoyles perched atop the gabled roof of the Festivity golf course mansion, despite the town covenants prohibiting such things. Leo liked eye-catching cars. Maxwell Harris liked eye-catching everything.

The housekeeper showed him to a formal library complete with high-backed chairs, ottomans, a fireplace (who needs a fireplace in Central Florida?) and a wet bar. Built-in floor-to-ceiling bookshelves displayed classic works of fiction in hardbound editions, complete with gold filigree on the bindings. Leo doubted anyone had ever read them. The impressive collection of half-empty cognac bottles on the bar was obviously frequently handled, however.

He made a show of seating himself, stretching his legs out across a polar bear skin rug.

Good God, did the man have no taste at all?

Leo waited until his escort left, then slipped out the door and sneaked down the hall. He didn't have time to waste hanging around an empty library. A check of his calendar app reminded him he had a real appointment for a client reading in less than an hour.

Shouting stopped him in his tracks.

He stood, listening, cupping a hand around his ear to make out the words, but with little success. Definitely a man and a woman, and from the intonations and pitch, the man would be Max.

Leo crept onward, determined to fake a wayward trip to the powder room should anyone inquire what he was doing wandering about.

The voices grew louder as he approached a set of swinging doors leading to what he assumed to be the kitchen. From here, he could hear every word.

"—were you doing, then?" Max. Followed by a thwap of something pliant against a solid surface—a magazine slapping a counter, maybe? That's what it sounded like.

"Shopping for a bikini," came the plaintive female response. "Because you said you liked the way I looked in one, and mine has faded. I've had it since before the wedding."

Leo had never met the most recent Mrs. Harris, but he pitied anyone who ended up married to a brute like Max.

"Then go to a fucking store!"

A squeak followed—a chair dragged across tile—and someone sat down, followed by muffled sobbing. "Y-you don't want me to go anywhere without you, and y-you hate shopping."

"What I don't want is you leering at a magazine filled with pictures of half-naked women. You a dyke or something?"

Leo took a step backward. Wow. Okay. Time to beat a hasty retreat.

He turned, just as he heard a loud slap, followed by more sobbing. The sound of a farther-away door opening came right after, then some angry words in shouted Spanish—the housekeeper entering the argument. Before Leo could escape, the swinging doors on his side of the kitchen flew outward to crash against the hallway walls and the Hispanic woman appeared.

They stood, staring at one another, both equally surprised by the other's presence. The housekeeper recovered first.

"See who you want," she informed Leo. "I quit."

Max appeared in the kitchen doorway. Behind him, Leo made out the wife, seated at the butcher block table, one hand pressed to her reddened cheek. Long black hair fell halfway down her back. Even with the injury, she was lovely. An open catalog lay before her, pages crumpled and torn.

"You say anything about this to anyone, I'll have you deported," Max said, pointing at the housekeeper.

"I'm legal, *hijueputa*!" she shouted back, giving him the finger over her shoulder. The other hand clutched her purse to her side. Under her breath she added, "Stupid American." Her tiny feet pattered down the corridor. A few seconds later, the front door slammed.

Max levered his gaze on Leo, who took another involuntary step backward. "Take care of that," Max said, tilting his chin in the direction she'd taken.

"You don't mean permanently, do you?" He wasn't killing anyone else for Max, on purpose or by accident, ever again.

The investment banker heaved a put-upon sigh. "Just keep her quiet."

"Twenty thousand dollars."

"Done."

When he didn't move, Max raised his eyebrows.

"I'll mail her the targeted silence charm. Don't worry," Leo said, "she'll open it. She's the type to read every piece of junk she receives. And if she speaks to someone before then, the charm will cloud that person's memory too."

Max headed off at a brisk pace, Leo falling into step behind him, the wife's sobbing fading as they got farther away.

"What are you doing here?" Max asked, pushing into the library. He shut and locked the door behind the two of them.

Leo didn't care for that one bit, but he hid his discomfort by moving to the bar and pouring himself a cognac. "I, uh, was thinking about the specifics of that curse you placed on the charm. I need to know why it's continuing to hurt people even though it should have been nullified after one... unfortunate incident. What, exactly, did you tell it to target?"

Max sat down in the closest chair, crossing his arms over his broad chest. "I told it to target my wife."

"Are those the exact words you used, 'curse my wife'?"

He leaned forward in his seat. "I told it to kill the dyke lesbian bitch."

Whether or not the curse should have been strong enough to do that, that's exactly what it did. And they were back to the whole lesbian thing.

Max turned away, mumbling under his breath, "Fucking cheat."

Taking a sip from his glass, Leo paced behind the bar. It would make a decent shield, should his client suddenly come after him. "So, she was cheating on you."

"Of course she was cheating. What did you think? I just randomly wanted her dead? What kind of man do you think I am?"

A murdering, abusive, paranoid.... Oh. Of course.

"Your first wife had an affair with a woman," Leo said without thinking.

Faster than Leo could move, faster than he could blink, Max stood before him, leaning over the bar, his

massive hands gripping Leo's neatly pressed shirt collar. "My wife was *leaving* me for a woman. A woman
I'd known nothing about, because I damn well wouldn't
have married her if I'd had a fucking clue. A woman
she'd been with for months before we got married. She
showed me pictures!" If he kept shouting that way, he'd
have a heart attack. Red-faced and sweating, he was
easily the scariest thing Leo had ever seen, and in Leo's
field, he'd seen some scary shit.

Leo's own pulse sped up. He wondered if he'd be
better off if the man did drop dead right now. Max's
current wife certainly would be.

"I built this house for Kat, bought jewelry for her,
fucked her senseless every goddamn fucking night."

Yeah, sure you did.

"And she was leaving all that, all *this*," he said,
releasing Leo to wave a hand around the luxurious library, "for a fucking broke construction worker…."

Who had to be Flynn Dalton. Leo's mind raced as
he processed all the details. That's how Max "knew of"
Genesis's girlfriend when he saw them together at the
lake. He'd seen Flynn's picture in his wife's hands and
had her investigated.

And, Leo was willing to bet, if he checked deeply enough into the histories of the other women who'd
died in Dead Man's Pond, he'd discover they preferred
female company to male.

Somehow, some way, Max had imbued the cursed
charm with a hatred of all homosexual women, and the
lake was collecting them, one by one.

Chapter 15
Trouble in Pseudo-Paradise

SATURDAY NIGHT and Sunday pass without incident. Gen sleeps wrapped around me, claiming her energy will keep Kat's spirit away.

Whatever. I just like the feel of her body against mine. It's a win-win.

Still can't help feeling like I cheated on her, though.

We talked about how to deal with the situation. There's every possibility the sex *was* the message, and now Kat will leave me alone. One last roll in the sack. One last goodbye. I'd like to think I'm done with ghosts, but I doubt it.

And none of that explains the deal with the lake as a whole. Why is it collecting victims? And why are the majority of them women?

I can't get those answers. Kat isn't talking to Gen. I have no desire to talk further with Kat's husband. Not much else we can do.

Sunday night I receive a text from Tom letting me know the company bowling group isn't playing. No surprise there. Bowling costs money, and laid-off employees need to watch every dime. Besides, with my bruised ribs, swinging sixteen pounds would hurt like hell.

But it presents a problem, one I'm going to have to deal with repeatedly over the next few days or, God forbid, weeks.

Gen knows my schedule. Sunday night is bowling night. It's why we can't go out on Sundays, though she often comes to the lanes to watch me wipe the floor with my teammates and opponents. She says she loves the way my back and arm muscles flex when I throw a bowling ball. I'm powerful yet graceful—her words.

I like how she strokes my ego… and other things.

I don't want her to know I've been laid off. She'll offer to loan me money and act all weird if I refuse. Bad enough I'm using her for transportation and temporary housing.

I don't want to use the injury, either. Having her take care of me is great for a little while, but the babying gets old fast.

I luck out when she tells me she has a client coming and can't watch me bowl. I scramble for words when she offers the car, concocting a quick story about catching a ride with Tom. I suppose I could just borrow her car and drive around for a while, but then I'd waste gas, and I'm responsible for whatever happens to the Charger. Damn, I hate lying to her, but it beats dealing with her pity.

At six fifteen I wave goodbye and trot out the door with my bowling gear. I keep right on trotting, around the corner and into a little beer-and-wine bar next to the pizza place. One wouldn't think a town like Festivity would be large enough to support two drinking establishments, but hey, if I could afford fine wines, I'd want a place like this to drink them in too. Dark, classy wood decor, soft jazz playing—completely different atmosphere from the pub and less grating on my frazzled nerves.

I forego the outdoor seating, just in case, and take a table with a good view of the entrance, by the back exit so I can slip out if necessary. Then I order a soda, since the cheapest beer is five bucks, pull a suspense thriller novel from my bowling bag, and wait.

I don't fit the norm here, and I catch a few odd looks from the regular clientele, still in their Sunday-best suits and skirts. That's Festivity for you. Church Sunday morning, kill a bottle of wine, often all on your own, Sunday night.

The pub would suit my attire better, but with Chris managing the place, Gen would find out. Besides, despite being Sunday, tonight is cougar night—the night all the older women flock to the pub in too tight, way-too-revealing outfits and try to pick up much younger men while gyrating to all the latest rave music.

No, seriously.

Two hours later, I've drunk four sodas, read six chapters, though none of it has really sunk in, gone to the bathroom twice, and had the waitress slip me her phone number. Okay, the Gay Pride sticker on my bowling bag is kind of a giveaway—a giveaway that Kevin Taylor Jr. totally missed at the lanes. At least she isn't mad about me holding down a table for two dollars and fifty cents plus tax and tip. And she's cute. Strawberry blonde with a tiny waist. If I weren't head over heels for Genesis, she'd totally be my type.

Regardless, I don't want to lead her on by sticking around, and it's time to head out, anyway. I creep into the apartment, heading straight to the bedroom so I don't interrupt Gen with her client. Must be an emergency appointment, coming in that late. The older gentleman has his back to me, seated on the floor cushions, and he's so intent, his tone so distraught, he never notices me there. Gen inclines her head when she spots me and offers a brief smile as I walk by. My stomach muscles tighten with guilt.

My bowling night routine includes a shower, so I take a long one, toweling off as Gen comes in. She's radiant tonight, her long skirt swirling about her delicate ankles, the lacy black T-shirt tucked in at her trim waist, her red hair glowing in the flickering candles.

Her eyes sparking with fury.

Uh-oh.

She has my jeans dangling from one hand, and she holds them up in front of her like a shield for a second, then hurls them at my face. I drop the towel to catch them and stand before her, naked and confused—a state becoming more and more familiar.

"What the hell, Flynn? I share my apartment, I share my bed…."

"Uh…." I drag my pants up my still wet legs, no underwear, but at least I'm half-covered.

"If you wanted to see other people, well, I wouldn't have liked it, but we could have discussed it." She swallows hard. "I guess."

I stand there, blinking at her stupidly. Is she counting Kat as "other people?" Yesterday she assured me I wasn't cheating, no matter what I believe.

Wait. Maybe she's possessed. That might make sense. "Um, Kat?" I ask.

"What?" It comes out as a startled, furious screech.

Nope, not possessed. But a helluva lot angrier.

I close my eyes and count to five. My instinct is to sit on the bed, but I suspect Gen will shove me off, so I place myself on the floor. At her feet. Back against the wall. Submissive.

Keeping my tone as calm as possible, I say, "I lied. I'm sorry. Bowling got canceled, so I went for a soda. I have absolutely no idea what else you're talking about. Please tell me."

Gen throws her hands in the air. "Bullshit! Bowling didn't get canceled. You skipped it. To pick up Arielle at the wine bar." Her face turns as red as her hair. Her eyes shine with barely held back tears.

Arielle. Who the hell is—? Oh.

I cast about the room, spying the half-full laundry basket by the door. She must have come in, collected my dirty clothes, and emptied the pockets of my jeans, including the one with the waitress's name and phone number and a lipstick imprint on the rolled-up napkin.

God, this is so screwed up.

I slow my speech, saying each word as distinctly as I can. "I. Am. Not. Cheating. On. You." When I'm certain I have Gen's attention, I continue. "I have no interest in Arielle. I just took the napkin because I didn't want to hurt her feelings. In fact, as soon as I figured out she was flirting with me, I left. I didn't go bowling because yes, it was canceled. It got canceled because I got laid off. Everyone in the crew got laid off. We're all out of work." I can't look at her. I can't face her pity. I focus on the cream-colored carpeting between my bare feet. "I didn't tell you because, well…."

Gen drops herself to sit on the floor beside me. In my peripheral vision, she leans against the wall, facing forward. She spends a long moment staring across the room while my heart blocks up my throat. "You're out of work?" she says at last, voice very small.

"Yeah. But you can call Tom if you don't believe me. I wouldn't blame you. I did lie. I just didn't want sympathy or handouts."

Gen lets that sit on the air for a minute. "Why did you call me Kat?"

"Um…." I press my chin harder into my chest and mumble, "I thought you were possessed."

Longer pause. The wall behind me vibrates a little, then a lot, until I wonder if we're having a freak Florida earthquake. I look at Gen. She's doubled over, shoulders shaking, little whimpering noises escaping from her throat. When she meets my gaze, tears stream down her cheeks, making me hate myself all the more.

"Gen, I—"

"*Possessed*? By *Kat*?" She breaks off, unable to continue speaking, and I realize she isn't crying. She's laughing. "That must have seriously freaked you out."

I wait until she regains control, wiping her eyes on the back of one hand, resting the other on my bare shoulder.

"That's not something you really need to worry about. I've never met a spirit with the strength to possess me…." She pauses and shrugs. "I suppose it's possible. I'm not egotistical enough to think otherwise. But it would probably take a ghost who was a psychic in life to have that kind of power in death. I'm assuming Kat was no psychic."

"No, not psychic." Kat couldn't even tell I was in love with her.

"Okay. I'll let the phone number thing go. But," Gen says, stabbing a finger into my chest above the breastbone, "the lying must stop. Right now. People who love each other don't lie."

Gen, however, is well aware of how much I love her, even if I don't say it enough. Or at all. Gen always seems to know how I feel.

"And the next thing we need to discuss is your financial situation."

Then again, maybe not.

Chapter 16
Drowning Sorrows

I'M FINISHING my fifth beer in the pub when Chris notices me.

Actually, I think he's been aware of me the entire time I've been sitting at the end of his outdoor bar, soaking in the night air and watching Festivity's varied clientele from relative privacy. Background noise and a variety of news and sports on flat-screen televisions help me not to think too much. This is a Yankees bar. And there's a game on. Yanks vs. Red Sox—a major event. I'm more of a football gal myself, but I follow the leading teams in most sports.

Chris plops himself down on the next stool over and folds his arms on the polished wood surface.

"Waiting until I'm half-drunk before risking me, huh?" The slur of a couple of my words surprises me. Maybe I've had more than five. I'm not a lightweight, but I don't down six-packs regularly.

He nods. "You're difficult enough sober. I've never seen you drunk. Does alcohol mellow you, or are you the angry type?"

"I'm not difficult."

At his raised eyebrow, I shrug. Okay, maybe I'm a little difficult. But I don't try to be. I focus on his real question.

"Mellow, I guess. I don't do this a lot. When I do, I've gotta be pretty upset or pissed, so I go all out. I don't end up remembering much."

The bartender, a pretty brunette in a red button-down shirt and tight thigh-length black skirt, places another vanilla porter in front of me. Chris waves a hand in a subtle gesture, but even buzzed, I catch it. It's the "slow her down" signal.

Part of me wants to bite his head off. I don't need babying. I need forgetting. I need haze so thick I can stop thinking and sleep through half of tomorrow. But it's Chris, and I love him like a brother, so I let it go.

"So," he says, that goofy grin of his so infectious it makes me smile a little, "are you pissed or upset, then?" His expression sobers. "Gen's pretty upset herself, you know."

"I know." I drop my forehead on my crossed arms. "She told you?" It comes out muffled, but he gets the gist.

"Yep. She told me all about what a prideful, arrogant bitch you are."

My head jerks up. "What?" I'm half off the stool before his hand closes around my bicep and he pulls me back. My fingers curl into fists. Chris isn't a big guy. Brotherly or not, if he wants a fight….

"So much for mellow," he says. "Calm down, Dalton. Drink your beer and listen for a change. And yes, I'm well aware I'm taking my life into my own hands, here."

I take a deep breath and sink onto the stool. It's an effort to unclench my grip and wrap my fingers around the cold, sweating bottle. The icy liquid chills me from the inside out. I expect a continuation of the argument I left upstairs....

The whole "we need to discuss your financial situation" argument.

Totally out of the blue and just when I thought things had settled between us, Gen had to go there. She wants me to move in. She wants me to look for some part-time work.

She wants to take care of me when I should be the one taking care of her. And myself.

It ended with me mad and her hurt, just like those conversations usually do.

A quick glance at the outdoor Yankees clock tells me it's 1:00 a.m. I've been down here for two hours. Looks like it might be another couple before I get to bed. Not sure where I'm sleeping either. I still have my key to Gen's place, but she probably doesn't want me there right now.

"Do you love my sister?"

The question slaps me in the face. I stare at Chris, then close my eyes. "Yeah."

"No matter what?"

It's an odd choice of words. An odd question. But I nod.

"Good. Now the harder one. Do you want to spend the rest of your life with her?"

My eyes snap back open. "What is this, an interrogation?" Across the bar, a group of guys cheers and shouts. Guess the Yankees are winning tonight. I'm glad somebody is.

"*You* love my sister. *I* love my sister. I don't want to see her hurt. It's a fair question."

It is.

"I think so."

Chris shakes his head so fast his longish bangs flop into his face. "No 'think.' Yes or no."

It isn't that I don't know. I shift on the seat, the vinyl creaking under my ass. The beer tastes harsh and bitter.

"Yes," I say. Heat floods my cheeks.

The baseball fans groan and swear. A couple exchange money. I can't make out the bills from where I sit, but I guess twenties, fifties, and hundreds. It sickens me, the way they throw their wealth around.

I'm agonizing over the tab I'm racking up, even with my "friends and family" discount, and they're waving enough cash to pay my rent for a month. Sometimes I hate Festivity.

"Question three," Chris says, dragging my attention back and raising three fingers. They blur for a moment, becoming two, then four, and I rub my hand over my eyes. "So you're considering asking her to marry you?"

Might as well get this over with fast. "It has crossed my mind." To be honest, while I only think about a future with Genesis in it, I haven't really considered formalizing our union. It just hasn't seemed… necessary. Gay marriage hasn't been legal in Florida for that many years, and I've seen a bunch of folks rush into things, spend a lot on elaborate ceremonies. But I bet Gen wants to make it official, or at least wants to talk about it.

"I'm not trying to put you on the spot, Flynn. I'm making a point. If you married Genesis, you'd share an apartment, right?"

Uh-oh. I'm walking right into a trap, but the gate already slammed shut behind me. "Yes…."

"And if one of you lost your job, you'd let the other support you until you got back on your feet." He holds up a palm to forestall any argument I might make, not that I can think that fast while this drunk. "You'll find other work, and you'll contribute to the bills as best you can. I need some more waitstaff. Gen wants to hire an assistant to handle appointments and record keeping."

"It's not enough. It's not the same. I don't want to be kept. I don't want to take advantage."

Chris picks up my beer and takes a sip, then frowns. "How can you drink this sweet crap? Look," he says, pointing a finger at my chest, "in every reasonable sense of the word, you're Gen's spouse. Spouses help each other. Everyone needs a hand once in a while. She makes more in a week than you do in a month, and you're going to have to deal with it or cut her loose. Period."

I blink at him, then think about his words. Is that my hang-up? God, I'm acting like a 1950s husband. The man of the house. The breadwinner. Can't let the little wifey work. Can't let her earn more than I do or my reputation with the guys will be ruined.

I *am* a prideful, arrogant bitch.

Chris barks a laugh, and only then do I realize I said that out loud. "That," he says, "is why I'm not kicking your ass right now."

I let my gaze wander over him from head to toe. In a fight, he would be the one getting an ass-kicking, and we both know it. His blush tells me he reads my mind.

"So you'll move in?" he asks, changing the subject.

"Yes."

"And you'll take the part-time jobs until you find something else?"

"Yes." It comes out as a growl. Nothing I hate more than working in the service industry. I am so not a people person.

Chris ignores it. "Good." He throws an arm around my shoulders. "Better get to bed, then. You start at eight for the breakfast shift."

I groan, reaching for my wallet, but he places a hand over mine.

"Don't worry. I'll take it out of your first check," he says with a grin.

I still toss a few bills down for tip. I'm halfway to the gate leading to the sidewalk when he calls, "Hey, Dalton! I'm really glad you can be taught."

Oh, I can be taught. I just wish I'd learn a little faster.

Chapter 17
Making Up Is Hard To Do

I ENTER the apartment to complete silence. Street-lights cast an eerie glow across the living room from the window. Gen has shut the bedroom door—an obvious "keep out" sign for me tonight. Out of curiosity, I try the knob anyway. Locked. No surprise there.

I throw myself on the larger couch, feet dangling over the armrest. It's the longest five and a half hours of tossing and turning I've ever spent. My brain won't shut down. I worry about money, Gen, my new jobs, and spirits. Without Gen to block Kat out, I'm at my dead ex-girlfriend's mercy.

I don't like being at anyone's mercy. Not one bit.

At some point I must doze off, because the cell phone alarm I set wakes me up with the most annoying sound I could choose—roosters crowing—and at the highest possible volume. Dear God, I would never survive on a farm.

At least nothing dead touched me during the night.

Gen's door is still shut, so that means splashing my face in the half-bath's sink, using water to smooth my hair down, and chewing a piece of gum to freshen my breath. Thank goodness I took that shower last night and changed clothes afterward. Well, sort of. I still wear the same jeans, and no underwear.

Commando it is, then.

My head pounds like a sonofabitch, so I grab a couple of aspirin from the kitchen cabinet and swallow them with a glass of orange juice. It isn't until I'm on my way out that I notice the blanket on the floor by the couch.

It's pink and fuzzy—one of those thin summer blankets people use for when the air-conditioning cuts on too much during the night. I remember throwing it off when I got up, but it wasn't there when I went to bed, and I was too out of it to register its sudden appearance.

I'm running late, but I take the time to fold it neatly and lay it outside Gen's bedroom door. After grabbing a pad and pen, I write a quick note: Thanks. Really sorry. – Flynn, and a smiley face, and leave it on top of the blanket.

Then I hurry down to my first day working at the Village Pub. Yippee.

THE MORNING is a whirlwind of washing pots and pans, dumping garbage, and cleaning counters. Apparently these are the least-desirable tasks the staff performs, and I get some sympathy from the other workers, but I don't mind. It keeps me busy, I eat lunch for free, I don't have to talk to many people, and I'm making money again—a whopping eight dollars an hour and no tips. Yeah, that's the downside.

Eventually Chris plans to make me a server, but my jeans and "Yet despite the look on my face, you're still talking" slogan T-shirt aren't what he prefers his staff to wear when interacting with Festivity's residents. Laughing, he takes my locked-out-of-the-bedroom explanation in stride and uses me in the kitchen until I can buy black slacks and a white shirt.

At four, he waves me out of there with a reminder to show up again the next day, Tuesday, at the same time, and I'm free.

Fresh air and sunshine revive me as I walk out the rear exit. I don't go upstairs. This is prime appointment time for Gen, and I haven't had a chance to offer myself as her secretary yet, so I'd be intruding.

I take a long stroll around the downtown lake, but even though this isn't Dead Man's Pond, it gives me the creeps, and I only do one lap. When that fails to loosen me up, I ask Chris to borrow his car again, drive out of Festivity, and head for the closest pawn shop.

Most people don't realize pawn shops offer great gifts for very little money. Used video games, electronics of all kinds, jewelry—good stuff at reasonable prices.

I call my bank before going in. Nine hundred odd dollars and some change—what's left of my last paycheck plus the money from my truck. Two hundred will satisfy my hotel to the end of the week, but I'll have to get my belongings out of there by Friday. That leaves me about seven hundred to work with. I still owe Gen tow truck money. I also want to contribute something to the rent and food and utilities, so I need to watch what I spend.

Forty is going toward a bicycle. When the company does pick me back up, I can use it to get from Gen's place to the site. And if no one buys out that contract, well, at least I can bike to the store or the bank, take care of all those pesky little household chores without hitting someone up for a car.

Like a proper housewife.

Stop it, Flynn.

This pseudo-spouse thing will take some getting used to.

As I pay, the sparkle of gold and gems in the counter case catches my eye. Necklaces, bracelets—those thin ones with lots of diamonds that rich people call "tennis" for no apparent reason.

Engagement rings.

I came in to purchase a bike and a present for Gen, something to add to my apology. But hell, why not go all out? She wants commitment, I can give her commitment.

I can.

Like Gen said, I play for keeps. And lately when I let my mind wander into the future, I imagine the two of us growing old and gray together. But this….

My throat goes dry and my palms sweat when I point to the row of the cheapest rings and ask to see them. The guy behind the counter, a thin old man with gray hair and sun-marked skin, raises an eyebrow at me, but he pulls out the ring holder and sets it in front of me, keeping one hand on the velvet-lined tray holding six different ones, like he thinks I might snatch the lot and make a run for it.

Maybe I'm not quite ready for the tux and the "Wedding March," but there's no reason why we can't be prepared for that eventuality.

"Boyfriend making you pick your own?" the sales guy asks, tugging his pale green T-shirt bearing the store's logo into place over his skinny frame. He's pretty well-groomed for a pawn shop salesman. I note his neatly trimmed nails and clean-shaven face. The T-shirt and jeans seem out of place on him, and he doesn't look comfortable. Maybe a new hire, a retiree looking for something to do. "He shoulda come in with you, but it's smart, really. You're the one who has to wear it. I hope he plans on paying you back," he adds with a grin.

"You have a lot of them," I say, not in the mood to correct his misconceptions. "That's sad. Broken engagements, pawned rings."

"Yeah." He drags a stool over, figuring out I'm going to dither for a while, and seats himself on it. "Young girls, mostly, jumping into things, rushing. Stay free as long as you can. That's my motto. Plenty of time to tie yourself to someone else. Rushing causes mistakes to be made."

If this old man is still free, he's going to stay that way for the rest of his life. And that's just as sad.

He leans in, and I smell pricey cigars mixed with expensive cologne. Definitely out of place here. Strong, but not unpleasant.

"What's he like, this guy of yours? He treat you right? Busy all the time, huh? Working a couple of jobs?"

Okay. Enough is enough.

"I don't have a boyfriend. It's not actually for me. It's for my girlfriend."

"Your... oh. Oh! Huh." He slaps the counter with his palm. "Well, good for you. Glad the damn government decided to stop controlling who can marry who."

He rants for another minute or two about gay marriage, gun control, and a couple of other issues I don't follow while I examine each ring. I'm very glad we're alone in the store.

Contrary to my previous beliefs, engagement rings are pretty similar to one another. Gold band. One stone, though that stone ranges in size and shape. Then again, maybe only the cheap ones are so plain. I'm sure I've seen elaborate rings with multiple diamonds, engravings, designs making them stand out.

Like Gen.

I want something special, but I'll never afford what she deserves.

The last one I pick up is the most unusual—instead of a plain round ring, it has some sharper angles to it, some character, and a small but real (not cubic zirconia) diamond. It's matched with a simpler band, but still with those edges; the two, the engagement ring and the wedding band, fit together where the edges match.

"This set," I say. "How much?"

"Five seventy-five."

Too much.

He must read it on my face because his softens a little. "How much can you afford?" he asks, checking the store to make certain there are no other customers to overhear him.

There's no one else, no shoppers, no other staff. That's a little odd, but times are tough. The business probably can't afford extra help.

Nothing, I want to tell him, but I say, "Five hundred." That leaves me about a hundred and sixty dollars to give Gen this week until Chris pays me. I shouldn't be doing this at all, but I get the feeling it will mean a lot more to her than a little rent money.

"Done," the guy says, grabbing my hand and shaking it once. "Now you go out there and make a statement."

"Um, sure." Whatever. So long as he doesn't charge me full price. I end up not buying the bike. Still need clothes for work, and it wouldn't have fit into Chris's sedan, anyway.

But even without it, I feel overloaded with the plastic ring box shoved into my jeans pocket. I've bought her an engagement ring, but giving it to her is another thing entirely. I don't even want to consider the wedding band at this point.

And God, what if she says no?

Chapter 18
It's a Dying

GEN ACCEPTS the bundle of Walmart carnations I give her as a peace offering, placing a light kiss on my nose before taking them to the kitchen for a vase and water. The ring box in my pocket presses hard against my thigh, one corner digging a groove into my skin.

Yeah, I'm a total coward.

She's forgiven me. Chris told her I agreed to share a roof and work for them until something better comes along job-wise. Not that the ring is meant to guilt her into forgiveness. I know it's a whole lot more than that. But I can't seem to find the same determination I had at the pawn shop now that I face the real possibility of rejection.

I hang my new work clothes in her bedroom closet—*our* closet—the action awkward and strange. The black trousers and white button-down look stark next to her tie-dyes and lace. I slip the box out of my pocket, find a dusty pair of shoes in the farthest back corner, and stuff it into the toe of one of the black patent-leather pumps. By the time I take a shower and switch T-shirts (and add underwear beneath my jeans), a mouthwatering smell of pasta and sauce wafts from the kitchen archway.

The growling of my stomach reminds me I haven't had dinner, and a glance at the wall clock, also showing the phases of the moon in case I'm interested, tells me it's eight.

Gen leans out, scans me from head to toe, and frowns. "We've got thirty minutes to eat. I have an emergency reading tonight, and I'll need you to greet her and settle her on the couch while I freshen up."

Right. Because I'm her assistant now. Got it.

Her eyes linger on my Pink concert tee.

At first I think she's admiring my chest, which is fairly ample, though nothing compared to hers. I like to spend long, leisurely minutes lying beside her, playing with her breasts until she yells at me to head back to the players' bench or go for the touchdown. (Yes, I'm bringing Gen around to liking football.) Then I realize she's scrutinizing the shirt—once again not quite professional attire.

"When are you moving the rest of your stuff over?" Gen disappears into the kitchen before I can answer.

"Tomorrow night I'll start, if I can borrow a car," I call. A quick trip back to the closet puts me in the white button-down, and I join her at the round wooden kitchen table a minute later. "Better?"

She smiles, and it brightens the whole damn room. "Much. Don't worry about the jeans. Like I said, this was a last-minute thing, so it's okay for you to be a little casual."

I wasn't worried.

I scoop slices of lasagna onto white plates with blue flowers around the edges. The carnations in the glass vase between us make a nice centerpiece.

Nesting. Gen's nesting. Well, she isn't pregnant, but knowing I'm moving in seems to have a similar effect. She reaches around and ties a napkin over my shirt.

"Domestic much?"

"Red sauce and white shirts always find a way to meet."

That wrangles a laugh out of me, and we settle in to eat dinner.

It's homey and nice, reminding me of family meals when I was a kid back in New Jersey. Just me and Mom and Grandma around the table, chatting and sharing our day. Before Grandma died and Mom sank into her first real depression. The one that never really ended.

Dad left when I was four. I barely remember what he looked like, and Mom burned all the photographs. Sometimes I wonder if that's why I'm so determined to have a permanent relationship. I'm never doing to somebody (to *Gen*, I correct myself) what my dad did to Mom and me.

Or what Kat did to me later.

"Hey, you in there?" A hand waves in front of my face. I'm ignoring her.

"Sorry," I mumble around a mouthful of green beans she's managed to sneak onto my plate. They aren't so bad covered in tomato sauce and parmesan cheese. "So what constitutes a 'reading emergency'?" I ask, not wanting to dwell on my childhood woes.

Gen's smile fades. "Death in the family. Unexpected. Slip and fall." Tears glisten at the corners of her eyes. Gen always takes her work to heart. Sometimes I hold her, crying, for hours after an emotional reading. "It's the client's daughter. Since she was young, her mother doesn't think she had prepared a will, so she wants to find out, and also say goodbye."

"Oh." And I'm supposed to entertain this grieving mother while Gen gets ready? "Gen, I'm not much for small talk. People make me nervous. What am I going to say to her?"

The smile returns, soft and sweet. "You're a human being, Flynn. Express your sympathy. Discuss the weather, Festivity, whatever. It won't be more than five minutes so I can rid myself of garlic breath." She points to me with one of the breadsticks, smothered in butter and garlic. "If you're lucky, she'll be late."

The doorbell rings; then the knocker sounds.

These days, I'm never lucky.

A wicked grin flashes across Gen's face. "All yours," she says with a grand flourish toward the front door. She disappears into her bedroom.

"Wait! What's her—" Name. Right. Well, now I have something to ask this woman. No, I'm supposed to be the assistant. I should already know her name. I steal a glance in the appointment book Gen keeps on a stand by the entry, but it isn't there.

Because it's last-minute. Right.

The bell sounds again.

"Flynn…," Gen growls from the bedroom.

"Got it!" I shout back. Real professional. Sigh.

I paste on what I hope is a believable smile and throw the door open wide, scaring the bejeezus out of the fiftysomething woman clutching a purse to her chest and raising her hand to knock once more. She stumbles backward, bumping the balcony walkway railing, and I grab her arm to steady her.

"Oops, sorry. Didn't mean to startle you," I say.

She blinks liquid brown eyes, red-rimmed and shadowed from little sleep. Her skin shines pale beneath the building's exterior security lights. "You're not Genesis," the woman accuses, pointing a painted nail in my direction.

I resist the urge to congratulate her on her astuteness and instead lead the way inside, hoping she'll follow. She does.

"I'm her new assistant, Flynn Dalton. May I take your purse and hat?"

The client scans me, pursing her lips at my sneakers and jeans while passing me the Coach brand bag (not a knockoff) and a bright pink sunhat, though why anyone would be wearing a sunhat at eight thirty at night is beyond me. I place both beside the appointment book on the table.

She fluffs her graying hair in the entry hall mirror and turns to me, eyebrows raised.

Oh. Right. "The powder room is there, if you'd like to freshen up." I wave behind her. Maybe she'll go in there and stay until Gen comes out. Then again, I can't remember if I cleaned up after myself when I took care of the basics this morning. A glance over her shoulder shows me puddles of water around the porcelain sink and a discarded T-shirt hanging on the towel rack.

Crap.

"No, I'm fine."

Thank God.

I lead her to the living room, as if she can't find her way the whole five feet by herself, and nod toward the larger couch. Then I busy myself setting things out the way I've seen Gen do it: tossing the pillows on the floor (well, they are *throw* pillows, right?), lighting the candles, and fetching her well-worn deck of tarot cards from a closed cabinet by the easy chair.

Tingles run through my fingers when I touch them, jolting me from nails to wrist, and I almost drop the whole deck. As it is, the top two cards escape my grip and flutter to the carpeting, landing faceup.

The Tower and the Lovers.

My heart rate picks up as the client (still don't know her damn name) sucks in a sharp breath, then lets it out with a little laugh. "You aren't a reader, are you?" she asks.

"No, I'm not."

"Good."

Yeah. I've been around Gen long enough to know the Death card doesn't mean death, but change. However, the Tower, with its macabre image of bodies jumping off and plummeting to an unknown doom, does indicate someone's demise. And the Lovers, well, that one explains itself.

Chapter 19
For Love or Money

GEN TAKES her sweet-ass time "getting ready" for the reading. I gather the fallen cards with still trembling fingers and place them next to the pillows as fast as possible, then try to ignore my odd reaction to them. As she suggested, I make small talk about the weather, Festivity, and whatever, which lasts all of two minutes.

"Can I get you anything? Soda? Tea?" Anything to give me an escape from the living room?

"You *may* get me a cup of tea, yes. That would be lovely."

Ah, grammar Nazi. I'd lay odds she worked as an English teacher.

In the kitchen, I stare at the counters and cabinets, with absolutely no idea how to "make tea." If I want caffeine, I'm a Coke Zero kind of gal. But I've seen Gen do it, and it isn't hard, right?

It only takes me three tries before I find the shelf with the teapot, and another two to locate the little baggies. "Um, Earl Grey, ginger, or vanilla?" I call out.

"It's night," she says by way of an answer.

Riiight. And which one is the most… night-timey?
"Um, vanilla, then?"

"Please."

Okay. I get the water going. Gen *still* hasn't emerged from her… *our* room.

I smell a rat.

This is a test. I hate tests. And Gen and her brother have been testing me a lot lately. I'm damn well not going to fail this one.

When Gen finally returns from the bedroom, I've set out the fine china teacups, the sugar bowl, and lace doilies to place things on. I have my legs crossed and my pinky extended, and I'm discussing the current state of education with her client (whose name, by the way, is Mrs. Pinkerton. Snort. And yes, she'd been a teacher for over thirty years, and her husband was a surgeon, which explained the Coach purse).

You could hear the thud Gen's jaw makes when it hits the floor.

I wink at her as she crosses to us and offers an apology with the excuse of having to take an urgent phone call—family business. Yeah, right. Gen's remaining family is Chris, and he never calls. He just shows up at the door.

"No trouble, dear. I know this was last-minute, and I so appreciate you working me in. Besides, I was having a lovely conversation with your new assistant, here."

Mrs. Pinkerton has done all the talking, but that seems to be the real trick, and I'm happy to take her mind off the loss of her daughter. Twenty-eight years old. My age. Fell in the shower. Geez.

I think about my near plummet at work and swallow hard, getting a taste of what Gen must have felt watching from below.

"Well, I'll just be leaving, then…." I stand and turn toward the bedroom, but Gen stops me with an upraised hand.

"Actually," she says, a wicked gleam in her eye, "if it's all right with Althea, I'd like you to stay. You should familiarize yourself more with the process, now that you're working here and all."

"Oh, it's fine by me," Althea Pinkerton says, gesturing toward the couch she vacates and easing herself onto the floor pillows. It takes a full minute for her to manage the cross-legged position, and I might suggest to Gen that she provide some alternate seating arrangement in the future.

I glare at Gen, but she has a point. We discuss our jobs with one another, but my phobia of all things supernatural has prevented me from observing her, with the exception of the occasional street festival. And even then, I've only seen her read tarot. I've never seen her actually channel a spirit. I need to suck it up and deal.

Pasting on another smile, I settle on the couch, rest my elbows on my knees, my chin in my hands, and wait.

Gen has explained that she isn't a typical psychic insofar as her methodology is concerned, but there's a wide range of skills and talents and ways of using them. Some can mix potions. Others read minds or move things without touching them or catch glimpses of the future. Some walk through the spirit world while deep in meditation, and still more see into people's past lives. However, most psychics read tarot or channel the dead.

She combines both of these.

Gen uses the cards to "tune in" to her clients and the loved ones with whom they wish to communicate. She begins by giving a simple reading: an overview of Althea's personality, where she's been, where she is, where she's going. Gen asks leading questions. Althea answers. The Death card and the Tower both make appearances.

When Gen's fingertips brush the Tower, she… changes.

I sit straight up, my blunt nails scraping my jeans, as the transformation occurs right in front of me. Gone are Gen's posture and mannerisms, the way her hands move, replaced by… someone I don't know.

But Mrs. Pinkerton does.

"Isabelle?" she asks, voice wavering, eyebrows drawn together.

Gen's head comes up slowly, gaze rising from the cards to Mrs. Pinkerton's suddenly pale face. "Mother?"

Holy shit.

It isn't Gen's voice. It's several pitches too high to be hers. And the way she cocks her head to the side. Not Gen. Definitely not Gen. My chest constricts. I can't breathe. Gooseflesh rises on my arms and neck. I want to grab and shake her until this stranger, this *apparition*, gives me back my girlfriend. I shift my grip to the armrest and the cushion. It's everything I can do to remain on the couch.

"Bella, baby, is that you?" Althea reaches out with her fingertips, holding her hand mere inches from Gen's arm, then thinks better of the action and drops her hand to her side.

Gen blinks, unfocused, her face a mask of confusion.

She's told me that spirits get confused when they're channeled. It disorients both the ghost and the medium. And sometimes they don't realize they're dead or understand why.

Gen's expression clears, her focus sharpens, the ghost looking out through her eyes.

"I'm… I'm sorry, Mama. So sorry. I should have been more careful."

"Oh, sweetheart." She breaks down then, the grieving mother, tears coursing over her cheeks. "It was an accident. Not your fault. Nothing was your fault."

To my utter shock, I feel wetness on my own face and swipe it away on the back of a sleeve.

They speak for a good half hour, this mother and daughter, sometimes crying, sometimes laughing over a shared memory. Althea eventually asks about a will, though she's obviously hesitant to mention something so cold and material.

No, Bella didn't have one, but she'd like half of her estate (twenty-eight-year-olds have estates?) to go to her parents and the other half to a charity for retired racing greyhounds, of all things.

I glance from one to the other. Gen's a huge supporter of animal rescue groups. If this is a ploy on her part… but no. Bella's mother nods vigorously, telling me that her daughter always felt so sorry for those poor mistreated racing dogs.

I feel terrible for even thinking Gen might use a desperate client to accomplish her own goals. No, Gen performs a much-needed service here. And she's amazing at it.

Then, as quickly as she came, Bella goes. Three of the six candles blow out simultaneously, drawing a shriek from Althea and a gasp from me. Gen slumps where she sits, shakes herself, and stretches her arms high above her head like she's awakened from a long nap.

"You okay?" I ask, rising and placing my palm on her shoulder.

She blinks up at me, dark circles under both eyes. What she does, it's hard on her. I've seen the emotional aftereffects, but I never noticed the physical strain before.

"I'm fine," she assures me, voice cracking a bit. "But I could use some water."

While Mrs. Pinkerton thanks her over and over and they handle the payment, I go to the kitchen and stand at the sink, taking breath after shaky breath. I splash cool liquid in my face. My hands shake when I fill the glass. I have to wait several minutes until I can carry it without spilling.

When I return, Althea is telling Gen how much like her daughter I am.

I just watched my girlfriend channel a woman's spirit. A couple of nights ago, I was sexually assaulted by my dead lover's ghost. It's been a really hard week. I'm not thinking clearly.

"Oh, so your daughter's gay?" I ask.

"What? No!" Mrs. Pinkerton turns from Gen to me and back again, horror and shock warring for dominance on her face.

I close my eyes and sigh. So much for passing that test.

Chapter 20
To Hell and Back

EVERYTHING GOES pretty much downhill from there.

Gen, her stride stiff and controlled, her face rigid with the effort of not laughing in the presence of this woman who has lost her daughter, walks the sputtering Mrs. Pinkerton to the front hall. Once she shuts the door and Althea's high heels clatter down the closest set of exterior cement stairs, Gen falls into me, a helpless victim of her own hysterics.

She can't breathe, can't speak, can't even stand without my support, she laughs so hard. I should be mortified, but I chuckle with her, relieved she laughs rather than yells.

"You're not mad?" I manage to sneak in during a lull in her mirth.

"Flynn, I swear, you're going to be the death of me."

The remaining candles go out.

Really, people should know better than to say things like that.

"Um, Gen?"

In my arms, she goes rigid. Her skin chills beneath my hands. The temperature drops by ten degrees or more. "We're not alone," she whispers, breaking away.

Kinda figured that one out on my own.

I track her by sound as she crosses the room, heading, I assume, for the heavy front curtains to open them and let in the streetlight from the road below. The zing the fabric makes as she yanks one curtain aside might be the most wonderful noise I've ever heard. A beam of light casts its path through the pitch-dark living room. I follow it to the corner nearest me.

Where Kat stands.

From the far side of the lake, I hadn't noticed the way her clothing and hair clung to her, soaked through with water, but here, this close, I can see every gruesome detail. She still wears the tan slacks and fuzzy sweater, pale green, I think, though in the yellow light it's hard to be certain of the color. I don't want to take my eyes off her for a second, but curiosity has me following droplets when they leave her skin… and vanish before hitting the floor.

That explains why the bed hadn't been wet from her previous… visit.

She takes a step toward me, feet squishing in her leather shoes. I'm not sure if it's water or tears running down her face, but her depthless eyes hold an eternity of sorrow. I shiver.

"What is it you want?" Gen asks, arms folded across her chest. She's pissed, and I'm impressed. Her voice never wavers, while I can't even get my own mouth to open. Then again, she's used to this sort of thing.

Up until this moment, I was sure Kat knew Gen was in the room. Kat's head snaps to the side, her dead eyes fixing on my current girlfriend's face. A look of rage replaces the hopelessness of a moment before. Sparks flash in her eye sockets. She moves fast, heading straight for where Gen stands.

Without thinking, I throw myself between them, blocking Kat's apparition seconds before it intersects with Gen.

"Flynn, no!" Gen screams, grabbing my forearms at the moment of impact.

Kat's spirit literally slams into—*into*—me.

My blood turns to ice. Pressure builds and builds from within, a thousand maggots crawling beneath my skin. Needle-covered maggots. With teeth. Chewing their way through flesh, muscles, bone, while I writhe and twist and struggle against their invasion.

"Let her go!"

It's Gen, but I barely hear her over my own screaming. The sensation creeps, wriggles, and squirms to the outermost tips of my extremities, to the innermost centers of my heart and brain. And then my body is no longer my own.

The maggots force their way up my throat, moving my lips and tongue to produce one word—one word emerging from my mouth in Kat's voice.

"Mine."

Gen said a spirit like Kat can't possess her. Kat isn't strong enough to overcome Gen's psychic defenses.

She didn't say anything about Kat's ability to possess *me*.

Chapter 21
Crosstown Blues

YOU WANT something done right, you have to do it yourself.

Max drove the shovel deep into the soft dirt at the far edge of his golf course property. No one around. Clubhouse closed at dusk. Nothing but rolling miniature hills, flags stuck in holes, sand and water traps, and the occasional deer or wild boar.

He swatted at a mosquito and tossed the shovelful over his shoulder. Sweat trickled down his chest and beaded on his brow.

The body lay wrapped in garbage bags at his side.

Dumping Amanda in a water trap would have been easier on his sore back, but he'd had enough of water. No one would find her here.

He'd wait at least a week before reporting her missing. No one would know the difference. She rarely left the house. He allowed her few friends, all of them older, heavier, uglier.

Then it would be—he came home from work. No sign of her at the house. No idea where she'd gone. Car still in the garage. Nothing disturbed. No forced entry.

Some of the neighbors would suspect a crime had been committed, but not by him. Not by the man who gave to charity and helped build playhouses for needy kids. The man whose first wife had tragically died in a horrible car accident to which he could not (had better not) ever be connected. Other neighbors might think Amanda left him, and he'd have to live with that embarrassment. But it beat the inevitable alternative—that she *planned* to leave him sometime in the near future for yet another fucking dyke.

Swimsuit magazines, fashion magazines, long hours in front of the TV watching *Dancing With the Stars*, all those girls in skimpy costumes. Amanda loved figure skating. Every winter. Every broadcast. Especially the female soloists.

She said she used to skate when she lived up north, said she competed in college.

Bullshit. Max knew the truth.

She liked watching them, those women.

He kicked at the black-plastic-covered body at his feet. "Not watching them now, are you, bitch."

His athletic shoe dislodged the bag, revealing half of Amanda's face—pale skin, wide, terrified eye, mouth agape. He'd caught her by surprise, his hands going to her neck as she sat in her favorite chair. A few soft, kneading strokes, the pretense to a massage and more, then a quick grab and a twist to the right, a wet pop. Done.

No screaming. No blood. Simple. Should have gone about it that way the first time around.

When the hole became deep enough to discourage curious scavengers, Max dumped the body, bags and all, into the opening and filled it in.

Now to fetch the seven boxes of petunias he'd purchased. Purple ones, pink ones. Amanda loved petunias, and he intended to plant a row along the property line, right across her grave.

In case anyone wondered at the disturbed dirt, the recently used shovel, the muddy shoes.

Everyone loved petunias.

Chapter 22
Inner Strength

"Mine," Kat says again with my voice.

My voice. Mine.

"She was never yours. You let her go. You threw her away," Gen says, hands still wrapped around my forearms. I think the contact hurts her. Her mouth twists in a pained grimace. "Hang on, Flynn."

Gen does… something. Jolts like tiny electric shocks prickle my skin where she touches me. The maggots retreat from the new and almost-as-unpleasant sensation, squirming down to my fingertips and disappearing in little sparkles of light that drop from my hands, winking out before reaching the floor. But Gen's tired from the earlier channeling. The process is slow, too slow, and the pain is too great. I'm suffocating, my lungs constricting as if Kat has forgotten to make my respiratory system function. I'm no longer certain my heart is beating.

But my nerves and brain work fine. I'm aware of every moment of torture, though my vision swims a bit from lack of oxygen.

And something in Gen's touch changes. For a half second, her eyes roll back into her head. Then she blinks and her focus narrows, her irises going almost black, like the darkest forest.

Holy mother of God.

"What do you want?" Gen asks.

Who gives a fuck? I know what *I* want. I want this thing out of me. And I want Gen to stop doing whatever the hell she's doing. Even if it works, even if she helps me, it feels... wrong.

"Get it out," says Kat's voice, an eerie echo of my thoughts.

Waves of anger and confusion mix in my mind. I can't tell which are my feelings and which are Kat's, but they overwhelm and bury me.

"I'm trying, Flynn. I'm trying," Gen says, but her brow furrows, and even through the pain, I understand why.

It was Kat's voice that said "Get it out," not mine. Kat feels bound and determined to stay. Why would she tell Genesis to get her out of me?

Enough of this shit. I'm getting torn apart from the inside out, and they're having a chat.

I reach into myself—no idea what I'm doing; it's all instinct. Pushing outward from my center, I thrust and shove and *force* this thing from my body. She fights me. The creeping crawling intensifies. My will against hers. But I'm stronger. I've always been stronger. I identify that which is hers and that which is mine. Separate her spirit from my own. There's a flash of light, an audible *pop*, and then she's gone.

Air, cold, sharp, and wonderful, rushes into my body. I suck in lungful after lungful, panting like I've just had the best fucking orgasm of my life with absolutely none of the pleasure. My heart thuds wildly. No, it wasn't beating before, and it pounds and aches now, struggling to catch up with the beats it missed.

Dizzy and nauseated, I sink more than fall to the carpet, Gen following me down, not letting go. The impact with the floor presses my warm, wet jeans against my chilled skin.

I close my eyes. Holy mother of fuck, I peed myself.

Faint mewling noises reach my ears, along with Gen's voice, telling me over and over that I'm okay.

The mewling comes from me.

Get it together, Flynn. Come on. Get a grip.

My head presses against Gen's shoulder. She's pulled me into her lap. I open my mouth to say something, but I shake so hard, my teeth clack together.

Try again.

"I'm… I'm…." Incoherent. That's what I am.

"Don't talk. Just breathe. In and out, in and out." She rubs my back and strokes my hair.

Yeah, breathing is good. Let me just do that.

Pounding sounds on Gen's front door, loud and insistent. Both of us tense, then relax at the rattling of a key in the lock.

Chris. Besides the two of us and the off-property landlord, he's the only other person with access to this apartment. The door flies open, slamming against the interior wall, and his silhouette stands framed in the entryway, backlit by the parking lot lights.

A click and the living room lamps spring on, blinding us. I turn my face further into Gen's body, shielding myself from the glare and Chris's inevitable shock and sympathy.

"What the hell?" He pounds over to us, and his hands find my shoulders. "Flynn?"

I can't respond.

"Gen, what the hell happened? Some of the kitchen staff reported screaming up here."

"That… would have been me," I say miserably, voice muffled against Gen's blouse.

Gen's breath rushes out of her in a whoosh of air. I guess she's relieved to hear me speak at last and make sense doing it.

"We had a little visit from the dead girlfriend," she explains.

I lift my head, to reassure her further if nothing else. Chris stares from one of us to the other, settling on Gen's face, and I immediately see why. Her eyes are still green/black.

Then she blinks and the darkness vanishes, the brilliant green replacing it as if it were never there. Maybe it wasn't. I'm so out of it, I barely know my own name. But Chris saw it too.

"Gen…." His voice wavers. I've never heard fear from him before.

"Later." The command leaves no room for argument.

Chris sighs, shifting his attention back to me, then does a double take. "Why are you wet?"

I drop my face back into Gen's shoulder. My groan is the only response.

"Help me get her into the bathroom," Gen says. I can picture the "shut up already" look on her face.

Without asking this time, Chris slides his arms beneath me and picks me up. It's an effort. I'm taller and possibly heavier than he is, but with Gen's help, we end up in the bedroom, then the master bath. Setting me on my feet is a mistake, and I grab for the sink, hanging on to keep from hitting the tile floor. Chris places his hands on my waist, steadying me.

When Gen fumbles with my belt buckle, I stiffen. "I can do it." And I prefer to do it in privacy.

Her expression shows her sincere doubt, but she lets go and moves to turn on the shower. I meet Chris's eyes in the mirror over the sink. Oh my God, I look like hell.

"I don't care if you're the brother I never had. I'm not stripping in front of you."

He chuckles, but it's strained, and he keeps darting glances at his sister. "Ah well, one more missed opportunity." To Gen he says, "I think she's doing better."

Not much better. The dark stain on my jeans floods my face with heated embarrassment. I've left similar wet spots on both Chris and Gen's clothing. And the carpet. Gen's beautiful cream-colored carpet. "I'm sorry," I whisper, chin dropping to my chest.

"I'll take it from here," Gen says, shoving Chris out the door. "Go on. I've got it."

"You sure?" He doesn't want to leave us alone. But is it me he's afraid for, or Gen? Gotta be me. Gen seems none the worse for wear. In fact, all traces of her earlier exhaustion have faded.

"Yeah, I'm sure. Shoo."

The door closes behind him with a soft click. The front door doesn't follow, though, so it looks like he's sticking around, hanging out on the couch until he's sure I'm all right. Humiliating or not, it warms me to know he cares.

Pots and pans rattle in the kitchen.

Or maybe he's making himself a late-night snack. Chris is a bottomless pit.

Gen tackles my belt for the second time, not giving up despite my faint noises of protest. Yellow stains mark the tails of my new white shirt where it was tucked into my pants. Seventeen dollars down the drain.

"It'll come out," she assures me, following my gaze. "Bleach works miracles."

I kick off my shoes, then step out of the jeans.

"Speaking of miracles," she says, pulling off her own shirt and skirt, "how did you do that, anyway?" It's nonchalant, that question, though I sense the intensity beneath her words.

"Do what?"

Gen waggles her fingers in the air in front of my face. "Drive her out. I started to pull her from you, but you already had it. You shouldn't have been able to do that."

I remember the pushing and the pressure, the sense of wills colliding, and anger, so much anger. "I grabbed and I shoved. It just felt like the right thing to do to get her... out of me."

"Huh." Both of us naked now, she takes my hand and draws me gently into the shower after her. It isn't that big a space, and our bodies brush constantly. Any other time I'd be totally turned on by the sight of the water rushing over her curves, glistening on her fair skin.

Not tonight.

"And no one in your family has ever claimed any psychic ability?" She picks up the shampoo from the side shelf, pours a puddle of the coconut-scented liquid into her hand, and begins massaging it into my scalp.

I close my eyes and sigh. It feels so good. Every way she touches me feels good. The tightness in my chest eases little by little.

"Nope, no one," I say, answering her question.

"How about your father?"

My eyes snap open; the tension returns. I brace myself against the tile, palms pressed to the shower walls on either side of me. "I don't know anything about him. I don't want to know."

"Okay," Gen says softly. Then again, "Okay." She pulls my arms down to my sides.

We're silent for several minutes, me letting her rinse my hair, soap my body, and rinse again, being extra careful around my damaged ribs and still swollen knee. The trembling in my limbs finally stops, and I'm able to use the soap on her, taking my time cleaning the mess I've made.

"What about you?" I say, having worked up the courage to ask. "You scared me a little in there. Your eyes went… dark, like night in the woods."

She turns from me, letting me soap her back, but I get the feeling she doesn't want to meet my gaze. "I drew on some extra power, that's all."

I frown. "Extra power? But where would it come—?"

"Not now, Flynn," she snaps, startling me. She must feel me jerk against her because her tone softens. "Sorry. I don't want to discuss it, any more than you want to talk about your dad. It's just too hard right now. Okay?" She shifts around to look at me, waiting.

It isn't, really. Gen's always willing to talk to me about personal things, even when I'm not. But having just refused her myself, I can't push it. "Okay." Besides, I've caused her enough problems for one night.

"That was a really stupid thing you did," she says, echoing my own thoughts. "Kat couldn't hurt me. If you'd let her come, I could have driven her off. Instead...."

Instead I went and got myself possessed by a fucking ghost and scared the hell out of the neighbors, Gen, and myself. Tears mix with the water running down my face.

I don't know how she can tell them apart from the spray, but she does, and she pulls me in close until we press tightly together. "Aw, Flynn, I didn't mean it like that. It was sweet, and really brave. I know how much all this terrifies you, but you threw yourself between us like it was nothing. I just don't want you to take that risk again, and it put me in a... difficult position. If there's a next time, and hopefully there won't be, let me deal with it. This is what I'm good at, remember?"

I remember. I remember how she helped Mrs. Pinkerton reconnect with her daughter, how she helps dozens of people who come to her, needing comfort and closure. She's incredible.

"And I'm not good at anything." I think of the rings hidden in the toe of that abandoned shoe and stifle a laugh. Why would she ever say yes? What can she want with a screwup like me?

Gen shoves me away from her, holding me at arms' length, the water pouring in a stream between us. "Stop it," she says, lips tight, eyes flashing. "Stop it right now. You build things. You create homes for people. You construct places for children to laugh and play. I could never do what you do. And what happened out there—" Gen waves a hand in the direction of the living room.

I shiver and hope it's a reaction to my body being out of the warm water, not more fear.

"—you handled that as well as anyone possibly could, and better than most."

I shake my head, but she grabs my cheek and stops the motion.

"I served on the board, remember? I've *seen* what happens when channelings go wrong, when things get out of hand. Forget what happened to your body. Think about your mind."

Gen leans her forehead on my shoulder, and only now do I realize she's trembling as well, trembling hard. I find the small of her back and press her to me.

"Most people never regain their sanity after something like that," she whispers, just loud enough for me to hear her over the water. "You aren't just sane and whole. You drove her *out*. With no training, no guidance, you pushed her away. You're amazing."

She wraps her arms around me, desperation in her tight embrace.

"And I love you," she finishes, shoulders shaking.

"I… love you too."

Her sharp intake of breath surprises me, but I guess it shouldn't. I've told Gen's brother I love her. I don't think I've ever actually said it out loud *to her* before now.

I've always been afraid of what she'd say in response.

"Then you won't leave?" She looks up at me, as frightened as I've ever seen her, and my heart skips a beat. That isn't the response I expected.

"Why would I do that?"

"The ghosts, the craziness, all this scary crap."

The darkness I saw in her, darkness I have to trust was nothing because she doesn't want to discuss it. Yeah, I can see why she thinks I might bail. Wrapped in all my insecurities about losing Gen, sometimes I forget she has the same fears about me. Different reasons, but the same damn fears.

I brush a strand of damp hair out of her eyes and place a light kiss on her lips. "I'm not going anywhere." Not for as long as she'll have me.

Chapter 23
Another Day,
Another Memory

"Didn't expect you in today," Chris says, turning from a pyramid of napkin-wrapped silverware he's been rolling. "You can have the day off, if you need it."

Behind him, a couple of guys load the dishwashers while two women wait their turn behind a third to type food orders into the main computer. There should be more staff. They're short-handed.

I chuckle, the sound coming out fake and forced. "Take my second day of work off? Yeah, that would look great to the boss."

He crosses to me, placing a hand on my shoulder. "I'm the boss. Do what you need to."

I stare at the unwashed dishes in a nearby bin. "I need to work," I mutter. "I need to get my mind off things, keep busy." I need to not think about what "get it out" meant when coming from my lips in Kat's voice. And I need the money.

Chris's eyes run over my shirt and black pants, the top fresh from Gen's laundry, clean and ironed. "Okay.

You can shadow Monica for the breakfast shift the next couple of days. By Friday, I'd like you taking your own tables."

"Got it." I head for the door leading into the pub's main seating area, then pause. "Thanks." I infuse the word with as much gratitude as I can manage, both for now and the night before, then push my way through the door.

The day passes in a blur of food and drinks, one spilled lemonade, one stiffed check, and three trips outside to stop panic attacks.

I stand beside the waste disposal bins, sucking in air through my mouth so I don't have to inhale the pub's refuse. One sniff of stale beer and moldy pretzels will send me over the edge and I'll add to the puddles of God knows what flowing around my shoes.

"Hey!" a familiar voice calls from above.

Glancing up, I spot Gen, leaning over the rail, smiling and waving. I swallow hard, smile, and wave back, then point toward the pub and walk inside. Much longer and she would see right through me.

We talked earlier this morning as I got myself ready—me taking a second shower and her trying to convince me to stay in bed.

"She's not coming back, right?" I asked, raising my voice to be heard.

"Not right away. That kind of… self-exorcism… takes a lot of a spirit's energy. And I doubt she'll do it in public. Too much interference."

I didn't know what that meant, but it sounded good. "All the more reason for me to be at work. I'll be with lots of people."

"But not with me."

She was angry because I wouldn't take it easy and because she wanted to be near me, just in case. "I can't hide behind you every minute of every day, and I can't stay in the apartment until we figure this out. I'll go crazy."

"You almost did," she said, handing me a towel.

The fear returned to her eyes. Dammit, I hated scaring her, and I understood, but…. "I'll be fine," I told her. "Tonight I'll move my stuff over."

She brightened at that.

"And we can make a plan."

Gen let me go, but somehow she's managed to be on the balcony walkway during every one of my freak-outs. I wonder if Chris is calling her when I slip out the back door.

After work, I change to jeans and a T-shirt, borrow Chris's sedan since it has more room than Gen's Charger, and drive to Kissimmee to pack up my hotel room/suite. Not that I own much. Between the passenger seat, the back seat, and the trunk, I'll be able to load everything in one trip.

A quick stop at the front office gets my account settled. They're sorry to see me go, and I don't blame them. Compared to most of their clientele, I'm a responsible, dependable tenant. I never missed a payment, I didn't make noise at night, and I wasn't mixing batches of meth in my bathroom and burning the whole place down.

Though that might have been an improvement.

By late afternoon, I'm casting one last glance around the single sitting/sleeping room combo, all the drawers in the battered wall unit open and empty, the closet devoid of clothing, the shelves bare of my few knickknacks, mostly given to me by Gen to "brighten up the place."

No memories to take with me… except one.

A small smile creeps across my face.

I WAS coming out of the hotel lobby when I spotted Gen climbing from her car. My first instinct was to turn around and dart back inside, but she'd seen me, and she waved, a bright smile on her face and wine and flowers clutched in her hands.

Oh crap.

I knew I shouldn't have let her drive me home the other night, but I'd had one beer too many to safely get behind the wheel of my truck, and the run-down Sunrise Suites didn't look nearly as bad in the dark with its recently replaced blue neon light accents and a fresh coat of beige paint on the front building.

I fixed on a smile and headed straight for her, hoping to head her off and put her back in her car, but she was crossing the parking lot. "Flynn! Hey!"

"Hey," I said, stopping her forward motion with my body. "Um, what are you doing here?"

She held the flowers and wine higher and waved them in front of my face. "Visiting," she said with a little laugh, like how dense could I be.

With one arm, I tried to turn her toward her car. "This really isn't a good time."

Three months. We'd been together three months. Not nearly long enough to prepare her (or me) for this.

Gen squirmed out from under my arm, making for the lobby. "What, you have another girl in there?" She laughed again, totally joking.

When I made no move to follow her, she stopped and turned slowly back to me, her smile faltering.

"You don't, do you?"

"No."

The smile returned. She crossed back to me quickly. "Good." It was still too early in our relationship for her to understand the full extent of my PDA issues, and she raised herself up on tiptoe to plant a kiss on my cheek.

"Dalton!" The shout came from the lobby entrance, where the hotel manager stood, arms crossed over his chest. He glanced pointedly from me to a few clusters of full-price-paying tourists staring at me and Gen from the luggage drop-off zone.

Shit.

Jarod wasn't a bigot. He knew my preferences and couldn't care less. But he worked for the hotel chain, and their "image" did not include lesbian couples kissing in the parking lot.

I could not get evicted from this hotel. It was one of the cheapest places in town, and most of the others were full up. At that time, in Florida, it had been legal to fire someone for being gay. (Still is, actually.) I was sure the powers that be could have found some excuse to kick me out of my room too.

I nodded to Jarod, grabbed Gen by the wrist, and hauled her around the corner of the front building, down the side of the left-hand two-story wing of guest rooms.

When we were well out of sight of the gawkers, I stopped. "Gen, why are you doing this to me?"

"You mean visiting you?"

My growl of frustration earned me raised eyebrows from my girlfriend, along with a healthy dose of hurt and confusion. "Fine. You want to see where I live? Let's go." I dragged her onward, down the long wing of nice rooms with beach towels and bathing suits drying on the railings out front. The cars in the spaces thinned out the farther we went; fewer and fewer of these rooms were occupied, creating a buffer between the tourists and the year-round residents.

When we turned the next corner, Gen stopped in her tracks. "Flynn...."

Yeah. It was that bad.

What a lot of people didn't know was when hotels couldn't fill all their wings, they dedicated one (usually the rearmost one) to homeless families paying week-to-week. These rooms received no maid service, no renovations, rarely got visited by maintenance or exterminators. Paint chipped off the crumbling exterior walls. Doors were stained with rust or mold. The residents blasted loud music, smoked all sorts of things inside and out, made and sold drugs, and spent a lot of time on the balconies yelling to and at one another. Families of up to eight crammed themselves into the slightly oversized single rooms that dared to call themselves "suites" because they had couches as well as a bed or two.

I was better off than almost everyone living there, but it didn't matter.

Gen's gaze landed on my truck, parked outside the corner unit. She took a steadying breath and stomped to my door, good old number 193.

Then she noticed the police tape blocking off the adjacent room.

"What... what's that for?"

"Suicide," I told her. "These places get one every couple of months or so. Nice guy. Laid off. Family left him."

For a long minute, she studied my face. I didn't have to be psychic to know she didn't like what she saw there.

There was another reason why I didn't want Gen to read my tarot cards—one beyond my fear of all things supernatural.

I was really, really scared about my future. And I was scared she wouldn't be in it. Hell, sometimes I was scared *I* wouldn't be in it. Not that I was the suicidal type, but living like this… it got to people.

It got to me.

And my family had a history of such things.

My voice dropped to a whisper. "Now you see why I didn't want you here."

"Open the door," she said, low and even. No inflection. No pity. Just a single command.

Moving on autopilot, I did it.

I let her go first, standing behind her in the doorway while she took in my accommodations. No clutter. No mess. I kept my place clean. The bed was made, but gouges marked every piece of furniture. The TV was broken, its glass screen cracked. The bathroom door hung at an odd angle, impossible to close, let alone lock. Horrible grating noises came from the ancient air conditioner.

She set the wine and flowers on the TV and faced me.

"Come here," she said.

I obeyed. Reaching behind me, she swung the door shut.

Then she kissed the hell out of me.

She had me half-undressed before I even registered the removal of my clothing. I was breathless when she backed me to the bed and pushed me down on its lumpy, creaking mattress. "Here?" I managed to squeak out.

I never squeaked.

"Here," she said firmly.

She laid me down, covering me with her body. Her hands found my jeans and underwear, and soon I was naked beneath her.

"Why?" I gasped, when her knee worked its way between my thighs.

"Because," she said, her grin fierce, "I'm giving you something to think about. Something to picture every time you come home. Something I intend for you to never, ever forget."

For the next nine months, every time I opened my room door and my eyes fell on that bed, I smiled just a little.

THAT DOESN'T mean I ever learned to like it.

So not fair. When I was working steadily, I brought in over forty thousand a year. Not Festivity money, but enough for a decent one-bedroom condo in Kissimmee. Now I make barely half that much and I'm forced to live in this dump.

Gen insists I have nothing to be ashamed of.

But I *am* ashamed of it. Her place is a paradise by comparison, her neighbors showered and clean-clothed and not smelling of stale cigarette smoke and pot. I don't want to be kept, but I don't want her here.

She deserves better.

Even the apartment over the pub is way beneath her means. With what she charges an hour—over two hundred dollars—and her steady stream of clients, she can afford one of the larger Festivity mansions. But she likes to be close to her brother, who has the apartment next to hers, and she says she doesn't need more.

Much of what she takes in, she donates to charity. Yeah, those rescue dogs make a killing off my girl.

I turn toward the door, the last box containing my against-the-rules hotplate (okay, so I'm not the model tenant they think I am), some plastic dishes, and a couple of mugs, all of which I intend to give to the nearest Goodwill, and come face-to-face with Max Harris.

Chapter 24
Unlikely Employer

THE BOX drops, the mugs shatter, and I'm in a defensive stance before he utters a single word. Self-defense classes in college. Living where I've been, they're good skills to have.

"What do you want?"

Harris straightens the jacket of his gray business suit, his gaze roving over my position before he offers a predatory smile. "Is this how you greet all your customers?"

I let myself relax minutely, but I'm not turning my back on this man. He hates me. I'm not positive why beyond the whole gay thing, but knowing the connection we share with Kat, I have a few guesses. "Customers?" I ask, his words sinking in.

"Dog houses. You build them. I want one."

I crouch to pick up the fallen box, my eyes still raised to his face. "I have a website, with a phone number. You could have called me." Instead of startling the shit out of me.

Instead of trying to intimidate me by showing me that you know where I live.

Or *had* lived. Moving in with Gen looks a whole lot better now.

"I like to do my business in person."

Yeah, I just bet you do.

He isn't moving, but I'm not letting him in, so I push my way past him and onto the walkway. "Heading out. This needs to be quick." Because I can only stand so much time in his presence.

"How much?" he asks, stepping out with me. I reach around him and shut the hotel room door, hearing it automatically lock behind us both.

I study him. He's actually serious. "How big is the dog?"

A pause. "Big."

I roll my eyes. "You need to be a little more specific than that." I can't believe I'm considering this, but he's rich. A couple hundred for a doghouse will go a ways toward Gen's rent. Not a long ways, but it's something. Besides, it might give me a chance to talk to him, figure out what Kat wants from me and what she meant by *get it out.* "Breed?"

Another pause while he shifts his weight from one foot to the other. "Mutt. Rescue."

Rescue, huh? Maybe this guy isn't all bad.

Or maybe he's making this shit up. My bullshit meter registers off the scale. I can't fathom why, though. To come all the way out here just to make a cruel joke in the form of a false job offer? It doesn't wash.

"Height? Weight?"

Harris holds his hand out about waist high. "This tall. I haven't placed the dog on my bathroom scale."

Because, heaven forbid, an animal should enter your clean bathroom, right? "Okay, I can work with that, but I'll need more accurate measurements if we agree on a price." If he is telling the truth, it's a fuck-ing big dog. Good. Big dog means big doghouse means more money for me. He doesn't strike me as the pet type, but maybe it's for extra security. "You have a de-sign in mind?"

"Whatever's standard for dogs."

Well, that simplifies things. And reduces the cost to me, and therefore to him. Damn. "Red-and-white paint?" Classic Snoopy.

"Sure." Another pause. "You do on-site work?"

I blink at him. "On site?"

"Will you come out to the property and build it? Or will you bring it already constructed?" He speaks slowly, as if explaining things to a small child. God, I hate this man.

"I'll...." I can do either one. Normally, I will build first and drive it over in the bed of my truck. Only I no longer have a truck. "I'll work on site," I tell him. "Four hundred. In advance. Plus materials." I never ask for payment up front, but if this is some kind of joke, I want the money in hand. "That's a rough estimate. After I see the dog, I'll let you know if there'll be extras."

It's already an exorbitant amount, almost twice what I usually charge, but I don't give prices on my website. It just says, "Call for pricing." Or, hey, drop in on my fucking doorstep. For this, for making me break my two favorite coffee mugs, and for the way he treated me out at Central Florida Lumber and Tile, I'm goug-ing him. He can take it or leave it, and investigating be damned.

"Fair enough," he says. He reaches into his pocket, pulls out a leather wallet, and from there, removes a stack of hundreds.

I juggle the box with one arm and let him peel off four crisp hundred-dollar bills and lay them neatly across my palm. I focus on his fingers instead of the money, willing my hand not to shake at the amount of cash. He has dirt under his fingernails. Harris follows my gaze and shrugs.

"Gardening."

Rescuing dogs *and* doing his own gardening? Maybe I really have misjudged him. "Pick one of the basic designs off my website. I list the materials I'll need right there. When do you want me?"

"Tomorrow. Two thirty. Be on time. Address is in Festivity's online directory."

Then again, maybe not.

Chapter 25
Unromantic Reunion

"GENESIS DARLING!" Leo stood on the doorstep to her apartment, hands spread and waiting for an embrace that would never come. Pouting, he lowered his arms.

"Come in." Gen stepped back, allowing the enemy to enter her home. A quick scan of the parking lot below revealed no sign of Chris's sedan. Good. She didn't need Flynn showing up right now.

The idea of Gen in the same room with a handsome man, especially when the man was Gen's ex-lover, would send Flynn into jealous, insecure fits. And worse, Flynn didn't know Leo was her ex. Not that she'd hidden it. It just hadn't come up. Hadn't seemed to matter. Right?

Like she hadn't told Flynn about her dark magic addiction. The two were connected. Leo had tended toward the dark even when they were dating. Gen neither needed nor wanted the temptation and exposure.

Leo made a beeline for the living room, removed his light jacket, and tossed it over the armchair. After kicking off his shoes, he propped his feet on the coffee table. "I knew it was only a matter of time before you ditched the Amazon and came to your senses."

"No one's ditching anyone," Gen said. She grabbed his feet and shoved. "Manners. You don't live here anymore. You're a guest." She took the couch, perching on the edge of the cushions. Maybe this hadn't been such a great idea.

"I'm wounded," Leo said, placing a hand over his heart and falling against the back of the chair. He glanced toward the window and cocked his head. "New curtains?"

Gen blew out a frustrated breath, her bangs lifting and falling on her forehead. "I swear, you are the gayest straight man I've ever known."

He laughed. "Coming from you, I'll take that as a compliment." He crossed his legs and studied her. "So, if you didn't invite me over to show me curtains—too flowery, by the way—or beg me to come back to you, then why am I here?"

"I want to know what you were doing at Dead Man's Pond."

Silence. And if that shut Leo up, then he was into something.

"I was investigating the accidents there," he finally admitted.

"Why?"

"Because a client hired me to."

Gen considered that. "Let me guess. Max Harris."

Leo jerked in his seat, a dead giveaway. "I don't have to discuss my clients with you. As I recall, professional differences were one of the many reasons we broke up."

"*We* didn't break up. I threw you out."

He slipped a hand around to his ass and rubbed it. "And quite roughly too."

"You were messing with black magic," Gen said, standing and pacing in front of the "too flowery" curtains, "going against everything we believed in."

"No," he said, pointing a finger at her. "What *you* believed in. What *I* believe is that we should benefit from every source of power at our disposal. We have gifts. We should use them to better the lives of others."

Regardless of the cost to some.

"Better your own, you mean," she said, stopping and facing him. "That McLaren is hideous, by the way." For some, like her, the power created the addictive factor. Using it felt good. For others, the addiction stemmed from wealth.

"I don't see you suffering." Leo glanced pointedly around the room, at the Laura Ashley decor, the expensive artwork.

She sighed. No point in telling him about the charity donations. He either wouldn't understand or he wouldn't believe her. And she did live well. "Bottom line, Leo. Did you cast some sort of spell at Dead Man's Pond?"

"I don't kill people, Gen."

Huh. Not quite an answer to the question she'd asked. Leo excelled at half-truths. She knew from experience. But he could be being honest. Dark magic exacted a cost, depending upon its use. She'd used it to heal; it had, apparently, taken a life in return. He used it for monetary gain. Someone close to him had likely gone bankrupt, considering how much wealth Leo had accumulated. But that wouldn't explain Dead Man's Pond.

She tried a different question. "What about ghosts? Seen any out there?"

He sat up straight and stared at her. "Ghosts? What ghosts?"

Genesis considered her options. If Leo *was* behind the accidents somehow, then he was responsible for a dozen or more deaths. If he wasn't, and he truly was just investigating for a dead woman's husband, which made some sense—it was the sort of thing psychics got asked to do all the time—then he'd make a powerful ally.

And no, she was not, *was not*, bringing him in on this to be closer to the dark magic she felt sparking from him.

"Katherine Harris," she said, watching for his reaction. "She's back. And she's pissed."

Chapter 26
Visitation Revelation

LEO FELT the blood drain from his face. Ghosts weren't his area of expertise—one of the reasons he'd resorted to dark magic, actually. Oh, he had some talent. A greater-than-average percentage of his tarot and palm readings proved accurate. And he had a way with charms, curses, and spells… sometimes more of a way than he planned, but that was beside the point.

However, he'd never been able to channel spirits the way Genesis could. The dead gravitated to her. They wanted to talk through her. They… liked her.

And they avoided Leo like the plague.

On the rare occasions he managed the feat, apparitions had an annoying tendency not to want to leave. That's when he started faking communications from beyond and focusing on the darker things he was good at.

That's when Genesis had kicked him to the proverbial curb.

"How pissed?" Leo asked, attempting to control the waver in his voice and failing.

Genesis smirked at him. She knew exactly how he felt about ghosts.

"Pissed enough to attack me last night." She paused for emphasis. "And possess Flynn."

"P-possess?" If the Harris woman still had control of Gen's new girlfriend, if Katherine started talking about how she'd ended up at the bottom of the lake, well, things were looking worse and worse for his continued existence, both as a practitioner and potentially as a living, breathing human being.

He was beginning to regret the day he took Maxwell Harris on as a client.

Gen turned for the entry hall and waved over her shoulder. "Put your shoes on," she said, taking pity on him. "Let's hit Starbucks. You look like you could use some caffeine, and quite frankly, so could I."

He followed her on unsteady limbs, not missing the way she checked her cell phone and scanned the parking lot before heading down the exterior stairs. Who was she looking for? The girlfriend? Flynn?

Who named a girl Flynn, anyway?

Festivity's Starbucks sat across the street from the Village Pub, on a corner overlooking the downtown lake, but Leo took no pleasure in the view. He'd had quite enough of lakes and ponds and hell, puddles, if they contained curses, bodies, and ghosts.

Genesis insisted on an outdoor table, and he chose a seat facing away from the water while she went inside and bought their coffees—her treat since she'd invited him. Very generous of her.

He waited, twisting his hands in his lap and going over the things Gen had revealed. Worrying for nothing, he told himself. If Katherine Harris still had possession of Flynn's body, Gen wouldn't be out casually having coffee at Starbucks. No. She'd sense the spirit's continued presence and be doing everything within her annoyingly extensive power to drive it out.

And if Katherine had said anything about Leo's involvement in the pond's curse, he wouldn't be sitting at Starbucks either. He'd have been picked up by the Registry board by now.

A general shifting of bodies and an underlying current of unease ran through the Festivity coffee-drinking crowd. As usual in the late afternoons, customers filled most of the outside seating, some chatting or texting on their phones, others tapping away at their laptops, a few engaged in real live face-to-face conversation. They wore business suits or Bermuda shorts and flowery shirts, the locals mixing with the tourists, but all of them well-dressed and well-off.

Festivity's Starbucks didn't attract the homeless.

But that's what just stepped foot into the wrought-iron gated courtyard.

Talking ceased, and all eyes followed the dirty, ragged, heavily bearded old man as he crossed the open space and took a seat at the one empty table in the corner—the one closest to Leo. Body odor and the scent of stale beer wafted from the man. He grabbed a discarded newspaper and spread it out before him, mumbling to himself. Only the words weren't part of any journalistic masterpiece.

They were spells.

Broken, disjointed pieces of spells. Spells in Latin and Greek, Gaelic and Norse. None of them complete. All of them familiar.

Because they belonged to the dark arts.

Leo peered at the face, searching behind the beard and grime and sun-weathered, wrinkled skin. "Ferguson…," he breathed.

The man's head jerked up, milky eyes unfocused, then zeroing in on Leo. He smiled a smile of yellowed, broken teeth, not-quite-recognition dawning in his expression.

Oh dear God.

A shiver ran through Leo's body. He twisted away, breaking eye contact with the man, the *mentor* who'd first recognized his talents, showed him the limits of his skills… and how to supplement them.

They'd last spoken right about the time Genesis had thrown Leo out. Ferguson feared the Registry knew about his indiscretions. He'd laughed, said he was going away for a while on a much-needed, well-deserved island vacation.

Leo had thought him still there, soaking in the sun, spending his fortune on drinks with little umbrellas, served by bikini-clad women.

But here Ferguson sat, unwashed and penniless and babbling incoherently to himself.

The National Psychic Registry had caught him after all and exacted their punishment.

Without waiting for Genesis's return, Leo stood and fled the Festivity Starbucks.

Chapter 27
Hazardous Ground

AT SEVEN thirty, the summer sun is just beginning to set. I should call Gen, let her know I'm on my way… home… still feels weird. Instead, I turn on the perimeter road around Festivity and head for Dead Man's Pond.

I stop by the construction site first, hoping for some signs of life, but locked gates block the dirt access, and a sign hanging off it reads, "Closed. No Trespassing." Guess they haven't sorted out their financial issues or found a new backer for the project yet. Well, it has only been a few days.

At twilight, I park at the lake, a couple of yards from the picnic table where Gen and I made out.

Nothing.

No activity whatsoever, save for a couple of evening joggers who wave as they bounce past and a few wild turkeys waddling into the underbrush.

What the hell am I doing here? I should be running too, as fast as I can, in the opposite direction. Instead, I begin a leisurely stroll around the lake. My legs appreciate the exercise. Waiting tables keeps me hopping, but it doesn't stretch out my body the way construction work does.

I realize, when I'm about a quarter of the way around Dead Man's Pond, that I'm looking for something, some clue as to what is happening in my suddenly fucked-up life.

In less than a week, I've lost my truck and my home, seen and been possessed by a ghost (the ghost of my ex-girlfriend, no less), and had more relationship problems than I've had in a year.

I pause, leaning against the nearest palm tree, pulling first one leg, then the other up behind me to work out the kinks in my muscles. My bruised knee complains, but not too much. It's healing. Ribs feel better too.

Good thing I changed clothes after work. I'm sweaty from packing and carrying and walking, but it's the good kind of sweat, the kind I already miss, like after a hard day on the site, and the fact that I pulled on a faded RPL Construction logo T-shirt doesn't help my mood any. After checking for any more evening joggers, I lift the bottom of the shirt and wipe my brow, then frown at the cracked iron-on logo with the crossed hammer and saw. Things will work out. They have to.

The sun dips below the horizon while I stand there. A clank echoes across the water as the Festivity sign's spotlights come on. They light the planter and concrete barrier between the road and the lake, a few misdirected beams casting across the pond's dark surface. Crickets and frogs take up their nighttime songs.

How can a place so beautiful and peaceful be so goddamn fucking scary?

Going back the way I came would be shorter, but I like to finish things I start, so I keep moving clockwise around the lake. At the halfway point I think better of it. It's dark here, the spots not quite making it all the way to the far side, and I stand right where Kat's ghost appeared when Gen and I saw her.

I search the sandy ground, half expecting footprints or heel marks from her black pumps, but ghosts don't leave traces of their passing.

People do.

In the moonlight, I spot the men's shoe prints leading across the sand, then two hollowed-out areas where someone knelt by the water's edge. My hand goes to the car keys in my pocket, pulling them out and slipping them between two knuckles to use as a makeshift weapon. Turning in a slow circle, I scan the trees and bushes but see no one. It hasn't rained in days, so these marks could have been left an hour ago or yesterday or last week.

My muscles relax and I put away the keys. I'm about to move on when I notice the glow.

It flickers at the center of the lake, dim and dull and so faint I have to squint to be sure of its existence. A glance at the sky confirms it isn't a reflection of the moon, which has vanished behind a cloud. No, this is something else, something issuing up from the lake's bottom, but judging from the gradual increase in its brightness, it's either growing in intensity or rising toward the surface fast.

It's the same glow I saw the night of my accident. The same one I observed after we saw Kat's ghost, though I'd been in no condition to investigate.

It shimmers and shines, undulating with the slight breeze's ripples across the water.

It's beautiful.

Like that first night, tendrils of fog curl up from the surface, their misty white fingers glowing in the ephemeral light. They reach toward me, beckoning. If they could only touch me, they would suffuse my soul with cooling peace.

My body flushes, heat searing through me like a raging fever. More sweat beads on my brow, drips down my back and between my breasts, leaving damp, dark patches on my T-shirt.

I'D BEEN sick for days, though I wasn't sure how many. In my fever-hazed mind, they all blurred together into one sweaty, vomiting stupor.

It was January, and Gen and I had been together six months. Long enough for her to have me halfway figured out. She didn't grab my ass in public anymore, didn't plant kisses on my cheek in parking lots or squeeze my knee in restaurants.

She didn't visit my apartment.

We spent New Year's Eve together, cuddling on her couch, watching the ball drop in Times Square and drinking cheap champagne swiped from the Village Pub. I slept over and woke up with a massive headache I attributed to the not-fermented-in-the-bottle alcohol. It took intense concentration to drive myself home, and by the time I arrived, I'd pulled off twice to throw up.

Not the alcohol. The flu.

I called in sick on January second, despite having a steady contract for at least the next two weeks working on a combination gas station and convenience store.

Gen and I were supposed to catch a movie on the third, but I canceled, claiming I had to work.

Yeah, I lied to her even then.

If I told her the truth, she'd hurry over to take care of me. It wasn't just selfishness on my part. In addition to not wanting her at my hotel, I didn't want her catching whatever I had.

I didn't count on it knocking me flat.

The back wing of the Sunrise Suites had air-conditioning but no heat. In a rare Central Florida cold front, the outside temperature plummeted while my fever crept up and up—102, 103, 104. Tylenol and Advil had little to no effect, and I kept throwing them up, anyway. I half expected the mercury to explode from the end of the thermometer clutched in my trembling hand. I lay shaking, huddled under my thin Walmart blanket and a sheet, cotton pajama shorts and tank top soaked with sweat.

My provisions ran low, the last boxes of Lipton soup and Nestea nearly empty of packets and bags. Not that I could keep much down other than water, and even that was iffy.

It took every ounce of strength I had left to walk, then crawl between the bed and the tiny bathroom. My head pounded; my stomach cramped so badly I was bent double. Eventually I dragged a pillow in with me and propped myself against the chipped-paint wall.

Fever brought hallucinations.

One cockroach crawling across the tile became dozens, then hundreds, swarming over my body, filling my mouth and nose and every other orifice my demented brain could imagine. The bathroom walls closed in, trapping me with them. No escape.

Not real. It wasn't real.

I fumbled for the faucet, most of the water spilling from my cupped hand before I could splash it in my face or bring it to my cracked and bleeding lips. Nausea struck, painful and sharp, and I dry heaved over the porcelain bowl, nothing left in my stomach to expel.

It occurred to me I might be dying.

On the nightstand by my empty bed lay my cell phone. It might as well have been in New Jersey.

The pounding in my head was so violent I swore it shook the walls. And someone called my name from a long distance away. It sounded like Genesis, and I smiled. Of course I'd hear my psychic lover's voice as I faded from this life.

The voice stopped, and for a long time there was nothing—then the creaking of the hinges on my hotel room's door.

"Flynn? Flynn, are you here?"

I was too weak to call to her, my throat too raw from vomiting, but the bathroom light was on. Surely she'd—

"Flynn!" A second later she knelt beside me, her blissfully cool palm pressed to my forehead, her face a mask of concern, and tears forming at the corners of her eyes. "You're burning up. How long have you been like this? Can you stand?"

"I know, don't know, and no," I answered, my voice a croak. "Water?"

She disappeared, and for a horrible moment I feared I hallucinated her too. Then she came back with one of my mugs, filled it from the sink, and raised it to my lips.

"How'd you get in here?" I managed.

"Bribed the desk clerk. He remembered me from last time." Gen waved a hand in dismissal. "Never mind that now. We need to get you to a hospital." She took the mug from me and set it aside.

My body stiffened and I shook my head, though it was more of a loll. "No. No hospital."

"Flynn…."

After six months, I knew that tone. She was about to lose her temper. But it didn't matter. "No insurance," I told her. "No hospital." Two years before, working full-time, the crew had a group plan, but since the housing crash it got cut more and more until we lost it altogether.

With what medical care cost and what little I made, I'd have been in debt for the rest of my life.

"I'll pay for it," Gen said.

It took tremendous effort to raise my head and look her in the eyes, but I did it. "No," I told her. "You won't."

Her gaze locked with mine. No matter how much we'd learned about each other in six months, that was the one thing she had yet to understand. No charity, no handouts. It was a deal breaker.

And something in my face made her believe that.

"Damn you," she breathed.

Then she slid her arms beneath my sweaty armpits and dragged me across the cracked tile.

Into the shower.

I didn't grasp her intention until she reached for the handle and threw it all the way to the right.

Oh fuck.

Freezing liquid struck my burning body like a thousand ice picks. My back arched as I tried to twist away from the spray, but Gen held me down, water soaking through both our clothes, dripping into my nose and mouth.

Lowering my temperature in a mad, cold rush.

SCREECHING TIRES jerk my head away from the light under the lake. I blink stupidly into the darkness, confused and disoriented and wet from the waist down.

What the hell?

I stand up to my belt in the water, drawn in and distracted by the shimmering, flickering, beautiful….

The screeching ends in a tremendous crash, the Festivity wall caving in and something black and metal hurtling through.

Concrete and rubber, plastic and steel go flying in all directions. Instinct takes over, and I throw an arm across my forehead to protect myself, even though I'm much too far away to be harmed. The car plummets down the slight embankment on this side of the sign, its wheels driving it forward and into the water.

Ohfuckohfuckohfuck. The wave from the impact sloshes over my head, soaking me entirely. I blink away the muddy muck, searching, searching, then finding the vehicle once more. Even as I watch, the headlights, then the hood, then the roof disappear beneath the lake's surface, and my heart sinks with it.

Chapter 28
Sinking Fast

I GRAB for my cell phone even as I take off at a dead run, racing around the lake toward the sinking car. Wet jeans weigh me down, every inch of fabric clinging to me and twice as heavy with the addition of the water. My shoes pound on the packed sand, kicking up clods of it where it clings to the soaked leather and squishing with every step. I punch 911 on the keypad and trip over an exposed tree root, staggering three steps before I right myself and keep going.

I hit Send and hold the phone to my ear. My breath comes in sharp gasps, bruised ribs now deciding to announce themselves, and I hope the emergency operator will understand me when the call connects.

Only it doesn't.

Trying to watch my path at the same time, I hold the phone out in front of me. A dark screen reflects my panicked expression, cast in half-broken spotlights and what little light comes from the moon and stars overhead. Droplets of water drip from the phone's casing.

Fuck.

It was in my pocket. My pocket was below the water line when I decided to go wading in the lake—and at some point I need to examine that action a little further, but not right now.

I've drowned my damn phone.

Hoping it will dry out, I shove it back in my jeans and start stripping as I run, for once not caring who sees me. In fact, I'd give anything for a large crowd, preferably made up of police, firefighters, EMT's, and scuba divers in full gear.

But it's only me.

I have no idea how deep the pond goes, but from construction sites with bodies of water on them, I know many Florida lakes are deceptive, dropping off sharply after a few feet to surprise and drown would-be swimmers. I'll need all my strength and as little weight on me as possible to have even a slim hope of swimming to the sunken car and its occupants. Clothes are an encumbrance I can't afford.

I'm down to undershorts and sports bra, both white and see-through when wet, dammit, when I reach the rear of the crumbled signage wall. On the other side, cars pass on the street, some pausing before driving on toward town, but none stopping. I guess seeing a hole in the Festivity sign is such a common occurrence, no one bothers to check out how recently it may have been made. Like ten minutes ago.

Ten minutes. The car has been under the water for almost ten minutes, and no sign of anyone coming up.

If the windows in the vehicle are down, the driver and passengers are dead. If they're up....

I pick my way over the crash site. Metal and fiberglass, the whole front bumper, one side mirror, but no pieces of windshield I can identify. Watching so I don't cut my bare feet on anything sharp, I run to where I parked Chris's sedan.

It's far enough to the side that the debris missed it. One less thing to worry about. Then I realize the keys are in my jeans and my jeans are a quarter of the way back around the lake.

For fuck's sake, I can't get a break tonight. Or last night. Or, apparently, any night.

Grabbing the closest chunk of broken concrete, I smash in the rear passenger side window. It takes two swings, not boding well for what I'll need to do underwater. Bits of bluish tempered glass shower the back seat and the boxes full of my stuff from the hotel.

I fumble for the inner lock and open the door, then scramble around for my toolkit. It's on the floor, and the vision-friendly gradually illuminating dome light doesn't help my search. At last I come up with what I'm looking for—my hammer. Prize in hand, I return to the water's edge.

Still no sign of life other than lizards and frogs, though a steady stream of bubbles floats up from beneath the rippling surface, and the headlights still glow down there, somewhere.

Not good. Bubbles mean escaping air.

I don't wear a watch. Without my cell, I have no idea how long it's been, but time ticks in my head like a bomb.

I try not to think about what else might be in the lake as I wade, then dive in, the water cold on my run-heated skin. It isn't so easy, swimming with a hammer clutched in my fist, but I'm a strong swimmer—high school diving team as well as the gymnastics—and I swam every day at the hotel pool before I met

Genesis. Since her parents' deaths by drowning, she avoids the water, and out of deference to her, I do too, but my body remembers.

Small fish dart out of my path, and slick leaves curl around arms and calves. At least I hope they're leaves. We get gators in Florida, and snakes, some of them poisonous. I jerk and kick myself free and keep going.

It isn't as difficult to see as I'd feared. The headlights draw me on like two beacons, straight to the car's passenger side. No sign of anyone there, which is good, since I doubt I can rescue more than one person, if that. However, the window is a spiderweb of impacted glass, and bubbles flow away from it in several thin lines like strings of tiny pearls.

Then I'm kicking upward, hard and fast, my head breaking the surface, my mouth gulping in lungfuls of cool night air.

I swim a couple of yards to where I guess the driver's side will be beneath me and dive again. But when I reach the right depth, the car has moved, rolling down the inclined lake bottom, deeper under the water. As I swim after it, it stops, but it's only a matter of time before it starts rolling again.

The driver's-side window is fractured like the other, and I heave a mental sigh. I can just make out a woman, head pressed into the marshmallowy airbag, face turned away from me. Some dark stains mark her big white cushion—blood. She isn't moving. I can't tell if she breathes.

I draw back the hammer, fighting water resistance and my own churning legs trying to keep me under, when she suddenly twists, her head coming around, her wide brown eyes staring right into mine. It startles me so badly, I let out an underwater shriek, all my air escaping in a huge bubble that floats serenely away.

If I had the leverage, I'd kick myself.

I reach the surface once more, expel all the air I have left, then take a massive breath and head back down. The car shifts a little farther, and the woman claws at the inside of the door when I reach her, screaming something, or maybe just screaming, though I can't hear her through the water and glass.

She sees me and gestures frantically, shaking her head and pointing at the door, which refuses to open. I wave through the window, indicating she should get away as far as she can toward the opposite side of the car. When she's shifted a few feet, I draw the hammer back and slam it against the window as hard as I can.

One hit, two, three. The already-weakened window bursts inward, glass and water flowing to fill the car in a torrent. The driver—and holy shit, I recognize her now, Arielle, the waitress from the wine bar—struggles in the current, pushing past the airbag and reaching for me with both hands. I let the hammer go and grab her wrists. She latches on to mine, and I pull, hooking my feet within the window frame of the car's exterior, yanking with all my might.

My lungs burn. The car continues sliding deeper. Much more and I won't make it back up before I run out of air, but I can't leave her for another breath. The car is fully flooded, and she's stuck between the bag and the seat. If I leave her, she'll drown.

Thank God she's skinnier than I am. Her body works itself free, blasting forward in a blinding cloud of bubbles, silt, and floating garbage escaping from her car: papers and a McDonald's bag, a hairbrush, her purse. I lose my grip and flail without direction, tumbling over and over.

When I right myself, I've sunk deeper, the lights on the surface impossibly far away. My chest hurts. My bruised ribs scream. My legs kick hard and fast, and something grabs my ankle.

More underwater shouting, more lost oxygen. This time rightfully so. A buzzing fills my head, like a swarm of angry bees penetrated my skull and got stuck in my brain. My vision doubles, and it has nothing to do with the distortion of the water. I twist and come face-to-face with Kat's ghost, her pale, cold fingers clutching and grasping. No sign of Arielle. Wherever Kat's essence touches me, my skin turns to ice, and I realize she's holding me under, preventing me from saving myself.

I kick hard, pushing her off with both body and mind, trying to thrust her away from the inside out like I did in Gen's apartment. Her anger suffuses me, ratcheting up my own and giving me strength. My injured knee threatens to give out. My chest hurts with the effort not to suck in a lungful of water.

Then my hand hits open air, followed a second later by my head, and all traces of Kat vanish. Arielle breaks through a moment after, both of us gasping and spitting, flailing around in the murky dark. She starts to go under again, and I flip her around to wrap my arm from behind, pressing it across her chest and swimming with my other arm while I drag her toward shore. I'm tired, so tired now, the day's events, hell, the week's, catching up with me. My eyes focus on movement—lots of movement. People running, staring, pointing. Flashlights aim at us. I spot some uniforms, police, I think. Two of them jump in and take Arielle from me.

A third meets me as I stagger out and wraps me in a scratchy brown blanket that smells like musty piss. He eases me down onto the sand and crouches beside me, waiting for me to catch my breath enough to talk.

While I pant and heave and spit, I scan the lake. No sign of Kat's ghost. With my lack of oxygen, maybe I hallucinated the whole thing. Then again, no one here would see the spirit except for me.

I turn to the cop and realize it's the same one I punched last week. He still has the shiner I gave him. Must be reunion night at Dead Man's Pond. I wish for a beer and a bonfire, the way I shake from cold and adrenaline.

He takes out a notepad and pen, seriously old-school, and I dictate a statement while he writes it all down, asks me to repeat it, and checks it twice. More lights spring up around this side of the lake—spots cast from a news van parked beside Chris's car. In the time I talked to the police, the media got wind of this story.

One of the ambulance guys checks me over and suggests I go to the hospital, but my insurance status hasn't improved, and I wave him off. He shrugs, praises me for saving a life, and wanders back to his vehicle.

I just saved a life.

Another cop arrives with my clothes gathered in his arms. He helps me shake off the dirt and sand, then holds the blanket up so I can get dressed behind it. It takes a long time. My jeans are soaked from my pre-swim wading, and I have to yank and pull and wriggle them over my hips, doing the wet-denim dance. My dripping bra shows through the otherwise dry RPL Construction T-shirt. Oh yeah, I'm ready for the cameras.

I go for my cell phone, pulling it out and checking for signs of life, but it's still dead. Dammit, I need to call Gen before she freaks. I glance around at the gawkers, hoping for a familiar face and a phone to borrow and get sidetracked by the media.

In the span of fifteen minutes, I go from a drowned-rat broke construction worker to a drowned-rat broke hero. They shine lights in my face, practically shove a microphone down my throat, and follow me when I head for the back of the ambulance to check on the woman I saved.

Arielle is there, sitting up, the attendant finishing off affixing a bandage to a cut on her forehead. Her strawberry-blonde hair flops across her face, some of it matted with blood, but she focuses on me well enough and waves me over, smiling broadly.

She describes the accident as I approach. "—don't know! The gas pedal stuck down and stayed down."

Yeah, I know the feeling.

The attention of the reporter standing behind me ratchets up a notch with the anticipation of what we'll say to one another.

"When I slipped you my number the other night, I didn't think we'd meet up here," Arielle says, laughing.

Definitely not what the reporter expected, but apparently even better, because she steps in so close I can barely move.

I turn to her and her cameraman, raising both hands in a gesture of surrender. "Come on, guys, back up a little, huh? Give a girl some room to breathe." When I look again, Arielle's right in front of me. She leans in and plants a solid kiss on my lips.

"My hero," she says.

It's my worst PDA nightmare, caught on camera, probably being broadcast live across the county, and for all I know, the whole state. My face flushes crimson. I'm taken completely by surprise, no idea what to say. What I come out with is, "I have a girlfriend."

Arielle's smile falters, but she recovers fast. "Well," she says, "she's a lucky woman."

That might be, but *I'm* not feeling so lucky as I notice said woman staring at me from beside the front bumper of the ambulance. I don't know how long Genesis has been there, but she has to have witnessed the kiss, because she turns and walks away without a word.

Chapter 29
Aftereffects

"GEN!" I chase after her. My sore knee twists, and I end up slamming into the side of the ambulance. One of the local onlookers steadies me with a hand on my arm. The news crew closes in again. I try waving them off as politely as I can, but they ignore me. And Genesis has disappeared.

I've already been interviewed, filmed, and embarrassed. Just past the half-demolished Festivity sign, I hear the familiar roar of the Charger's V8, but the reporter blocks my path.

Turning head-on to the camera, I fix the woman with my iciest glare, lean in to her microphone, and say, "Back. The fuck. Off."

She jerks as if I've slapped her, hand clamping over the mic, and I wonder if I just cursed her out on live TV. Then I'm running, limping really, for the main road.

The Charger's taillights vanish into the darkness down Festivity Boulevard.

An hour later, I make it "home."

That's how long it takes to get clearance from the cops to leave the scene, find some plastic to spread over the driver's seat of Chris's sedan so I don't get it wet with my still damp clothing, and locate a late-night parking space behind the pub.

When I go inside the bar, everyone turns from the four mounted televisions, each tuned to different local news stations who've picked up the story, and all of them featuring me in one way or another: me walking out of the lake in my underwear (oh God), me dripping wet and telling how I broke the window and pulled Arielle out, and an oh-so-fabulous shot of me in Arielle's arms being seriously, intensely kissed. Okay, she's one hell of a kisser—not as good as Gen, but hot.

The patrons start a spontaneous round of applause. Several offer to buy me drinks. A few shake my hand or clap me on the shoulder. A couple of women and a number of men eye me speculatively. At least my T-shirt has dried.

The one person I need to see, however, isn't congratulating me. He's watching a replay of that damn kiss. It's a shot taken from behind, so Arielle looks very happy, and I seem very involved in the moment. My hands held out to the sides, carefully not touching her, are completely cut off by the bottom of the screen.

"Chris…."

The news cuts to commercial break and he turns, glaring, accusing. The waitstaff around him fall silent.

And I'm suddenly exhausted, furious, and fucking sick of apologizing.

I storm up to my temporary (maybe very temporary) boss and slam his car keys on the bar.

"I broke the window on your car. I'll pay for it. I broke it to get at my hammer because I didn't have the keys. I used the hammer to save a girl's life. She thanked me. You know how I goddamn feel about Gen. By now, so should she. Maybe you both would have preferred I let that girl die."

I point a finger at the television. My hand trembles with my anger. Blood pounds in my ears, drowning out the same odd buzzing I experienced in the lake. The image on the screen doubles for a moment, then refocuses, like there's a brief transmission interruption. "You know there's two sides to everything. You saw one. If you and your sister have any faith in me at all, you should already know the other. And if you don't, I don't know what the hell I'm doing here."

The fire fades from his eyes. He opens his mouth to say something, but I don't stick around for it. Instead, I leave the Village Pub by the nearest exit.

Chapter 30
Fears

I REGRET leaving the pub as soon as I'm outside. Chris probably means to apologize. I should give him the opportunity. But there's no going back now.

I grab my toolbox—the most valuable thing I own minus a hammer—from Chris's unlocked car. Not much point in locking it with the window broken. I'm not worried. The parking lot is well-lit, and Festivity pays extra for regular police patrols through the community.

With no idea what to expect, I let myself into Gen's apartment. Yeah, it's back to being *Gen's* apartment until we get tonight sorted out.

If I had anywhere else to go, I would do it, but it's after midnight, and any friends I might have called wouldn't thank me for waking them.

The living room lies dark and quiet, but the open curtains allow me to see. The closed bedroom door tells me our relationship's current status and sends another wave of anger through me. One of the outside streetlamps buzzes, a bulb about to burn out. My eyesight blurs like I'm fighting back tears, but when I swipe at them, they're dry. Weird. Then I spot the note on bright yellow paper lying on the coffee table.

I set the toolbox down and approach it like I'd approach a live wire. Angry as I am, I'm still not ready to end things. Not by a long shot.

What if she is?

Lifting the scrap by a corner, I take it to the window to read.

"We need to talk. Gen."

That doesn't sound good. We needed to talk at the lake. Now things have had time to sit. And worsen.

I cross to the bedroom and try the doorknob. Closed but not locked. Should have checked it when I first came in.

Bathed in moon and starlight from the bedroom window, Gen is the most beautiful thing I've ever seen, like some fairy-tale princess. She lies atop the sheets, her spaghetti-strap white satin nightgown covering her from chest to midthigh and hugging all the curves between. Her red hair curls in soft waves across the pillow, her lips parted slightly in sleep as if she's waiting for a kiss to wake her.

I'm no prince or knight in shining armor, but I kneel beside the bed and touch my lips softly to hers.

She kisses me back, hard, then awakens fully and pulls away.

Not good at all.

Sitting up, she studies my face in the dim light, searching for who knows what.

"I was not cheating," I say. "Hoped you'd know that."

She draws back a little farther and blinks at me. "I do know that. I knew it with the whole phone number thing too. I just wasn't thinking, and the lie didn't help." She manages a laugh, but there's no humor in it. "I saw the look on your face when that waitress kissed you. Your eyes went so wide, and your hands were flailing like you were about to take flight."

"Then what... why did you leave?" It comes out more plaintive than I want. I never sound like this.

Gen sighs and reaches around to prop a pillow behind herself. I stand and lean against the dresser, waiting. Joining her on the bed feels like the wrong move right now.

"I was heading out to grab us some pizza," she begins. Her gaze goes distant, not focused on me at all, but on whatever happened earlier. "I was halfway down the stairs when I felt... you."

"Huh?" Oh, very eloquent, Flynn. You should write speeches instead of waitressing at the pub.

"I was cold, wet, suffocating. It wasn't me. It had to be you. I felt the ache in your knee and the pain in your ribs, and I knew." She breaks off and swallows hard. "I knew you were in trouble."

A shiver runs down my spine. This is too weird, but I believe every word she says.

"It was like... like the night my parents died." It comes out a whisper.

Oh.

Gen told me once about losing her folks, how she awoke in her bed, a terrified sixteen-year-old, her screams choked off by a constriction in her throat she could not explain. She stumbled to her brother's room and shook him awake because she could not speak. She turned blue right in front of him, collapsed, and lost consciousness. He called 911. Their parents were on a weekend getaway, leaving him, nineteen at the time, to watch over Genesis.

They took Gen to the hospital, where she recovered by morning, but her parents had drowned in a boating accident that same night. And she'd known. She'd felt it all as it happened. Clairvoyance, she called it. One of her several talents.

People think being psychic would be so cool. Watching how it affects Gen, and how it's touched my own life, I don't ever want those kinds of powers.

"I didn't mean to scare you," I say. But I do it. I do it all the time.

"I wish you'd called."

"Tried to. Dunked my phone."

Another small laugh escapes her. "Yes, you'd do that, wouldn't you? You are one to jump in with both feet."

I don't tell her how the light in the lake caused the damage to my cell, how it drew me in without me realizing it. Let her think I did it during the rescue. She has enough to stress about.

I don't mention Kat's ghost reappearing either.

"I nearly wrecked the Charger trying to get to you," she continues. "I saw Chris's car and the broken wall, and you weren't anywhere around. There were police and ambulances…." She trails off. "And then you were there. I should have talked to you. But I couldn't speak. I was just so relieved… so relieved to see you. And so angry that you'd scared me so much. But proud too. Really proud. I want you to know that, Flynn."

Uh-oh.

"Because I'm not sure… I'm not sure we can keep seeing each other."

Maybe she isn't sure, but I am. I'm sure that something inside me just died. "Gen…." I don't know what to say. She's right. I scared her, and I'll keep scaring her. I work in construction. I take risks. And I'm not likely to change.

"My parents' deaths almost killed me. I can't go through that again."

And just like that, my anger returns. Someone needs to fix that fucking streetlamp. The buzzing bulb almost deafens me, but I shake my head and force the distraction away, blinking to focus on the more immediate problem in front of me.

"So that's it? We're done? Fine." I storm to the closet and yank the few things I've hung off the hangers.

What the hell am I doing? She said she "wasn't sure." She didn't actually say we're through. If we talk, we might work things out. But I seethe with rage.

"Flynn…." Tears strain her voice, but I don't care. I want to hurt something. I want to hurt *her*.

And I have no idea why.

"No," I hear my voice saying. "I thought you were braver than this. Last night—" God, was it only last night? "—you're begging me not to leave you. Now you're calling it quits?"

The blanket rustles as she shifts on the bed. "I can lose you like this. I can't lose you to death."

"Everyone dies, Gen!" I whirl on her, facing down her fears with cold, hard logic. "If not me, then the next person you invite to move in and then dump. People get sick, or fall off buildings, or drown. But everyone fucking dies. And unless *you* plan on dying alone, you're going to have to deal with that."

Clothes bundled under one arm, I storm out of the room, grab up my toolkit, and slam the apartment door behind me.

I'm halfway across the parking lot before I rein myself in. What did I just do?

And where the hell am I going?

The rage fades as fast as it came. I turn in a slow circle, the night air chilling my skin.

Festivity has two hotels, one on the edge of town and one about a block away overlooking the central lake, neither of them with rooms under two hundred a night. I remember the four hundred-dollar bills in my pocket and feel for them to make certain they're still there after the night's activities.

They are. But even under these circumstances, I'm not springing for a Festivity hotel room.

I have to hike three miles out of town to the touristy road that skirts Festivity before I reach a Motel 6. The desk clerk, a teenager who probably dropped out of high school, eyes me nervously when I come in, limping and carrying tools and clothing. Then he straightens. "You're the woman off the news! The one who rescued that girl from a sinking car."

"Yeah, that's me." And despite feeling horribly guilty about the impulse, I wish it wasn't. Not that I want Arielle to have drowned. I just wish somebody, *anybody* else had saved her.

The memory of Kat's hands holding me underwater send me staggering into the nearest lobby chair.

Why would she have tried to stop me? Why did she come back to make love to me in Gen's bedroom and then try to kill me at the lake?

Ghosts get confused sometimes. They don't always make sense.

Yeah, that's for sure.

"Jesus, you okay?" The clerk rushes from behind the desk. It's late, nobody else around. He grabs a paper cup and fills it from a cooler, then brings it to me.

"Rough day," I tell him, setting aside my bundle and taking the water.

The kid laughs. "I'll bet. Need a room?"

I nod, biting back a snarky remark about enjoying the lobby decor: Disney attraction posters, fake plants, racks of brochures, an empty popcorn machine still smelling of waxy butter.

He slips behind the desk and returns a minute later with a card key. "Number 125. On the house," he says. "Hero discount."

I give him a look.

"Don't worry. My dad's the manager. Heroes deserve to be rewarded."

Maybe they do. Maybe they don't.

An image of Genesis lying asleep on her bed in the moonlight comes to mind, and I blink away tears.

I hold it together until I reach my room, ground floor, between the elevator and the ice maker. The key sticks in the slot and the door has warped, forcing me to kick it open to reveal a space smaller than my previous hotel residence. Bed, dresser, television. Bathroom with a tub/shower combo, sink and toilet. The most basic necessities but clean. And free. Two of my favorite descriptors.

The rumble/screech/ding of the elevator almost cancels out the rattle/bang of the ice maker. Mercifully, they both drown out my choked sobs as I throw myself facedown on the bed and cry myself into an exhausted sleep.

Chapter 31
Full Circle

I'M DISORIENTED when I wake up. Sunlight streams past orange-yellow curtains. It's a hotel room, but not the one I've occupied for the past couple of years. I'm fully dressed, my jeans stiff, my shirt smelling of dank mold. I'm not a drooler, but the pillowcase clings to my cheek. A pile of discarded clothing lies atop my toolbox by the nightstand. My phone sits on top of the stand, its battery pulled and resting next to it.

Memories of the previous night flood in.

My dead ex-girlfriend tried to kill me. I saved a life.

I broke up with Genesis.

My sharp intake of breath catches on a sob, and I bury my face in the pillow. Well, now I know why it's damp.

Our final conversation replays itself in my mind. I don't know what I was thinking, yelling at her, walking out. Of course she was scared. She almost lost me, and she felt it. *Felt it.* Geez. Could I have been any more insensitive?

If I'd talked to her, reassured her like I did when I almost fell off that roof, we could have worked things out.

Instead….

Instead, I'd ruined any chance of a continued relationship.

My eyes go to my phone, but of course she can't call me. It's dead. She might have left a voicemail, though. With shaking fingers, I pop the battery back on, press and hold the power button down, and wait.

The screen lights up. The message indicator doesn't.

Even if it works now, I can't call her. I have no idea what I could say to make up for the way I behaved.

Which leaves me alone and broke in yet another hotel.

I want nothing more than to pull the covers over my head and lie there the rest of the day, but responsibility won't let me. I have a doghouse to build. I've already been paid for it. And whether I like Max Harris or not, word can't get out that I stiffed someone on a job.

Besides, going to his residence might provide some clues about why Kat's haunting me, and working with my hands will help keep my mind off Genesis.

Maybe.

Probably not.

I shower and change, then stop by the lobby and check out, leaving a laundry bag of my clothes behind the desk for them to hold until I get back. Not sure where I'm spending tonight, probably here again, but I should try to find an even cheaper place if I can. Given the demand, my previous hotel has likely filled my vacated room.

It's a long walk back to Festivity, especially carrying a toolbox.

Chapter 32
Sage Advice

LEO STOOD at the lake's edge, as far from the mob scene of police and now a tow truck as he could get. With the morning light, divers could descend to the waitress's car and hook up the winch. He hoped she had good insurance.

He'd been there last night, too, when the news broke that another vehicle had ended up in Dead Man's Pond. And he'd breathed a sigh of relief when he saw that construction worker drag the driver toward shore.

That construction worker. Flynn Dalton. At the center of everything. What the hell had she been doing at the pond last night?

Unobserved, hidden by bushes, he'd watched her walk the trail around the lake. Watched her stare into its depths… and walk into the water. He'd opened his mouth to call to her when the car crashed through the Festivity wall.

Damn, the lake wanted her badly.

What had she seen? What had drawn her in? He'd searched but found nothing, and yet Flynn had seemed fixated on something beneath the surface.

The charm. The cursed charm. That had to be it, and yet, Leo could not see it, could not sense it. And he needed to. Before someone else died.

"What did you do, snit?"

Leo whirled, coming almost nose to nose with Ferguson. The old man staggered backward into a thorny bush and yelped, then reached out a weathered hand and slapped him on the arm.

"Never could keep aware of what was around you. Damn miracle the Registry hasn't hauled you in for 'conditioning' already."

Leo cocked his head at his former mentor. Ferguson had trimmed his scraggly beard and combed the mats from his hair. His skin glowed red from a recent scrubbing, and he wore clean clothes. "You're... not crazy?"

Ferguson barked a laugh. "Oh, I'm crazy, all right. Crazy as a fucking loon. Crazy with moments, even days, of painful, uncomfortable sanity. Just enough of them to remind me of what I've lost. I 'corrupted' the youth. Twisted your poor, innocent little mind. Permanently nuts is too good for me." He laughed again, a long cackle that had Leo searching for the clearest path of escape.

He saw none. Ferguson had him backed to the water's edge, and he damn well wasn't jumping in the pond. Whether it preferred lesbian women or not, he still had Katherine Harris's ghost to consider, and Leo didn't doubt for a minute that she'd love to get her ephemeral hands on him.

"So I ask you again, snit. What did you do? You know they know about you, don't you? Caught me, so they know about you. And they've been watching. Watching for almost a year."

Almost a year. So, the Registry got interested in him after he made the cursed charm. Okay, that was good. Leo raised his hands in surrender. "What makes you think I've done anything? It's a nice sunny day. I'm at the lake. The activity caught my interest." He nodded back over his shoulder at the grinding winch, now dragging the water-filled car up onto the bank. Little waves created by the emerging vehicle lapped against the shore.

Before Leo knew what happened, Ferguson placed both his palms on Leo's chest and shoved, hard. He tumbled over backward, landing on his ass in the pond. Water soaked through his neatly pressed khakis, then his undershorts.

"Don't fuck with me, snit. All those 'accidents'? All those dead bodies? And you here? I know damn well you have something to do with it, specifically because *I* don't. Three psychics in the Festivity area, one of them a goody-two-shoes. Then there's us. Any bad shit goes down, it's you or me, kid." Spittle spattered from the corners of Ferguson's mouth, adding to the general wetness of Leo's trousers.

"I... I...."

"Can it. You don't want to tell me, that's your funeral." Ferguson blinked. "Or in your case, your asylum. But let me warn you anyway. Your client? He's crazier than I am. And that's saying a lot."

At Leo's raised eyebrows, Ferguson cackled again, reached down, and hauled him out of the water. His underwear squished. His socks squelched. Disgusting.

"Yeah, I've been keeping an eye on you for a while now. Ever since I made it back from the islands. Maxwell Harris? Murderous, vicious, evil sonofabitch. At my worst, I wasn't as dangerous as he is. And if I can earn some sanity points with the Registry by warning you, then I'm going to do it."

Leo studied the old man's face, the darting eyes, the twitches and tics in his forehead and right cheek. Ferguson's arm muscles bulged and tensed beneath his short-sleeved gray button-down. He held his shoulders rigidly back, as if doing so might hold the crazy in.

Under no circumstances did Leo want to end up like this.

"I made a bad-luck charm," he muttered, digging a groove into the wet sand at his feet. "Wasn't meant to kill anybody."

Ferguson turned his head and spat. "Dammit, boy, how many times did I tell you how unstable those are? You curse it?"

Leo's voice dropped to a whisper. "The client did."

His mentor threw his hands in the air. "Even worse. You make a charm, you set the curse yourself!" He stabbed a finger into Leo's chest. "Never listened. Never paid attention. Always thought you knew better than me. Now you got more than you bargained for."

Leo's own anger rose. "You taught me to go for the money. Harris paid me. He paid me a lot."

"How much?"

"One hundred thousand dollars."

More maniacal laughter. Right in Leo's face. In his goddamn face!

"And you didn't think, just for a minute, that a man paying that much might have murder on his mind?"

"I didn't—"

"No, of course you didn't." Ferguson paced up and down the narrow beach, waving his hands and muttering under his breath.

Half of what he said were unfinished spells, the other half coherent, if colorful, profanity. He completed five or six full paces, then spun to stare across the lake, speaking more to it than to Leo. "Didn't expect anyone to die. Now you're stuck. What're you going to do about it?"

Crazy or not, Ferguson knew far more than Leo ever would. Maybe his mentor could still be of use. "I've tried to locate it. It's at the bottom somewhere, but I can't see it. I feel it, but...."

"Got yourself into quite the fix, sending it into a lake. Only the cursed can see it, snit. Now what're you gonna do, eh? What're you gonna do?" The old man fell to his knees, grabbed up handfuls of sand and water, and threw it over himself like an ancient baptism.

What indeed? Only the cursed. Like Flynn Dalton.

Well, now he knew what had drawn her into Dead Man's Pond.

"Find yourself a dyke. Dyke can block the flow.... Damn her, dam the evil water, down and down and drown and drown."

So much for moments of painful sanity.

Leo crept behind the punished psychic, wincing at each squish and squeak of his ruined leather shoes, but the old man never turned from the lake. "She's there, walking in, walking into the home of death."

Huh? He glanced around the lake, eyes following the path encircling it, but saw no sign of the construction worker.

"Builder of bitch houses, taking the maximum penalty, death to the max. All well and good. A hairy situation." The babble grew less and less coherent.

Bitch houses? Doghouses? Leo remembered Max mentioning the Dalton woman built custom doghouses. Death to the max. Well and good. Maxwell? Hairy situation. Harris? Was Ferguson trying to tell him Maxwell Harris meant to kill Flynn Dalton?

Into the home of death. Shit.

Flynn Dalton was at Max's golf course mansion.

Leo took off at a run for his orange McLaren. He couldn't bring back the curse's victims, but assuming the Registry did someday find out about that, he could at least keep his record from getting worse.

And if they never did discover what he'd done? Then saving Flynn might earn him some brownie points.

Chapter 33
In the Doghouse

I MIGHT not care for Maxwell Harris, but I adore his dog.

When I arrive at his house (his mansion, and oh holy shit it's huge, overlooking the golf course, with pink-and-purple petunias delineating the property line and a whole bed of them in the back), the asshole has "Katy" on a long lead, tied to a tree in the backyard. The poor thing, a husky/shepherd mix with a thick coat entirely inappropriate for Florida, has no water in her bowl.

Immediately, my claws come out. I want to yell at Harris, want to scratch him with my long fingernails.

Except I don't have long nails.

While he babbles about the property and the "idiot" dog, I stare at my hands and take deep, even breaths. My blunt fingernails need trimming to keep them appropriate for my work, but they aren't long by any standards.

What the fuck?

Somewhere nearby, one of those bug zappers buzzes. Church bells ring in the distance. A pair of squirrels chitter to each other. Sweat drips in my eyes, blurring my sight. I wipe it away on my sleeve, wanting to keep a close watch on everything Max does.

He heads inside the garage to get some things, and my anger subsides while my nerves take over. Everything about this screams setup, but what's he setting me up for? He doesn't like me, but he hires me. Could he be just as curious about me as I am about him? No, that doesn't feel right. He hates me, so he's already made up his mind about me.

No answers. Lots more questions.

I take a minute to fill the dog's empty red plastic container from a spigot attached to the outside of the Victorian-style home and stick my head under for good measure. I walked a couple of miles carrying my tools, and it's damn hot. Maybe that's all my weird impulse had been—the heat.

Katy watches me approach with her head down on her white paws and her tongue lolling out the side of her mouth. When I place the dish within her reach, she laps from it until it's half-empty again, then laps me, laving my face with happy doggie drool until I have to push her away or drown.

She's a real sweetheart, but when Max comes out the side door with the box of building supplies, she whines and cowers behind me.

Could be she doesn't like men. She's a rescue. A man could have hurt her.

Or maybe she's smarter than I am.

"So," I ask, taking the box from him and setting it on the ground, "why 'Katy'?"

"She's a bitch and I can tie her up," Max says. Then he laughs, making the bald statement a joke.

It takes me a minute to get it. Katy. Short for Katherine, like Kat.

Despite my own negative feelings about my ex, it isn't funny. And it speaks volumes about what their relationship must have been like before she drowned in the lake.

More and more I'm guessing Kat told her husband about me. I can't imagine why she'd have done that, but nothing else explains this kind of animosity toward both of us. She went back to him, but maybe he couldn't handle her having been with anyone else.

If her death hadn't been ruled an accident…. Then again, Gen pretty much figures it *wasn't* an accident. We just don't know how it *did* happen.

My instincts scream to get the hell out of here, but where else will I have any chance of finding answers? I definitely don't want to head back to the damn lake. I scan the yard for any sign of Kat's ghost, but nothing looks… ghostly… to me. *Come on, Kat. Give me a clue here. Why did you show up? Why did you try to drown me? And what did you mean when you used my voice to say, "Get it out"?*

"Hey! Hey, you stupid dog. Get away from there." Max hauls on the lead, dragging Katy away from the petunias where she's started digging, and practically strangling her in the process. The poor dog gives a little yelp.

"So," I say, taking a hold of another section of lead and casually pulling it away from Max, "where do you want the doghouse?"

He releases the rope and aims for the house, waving offhandedly over his shoulder. "Wherever. Just keep her away from the flowers." Turning back to me,

his face splits into a wide grin. "My wife *loves* her petunias." He disappears through the side door.

"Wife, huh? Didn't waste any time, did he?" The
dog barks once in response.

I set to work on organizing my tools and the materials Max provided while I run through things in my
head one more time. My guess is Kat is angry about her
lake accident. Who wouldn't be? And she's cursed the
lake and any woman who comes near it, if I believe in
that sort of thing. And having known Gen as long as I
have, I do. But how do I fit into it? And why does Harris
hate me so much?

No answers, and no Gen to help me. Harris won't
talk to me, but... maybe his current wife will. If I stick
around long enough to build the doghouse, she might
come out of the mansion and I can get her attention.
Then again, how will I start that conversation?

Um, hi. I'm your husband's dead wife's ex-lover.
Can we chat?

Maybe not.

I pat Katy on her big furry head and scratch behind
her pointed ears. She leans against me, rubbing her face
on my jeans. Damn, I could grow to love this dog.

Music carries from an open window on the second
floor—smooth jazz. But I don't see anyone. No sign of
the wife. Or kids, for that matter.

I can't imagine Maxwell Harris with kids, God
help them. Hopefully, he hadn't had time to produce
any with either of the women he married.

I construct the doghouse beneath the large banyan
tree Katy's tied to, on the far side from the bed of flowers. By lunch, the cozy home is standing but unpainted,
sweat drenches me, and Katy lies watching my every
move.

My stomach growls, but I didn't think to bring a sandwich, though I grabbed a bottle of Gatorade from hotel vending before I set out this morning. It's warm but wet, and I chug half the container, taking a break with Katy in the shade.

While I'm at it, I give Genesis a quick call, which, of course, goes straight to her voicemail. I swallow hard.

"Hey, Gen. I'm… sorry about last night. Not sure why I said what I did. *Am* sure I can't get through all this without you. Give me a call, please?" Katy adds a bark to the message, and I drop the connection.

I lean back, resting my head on the dog's soft flank. "If nothing else, maybe she'll call to ask where the dog came from," I tell her.

After capping the remainder of the Gatorade, I return to work, painting the house in red with white trim and adding some little touches Harris hasn't paid for, because, dammit, I like the dog a lot. Instead of a simple opening, I install hinged swinging doors to protect her better from rain or wind and a little window, also with swinging panels, that she can stick her head out of, if she chooses.

I down the rest of the Gatorade while the paint finishes drying, then let Katy inside to see what she thinks.

It needs bedding, but I've built it extra large, and there's plenty of room for her to turn around three times before lying in a smoothly sanded corner. I refill her water dish and set it inside with her. She barks a couple of times and licks my hand.

"Max!"

The shout comes from behind me, loud and close, and I jerk upward, my head in the doghouse, my butt sticking out the front opening. My skull slams into the swinging doors' frame, and I back out, rubbing my head and scowling.

I freeze.

Max Harris stands over me, a shovel in his upraised hands. Behind him, Leopold VanDean finishes what must have been a brisk run across the yard. He's out of breath when he reaches us, panting and resting his hands on his knees.

I glance from the shovel to Max and back again. "Problem?"

For a moment he stares at me, then lowers the garden tool. "Wasp," he says, gesturing toward the ground beside me.

I don't see one, and I don't believe him. But the only other explanation….

The only other explanation is unthinkable.

And doesn't surprise me in the slightest. Because it feels right. And it fits. When I crawled out of the doghouse, Max Harris planned to hit me with a shovel.

Inside the red-and-white structure, Katy growls, long and low. "Shh," I tell her, appreciating the sentiment, but not wanting her to get in trouble with her master.

"I'm assuming you wanted something," Max snaps at Leo. If looks could kill….

"Yes. I have new information. On that assignment you gave me." He casts a glance in my direction. "Nice work, Flynn. A real masterpiece. Simple yet classic design. Lovely workmanship."

"Um, thanks."

"So," Leo continues, "if you two want to settle up accounts…."

"Oh, we're settled. Payment in advance." I stand, brushing grass from my jeans. Gathering up my tools, I shove everything helter-skelter into the toolbox—not my usual MO. I treat my tools the way I'd treat my hypothetical children. They're my darlings and my livelihood. But I'm getting them, and me, the hell out of here.

I pass Leo on my way off the property.

"Thanks," I mutter under my breath.

"Don't mention it," he returns, with all seriousness.

For whatever reason, Max Harris just tried to kill me. And Leopold VanDean just saved my life.

Chapter 34
New Gig

"SO, YOU'RE out of work again? That sucks."

I sit in the Kissimmee Lanes bar, my waitress friend, Allie, straddling the chair opposite me, the rest of the place empty except for her bartender boyfriend, Steve, and a few guys drinking in the corner. She's especially hot today, hair in an elaborate braid and minimal tasteful makeup. It works for her and turns her white button-down and black skirt into almost a French maid look.

I've been pouring out my sorrows while she pours me more beer. The place is dead on early Wednesday nights, so I know I can talk her ear off and not get her in any serious trouble with the management.

"Yeah, twice over. Had two part-time gigs after the construction site closed, but one's with Gen and one's with her brother, so I'm guessing I'm fired from those too." I've also gone over my romance issues. Allie's a very sympathetic listener. Knows when to nod and when to smile and when to interject some helpful advice.

Except tonight she's kind of at a loss in the advice department.

"Well," she says, "I can't help you with Genesis. You've screwed that one up royally. But I might have a solution to your employment problem. The kid who works the rental desk quit yesterday. I'd be glad to put in a good word for you. Doesn't pay much, but it's something."

I smile at her. "That would be great. Thanks."

"And you can crash at my place for a while. I've been spending most nights at Steve's, anyway. I'm sure he won't mind me making my visits a little longer in duration."

Outside the bar in the main area with the bowling lanes, something buzzes again and again—some kid standing on the foul line at the end of the approach. I blink away blurred vision, exhaustion taking its toll, and consider Allie's offer.

"Me sleeping in your bed? With or without you, that's pretty hot."

Allie goes silent, the grin dropping from her lips. She sits back on her seat and fixes me with a long, hard stare.

Oh my God, I said that out loud.

"Allie—"

"Flynn, I know you're going through a lot. And I know you've always found me attractive."

My eyebrows fly up.

She waves a dismissive hand. "Hey, I'm not blind. I'm also sexy as hell, and you're gay. And I've never had a problem with that. But if you're going to hit on me...."

My face flushes with heat. "I'm not... I didn't... I have no idea why I said that." It's the truth. I respect her, her boyfriend, and her preferences, and I'm not an idle flirt. I've dated women who were, Kat being the most obvious of them. Even with her hand holding mine, she'd shamelessly hit on any attractive woman who walked by, and some who weren't so attractive. But I'm not like that, not with someone else's girlfriend in a public bar, even if there are only a couple of other customers around.

Allie's eyes narrow on my face, which must be three shades of red by now. She nods slowly. "Fine. I'll chalk it up to the beer and your mind being elsewhere. But seriously, Flynn, if you value our friendship, don't do that again. I'll still put in that word for you, but… I don't think lending you my apartment is a good idea." Grabbing her order pad from the table, she stands and retreats behind the bar, putting two feet of solid wood between herself and me.

Great.

She casts a quick glance in my direction, then fastens two more buttons on her shirt.

Even better.

Steve wanders over to her, wiping a glass with a bar rag. He leans down and whispers something in her ear, but she waves him off. Well, at least she isn't telling her boyfriend that I flirted with her.

I flirted with Allie. I walked out on Genesis. I think I'm losing my damn mind.

Unable to deal with her avoidance routine, I toss a few bills on the table—with a generous tip—grab my half-empty glass of beer, and head out to the lanes.

The brighter lights, thudding bowling balls, and crashing pins start a headache throbbing in my temples, and I clench my teeth on the pain. I'd love to play a few rounds, take out my aggression on something inanimate, but my equipment lies in Gen's closet. I rescued my tools and an armload of clothes from her place, and nothing more.

I'm contemplating all the cons of using a house ball and renting shoes when a rough hand falls on my shoulder and spins me around. The sudden motion causes me to slosh my beer into my own face and down the front of my T-shirt, so I'm already annoyed before I come face-to-face with the grabber—Paul. The new guy from the construction site.

The one who can't stand me.

He should take a number.

Though to be honest, I'm not working at winning any popularity contests these days.

"Problem?" I ask, lifting the dry hem of my shirt to press against the damp stain. Yeah, it doesn't make sense. Now I have *two* wet spots. But it gives me something to focus on besides Paul's angry face.

"You're my problem," he says.

Why doesn't that surprise me at all?

What does surprise me is his palms slamming against my shoulders and shoving me backward. I stumble across the wide center aisle separating the two rows of bowling lanes. My glass goes flying and lands with a thud on the multicolored carpeting covered in smiling bowling pins. My hip bumps a rack of balls so hard that three of them fall and bounce/roll away. And it hurts.

"What the fuck?" That comes out a little louder than I plan. A couple of families turn from the computerized scoring desks to glare at me. Right. Get annoyed about my cursing. Never mind some guy's beating up on me without provocation.

I rub my sore hip and step away from the rack. Raising one hand palm out in a placating gesture, I swing the other around and catch him in the face with my fist. Paul staggers back, putting a more comfortable distance between us.

"This is about fetching two-by-fours?" Talk about holding a grudge. It's been a freaking week since I ordered him around at the site. And besides, he deserved it.

"Hey! Break it up or I'm calling the police!" The manager, shouting from where he's temporarily manning the rental desk. Another real charmer.

I'm no damsel in distress. I can hold my own in a fight. But a little direct assistance would be nice right about now.

I guess I can kiss that job opportunity goodbye.

Paul snatches up the dropped glass and hurls it at my head. I block it with my forearm.

"You cost me that job. I needed that job." He charges me, but I sidestep him, causing him to knock down the rest of the bowling ball rack. Parents grab their kids and head for the front doors.

"What're you talking about? We're all laid off." Unless Tom fired him for his obnoxious comments after my accident. I don't like this guy, but I would've let those go.

He turns, panting, a trickle of blood running from the corner of his mouth. When he comes at me again, my college defense lessons rise up, and I strike out with a swinging kick that connects with his rib cage and forces him backward. All rage and no skill.

But plenty of brute force. He's bigger than I am. Taller and wider with meaty upper arms and large hands. When he makes another run, those hands wrap around my shoulders and throw me down.

I roll over the step leading to the slightly lower level of the lanes, across the uncarpeted floor, and slam up against the bolted-down seats. He's on me a second later, pounding me with his fists. "We're all laid off because of you."

"We're laid off because of bad financing," I shout, keeping my arms over my face to protect it from his blows. I manage to pull my knees into my chest and kick him off. He crashes into the scoring desk.

"Not the financing," he growls, spitting blood on the floor. "OSHA. The OSHA guys were there when you decided to go out on that beam without drinking enough water. Stupid, clumsy bitch. They saw your fall."

I'm halfway up, but at those words, I sink onto my butt and stare at him.

I remember Tom making a joke about his insurance not being able to afford a fall like mine, his strained laughter.

What if it hadn't all been a joke?

We keep an eye on inspection schedules, and everyone takes special care when the OSHA people come around.

Only, I crashed my truck a couple of nights before. I'm not keeping track of anything. And the inspectors haven't been by in a while.

"Look, Paul," I begin, but he's on me again before I can force the apology out. I guess some of the beer I sloshed is still affecting my vision, because I take a fist to my eye and another to my stomach. That buzz sounds over and over again. Seriously, parents, watch your damn kids. Don't let them cross the foul line and wander down the dangerous, oil-slick lanes.

Then the anger hits.

Blunt or not, my nails scrape down the side of his face leaving long red streaks. My knee comes up between his legs with all the force I can put behind it. With a shriek, he rolls away, cupping his privates with both hands.

Maybe Tom didn't tell me to spare me the guilt. Maybe it is my fault we're all out of work. But it was an accident. It could have happened to any of us. And I don't deserve to get beaten up for it.

Paul takes one look at my face and his eyes widen.

I pursue him as he scrambles backward on all fours, out onto the approach and then the lane itself. His hands and feet slip and slide in the oil, making him helpless to defend himself, but I stand over him, driving my work boot into his side again and again. The bowling alley blurs around me. I lose count of the number of times I connect. Then I'm grabbed and hauled away, kicking and shouting.

"Flynn! Flynn, calm down. Let it go." Steve shoves me into one of the seats, and cold water pours over me. I jerk back to see Allie holding an empty glass and shaking her head. "You all right?" Steve asks, holding me in place.

Little by little, I force my muscles to relax until he feels safe to release me. My cheek hurts, especially around my eye, which is half-swelled shut. "Yeah," I tell him, squinting.

"What happened? The boss says he started it."

And I finished him. Paul lies still, his eyes closed, and for a heart-stopping moment, I panic. Then he heaves a shuddering, wheezing breath.

Thank God.

"Work dispute," I manage.

The thuds of running feet herald the arrival of local law enforcement, and we're joined by four cops, the manager, and his assistant, along with a number of customers coming to gawk. Just like at the lake, one person's disaster is another one's entertainment.

I give them all the finger.

Not a smart move.

The finger and the hand attached to it are quickly cuffed to my other hand. One officer hauls me to my feet while another radios for an ambulance for Paul.

I struggle against the cops' holds, despite their repeated warnings, but I'm too tired and hurt to do much damage.

I'm in the back of a squad car and being read my rights before I realize I'm under arrest.

Chapter 35
Self-Analysis

I'VE NEVER been arrested before.

Kat was a couple of times while we dated. Once on a DUI, another on a drunk and disorderly at our local bar. She talked about it like her record was a badge of honor or a rite of passage. But she always had money. I look at it as a way to make myself unemployable.

I can't say I'm enjoying the new experience.

The good news? Paul isn't pressing charges. All the witnesses agreed he started the fight and had me on the ropes for a while, and the bruising on my face testifies to that story too. According to the cops, he went to the emergency room, got checked over, picked up some painkillers, and left, so even though I went overboard, he didn't suffer anything too serious beyond a cracked rib or two.

The bad news? I pissed off the cops by giving them the finger and resisting arrest, and they're holding me until they confirm no one wants to press charges and someone can come pick me up.

Guess where I'm spending my night.

I'm entitled to one phone call, and Officer Davies, a nice woman who remembers me from the rescue story the previous night, and makes it clear she supports me kicking the shit out of Paul, strongly urges me to use it to contact someone who can come get me and take responsibility for me. But who could I call? I've pretty much alienated every friend I have. I decline use of the phone.

It could be worse. I'd checked out of my Motel 6 room that morning and stored my belongings behind their desk, figuring I could check back in tonight if I didn't find anything cheaper. The manager made it clear a hero got one free night, but no more than that. Hopefully they'll hold my stuff until tomorrow. My tools are locked in Allie's truck from when she gave me a lift between Max Harris's driveway and the bowling alley, so those should be safe.

Presuming she doesn't throw them in the nearest dumpster for hitting on her.

Still can't believe I did that.

After enduring processing, mug shots, and booking, I'm told to change into pale orange coveralls, which look like they were once bright but have suffered too many washings. A featureless cinder block hall leads to the cells, and Davies opens one and gestures for me to step inside.

Oh goody. I'm sharing.

"Sorry," Davies says, and means it as she locks the bars behind me.

Two prostitutes (I guess from the overteased hair and abundance of heavy makeup since they're both wearing orange jumpsuits like I am) sit side by side on the bottom right-hand cot in a set of bunk beds, one crying and the other dabbing at the mascara running down the first's cheeks. The calm one might be fifty, the younger maybe eighteen, and that's stretching it. I wonder how they manage to make enough to survive.

Despite my own circumstances, my heart goes out to them. I've been poor and desperate, but I have a college education and a skillset that can get me odd jobs even when the construction company shuts down. I've never had to consider selling my body to pay for the necessities of life.

I take the cot on the bottom left and drop onto it. Sharp springs poke through the too thin mattress. Yellow sweat stains cover the caseless pillow. A couple of roaches lie belly-up in the corner while a second pair chase each other along the wall line. The air carries scents of bug spray and mold.

The warning buzz that sounds whenever the door leading into the holding area is opened rings over and over again. Busy night. I scrub at my tired eyes, trying to clear my sight, and focus on my roommates.

"So," I say, speaking to both women, "we've got some time to kill. How much do you charge?"

Chapter 36
Foot in Mouth Disease

I CLAMP one hand over my mouth and the other over my eyes and rest my whole head on my knees.

Stress? Yeah, I have tons of it. Emotional trauma? Yeah, that too. But the way crazy things spew from my lips, one would think I just developed a late onset case of Tourette syndrome.

Movement in the cell alerts me to the approach of one of the other women. I glance up to see the older hooker, hands fisted at her sides, staring down at me. Cheap, flowery perfume wafts in a cloud around her, nearly choking the air from my lungs.

"Don't know if you're drunk or high, honey, but we've got enough trouble. Keep your propositions to yourself or I'll shut your mouth for you, no matter how tough you are."

I refrain from reminding her that a cell block fight will also add to her troubles, and nod instead, muttering an apology. She peers at me, hard, then sits down beside me and motions the other girl over. A second later, I'm sandwiched between two prostitutes.

Not sure being assaulted by the ghost of my ex-lover was weirder than this moment.

I panic she might really want to take me up on my offer, when an arm falls across my shoulders. "You look like you're having a harder day than we are," the older woman says. She glances across me to the younger girl. "See what I been telling you? There's always someone worse off, and you need to pull up your big-girl panties and get through this."

Not thrilled with being the one "worse off" than a pair of arrested streetwalkers.

The girl nods, then wipes snot and tears on the shoulder of her coveralls. She sticks out a shaky hand. "Theresa," she says.

I take it, noting the bruised knuckles and scratches on my own. Hadn't felt those before, but they hurt like hell when she closes her fingers over them. "Flynn."

"Huh. Never heard that one on a girl before," the older one says. "I'm Fresca."

Never heard that one on anything but a soda can before, but I withhold comment.

She holds out her hand for a shake, but I pull mine back into my lap, settling for a girly finger wave instead, which still hurts. Her eyes narrow.

"What? You're too good to touch me?"

I display my damages for her, and she lets out a low whistle.

"Never mind. Between that and your face, I'm guessing you got yourself in a fight. Hope the other one looks worse than you."

"He does." I'm not proud of it. Oh, I'm not above defending myself, but I hit a man when he was down. Way down. And that goes against my moral code.

Or at least, I thought it did.

Another whistle. "He, huh? Well, good for you. Men got no right to touch without permission." She points a finger at the girl. "Or without paying. Even if yelling does get you caught."

Yep, it's been an eventful evening for all three of us.

Chapter 37
Connections

"AFTER EVERYTHING both of you have gone through this past week, you *broke up* with her?" Chris couldn't believe what his sister was telling him. He didn't believe it when she sobbed it over the phone, and he didn't believe it now that he sat across from her in her living room. But Flynn's absence in the apartment seemed to testify to the truth of the statement.

Flynn hadn't come in to work that morning, but Chris had given her Wednesday and Thursday off, so that made sense. He'd also shot her some dirty looks over her news broadcast kiss, grief she neither needed nor deserved, and he'd called to apologize. That's when Genesis had dropped her bomb.

They split up. At Genesis's request. Genesis, who never let a day go by without telling Chris how much she loved Flynn, how she wanted Flynn to move in, to spend her life with Flynn. Seemed like everyone had lost their minds these days.

Genesis sniffled, then burst into a fresh round of tears. From the puffiness around her eyes and their redness, Chris guessed she'd been crying since Flynn left the night before.

He glanced at his watch. After midnight. Gen had kept him on the phone for over an hour, being generally incoherent, before he finally offered to just come over and do this in person.

He passed his sister a tissue.

"Can you tell me why? Because, really, I don't get it."

Gen hiccupped. She always got the damn hiccups when she cried hard. "…. M-Mom and D-Dad," she managed.

"Oookay. Help me out here." Chris went to the kitchen and fetched her a glass of water while she composed herself. When he returned, she forced out a passable explanation for why she couldn't love someone who lived a dangerous life like Flynn did.

Let that sit for a while.

"So, you don't love her?" he asked.

"Of course I love her. But—"

Chris loved his sister. Very much. With their parents gone, she was his only remaining family. And her gift made things difficult for her. He remembered rushing her to the emergency room the night their parents died. He never wanted to go through that again.

He also didn't want her to live the rest of her life alone, regretting the decision she made last night.

His job to love her. His job to tell her when she was being stupid.

"But nothing. You already love her. The damage is done. Won't matter if you're seeing her at the time or not, if something happens to her, you'll be devastated. Everybody dies, Gen," Chris said softly. "It's not like she's a cop or a firefighter or a soldier. She's not a daredevil either. Opportunities to save someone's life aren't going to come up often." After a moment's thought on the last few days he added, "Hopefully."

Gen sipped her water and wiped her eyes. "That's pretty much what she told me," she admitted, "except she was shouting. She was so angry."

"Do you blame her?"

"No, but it wasn't like her. The shouting and grabbing things. She didn't even try to argue with me much. Just snatched up an armload of clothes and went."

"She didn't hit you, did she?" That would be a different story.

"No, but for a second, I wondered…." Gen shook her head. "No."

"Huh." Chris thought about it. "I don't believe she would have. Like I said, it's been a helluva week. And this isn't the first time she's been dumped by someone after investing a lot of emotion."

"I didn't dump her," Gen said, standing to pace the cream carpet. "I thought, maybe, she'd offer to, you know, change."

Ah.

Standing, Chris went and put a halt to the pacing, then wrapped his arms around Genesis and pulled her in close. She buried her face in his white work shirt.

"Have you *met* Flynn?" he teased, using her exact words from the other day. "You love her for who she is, and you know she won't change. Sometimes…." He tilted her face up to meet his eyes. "Sometimes you have to take risks to receive great rewards."

Genesis blinked at him. "That sounds like something Dad might have said."

"It was."

"Oh." She grabbed another tissue. "Flynn did try to call, left an apology on my voicemail. But when I tried to call her back, it just went to her messages over and over. That's when I called you."

"Well, there, you see? It'll work out, if you let it." Flynn could apologize. She did it pretty often, in fact, because her poor self-esteem made her think she was wrong a lot more than she really was. But it cost her some serious effort. If she'd gone through the bashing of her minimal ego and pride to leave Genesis a message, that was a very good sign.

"Unless she's changed her mind." Fresh tears welled up in his sister's eyes.

"Gen—" He'd been about to chastise her for pessimism when a sudden thought occurred. "You… you don't think this breakup might be payback, do you?"

She grabbed a tissue from the box on the coffee table and blew her nose. "What are you talking about?"

"The other night. The dark magic. I saw you, Gen. Could this be the price?"

A long pause while she considered, the red of a fierce blush creeping into her face. Good. Let it embarrass her. Whatever it took to stop her from using it.

After another moment, she shook her head. "No. I don't think so. I never actually did anything with it. Flynn beat me to it."

"Flynn? But how—?"

"She sees ghosts, Chris. Clearly, she has some untapped talent of her own."

But exactly what sort of talent was it? And which side of the magic spectrum did it come from?

The phone rang. Gen hiccupped. "That's the client line. C-can you get it?"

He pushed away his concerns for now. "Sure." Though what a client would be doing calling after midnight, he had no idea. Probably a wrong number. He grabbed the cordless from the holder just inside the kitchen.

It was Allie, Flynn's friend from Kissimmee Lanes. He'd bowled a few rounds with Flynn out there, getting his ass kicked every time, and had to buy a number of victory beers in the bar, so he remembered the leggy waitress quite fondly. Tonight she had a lot to say. After listening for several minutes and interjecting the occasional "Uh-huh" he hung up.

Gen had watched him throughout the entire conversation. He could only guess what his expression must have looked like, shifting from shock to concern.

He steadied himself. "Flynn's been arrested," he said.

"What?"

"Seems she got in a fight at the bowling alley. Sent some guy to the emergency room."

Genesis sank back down on the couch, head in her hands. "That doesn't make sense. Flynn doesn't start fights."

"She didn't start it," Chris said, "but she sure as hell finished it, beating on the guy way past him being down for the count. Started in on the cops, too, before they subdued her. Allie"—he gestured at the phone—"found a bunch of your cards in Flynn's tool box and got your number." Though what the waitress was doing with Flynn's tools, he had no idea. He shook his head. "Anyway, she thought you might want to know."

"She was going to take those cards to the little gift shops around town, leave some at each one." Genesis grabbed a white sweater from the back of a chair. "Let's go get her. I have some apologizing of my own to do." She sighed, then frowned. "And that still doesn't sound like Flynn. I can't see her hurting someone past what was strictly necessary to protect herself, and she's not stupid enough to go after a cop, even if she was drinking."

"She's had a really, really bad week." But Chris didn't buy it either. Something was going on with Flynn. Maybe not payback for use of black magic, but something bad. She'd lost it in the pub, too, beyond the anger she should have showed over his silent assumptions about that kiss. He thought about mentioning the episode, but at a second glance at the dark circles beneath Gen's eyes and the way her hands trembled buttoning the sweater, he decided to wait.

She had enough to worry about.

Chapter 38
Let Out

APPROACHING FOOTSTEPS wake me from an uneasy sleep. I'm not sure how I managed to doze off. Between the disgusting state of the bed and the snoring of Fresca and Theresa in the opposite set of bunks, I thought I'd never rest.

The feet come closer, and I wonder if we're getting another cellmate to bring us to full capacity. Swinging my police-issued booties to the floor, I sit up and lock eyes with Chris and a cop outside the bars.

I do a quick scan for Genesis, but they're alone, and my heart sinks. Don't know how Chris found out about my arrest, but I'm glad to see a familiar face, and... I study him... a friendly one. He smiles. Not too much. Like he's afraid to be too jovial under the serious circumstances, but I definitely detect a grin and the usual twinkle in his eyes.

I stand and approach the bars, but the cop gestures for me to keep back while she fiddles with the keys and inserts one into the lock.

"Didn't know we got middle-of-the-night visitors," I say quietly, not wanting to wake the ladies.

Chris glances past my shoulder at the hookers and snorts. "Looks like you've got plenty of company without visitors. Must have been entertaining. But no. I convinced the police to let us take you home."

The guard swings the bars open and waves me through, and Chris and I follow her down the hallway.

My face flushes hot, and I'm sure Chris notices, but, bless him, he doesn't rag me for it. He doesn't rag me for anything, actually, just walks by my side, a quiet, comforting presence. Then his words register fully on my sleep-deprived brain. "Us?"

He grins at me. "Yes, us. Gen's in the car. She balked at the doors, said the place gave off really negative vibes." His smile fades some. "To be honest, I think she's just scared to face you. Sounds like you two had quite a row last night."

The cop leading us hmmphs. "More fighting? Get some counseling." She opens the access door. The buzzer sounds. My vision blurs with anger.

"Hey," I start, "who the fu—"

Chris's hand comes down on my shoulder, hard. "She will, officer, thank you." To me he whispers, "Cool it, Flynn."

We arrive at the desk, and I take the opportunity to close my eyes and heave a few deep breaths. Cool it. Yeah. I've been needing to do that for days.

The cop fetches my personal belongings, and I duck in a bathroom to change clothes and gather my thoughts. When I emerge, it isn't a hallucination. Chris is still there, holding the door for me, and we walk outside together, around to the side parking lot.

Where Genesis waits.

God help me.

Chapter 39
Bits and Pieces

SHE STANDS by the sedan. Good thing they brought it and not the Charger. The sports car is hot, but I knock my head on the roof every time we hit a bump when I sit in the back seat, and I figure that's where I deserve to be in this trio, especially under the circumstances. Then I realize Gen's car isn't here because she probably feels unfit to drive, and my guilt multiplies by ten. Knocking me in the head a few times might not be a bad idea.

When my feet fail to propel me across the parking lot, Chris places a hand between my shoulder blades and gives me a gentle shove. "She doesn't bite," he says, then pauses midstep. "Well, not since she was three."

That earns him a snort from me. I start moving again.

Gen doesn't meet my eyes when we get to the sedan, just stares down her flowing tan peasant skirt at her pale pink ballet flats. I love those shoes, danced with her any number of times while she's worn them, sometimes to no music at all. Holding her in my arms, twirling her around. She's graceful and agile and beautiful, though she claims she's a natural-born clod.

Chris scans the well-lit lot. "Not the best place for a heart-to-heart, but I'll give you guys some space." He wanders back toward the main building, whistling off-key, his shadow casting lean and long in the overhead lights.

I scuff one boot on the concrete. "Seems like all we're doing lately is fighting."

"And making up."

I detect the note of hope in her voice and smile a little. My heart gives a leap.

"And making up," I agree. "I shouldn't have yelled at you. I shouldn't have stormed out. I should've been more sympathetic. I know how hard your parents' deaths hit you. But you went and said you loved me, and then you said—" I choke off, unable to repeat the worst words I ever heard fall from her lips.

"I said I wasn't sure about us," she finishes for me. Her head comes up. Her shining green eyes meet mine. "But what I really wanted was comforting, reassurance, whatever you could offer. I never should have used those words with you. Because I *am* sure. I'm sure I love you. I'm sure I want you. Always. And I should have thought about how those particular words would hurt. Especially used against you."

Because of Kat. Yeah, she hurt me then, and Gen hurt me last night.

One of the overhead parking lot lights buzzes. Suddenly things aren't nearly as well-lit as they'd been moments before. The shadows creep in, twisting and turning, making Gen's expression difficult to read.

My anger boils just below the surface, but I tamp it down. We're apologizing, not starting another fight, dammit.

"I don't know what got into me."

"I don't know what I was thinking."

Our words tumble over one another's, and then she's in my arms, holding me as close to her and as tightly as she can.

And then she isn't.

I'd closed my eyes, so when her body suddenly unmolds itself from mine, I have to open them to find out why.

Gen stares at me. In the overhead lights, she's gone pale. The slightest of tremors passes through her. I reach out a hand to steady her, but she backpedals.

What the hell?

"C-Chris?" she calls toward the precinct entrance.

A glance over my shoulder confirms Chris's location, by the front doors, chatting up a curvaceous female officer. Might even have been Officer Davies, the one who processed my paperwork, but I can't tell at this distance.

"Chris, I need you over here!"

Panic. That's panic in Gen's voice. And it causes a sympathetic rise in my own tension. Chris notes it, too, and he breaks off with the officer, heading at a brisk pace in our direction, his smile too tight to be anything but for show.

With a shrug, the policewoman goes back into the precinct.

"Gen—"

She holds up a hand, cutting off my words. I grind my teeth in response. If it were anyone but Genesis….

"What's wrong?" Chris asks, falling in beside his sister and glancing between the two of us.

With him there for backup, I guess she feels secure enough to talk to me. "Flynn, have you had any further contact with Kat or any other spirit, for that matter, since that night in our apartment?"

Well, at least it's still *our* apartment.

I have no idea what she's getting at, but Chris seems to, because he backs a step away and pulls Genesis with him, never taking his eyes off me. "That... would explain a lot," he says.

"Yeah, it would," she echoes, voice drifting off.

He glances at his sister. "She almost got into it with the releasing officer on our way out. I had to step in."

"Still standing here," I remind them, crossing my arms over my chest and rapidly losing my patience.

"Still haven't answered my question," Gen reminds me.

"Okay, yeah," I say, pacing the length of the sedan. "When I rescued what's-her-name from her car, I ran into Kat. She grabbed me. I got away. Pushed her out like I did before."

"And have you noticed any odd repeated sensations? Especially connected with your moments of anger? Things you could have explained away as naturally occurring? Because that's what you would have done, Flynn. The human mind seeks a rational explanation for the supernatural because it can't accept the paranormal as real."

I think about all the moments I've felt those furious surges... and the buzzing and vision problems that accompanied each and every one.

"Ohhhh... fuck...."

"Hold her, Chris," Gen orders softly.

Before I can react, he has my upper arms, and I growl into his face. "You realize," I say with complete control, "that I can take you."

Chris swallows hard, but it's Genesis who answers. "You realize," she says, "that you shouldn't want to."

And she's right. I love Chris, the brother I never had and always wished for. I've never wanted to hurt him, not really. But I want to now, and that's... very wrong. I can't hear over the swarm of bees in my head. I can barely see. My situation dawns on me, at last. "Am... am I possessed?"

Genesis shakes her head, and I let out a breath. "We really need to look into your family line later." She holds up one finger to stave off my rising argument. "You pushed Kat out, and again, you shouldn't have been able to do that without help. But this time," she adds before I can bask in relief, "you missed a piece."

Chapter 40
The Enemy of My Enemy

LEO STOOD on the fraying welcome mat outside Genesis's apartment, staring into the lightening sky and hoping no one saw him.

He laughed. Who was he kidding? No one in his right mind would be out at this ungodly hour.

Then again, Maxwell Harris qualified as pretty damn ungodly, and pretty damn not in his right mind.

Leo cast another quick glance down at the parking lot and all along the upper walkway. If Max or a friend of his spotted him here…. He shivered in the early-morning air.

Ravings aside, his old mentor, Ferguson, had been dead-on about Flynn's whereabouts, the threat to her life, and where that threat came from. Leo had no doubt Max meant to kill the construction worker. He'd killed his first wife, after all.

And Leo hadn't seen any sign of the second woman of the house during his last visit.

He needed to get out from under the crazy man's thumb.

He needed to do it without the crazy man turning him over to the Registry.

So, when Genesis called him at four thirty in the morning, he'd thrown on clothing and come. Indeed, rumpled slacks and a wrinkled polo, not to mention no socks or underwear, did not suit his image. Not one bit. He hadn't even bothered to comb his hair or brush his teeth. But he'd driven his orange McLaren to an empty space a block away and walked to Gen's apartment without hesitation. Because she needed his help.

And he was going to need hers.

The door swung open before he could knock a second time, and Gen stood in the entry, as worn and bedraggled as he was, though he doubted she'd gone to bed this night. She stepped aside so he could come in and he did so, ignoring her raised eyebrows at his disheveled appearance.

She took his hand, surprising him. It had been a long time since she'd willingly touched him. Oh, she must need him very, very badly. Tugging, she led him to the living room.

Where Flynn sat.

His own eyebrows lifted at the sight of Gen's latest significant other. Gone was the confident woman, the one full of strength ready to unleash upon him if he so much as looked at Genesis the wrong way. Instead, the construction worker appeared broken. She sat in the armchair by the windows, her head hanging down, her hands pressed between her knees. Her throat moved convulsively, as if she fought not to vomit. Her clothing bore a number of tears, some in awkward places revealing more flesh than the woman would have allowed if she'd been fully cognizant. Her skin sported bruises, some of them fresh, so not from her car accident or the rescue. She'd been in a fight, and recently. Genesis's brother, Chris, stood beside the chair, hovering, guarding, but Leo got the uncomfortable impression it wasn't Flynn Chris was protecting.

"What," Leo asked in a whisper to the woman at his side, "is it that you exactly want from me?"

"I want you to help me perform an exorcism. A partial," she corrected herself.

He stiffened. Exorcisms were bad enough—nasty, dirty, crawly things that lingered in the psychic resonance for days afterward, even with his somewhat limited sensitivity. He hated them with a passion, and Genesis knew it.

But partials....

Remnants of spirits, or "partials," as some psychics called them, were just as distasteful to the psychic "touch," if not more so, and required a certain delicate finesse to remove from a living host—a finesse Genesis should have possessed all by herself, unless... "How long has it been in her?" He glanced at Gen out of the corner of his eye, never taking his full gaze off Flynn.

The muscles in Gen's jaw tightened. "More than twenty-four hours."

And that explained that.

Caught immediately, a remnant could be extricated from a person by one good psychic. Given multiple hours to establish a foothold, it would take more than one to do it without permanently damaging the emotional and mental stability of the victim.

"This, my dear, is going to cost you," Leo said, his lips curling upward in a predatory smile.

She never looked fully away from Flynn, either, but Gen's expression was much different from Leo's.

It almost hurt him to see the pain in her eyes, and the love she had for Flynn far surpassing whatever she'd felt for him.

Gen would do anything to save Flynn. He had her right where he wanted her.

Part of him wished he didn't.

"How much?" Gen asked. "You know I can afford it."

"I don't want money," he said, sensing her tense beside him. "A favor, to be called in at any time, regardless of how large. And your word that you'll grant it."

Now she did close her eyes, trusting Chris to watch Flynn. "If it's within my power, if it brings no harm to another living thing," Gen said, "you have my word."

Chapter 41
Out With the Bad

GEN AND LEO crouch before the armchair, study-ing me as if I'm the newest specimen in their psychic laboratory. Chris hovers at my left shoulder, never leaving my side. His presence both comforts and in-timidates me.

"Why did you let it get ensconced?" Leo asks.

"I didn't know it was there. She didn't tell me," Gen answers.

"*She*," I say, pointing at myself, "didn't know. And I'm *still* here." They ignore me. No real surprise. So long as I'm even partially compromised, anything I say is suspect. I push down inside myself, like I did the last time Kat took up residence, but if part of her is in there, it's too small for me to, what, get a grip on it? Fuck if I know. I *feel* like me, like I'm in complete control, and yet I *know* I haven't acted like myself since my jump in the lake.

Kind of wish I could dive back in and never climb out.

Which serves to remind me that I'm really not myself.

I stop trying to get their attention.

"Didn't you feel its presence?" Leo asks Gen, incredulous.

"We hadn't touched," Gen says. "We had a fight." As if that explains everything. Maybe it does.

"I kissed you," I mutter.

Gen places a hand on my knee, recoils as if shocked, then forces it back down, applying a gentle pressure. Amazing how denim, thick material that it is, manages to enhance every bit of physical contact. "I remember," she says, "but I was half-asleep. Probably chalked the sparks up to your usual magnetism."

I wonder how serious she is, if she actually feels a connection to me through her talent, or if it's a figure of speech. Regardless of what she usually senses, her current smile is pained. Touching me at all is uncomfortable for her now, so I hold on to my curiosity. A moment later, I push her hand away. No use hurting her more than I must.

"So," Leo says, rubbing both hands together, "we should get started, then." He doesn't sound as eager as he pretends. "You say it's an anger remnant?"

Gen nods. "That's my take on it." She glances at Chris for confirmation.

"Yep. Anger. Lots of it. She tried to start a fight with me, had one with Gen, and then got into it with a coworker she ran across at the bowling alley, not to mention almost going after a cop at the station. Flynn's a bit volatile by nature, but she's been over-the-top."

Leo raises an eyebrow. He hadn't known I'd been arrested. Thanks so much, Chris.

"So, Kat's an angry bitch of a spirit," Leo says.

"Hey!" I start to rise. Chris shoves me deep into the cushions.

"Sit," he orders.

"Stay," Leo tacks on.

"Woof," I tell them both, swallowing the urge to growl. I hope Max's dog, Katy, is doing better than I am. No more buzzing, no more blurred vision. My head just hurts.

"If we're going to remove the partial, we need to know exactly what she's angry about," Gen says.

Leo blows out a breath and stands, then stretches each of his legs. Crouching hurts if done too long. "I'd think that'd be obvious," he says. "She's upset about dying."

Gen shakes her head. "More to it than that. General anger over her death explains some of the random fights, especially if she had unfinished business, but she's particularly aggressive towards me, both in and out of Flynn's body. Why?"

"Again obvious." Leo points a finger in Gen's direction. "Jealousy. You're the new love interest."

"But Kat gave Flynn up, got married. It doesn't make sense for Flynn to be the unfinished piece."

Leo wanders across the living room, pausing in the entry to the kitchen. "Unless she was heading back to her…," he mutters.

My head snaps toward him, difficult with Chris holding me in place, but I manage it. I lock eyes for the briefest moment with Leopold, but it's enough for me to get the impression that he knows something, and he isn't telling.

God, could it be true? Could Kat have been leaving Max Harris? Having met the man, I can understand why. But coming back to me?

I turn to stare at Genesis, desperately trying to hide the traitorous bit of hope that flares in my chest. No, not hope. Kat is long dead. But something. Something I shouldn't be feeling for my ex-lover. Gen stares back, the hurt evident. Guess I don't hide it very well. "It wouldn't have mattered," I tell her. But that would have been before I met Genesis. What would I have done if Kat had returned, apologized? I would like to think, after how much pain she caused me, I'd have told her to go to hell. But honestly, I don't know.

The pressure on my shoulders eases, and Chris seats himself on the armrest of my chair. "Gen, you always say ghosts get confused. Maybe Kat's forgotten leaving Flynn. That would account for her more… intimate… visit as well."

Leo's mouth drops open. Gen stands, walks over, and closes it for him. It doesn't stay closed. "Well, that *is* interesting. And understandable. I know there are times I'd like to forget our breakup and revel in another roll with my Genesis."

Chapter 42
Bachelor Number One

I'm UP and slamming Leo backward across the tile and against the kitchen counter before I even know I've moved. "You're the guy?" I scream into his paling face. "You're the one she broke up with?" Hell, I thought he was gay.

Chris tries to pull me off, but I shove him away, hearing him collide with something behind me. I'm strong, and whatever's going on inside me makes me stronger. Gen shouts at me to stop, but she's smart enough not to touch me, thank God. I don't even know why I, or Kat for that matter, is angry with Leo. He and Genesis are a done deal.

Except Gen never told me, and now he's here, in her apartment, helping her.

Helping me.

Measure by measure, I force the arm I'm pressing to Leo's throat to relax. He hasn't said a word, either out of fear or from lack of oxygen, and as soon as I release him, he grabs for the closest chair and slumps into it. One hand rubs his neck; the other reaches behind to his back, where he caught the counter edge.

"Yes, anger is certainly the correct assessment," he chokes out.

I drop into the chair opposite him, cross my arms on the table, and rest my aching head on them. I sense Chris's approach, but it's Gen's hands that find my shoulders, massaging gently. "He's no threat," she whispers. And I know she doesn't mean physically.

I groan in response. "Can we get this thing out of me now?" My arms muffle the words, but she understands me.

She always understands me.

"It'll take us a few minutes to prepare. You okay here?"

I nod, and Chris says, "I've got her." I raise my head and give him a grateful look.

Leo's seat creaks as he rises and moves stiffly into the living room. Genesis casts one more worried glance in my direction before following. Cabinets open and close. Lights are dimmed. Candles flicker through the archway.

Chris hands me a glass of water. I take it in a trembling hand. His has a bruise forming, and the knuckles are swelling. "I do that?"

Not me. Not me. Not me.

His sheepish grin confirms it before he speaks. "Slammed it into the dishwasher knob when you shoved me. It's no big deal."

But it is to me.

Chris is right. I'm quick to finish an argument, quick to return a punch if one is thrown at me. It's a character flaw I've worked on improving for years. But I don't start fights.

Except for once.

THE ROCK sailed through Gen's driver-side window, smashing the glass and scattering shards across the interior. Too far away to stop it, I had to content myself with watching from the upstairs walkway, but I took in as many details as I could.

I'd just stepped out with my morning coffee, something I liked to do when I slept over at her apartment. The February air burned the insides of my nostrils with its crispness—too rare an experience in Florida. While most natives huddled in their homes with heaters on high and fires burning in ridiculous fireplaces, I wanted to take advantage of every cold front we got. Not too many crazy Floridians like me.

Bad luck for the rock throwers.

Following the trajectory backward, I spotted the culprits, two older teenage boys, fleeing from the parking lot in their vehicle—a bright red NEV with "spinny rims" on the tires rotating the opposite direction from the wheels themselves. Wannabe gangsta adornments. Very noticeable. Very obvious. Very stupid.

I laughed, watching my breath cloud the air in front of me.

Not an amused laugh. An "I'm going to hunt you down without even breaking a sweat" laugh.

I waited long enough to see which direction the NEV took out of the lot. It was only just pulling onto the main road now. Because NEV's are slow. Really slow.

NEV stands for Neighborhood Electric Vehicle. Festivity crawled with them, literally. Open-sided glorified golf carts, they ran solely on electricity, made green activists happy, and had a top speed of twenty-five miles per hour.

They also couldn't leave Festivity. The speed limits were too high outside the town borders.

I grabbed my keys from the table inside Gen's door, left my half-full coffee cup in their place, and pounded down the stairs. The chill got chillier. I hadn't stopped for a jacket, and the wind cut right through my thin T-shirt, exhilarating me.

My truck sat next to the damaged Charger, and I paused to lean through the broken window and snag the rock off the glass-covered leather seat. My intention was to return it to the boys, maybe through their windshield, but definitely in a way guaranteed to make them pay for the vandalism.

The note stopped me.

Snapping off the rubber band, I unwrapped the crumpled paper from the chunk of concrete and read the one word printed there.

LESBIAN.

This wasn't random vandalism. It was hate.

My vision went red. Careful not to rip the rusting handle off the door, I climbed into my truck.

It didn't take long to find them. How many tricked-out red NEV's containing two teenage boys could there be in Festivity?

They were heading down one of the perimeter roads not far from the high school, only it was Sunday, and no one drove out there on weekends, especially not on a frigid early morning.

They saw me coming up behind them, glanced back over their shoulders as I tapped their rear bumper, and moved off to the side to get the hell out of my way while hurling curses at me.

I cut them off and used my truck to block them from reentering the road.

When I got out, they were standing in front of their NEV, one of those JESUS fish stuck to the front panel. Oh yes, they'd been behaving very Christian-like.

Then again, by many accounts, I guess they had been.

They were eighteen, maybe nineteen years old, and cocky as hell. One wore a football jersey from Festivity high. The other cracked his knuckles and looked me up and down. He sported an olive drab ROTC T-shirt.

Holding out the rock, I said, "You dropped this."

Football dude's eyes widened. "You're the lip-stick's butch."

Slang, TV, and smart mouths—the enemies of all homosexuals. Inwardly I cringed, outwardly said, "You'd better as hell believe it," and launched the rock.

It caught the knuckle cracker in the temple, and the fight was on. Outnumbered or not, I was stronger than either of them and more experienced in self-defense than both. The one kid might have had an army shirt, but he sure hadn't learned much from his classes. Ten minutes, two sweep kicks, and a lot of punches later, I stood over them. I was sweating despite the cold air, and panting like a racing greyhound, but with the exception of a few bruises and a swollen upper lip, I was unharmed. Couldn't say the same for the bleeding boys at my feet.

The football player had a broken nose, blood dripping and staining the front of his white-and-purple jersey. The other had bruised ribs and a sprained wrist, if it wasn't actually broken.

"We'll sue," he said. "We'll have you arrested."

"What you'll have," I told him, "is a check for the broken window in Genesis McTalish's PO box by tomorrow. I have your license plate number. I have your note in your handwriting. And I have your fucking rock." I picked it up from the road and tossed it into the bed of my truck, where it clattered a couple of times and lay still. "I think the local cops would much rather arrest a pair of hoodlums for a hate crime than believe a girl beat up two boys old enough to enlist in the military. And besides, with the other evidence against you, I'll just claim self-defense." I gestured at my swollen lip, which really did smart, dammit.

I left them there, sitting on the asphalt, and drove back to Gen's apartment in my truck. Made up a story to explain my minor injuries—caught some guy breaking into her Charger, ran him off after a brief scuffle. The check showed up on schedule with an apology attached, no mention of the rock, so I left it out too.

Yeah, it was another lie, but I had my reasons. Gen had always been comfortable with her sexuality. I didn't want to take that away. She never found out about the hateful note. No one as sweet as she was deserved to feel hated just for being her.

Chapter 43
Push Me Pull You

"WE'RE READY," Gen calls.

Chris leads me to the living room, hovering close, I guess in case I go apeshit again.

Gen has the place set up like any other of her tarot readings/seances, with a few notable differences. Someone shoved the glass-topped coffee table out of the way to make room for a second pillow on Gen's side, while the usual single cushion sits on the opposite side of the deck of cards. More candles than usual cover every usable surface: coffee table, both end tables, even the windowsill. Those flames have glass covers protecting them and keeping the closed curtains from catching fire.

I realize with a start that it's morning, broad daylight outside, well after six, but darkness shrouds the living room like night.

Lastly, a picture of Kat, the wedding shot from the obituaries, stands propped up by a small frame beside the tarot. Seeing it sparks a low rumble from my throat, but since no one grabs me, I must have held it in. I'm not sure if it's me angry at Kat or that part of Kat inside me furious with something in her bridal pose, but either way, the anger disconcerts me.

"Have a seat, Flynn," Gen says, keeping her tone light. She beckons me toward the single pillow on the client side of the cards.

And there I am, having that reading she always wants to give me. A real one, not some scam at a carnival. One I've been trying to avoid since the day we met.

No. Since the day my dead grandmother walked through a mortuary wall.

I can't think of worse circumstances under which to lose my tarot card virginity.

I force my body to fold into a cross-legged position while Leo and Gen seat themselves opposite me and Chris stands behind. I inhale a deep breath of his cologne.

"Leather Chaps," I say, guessing at the brand.

"Yeah…?"

"Nice."

"Flynn…."

My shoulders stiffen at the warning note, and I sit straight up. No way in hell I'd recognize a cologne by smell or bother to memorize its name. I don't even know which perfume Gen wears, only that I like the combination of orange and honey.

"The remnant's getting stronger," Genesis says, forehead wrinkled in concern.

"Let's get this over with," I say, and pick up the cards, shuffling them as I saw Mrs. Pinkerton do a few days ago. The well-worn pieces of plastic-covered cardboard feel warm and pliable. Twin cats stare at me from their back sides, one white, one black, both with green eyes like Gen's. I focus on their sleek bodies and try not to think about what I'm getting into.

"Shuffle until you feel ready," Gen instructs, her voice taking on that soothing monotone she uses when she reads.

"I'll never feel ready," I mutter. And then I do. My hands cease manipulating the cards as if of their own volition. I place the slightly uneven stack in front of her.

Gen picks up the cards. Leo places one arm across her shoulders. It's a practiced maneuver, one they've done before, and I bristle at the familiarity.

"Easy, Flynn," Chris says. "He's bracing her, lending his… minimal… talent to hers."

"Oh yes, thank you so very much," Leo puts in, glaring up at him.

"It's a steadying technique," Gen says. "He'll ground me so I don't get distracted calling her to you."

Right. Okay. I want Gen grounded. Don't want her mind wandering when—"Wait. Call her? You mean Kat? To me? Why? I thought we were getting her bits out, not inviting the rest of her in." Memories of her first invasion flood back, raising the hairs on my arms and legs—creeping, crawling, prickling, *hurting*. I move to stand, but Chris pushes me down. Getting a little tired of that.

"The only one who can collect the remnant of herself is Kat," Gen says, reaching to place a hand over one of mine. She gives it a light squeeze and sits back. "Once she's whole, Leo and I will drive her out in her entirety. It'll be fine."

"You've done this before, right?"

She doesn't meet my eyes. "No, but I've seen it performed."

"And it worked?"

A long pause. "The psychic wasn't properly grounded."

"And?" I prompt.

"Both she and the client suffered emotional breakdowns."

Terrific.

"Let's get this over with," I say, pasting on a trusting smile. Gen's looks equally fake.

She closes her eyes, takes a cleansing breath, and lets it out. Then she takes up the cards in her delicate hands and lays them out, one by one, in the cross and line pattern I've seen her use. As always, I don't know most of their meanings, but the one she turns over at the center, a muscular woman bearing a spear and sporting armor, resembles me to an uncomfortable degree. The one lying across it, also depicting a woman, less fierce and warlike, looks like Kat.

"You're a fighter, Flynn," Gen says. "She's strong, but you're stronger. You'll beat this." The monotone of her speech, resonating in the high-ceilinged living room (and why didn't I ever notice that odd echo before), lulls me into an almost semiconscious state as she continues to read the cards.

Family difficulties in my distant past, death and danger in my recent past, pain and danger in my immediate future, and—oh, lovely—a blank card for my distant future.

"Doesn't mean anything," Gen hastens to reassure me. "Just that it's unclear, uncertain. The actions you take from here forward are too unpredictable even for the tarot."

The Lovers and the Tower make a reappearance, drawing a gasp Genesis can't quite hide, though I pretend I didn't hear it. She's under enough stress, tense muscles, face pale, breath coming a little too fast. I worry for her, actually, and from the quick glances Leo keeps casting to the side, I suspect he's worried too.

We're nearing the end of the reading, and I don't notice anything different about how I feel. There's still a sense of underlying anger, barely controlled, but it's deep down inside me and no more intense than before. The one thing I do pick up, however, is the marked absence of any cards in the layout resembling or referring to Genesis. After the Lovers and the Tower, it's like she vanishes from my existence.

Or I vanish from hers.

Chapter 44
News to Me

THE SMELL hits me first—a dank dampness like wet, moldy clothing and stagnant water. I know that scent. It smells like Dead Woman's Pond—how I'll forever refer to it, despite what the town calls it. A breeze passes through the room, though the windows and doors are closed. Every candle flickers, even the ones protected by glass. Genesis shivers, and goose bumps rise on my arms. I stare wild-eyed into the shifting shadows, but other than the scattered flames, nothing moves.

Unlike the last time, Kat's spirit doesn't slam into me. It eases its way in, like a tiny garden snake sliding down my throat. I suspect she's been in the room awhile, slipping past my natural defenses an inch at a time, because when I do notice the odd heaviness, the pressure in my... soul, for want of a better description... it's too late for me to fight it.

Not that I'm supposed to.

"Don't struggle. Let her in," Leo says. "We need all her essence in one place."

Fuck you, Leo. "Gen...," I manage while my eyesight goes blurry, "not doing so well here." It's like looking out through two sets of eyeballs, and I gain an odd perspective of what a fly's view of the world might be like. My body rocks, wavering back and forth, its balance lost with my vision. Chris steadies me with hands on my shoulders.

Gen looks up from the cards, at me and through me, then nods once. She reaches out and wraps her fingers around one of my forearms. Leo grasps my other arm, and I clamp my hands on their wrists. With his arm around her shoulders, we make an unbroken human circle, Chris a minor extension off one side.

The moment Leo and I make physical contact, the rage surges, screaming and shrieking through me, coursing in my blood and pounding in my chest. I twist in their grip, muscles going taut, Kat struggling while I scrabble to regain control of my own movement. Chris's hold tightens, and he presses his legs against my back.

"Get it out!" Kat says with my voice. "Your fault. Yours." I face Leo, me a helpless spectator trapped within my head.

Gen's gaze darts between us. "Explain," she commands.

When the rival psychic fails to volunteer anything, she jerks her chin toward me. "Tell me. What's he done? Why are you taking Flynn? I may not like you. I may not have any respect for you. But I *can* help you." Gen's power flows into me, a cool soothing I recognize on an intimate level, encouraging, pushing, searching. I feel nothing from Leo. His skin bears a greenish tinge, and his gaze darts around the room wildly, mostly in the direction of the front door.

"Curse…. He made a curse. Only the cursed can see. Still there. Get it out." My breathing comes in short gasps. Whatever's happening inside me, it's taking a heavy toll on my physical well-being. "He killed me."

Leo's head waggles back and forth so rapidly I'm afraid it might disconnect from his neck. "Not me. Max. He set the curse on the artifact. Put it on her car…."

"But you made it. Oh God," Gen whispers, staring at him. "You *are* responsible. I knew you were tempted, that you experimented, but you actually did it. Did it knowingly."

"Not my fault. Not my fault. No one was supposed to die."

"I always knew the potential was there, but I never thought you'd really…. And you," she says, finding Kat behind my eyes, "you *were* going back to Flynn. That's why Max wanted you dead."

"Shut up!" I shout, using all my will to retrieve the use of my vocal cords. Both psychics stare at me like I slapped them across their faces. "This fucking hurts. Stop talking and do something." I sound a helluva lot calmer than I am, and a second later, my control is gone.

"This isn't over," Gen says to Leo, setting herself.

"You owe me," he returns, straightening where he sits.

Great. I'm stuck in the middle of an ex-lovers' spat.

"This is what that promise was all about?" She stares at him like he's grown another head, then mutters some curses I never thought I'd hear coming from Genesis.

I force a low growl past the constriction in my throat.

"Right. Sorry, Flynn." She bumps Leo with her shoulder. "Now."

More cool energy flows up both arms, tingling and teasing, easing the pain and pressure. The power from my right is stronger—Genesis proving she's the superior talent in the room. Leo's, while present, fluctuates in intensity, stopping and starting and eventually failing altogether. But when they release me and I shake out my fallen-asleep arm muscles, all sense of Kat's presence has disappeared.

"Gone," I pant, then flop against Chris's legs. Leaning my head back, I give him a weak smile.

Gen reaches across the scattered tarot cards to place her palm against my cheek. She closes her eyes. When she opens them again, she nods. "No sign of her."

I'm exhausted and nauseated, and the corners of my sight darken, but I can't faint just yet. As one, Gen, Chris, and I turn toward Leo, who has been inching toward the door since the exorcism ceased.

"You," Gen says to him, "aren't going anywhere."

Chris moves to grab him, and without his support, my body does what it's been planning.

I pass the fuck out.

Chapter 45
The Best Laid Plans

I AWAKE with a cold cloth across my forehead and eyes. Softness supports me, and the scent of lavender carries on an air-conditioning breeze, so I'm in Gen's bedroom. I pull away the compress with a steadier hand than I expect and force myself to a seated position.

Bright sunlight shines through the windows. The clock says nine thirty. So I guess I was out for a couple of hours at least.

Raised voices alert me to everyone else's location: the living room. Gen, Chris, and Leo argue, their tones rising and falling amidst shushing and noisily whispered reminders that I'm in here. I listen for a few moments, wondering if they're debating about me, but the words I catch don't give me that impression; they're just trying, unsuccessfully, not to wake me up.

I'm curious and semi-eager to join the discussion, but I still have on the same clothes I wore to jail, and my oily skin and matted hair demand a shower.

Three stumbles and a stagger later, I stand under the blistering spray, rinsing away the fear-sweat and grime. What day is it, anyway? Thursday. Right. Eight days from my crash into the Festivity sign by Dead Woman's Pond.

Eight days for my life to go completely to hell. Holy crap.

When I emerge, a cup of Starbucks dark roast with cream and sugar and one of their breakfast sandwiches wait for me on the bathroom counter. Damn, I hope Gen is the one who brought those in. Beneath hot water bliss, I hadn't paid much attention to what was going on outside the frosted-glass enclosure.

I eye my discarded dirty clothing in a pile on the floor, then wonder if Gen has a robe in her closet big enough to cover me. I don't remember anything but satiny stuff in the way of robes, but maybe she left a winter terrycloth in the back somewhere.

Peeking out of the bathroom, I spot Gen, seated on the end of her bed, a stack of neatly folded clothes in her lap—my clothes. And my work boots at her feet.

"How—?" I cross the carpet naked and take them from her. She scans me from top to bottom, appraising, smiling. She's seen me nude plenty of times, but damn if I don't blush.

"Closest, cheapest place, Motel 6 across route 192. Chris took a wild guess. You're lucky they still had your stuff behind the front desk. Said they held it an extra day 'cause you're a hero and all."

"Right." I don't feel like a hero. Between the old injuries to my knee and ribs and the painful bruising on my face, I feel like a total wreck. Taking the clothes, I duck back into the bathroom and change, downing half the coffee and the entire sandwich in intermittent bursts throughout the process. Clean underwear, a spare pair of jeans, and my Indigo Girls concert tee make me feel almost human. Stompy boots add that touch of invincibility.

With my still warm cup in hand, I return, but she's gone to the living room, where the argument begins anew. Okay. Time to insert myself into the fray.

Like I haven't been doing that enough lately.

"So," I say, leaning in the doorway, mostly so I won't fall over, "what's the plan?"

The trio looks up from their positions, Chris and Gen on the larger couch, Leo in the big armchair. Guess he's given up trying to escape.

Gen tosses me a hair tie, and I pull my wet strands into the familiar and more comfortable ponytail.

Behind them, stacked neatly against the wall, are my boxes of stuff from Chris's sedan and the bag from the Motel 6 sitting on top. Four boxes and a garbage bag to contain pretty much all I own, minus my bowling gear and toolbox. How sad is that?

Leo's voice pulls me from my depressing reverie. "We're thinking a two-pronged attack."

"Two prongs. Like splitting up? Oh yeah, that works great in all the horror flicks." One thing I know—I'm not leaving Gen's side, although the look she gives me makes me think I'll have to reconsider. "Be more specific."

"We need to go after Max, and we need to deal with the lake. According to the psychic screwup here"—Chris jerks his thumb at Leo, who sputters something unintelligible—"only a target of the cursed charm can actually see the damn thing. That means the only one of us who can dive for it is you, Flynn."

Oh, that's just ducky.

"Actually," Leo puts in, with glares from the others, "Genesis should be able to see it as well. It hasn't tried to pull her in the way it did with you—"

"Which you should have told me about, Flynn," Gen scolds.

I shrug it off. "You were already breaking up with me for being too reckless. I wasn't going to add a bow to that surprise gift."

She has the good grace to look away.

Leo clears his throat. "As I was saying, Genesis can probably see it too. She meets the criteria—gay female."

"But there's no guarantee of that," Chris says, brows drawn.

"I'll do it," I say before Gen speaks up. Chris shoots me a grateful look. No way he wants his sister jumping into that lake, and neither do I. Not that I'm thrilled about the concept. An evil, hypnotic, deeper than average lake isn't where I want to spend an evening, or a lifetime. "We may need diving equipment."

"I can cover that," Leo says. "I'm certified, I have several sets of gear, and I can give you the down-and-dirty version of the how-to guide—enough for one trip to the lake bottom with me as your buddy, anyway. Would have gone after the damn thing myself, if I could still see it. I can also handle keeping Flynn from succumbing to the charm's influence on her. Since I made it, occasional physical contact with me will make her temporarily immune to it." Leo gives me a cheeky wink. "See? I'm indispensable."

"I think the word you're looking for is 'insufferable,'" Genesis puts in.

He ignores her.

Partnering with Leo. Huh. Well, he already saved my life once. But that means....

"I don't want you anywhere near Max Harris." I cross my arms over my chest and fix Gen with my best glare.

Unfortunately, she's a much better glarer than I. Must be a learned defense mechanism. That and her cuteness.

"Trust me. I don't want to be near him. And hopefully I won't have to be. Chris and I will watch for him to go out."

"And why, exactly, do you need to go to his house?"

Chris doesn't seem any happier about it than I am, but he answers, "Evidence. We know he killed Kat, but we'll never find any proof that we can use with the police. Leo suspects he's also gotten rid of his current wife, who hasn't been seen in several days."

Leo jumps in. "We're hoping Kat's spirit, or the new wife's if she truly is dead, can lead us to something we can show the authorities, or anonymously tip them to conveniently find," he amends.

"And I'm the most likely one to be able to see or communicate with either of them," Gen says. "Leo isn't so good with the spirit types."

Leo apparently isn't so good with anything involving the psychic realm.

While Gen and Leo argue over what he might or might not be good at, I beckon Chris closer to where I stand.

"You'll look after her, right?" I say, keeping my voice low.

He stiffens. I offended him. He's her brother. She's his only family. He loves her more than air.

"Sorry. Of course you will."

"No," he says, letting his shoulders settle, "I understand. I'd be asking you the same thing if our partners were reversed. You gonna be okay with the screwup?"

I glance past him to where Leo now stands, wagging an officious finger in Gen's direction while she shakes her head and smiles a bemused smile. A flicker of jealousy flares in my chest, but I tamp it down. Now that I know about it, I recognize the couple they once were, and could never survive being on a long-term basis.

"I'll be fine. I was a competitive swimmer and diver in high school," I remind Chris. "I've done snorkeling. Scuba seems like the most logical next step. How hard can it be?"

WHEN WILL I learn not to ask optimistic questions?

The four of us go in two cars to Leo's mansion, not on the golf course like Max's, but in a secluded, one-way accessible corner of Festivity nestled among other million-plus-dollar homes, none of which can compare to Leo's.

"It's… a castle," I manage, climbing out of the Charger, gazing up at the block stone architecture, the Medieval-style turret, the huge wooden double front doors. And yet… I like it. He hasn't adorned it with anything gaudy or ornate beyond the basic structure. It's almost austere, forbidding.

"Every man's home should be," Leo answers, standing beside his own car in the driveway and grinning with pride. "The customers love it. Sets the atmosphere for my readings."

"Your mostly fake readings," Gen mutters, leading the way to the front door.

I'm half-surprised there isn't a moat, and I say so, but that, according to Leo, would be tacky. Instead, a simple stone walk winds its way up to the entrance. Leo slides past us, unlocks the doors, which swing open on what must be deliberately creaking hinges, and ushers us into a greeting hall fit for royalty.

Paintings hang in elaborate yet tasteful frames, many of them life-sized and full-bodied, ranging from four and a half to six feet in height. Faux torches in metal sconces line the walls, and a flick of a hidden switch sets them glowing and casting eerie shadows across the gray slate flooring.

I step to the closest painting, straining my eyes in the dim light to read the tiny plaque at its base: "Ricardo Oliverio—Wizard—Circa 1537." The portrait depicts a weathered man in a cleric's robe with olive skin and wrinkled hands. His gaze bores into me, and I take an involuntary step backward.

"Are these all…." I'm not sure what to call them. "Magicians?" I finish, waving a hand down the long hallway.

"Wizards, witches, warlocks, clerics, psychics, magicians. All pretty much the same thing. Though the ones hanging here are the greatest of their times, whether the non-magic user has heard of them or not."

Well, certainly I've never heard of Ricardo Oliverio.

Genesis groans at the posturing. "With the exception of your hideous sports car, you once described your taste as simple," she says to our host.

"Yes?"

"You're full of shit."

I sputter a laugh, and Leo reddens, though he denies nothing. I slip a comfortable arm around Gen's shoulders, and we fall into step behind him and follow through an archway into the room where he must entertain his clients.

A large circular wooden table dominates the center of the room, surrounded by eight high-backed, red-velvet-covered throne-like chairs. Well, I guess that beats sitting cross-legged on the floor. In the middle of the table sits an honest-to-God crystal ball, two candles, and a neat stack of tarot cards, all resting on a piece of black velvet. A cabinet designed for china and glassware instead holds additional accoutrements of Leo's profession: spare candles, many of them black, ornate candle holders, an ancient Ouija board propped upright on its side for display (though Gen has corrected my use of the term Ouija. It's a talking board. Parker Brothers coined its modern name), multiple crystals in a variety of colors which catch the "torch" lights and glitter with life of their own, and glass bottles in many shapes and sizes, each containing a different liquid.

"Come on," Leo says, gesturing over his shoulder toward another arch on the far side of the room. "Private areas are back here. We're still in the public spaces."

"Thank God," Chris mutters.

I stifle my snort.

A thick black curtain blocks the way through the arch, and we push it aside to find ourselves in a startlingly normal kitchen—so startling, in fact, that I stop dead in the entryway, dragging Gen to a halt, and Chris plows into the two of us from behind.

"What?" Leo asks, blinking innocent wide eyes as he pulls out one of the chairs at a simple table of whitewashed wood, kind of like the one in Gen's apartment kitchen. "Come, sit. I've got the diving gear in the garage behind the house." He points to a very normal back door I presume leads to said garage. Most of Festivity's garages sit behind the main buildings, preventing the potential eyesores from lowering property values. This one also keeps the neighbors from complaining about an orange McLaren.

Gen recovers first, disentangling herself from my arm and crossing the cheery yellow tile to the closest set of maple cabinets between the stove and the sink. "You still keep the tea near the stove like you did at my place?"

Leo places a hand over his heart. "Ah, you remember. Cups of tea, cozy pillows and blankets, wild, crazy—"

She elbows him, hard, in the chest, but not before another pang of jealousy mixed with sadness passes through mine. Not like we haven't had warm, cozy moments. I just want them all to myself. At least I no longer feel the urge to do him bodily harm. That rage left with Kat's spirit.

He goes to find his equipment while Gen heats water for tea. The next two hours are spent alternately drinking it, bickering over the final details of our sketchy plan, and trying to make scuba gear sized for Leo fit onto my somewhat larger and more muscular frame.

The wetsuit is flat out. However, it being July and all, the lake water, however cold, should not be freezing enough to deter my efforts to find the cursed charm. The tanks hang all right; their belt is adjustable. But when we go into the backyard to try things in his pool, me squeezed into a pair of Leo's swim trunks and my

T-shirt since we forgot my suit, we discover the weights he uses to hold himself beneath the surface lack sufficient mass to keep me under.

This necessitates a trip for Leo and Chris to the closest dive shop—no one lets Leo go anywhere alone despite his pledges of loyalty. But their departure gives me the opportunity I want to have a private chat with Gen.

I change back into my dry underwear and jeans, though I'm stuck with the wet shirt, and go hunting for her. "Hey," I say, after finding her in the "seance" room frowning at some of the items in the display cabinet.

"You know these are infused with dark magic, these candles, that crystal." She points out a bloodred, multifaceted piece on the third shelf up.

No, I didn't know, but it explains why Leo rushed us through this area.

"We can't do a thing about him without catching them in use."

"We" meaning the Registry board, I assume.

"And the one thing he *did* use, even if he says it wasn't his intention to kill anyone, I can't do anything about because I owe him a *favor*." The last she spits like a curse. To her sensibilities, I suppose it is one.

And she owes it because of me.

Well. This isn't the conversation I'd planned to have. Then again, when do any of my plans turn out the way I want? I hope tonight's goes better.

No, I'd thought to propose, actually, even without having the ring still hidden in the rear of her closet, tucked in a shoe along with the wedding band. No more wasted time. I want her to know how I really feel. But now there's this.

"I'm sorry," I whisper.

But she's no longer listening, her entire focus on the red crystal, which begins a soft, steady, pulsing glow. In the reflection of the glass front of the cabinet, Gen's green eyes respond with a glow of their own.

Chapter 46
The Other Shoe

OH FUCK me now.

Gen's hand rises to the latch on the cabinet. She goes for the crystal, which pulses even more brightly until the red seems to burn my retinas.

I'm about to do something stupid again, I just know it, but I can't let whatever bad mojo Leo keeps around have its way with Genesis.

Acting on pure instinct, I round the table to her side and step between her and the cabinet. For a second, nothing changes. Her flashing green eyes stare through me, unseeing, despite the fact that I grab her by the shoulders, then shake her.

Next thing I know, her hand swipes out, and her long, manicured nails rake across my cheek, deep enough to draw blood. It wells up in the wounds, warm and oozing, the cuts stinging on my already bruised skin.

"Ow! Shit, Gen!"

No time to whine about it. She throws her weight against me, slamming me into the glass doors and shattering at least one. I'm bigger and heavier than she is, but she catches me by complete surprise. The entire cabinet rocks with the impact, display items clanging and clattering on the disturbed shelves behind me. Sharp pain flares beneath my right shoulder blade, and more warm stickiness seeps into my thin T-shirt.

With my considerable strength, I could subdue her easily. Doing it without hurting her presents more of a challenge.

Releasing her shoulders, I grab for her wrists, taking a knee to my groin for my efforts. Regardless of having feminine rather than masculine parts, it hurts, dammit. The head-butt to my chest doesn't feel much better and knocks the wind out of me, preventing me from continuing to speak to her.

My seeking fingers close around her forearms, holding her away from me while her feet pummel my already-battered shins. I use a knee to shove her backward, still keeping my grip on her arms but putting a safer distance between us while I try to figure out just what to do with my suddenly crazed girlfriend.

"What the hell?"

I jerk my head toward the voice to find a stunned Leo and Chris standing side by side in the hall archway. Leo, the speaker, clutches a bag printed with "Dave's Dive Shop" in wavy blue script.

Taking in the scene at a quick glance, he passes the sack off to Chris and strides toward us, presses his fingers to Gen's sweat-covered forehead despite her twisting and wrenching, and mutters a few phrases in some archaic language. Gen's body goes limp, dropping like dead weight, and I scramble to catch her before she cracks her head on the hardwood floor. When I go to lift her into my arms, a tearing sensation across my back stops me cold.

A dull thud, the bag of dive weights dropping on the fine wood table, precedes Chris's hand on my shoulder. "Let me get her," he says gently. "You've got enough problems." He scoops her up, seats himself, and holds her on his lap, keeping her tucked to his chest.

"What did you do?" I demand, whirling on Leo and regretting the painful movement.

He ignores me, appraising Genesis like she's a particularly interesting specimen. "Broke its hold on her," he finally replies. "A hold it shouldn't have been able to get. Hmm."

I'm about to ask what he means by that when a wave of agony shoots from my injury, across both shoulders and down to my rib cage. Groaning, I double over.

Leo shakes his head at me, tsking under his breath. "I'll fetch the first aid kit." He disappears out the arch.

Contrary to my initial belief, Gen has not passed out. She blinks rapidly, gaze shifting between me and her brother while she processes what just happened. I know the moment she figures it out because she draws a sharp breath, her face pales, and her eyes find mine, then dart away.

I sink into the high-backed chair closest to them, hissing when I lean too far back and press the glass deeper into the raw wound. Reaching out, I touch her knee through her skirt. She trembles. "Hey, forget it. Evil shit. Consider us even. Not your fault."

Chris opens his mouth, but a quick, pleading look from Gen has him pressing his lips together. Don't know what that's all about, but Gen's my biggest concern right now.

"I'll get you some water," I offer, moving to stand.

"You'll stay put and let me remove the glass sticking out of your back," Leo says, returning with a double-sized white metal first aid kit under his arm. Guess with his track record, he probably suffers quite a few injuries courtesy of the magical/psychic realm. Smart of him to be prepared.

And nice of him to be concerned about my welfare, again.

"You're ruining my upholstery," he adds, frowning at the darker stains I've left on his chair coverings.

Yeah. Never mind.

Leo peels off my ruined shirt, and I moan at the sight of the torn, bloodstained concert tee, not to mention that I'm also seated in front of two men while I wear nothing more than a sports bra and jeans.

"So," he continues, setting about pulling the shard, gentler than I would have expected, "looks like I'm not the only one who's been naughty." I assume he refers to Genesis poking around his cabinet of baubles and artifacts, but his smug smile makes me wonder if I'm missing something. I want to punch the grin right off him, and from Gen's expression, I'm not alone, but I can't move while he has tweezers embedded beneath my skin.

"Leo," Gen says, a warning tone. Chris pointedly stares into an empty corner of the room, choosing not to involve himself for whatever reason.

"We could've been great together," Leo continues, oblivious. "You, me, and the black—"

"Don't!" Her shout causes me to jerk in place, and I stifle a groan as the glass bites further into my flesh. "Please," she adds more softly. "Please, Leo. If you ever cared at all…."

He glances from me to her and back again, eyes widening before he schools his features and closes his mouth at last. Now I'm sure I'm being kept out of some loop. The look I give Gen promises that we will discuss this when events aren't so hairy.

The remainder of the doctoring proceeds in silence. I can tell Gen wants to assist in fixing me up. Her hands twitch toward me, but she reins the impulse in and clutches them together in her lap, maybe afraid she'll do me further harm. I give her what I hope is a reassuring smile, but she avoids meeting my eyes or returning it.

When Leo shows me the piece of glass he removes, I'm stunned by its smallish size. Okay, it spans the width of my palm, but it felt like an entire windowpane. He looks around, shrugs, and drops the bloody shard on the table beside the dive shop bag. "I'll already need to get someone in to buff and polish it," he says at our raised eyebrows. Then he applies disinfectant, which has me sucking air through my teeth at the stinging, and bandages me with gauze and tape. "Don't think you'll need stitches."

Well, that's something.

"I'll see if I can find you a shirt that will fit."

"Do you even own a T-shirt?" I asked, crossing my arms over my half-naked chest and watching him depart once more.

Leo flashes me a grin fit for a frat boy. "Never said it would be a tee." He exits, chuckling.

BY THE time we tuck all the diving gear and other supplies in the miniscule trunks of the McLaren and Gen's Charger, it's already late afternoon. Instead of riding with Genesis, I sense she'd rather have Chris as her companion and climb in with Leo. She seems relieved by my choice, and I wonder how long her embarrassment over the seance room mishap will last.

As we tool through Festivity back to the apartment to pick up my swimsuit, I'm more than grateful for the sports car's tinted windows. I don't know many people in town, but I wouldn't even want a total stranger seeing me in the long-sleeved purple satin button-down Leo's lent me to wear. Gen swears it suits me, especially tucked into the jeans, and according to her, maybe with the addition of a black velvet vest on top, and I'm glad for that spark of her old self coming through, but I intend to return the garment as soon as possible.

The others wait for me in the parking lot while I run up and change, catching a glimpse of myself in the full-length mirror on the back of the bathroom door. It gives me pause. Dark purple sets off my light brown hair and… yeah, a black vest might be okay. Later.

I shuck my clothes and toss them on the bed, then dig through boxes until I come up with my one-piece racing suit that I'm proud to say still fits from high school. A little snug across the hips, but that's muscle, not fat. I toss shorts over top, wishing I'd shaved my legs more recently, and exchange my boots for tennis shoes. When I head downstairs, Leo gives me an appreciative once-over.

"Fine, athletic physique. Starting to understand what Genesis sees in you," he says.

"Starting to see why she dumped your ass. No, wait. That's been obvious from the beginning."

"Cute."

I scan the parking lot, finding the empty spot where Chris has parked Gen's Charger.

"They took off five minutes ago, I suspect an act on Gen's part to prevent you from trying to dissuade them from their plan of action," Leo says, forestalling my next question.

Something clenches in my chest, but I keep it off my face. No, I hadn't thought to stop them. Gen's a big girl, and I respect her decision to deal with Max Harris as she sees fit, no matter how much I wish I could be beside her. But she has Chris with her. With her powers, she will succeed in speaking to Max's most recent wife's ghost and probably get Kat to help her as well. They'll find the evidence they need to convince the police to arrest Max.

I just wish I'd had the opportunity to say goodbye. Because I feel far less certain of my own success in the night's endeavors, or my chances of surviving them.

Chapter 47
Into the Fray…
or, urm… Lake

WE PULL up at Dead Man's Pond just after sunset and take the dirt access to the narrow beach, Leo complaining all the way about damage to his McLaren.

"Seriously, dude, a little sand might dull all the damn orange," I say and laugh at the glare he gives me, as threatening as a chihuahua. Then I remember he's responsible, however unwittingly, for this whole mess, and I sober. This is one dangerous man, even more so for his lack of control over the scary things he creates.

Our arrival scatters a trio of deer, sending them leaping into the forest cover as if they can meld with the tree trunks or pass through them. Spotlights glow on the water's still surface, broken and irregular due to the unrepaired hole in the Festivity signage wall.

"Ah hell, we have company." Leo points out the window to another vehicle on the opposite side of the lake, a nondescript compact car I don't recognize.

I do, however, identify the woman chest deep and walking deeper into the water only a few yards around the lake's edge.

Arielle from the wine bar.

Of course. The pond tasted her. Now it wants her.

I'm out of the McLaren and running for her before Leo gets his door open. The water closes over her head as I reach the spot where she stepped in. Still in my shorts, but without my phone, which I thankfully left back in the apartment, I dive, swimming all out, using every ounce of strength and every breathing technique I know to get to her.

I collide with her body before I see it, the impact expelling the air from my lungs. Beneath the surface, her eyes and mouth are open. She's *inhaling* the water, oblivious to it, to the fact that she's freaking *drowning* and can care less.

Oh God, that could have been me.

Could still be, if I'm not careful tonight.

I wrap an arm around her torso, hauling her backward toward the shoreline, first swimming, then standing when the depth gets shallower. A quick look behind reveals Leo at the edge, tossing what look like his keys, wallet, and phone onto the narrow strip of sand. Though he has his wetsuit under his clothing, there's no time for him to strip. He casts a woeful glance at his expensive designer attire, then strides in to help me with Arielle.

"This is becoming tiresome," he says upon reaching my side, his trousers and shirt soaked through. The waitress in my arms sputters and coughs, water pouring from her mouth and nose.

"*This*," I remind him, "is your own goddamn fault. So shut the fuck up."

We're almost to the shore when I foolishly glance across the lake—and catch sight of the glow at its center. I'd been so focused on Arielle, I hadn't noticed it before. But it has my full attention now.

Beautiful. Peaceful. Serene.

My body shivers, wet and half-submerged. My limbs grow heavy. My arms release my burden, making Arielle flail, splashing and kicking water in my face, which I barely notice. Leo grabs her, hauling her away. My feet plant themselves in the silted bottom of the pond, then inch back out into the deeper water.

It wants me. It feels so good to be wanted so much.

Like I feel when I'm with Genesis.

Gen's face fills my thoughts, my heart, my soul, and, like I did with Kat's spirit, I wrench my body, twisting and shoving the lake's compelling force out.

"Little help here…."

I stare at Leo over my shoulder, catching his eye as Arielle punches him once in the face, taking them both under. I grab for her as she attempts to swim past, one hand catching in her long reddish-blonde hair, the other locking around her chest once more. My grip has to hurt her, and I'm sorry for that, but she seems to feel nothing, and her expression shows fierce determination to meet her doom at the center of the pond.

A few days ago, she passed me her phone number. She's single, unattached, lacking a partner to focus on and drive out the dark magic. Or maybe it wouldn't matter if she did have someone in her life. If Gen is to be believed, I have power of my own, and that's why I fare better than others in this craziness.

Sooner or later, I'm going to have to face that and deal with it.

Goose bumps crawl over my skin, and I shiver in the cooler night air.

But not tonight.

Leo's head pops up, his perfectly coiffed brown hair wet and stringy and hanging in his face, along with a good measure of snot and spit. He wipes it all away on the back of a hand, then shoves his fist beneath the water to rinse it.

With much growling and grumbling on his part, we manage to wrangle Arielle onto the sand. Her foot catches on something, maybe a banyan tree root, and down we all go, her lithe body falling atop mine, her breasts pressed to my own chest and her lips inches from my mouth.

She blinks, laughs a little, and says, "I'm dreaming about you again, right?"

"Me too," Leo sighs, admiring our current positions and grinning ear to ear. I growl at him.

Thank God Gen isn't here to see this. Arielle has all the right softness in all the right places. She's young, younger than Genesis, and she's been dreaming about me....

She can't compare to Gen.

"Taken," I remind Arielle, both flattered and flustered at once, "and no, you're not dreaming."

Reality slams into the waitress, hard. She shrieks, scrambles off me, and sits up, pulling her jean-covered knees into her chest. "Who are you?" she says to Leo. Her eyes dart to me, then the lake, then the car I assume to be a rental since hers got dunked. "What am I doing here? What's going on?"

We tell her.

Chapter 48
And Again

OKAY, ACTUALLY, *I* tell her. Leo waves his arms and tries to interrupt me at every juncture of the explanation, but I'm not having it. I don't like secrets, especially when those secrets involve life and death. Someone once said, "Well-informed is well-prepared," or something like that. Whatever. It applies now.

"Leave it to me to fall for the crazy ones," Arielle says. "You two are certifiable, you know that?"

Leo and I say nothing. He never said anything in the first place, but she lumps us together, and understandably so. I glance pointedly at the lake where the glow still beckons, offset a bit by the spotlights crisscrossing the surface, which ripples in a light breeze. She follows my gaze, stiffens, and shakes her head once, hard.

"Or maybe not," she says with a nervous laugh. "The last thing I remember, I was asleep in my bed. I have the apartment over the wine bar."

My eyebrows rise. Downtown apartments like Gen's are pricey and far beyond a waitress's pay grade.

She notices my expression. "Dad owns the bar."

Ah. That explains it.

"Next thing I know, I'm looking down into those gorgeous brown eyes of yours. And God, those muscles. I said it before. Your girlfriend is a very lucky woman."

A fierce blush creeps into my cheeks.

"Anyway," she says, kind enough to pretend she doesn't notice my embarrassment, "I can't deny that I'm here, and I'd be drowned... again... if not for your help. So." Arielle slaps her hands on her wet jeans, scattering little droplets across the ground. "I want to return the favor. What can I do?"

I shake my head, about to send the kid home. And yeah, the more I study her, the more she does seem like a kid. If she's younger than Gen, she's much younger than me, maybe twenty-one? twenty-two? I can't drag her into this mess. But Leo opens his damn mouth first.

"You can monitor the time and call for help if we need it." He passes her his cell phone. "I've got our friends' cell number on speed dial. No official types," he warns with a stern look. "They'd never believe what we're doing here, and if we did survive, they'd haul us off to jail or an asylum."

Yeah, he has a definite point, though I don't like the idea of cutting us off from potential rescuers. I assume by "friends" he refers to Gen and Chris, but I'm not sure what they can do if things go wrong underwater. Use magic, maybe? I get the vibe that Gen's skills extend far beyond seeing and speaking with the dead and driving them out of possessed bodies. It bothers me that she's hidden this whole magical world throughout our relationship, but I guess I understand why. If she'd told me, I would have freaked, no doubt about it.

Leo continues, "Our dive tanks aren't large, not pro-grade, so they only hold about an hour of air for each of us. Make sure you sit facing away from the lake." He unbuttons his soaked shirt and tosses it aside, then peels off his slacks, revealing the wetsuit beneath. "Now that you're aware of the situation, it shouldn't be strong enough to call you if you don't look at it. We don't want you getting pulled in again. One dramatic rescue is enough for an evening."

Arielle nods and shifts to put her back to the pond, sitting cross-legged with the phone clutched in both hands. She turns on the screen, displaying both the time and the power level, and nods again. "Good to go," she says.

"If we're not back in forty-five minutes, use the cell phone."

I shoot Leo a surprised look. Forty-five minutes is a long time to go get some artifact and come back.

"That's an outside estimate," he says. "I don't expect to take that long, but who knows what sort of trouble we might run into? I never expected any of this."

Great confidence builder there, Leo.

We stroll to the McLaren and get the rest of the gear from the trunk. Leo helps me put everything on right. One big downside of not having a wetsuit of my own is the tanks and weight belt dig into my bare skin, and the pressure against the cut on my back hurts like hell, but it can't be avoided. At least the bandages he put on are waterproof and provide a little cushioning.

"You shouldn't have told her about the charm," he scolds while fastening a final strap. "We keep our skills hidden, for the most part. The rest of the world isn't ready for actual witches and warlocks. Run-of-the-mill vanilla tarot-reading psychics are about all they can handle."

Is that what Gen is really? A witch? "Gen has a lot of power, doesn't she?"

He nods while I adjust the weight belt on my waist, trying to find a position in which it doesn't chafe and failing. "A *lot* of power. And a lot more skills than I can ever hope to attain, with or without the forbidden dark magic." He makes air quotes when he says "forbidden." Damn. He hasn't learned a thing from this fiasco. "She'll have to be careful if she doesn't want to end up like me."

Is that a threat? I jerk my head toward him. "What do you mean by that?"

Leo bites his lower lip—an odd nervous tic on a grown man. "Hers to tell, Flynn. Hers to tell."

Swallowing my growl of frustration, I follow him to rejoin Arielle at the water's edge.

Time to focus. "So what, exactly, am I looking for?" The glow should lead me to it, but I should still know what the damn charm looks like.

Out of the corner of my eye, I catch his frown. "Metal. Magnetized, so it may stick to your gear. Shaped like a pentagram with the initials L. H. S. engraved on it and an eagle. Harris's high school emblem. Some kind of debate club medal. It's also sharp. Careful you don't cut yourself on it. It's likely rusty by now."

Even better. "I get hurt or sick, you're paying the medical expenses."

He flashes me a genuine smile, perhaps the first I've received from him. "You pull this off without getting us both killed, and it will be my pleasure."

"Anyone tell you you're just chock-full of optimism?"

His grin spreads wider. "Genesis. All the time." His eyes go wide with sudden realization. "Could that have been sarcasm?" Then he laughs.

Snorting, I step into the lake, letting my gaze drift across the water to the ever-present glow. Its pacifying effects drift over me, but I fight them off, shaking my head.

Leo places a hand on my shoulder. "That will worsen the closer we get. So long as we're in contact with one another, at least sporadically, my magic should keep it from pulling you in."

"'Should' is kind of a scary word." We walk forward until we're waist deep. "And would that be dark magic you're using? And does it have a cost?" The memory of Gen's glowing green eyes makes me shiver. Damn, I wish I'd called her one last time before heading in. Then again, I wouldn't want to cause a disruption in whatever she's doing or give her presence away to Max Harris, not without a vital reason to do so.

I just want to hear her voice.

"No dark magic. You use light to fight dark, so that's what I'm tapping. No cost except a bit of fatigue. It's not my strongest suit…"

Nothing is his strongest suit, and my look says so. He ignores it.

"…but we should manage fine. Other than causing victims to drown, the charm has no abilities of its own. Synchronize your watch with mine."

I glance at the waterproof timepiece Leo lent me. "Eight thirty-seven." Later than I expected. But the summer sun sets late in Florida, and we have to do this at night.

"Got it," Leo confirms. "From here out, we're reduced to communicating by hand signals." He flips on a bright lamp strapped to his belt, and another on the side of his face mask. I do the same. The charm will light my way, but he needs illumination to see down there.

Both of us pull our masks into place and insert the breathers into our mouths.

The cold, murky water closes over our heads.

Chapter 49
Charming

THE CURSED charm shines like a beacon under the water and I head straight for it, kicking my borrowed flippers and churning up silt from the bottom of the pond. Not deep here. Plenty of small fish and floating detritus: leaves, sticks… car parts. A rusted headlight here, a door handle, bluish broken glass. They glitter in the light cast by our lamps as we pass.

Leo chugs along beside me, lagging a bit behind. He's a decent enough swimmer, but his less-developed arm and leg muscles aren't as accustomed to this type of exercise as my own. I ease up on my strokes, not wanting to leave him in my wake.

The deeper we go, the less sure of myself I become. One thing to splash around in Leo's backyard pool where the clear water reveals everything around me. Quite another to see only what is straight ahead, the view to either side pitch-dark unless I turn my lamps right or left. It's like swimming down a dark, narrow tunnel, the walls of which might collapse and bury me at any second. I falter and flail, taking too rapid breaths that rasp in my ears, bubbles from my breather obscuring my vision.

Breathing. Underwater. Impossible. Unnatural.

A brief flash of rationality tells me this might be the charm affecting my thoughts, stealing my balance.

Panic grips me, scattering my courage and determination like fish fleeing a great white shark.

And then Leo is there. He grasps my upper arms, hauling me around to face him through our masks. I never believed I could be so happy to see the bumbling little twerp of a psychic, but right now, if I wasn't dependent upon the piece of plastic in my mouth for air, I could kiss him. His eyes narrow in concern, his hands giving me a shake, gentle yet with enough force to snap me from my fear. When he recognizes my focus has shifted back to reality, he lets go, making the okay sign with his right hand and raising both eyebrows.

I nod, returning the universal symbol. Yeah, I'm okay. Now.

Until a coil of undulating black winds its way up from the lake's dark bottom, too far beneath us to make out even with the lamps.

What I take at first to be a narrow strip of rubber or debris doesn't float unguided and harmless past us. Instead, it chooses its direction with purpose, cutting through the water on a path intersecting with our own. It drives like a spear toward Leo's blue wetsuit-covered leg, producing a pair of sharp fangs at the last second before it strikes.

Too late, Leo spots the attacking water moccasin. Bubbles erupt from his breather as he kicks out the targeted leg, but the snake has him, its jaw clamping down, inserting its poisonous venom into Leo.

I'm too uncoordinated in the scuba gear to do more than watch, helpless to aid him, and not knowing how I can do so anyway without getting myself bitten as well.

A flash of metal catches the light from Leo's lamps, glinting off the steel blade of the knife that suddenly appears in his fist. I have no idea where he pulled it from, maybe a belt pouch, but he thrusts down with it, hard and fast, with more accuracy and sureness in the stroke than I would have given him credit for. A curl of dark blood swirls from the snake's body as it drifts away, lifeless.

Chapter 50
Done

I DO not like snakes. Not one bit. And I'm ashamed to say I flinch away from it, dead or not, before checking Leo's leg. It's more of an uncoordinated flail, and I'm sideways, unable to right myself, when I finish. Damn this scuba shit, anyway.

Leo grabs me, turning me in place so I'm upright, and holds up the okay sign.

Okay? Seriously? You just got bitten by a fucking water moccasin. He must be delirious already.

My mind races through articles I've read on Florida wildlife. Poisonous snakes, how long the venom takes to incapacitate a victim. Construction workers deal with a lot of newly tamed land, disturbing the local fauna, driving critters to engage with humans when they'd rather remain in their natural habitats. I feel for the animals. I take the paycheck, but I feel for them. But it means reading a lot of literature on dangerous species.

What I come up with isn't good, though I might be confusing one breed of reptile with another. My motto for snakes is you don't have to worry about the venom if you run so fast in the opposite direction they don't have a chance to bite you. But Leo's been bitten, and we need to get him to an emergency room, fast.

At least he can afford it.

I haul on his outstretched arm, urging him back toward the surface. The charm will wait. He'll require antivenom. The leg will swell....

Water moccasins don't swim underwater.

That little tidbit floats to the top of the crowd of reptilian facts. Those snakes keep their heads above water when they swim. They like lakes, sure. But they don't dive under.

So what the hell was this one doing down here?

We're twenty feet down at least, the signage spotlights a dim glow above but getting brighter as I pull Leo up inch by frustrating inch. He fights me, still pointing at his leg.

Fine. If he wants to die down here, I'll look at his goddamn leg. Because I'm sure as hell not making any headway with him yanking me in the opposite direction.

I flip myself under the water, angling my head toward his feet, aiming my lamp where the snake dug in with its fangs.

Nothing. Not a damn thing.

I push my face closer. If I strain my eyes, I can just make out two indentations in the rubbery wetsuit material. No punctures. No droplets of blood leaking out to mix with the water. I glance at Leo's face. He nods and smiles, miming the wiping of sweat from his brow. Then he gestures in the direction of the charm and indicates his waterproof watch.

Time. We've been under for twelve minutes. We're running out of time.

We continue on, deeper and deeper, the charm's glow growing and lighting everything it touches, for me at least. Brighter. Beautiful. Warm. So warm. And I'm cold.

The light brushes my skin, warming me, soothing me.

Leo's hand grips me by my ponytail, then the back of my neck. His icy fingers send a shock through my nervous system. I snap out of it.

We keep going.

I concentrate on other things: work, doghouses, bowling scores, snakes (not a good choice). Its bleeding body might attract other predators, bigger ones, like gators. I think about something else.

Genesis.

God, what must she be doing right now? With luck, she and Chris have found a mansion empty of Max Harris, contacted the local spirits, and figured a way inside. They'll locate evidence. Maybe a body.

A shudder passes through me, more out of sympathy than my own discomfort. Gen will not react well to a dead body. She can speak with the deceased just fine, but she can't watch serial killer movies, or, hell, crime dramas because the special effects prove too intense for her. Comic horror or classic are fine: zombies, werewolves, a good haunted house flick. But accidentally stop the remote on a documentary about surgical procedures and she'll toss her cookies quick.

At last I stop swimming. Leo pulls up beside me, eyebrows rising. Right. He can't see the charm, but I can. We're right over it, the glow so bright I wish my face mask was tinted.

I point straight down and he nods, spreading his arms wide, indicating I should grab the thing. Flipping myself over, I blink past the glare, then give up and close my eyes to feel along the silty bottom for something metal and pointy.

Which cuts through the skin of my palm like a knife through a baked potato.

I'd forgotten Leo's warning about the sharpness of the artifact. My blood flows in inky curls up through the water. My hand stings like a sonofabitch.

The moment I make contact with it, the glow extinguishes, leaving our hand lamps as the only guides on this horrific adventure. Fingers numbing, I have a hard time closing my fist. I switch the charm to my other hand, careful not to give a repeat performance of my injury, and hold it in front of the light, examining it.

Rust paints the hideous charm a brownish red, like blood. Lovely. I slip the thing into an empty compartment on my weight belt, noting how it adheres to the metal interior. Magnetized.

I flex the fingers of my right hand experimentally, frowning at the decreased mobility. Well, my tetanus shots are up-to-date. Working around nails and screws and saws all day, I don't take chances with that preventative, regardless of the extra cost.

Leo nudges my shoulder with his own. When I give him my attention, he points upward. I nod and kick my flippers, ready to evacuate the area now that I've added more blood to the water, but before I can get past him, he grabs me again.

What now?

It's an effort to stop my momentum and orient myself to look at him. He stares past me, aiming his lamp over my shoulder, his eyes wide and his breathing rapid, judging from the constant stream of bubbles emanating from him.

I rotate, letting him assist me.

Half a dozen dark strings curl in our direction, darting from the blackness where our lights fail to extend. The long, ropy things curve over and around one another, their dance elegant, graceful, serpentine.

Serpentine.

Oh shit.

Visions of an Indiana Jones movie send me reeling, thrusting myself backward as hard and fast as I can kick, Leo at my side, the knife out once more.

One aberrant snake I can accept. One freak that swam with its head beneath the water. But a half dozen? It's the charm controlling them. It has to be. There's no other explanation for their behavior.

We both backpedal, flippers flapping and stirring up bubbles and sand and plant life from the lake bottom. In the debris, I lose sight of the black monsters. A stringy vine catches my ankle, and I let out a soundless shriek around my mouthpiece before identifying it. Turning around and swimming upward and forward will propel us faster, but in the time we'd rotate, the snakes would have us. We're doomed, and from the look Leo gives me, he knows it as well.

He closes his eyes behind his mask, and at first I think he's given up, resigning himself to his fate. Then he opens them, and a brilliant green flash streaks through the water, cutting like a bolt of lightning, sending flickering sparks in all directions. I arch my torso, the light missing me by inches, and watch as three of the snakes caught in the flare ignite on contact, burst into brief flame, and turn to ashes, which disperse in our wake.

I wonder if that was dark magic or light, but I'm not knocking it either way. Maybe Leo has some competence after all.

I swim as fast as I can, hoping he's right behind me, when the first set of fangs pierces my bare right calf.

Fire, burning inside, flowing through my veins, worse than any pain I've ever experienced, bar none. And just when I think I might, *might*, not faint from it, a second set of fangs clamps down on my left shoulder, followed by a third bite in my neck.

Ohgodohgodohgod.

I claw at my body, tearing away the snakes, my useless right hand ineffective, my left flinging them from me to swirl like tiny tornadoes in the water at my side. Larger dark shapes loom in my peripheral vision, long snouts and longer scaly tails propelling them forward. Gators.

They undulate and waver, and it isn't the water distorting my view. My eyesight blurs. My breath comes in rapid gasps, each inhalation harder than the last, like sucking soda through a broken straw. My left leg kicks and my right hangs like dead weight from my hip bone. I'm heavier and gaining mass every second. A glance down shows the leg swelling, impossibly fast and getting worse. If my neck swells too….

Hands grab me and pull, yanking, dragging me upward toward the distant spotlights, toward air. Leo lets go to fight off the reptiles, knife slashing, magic flashing. Bubbles and blood fill the water around us. I'm tired. So tired. Too weak to maintain my position. I sink, but he grabs me again.

Nausea hits. I try to swallow it down, but it's no use, and I vomit, spitting out the mouthpiece with the contents of my stomach. When I take another breath, it's all water, and I'm sputtering and choking. And dying.

We break the surface, and I gag on water and air while Leo uses my tanks' shoulder straps to drag me to shore. He shouts, but I can't make out the words. A second pair of hands, feminine, Arielle's, take hold of my legs, and I scream when they lift me. Every motion, every touch sends acid through muscles and bone.

Arielle holds me upright while Leo removes the scuba gear from first me, then himself. She sobs and stares, face pale, hands ice-cold and shaking where they connect with my skin. Or maybe that's just me. "Help…," I manage through clenched teeth. The word comes out slurred, my mouth filled with cotton.

They lay me back on the sandy grass, gently as they can but still causing unspeakable agony. I scream again, but the sound cuts off in my swollen throat and the effort leaves me gasping. "Can't breathe." It's a hiss more than a statement.

A swath of green scales flashes in the corner of my eye, and Leo lashes out with both his knife and his power. Clods of dirt erupt at the gator's front feet. It growls and flees into the water. Arielle looks ready to faint.

That makes two of us.

When I vomit a second time, Leo turns me on my side so I don't choke. The act wears me out. I flop back, slamming my head on the hard-packed earth. I can barely keep my eyes open. Arielle dives for the cell phone she must have discarded when she came into the lake to help us. "Ambulance. She needs an ambulance. Oh my God, how many bites did she take?"

"Three," Leo says, studying me. "And no ambulance. Use the number I showed you."

She glares at him across my body. I dig the nails of my good hand into the dirt, anything to manage the pain. It isn't working. I twist and convulse, unable to escape. Come on, Leo. Come on. Do something.

"You're out of your fucking mind. Unless your friend is a miracle worker, she'll die without immediate treatment. My brother works at Animal Kingdom. He knows this shit. And so do I." Arielle punches three numbers on the phone.

I hope they're nine one one.

A second later she tries it again, and again. She shakes the cell phone, powers it down and then on, tries again, but her call isn't going through.

"I locked it out," Leo says, calm as a priest. "Right along with four one one, zero, and the numbers for local police and fire rescue just in case you should have those memorized for some reason."

Shit. I know he doesn't want a lot of questioning authorities out here, but I figured with my life at stake….

"That's impossible!" Arielle screams in his face, pure panic setting in.

"No," he says. "That's magic."

Chapter 51
Discovery and Betrayal

"You... son of a... bitch," I wheeze, squeezing my eyes shut against another wave of pain and nausea. When one bite eases off a bit, the other two take over. Constant agony. A glance down my body shows my leg twice its normal size, the skin around the puncture wounds an angry red giving way to black before returning to the normal pink farther from the bite. I guess my shoulder and neck are the same, though I can't twist my head enough to check. The swelling prevents much movement.

"Flynn, Flynn." Leo tsks. "Surely you've figured me out by now. I act on behalf of my own self-interests, perfectly happy to aid you when you're aiding me. I needed you to get the charm. I needed Genesis's promise not to turn me over to the Registry."

And he doesn't need me anymore.

Gen knew not to trust him. She wouldn't have, either, if she hadn't required both his info about the charm and his assistance in un-possessing me.

"Gen won't keep her promise if you let me die." In fact, she may kill you, you bastard. The memory of her glowing green eyes adds to the nausea from the snake venom. She has the power. She hates dark magic, but I believe she can kill, if something drives her to it.

I don't want to be that something.

"I have a first aid kit in the McLaren," Leo says to Arielle. "It's unlocked. Go get it."

I don't know what kind of oomph he adds to the command, but her eyes glaze over. Her knees tremble when she rises, but she stands and heads around the lake to the parked car.

"Now," he says, brushing away a strand of hair from my face that came loose from my ponytail, "let's be straightforward with one another." I want to flinch from his touch, but I can't move my head at all. "By no means do I intend to let you die. I will do everything in my power, and encourage you to use yours, to purge your body of the poison."

Not sure what he means by that, but I listen. I have no choice.

"In addition, I will contact Genesis. She's a talented healer. Assuming Max hasn't killed her—" His look grows thoughtful, and a smile plays about his lips. "—and that would be *so* unfortunate…. She can save you if you cannot save yourself."

And now I see it. The perfect vicious circle in his plan. If we all live, he has Genesis in his pocket, owing him that favor, perhaps even protecting him from Max Harris, should he live. If Gen and I die, even better if Genesis and Max kill each other, no one except Arielle and Chris, nulls whom I'm sure he can manipulate to forget all this, will ever know what he's done. "Why—" A fit of coughing, harsh and painful through my tight throat, cuts me off. I try again. "Why don't you just kill me yourself?"

He gives a delicate little shiver, but it appears genuine. "As I told Genesis on numerous occasions, I don't kill people."

No, you just sit back and let things run their course.

Chapter 52
Caught Out, Caught In

THEY PARKED the Charger two houses down from Max Harris's house and waited almost an hour until they saw him drive by in his expensive SUV. Not that Gen thought the man would recognize their vehicle, but it didn't hurt to be careful. No cars in the driveway, and a quick peek through the garage window showed it empty. No one home.

"So what now?" Chris asked.

"Now," she said, "we find a guide to get us in."

She closed her eyes, standing beside her brother in the shadows cast by security lighting on the mansion. He stayed silent, not intruding on her concentration. She reached for her power, harder without the tarot to ground and center her. Moments later, a tickling at the edge of her consciousness indicated the arrival of a member of the spirit realm.

"Gen...."

She opened her eyes and studied Chris. All the hairs stood up on his arms—the only way he ever showed any sensitivity to her talents or anything otherworldly. Behind him posed a woman, and posed was the correct word. Perfect hair, perfect makeup, designer clothes. She leaned against the stucco exterior, one hand on her hip, lips pursed in a pretty pout.

Not Kat. The second wife, maybe? Or, given Max's character, maybe some other woman he'd killed.

"You here to fix the bastard?" she asked.

"If we can find evidence."

Chris looked from her to the empty space she spoke to. He'd been around her long enough to know how she operated. It didn't freak him out that she talked to no one visible.

"My body's buried in the backyard," she said.

Genesis shivered. What must it be like to be a ghost, tied to an unfinished element from a too short life?

"Any proof attached to it?"

She shook her head, tossing her long, dark hair over her shoulder. "He pretended he was giving me a massage, then broke my neck. There might be evidence on the clothes he wore. Dirt from burying me? I think they're in the laundry room."

"Lead on."

They followed her to the rear of the home, where a large dog barked at them from the end of a long tether. That must have been the one Flynn built a doghouse for. It stood under a tree, freshly painted, the white trim glowing in the lights. Beautiful work, but Flynn always took pride in what she made.

A pang of concern turned her thoughts to Flynn. God, Gen hoped she was okay.

The ghost showed them to one of those fake bricks by the back door, the kind with a hollowed-out portion where a key could be hidden. Chris used it, wincing as the burglar alarm started beeping.

"Seven five six eight," the ghost said.

Genesis entered it on the keypad. The alarm died.

"Down the hall, in the laundry room. Look in the hamper. They're at the bottom."

"Thank you," Gen said.

"Just make sure he pays." With that, the ghost vanished.

Gen headed for the laundry, Chris on her heels, using a flashlight to show their way. They found the hamper, but it was empty. He must have done the washing or more likely had a maid do it.

Gen knew that, contrary to popular belief, ghosts didn't pay attention to everything all the time. Like living people, they got distracted.

They could call the police, leave an anonymous tip that there was a body in Max's backyard, but she would have much rather had something to tie him to the death directly. Hopefully, there would be prints on the body itself, especially if he didn't wear gloves....

The front door slammed.

For whatever reason, Max Harris had returned home.

Chapter 53
Power Within, Power Without

LEO FIDDLES with his cell phone, holds it to his ear, and frowns. "Voicemail. Well. That forces things in a different direction."

My hopes plummet. The pain spreads to my chest. I can't see, can't think. And yet, my worries focus on Gen. Is she just keeping quiet, or is she in trouble?

I can't help her.

Worse, I'm about to make her biggest fear a reality.

I'm going to die.

"Use your power," Leo says.

Oh yeah, like it's something I do every day. Like it's something I understand and *want* to do rather than running from it as fast as I can. Only I can't run.

"Don't know how," I grind out.

"Push. That's your talent. Use your inner spirit and push the poison from you, the same way you pushed Kat's ghost away."

I want to. Really. I want to live. But I'm so, so tired.

"Arielle…." If she returns with the first aid kit, maybe she can do something.

"Is hopelessly searching for a box of supplies that doesn't exist, and she will continue to do so until we're through here. No more exposing the nulls to our world. So get on with it."

Our world. Shit.

My eyes close, my mind wanders, my senses force their way past the pain and the constriction in my throat. Not sure if it's oxygen-deprived delirium or if I'm accomplishing my goal. Running on instinct again. Following my concept of self. Deeper. Deeper. Greenish-yellowish energy tarnishes the white. Hallucination? Interpretation?

Whatever. I *push.*

Hard. So hard. No idea if I accomplish anything. The pain blinds me to all else, so great, if it lessened, I can't tell.

Something trickles down the outside of my right calf. Venom?

"Good, good. Keep driving it from you. You're doing fine."

He sounds like some kind of demented birthing coach.

I keep pushing, but my chest aches, deep and throbbing with every beat of my straining heart. I still can't see, though I think my eyelids are open. I reach for another breath….

Nothing. No air comes through to my lungs.

Panic seizes me. My body jerks, arms flailing, sending arrows of anguish through the bite on my shoulder. My fingers turn to claws, scraping at my neck, desperate.

I'm sorry, Gen. I'm so sorry. I love you.

"Push it out, dammit!" Leo orders, but I have nothing left. "Do you want to die? Do you want to leave her? It might make things easier on me, but is that what you *want*?"

No. It isn't.

With every ounce of strength I retain, I *push*.

DARKNESS.

I'm standing, which seems odd. I shouldn't be standing, but I don't know why. And total pitch-blackness surrounds me. Where am I? I don't remember. I don't remember anything.

I know who I am. I have no idea how I got wherever the hell this is.

Fear has me throwing my arms out to the sides, but they don't reach far. My knuckles slam into two walls, the thuds they make echoing in what must be a pretty small space. More cautiously this time, I reach backward, maybe a couple of feet, connecting with a third barrier like the ones to my right and left, then forward and collide with a fourth; that one feels rougher, wooden, and when I knock on it, it's hollow. There must be open air on the opposite side. I shuffle my feet, clanging against something metal and knocking over what feels like a long stick.

My mind races. A box, tall enough to hold me, but not much larger than an oversized coffin? A shiver has me wrapping my arms around myself. I stand, paralyzed, not knowing what to do next, afraid of encountering something in the dark that might actually hurt me.

Light. The tiniest amount reaches my eyes. Now that they've had time to adjust, I realize the dark isn't total. Right in front of me, glorious light seeps through a space a few inches from the floor.

A door. I face a door. I fumble for the handle—the little light barely shows me the toes of my work boots (which also feel wrong, somehow). My fingers close around a knob and I twist.

It opens to reveal an unfamiliar hallway, the floor done in red Spanish tile. To my right is an ornate front door with frosted etched glass at its center. It's dark outside. It should be. It's night. Is that right? A pair of naked statues flank the entry. To the left, the corridor continues to a set of swinging doors that might lead to a kitchen. A winding staircase leads up to the second floor.

I turn around, discovering I'm emerging from a closet, complete with a mop, a bucket, a dustpan, and a broom against the rear wall. What the hell was I doing in there?

It has to be a dream. It's the only explanation. I'm in a stranger's house. The need to get out before someone spots me pushes me into action.

I head for the front entrance, work boots squeaking on the tile as I pivot. A familiar voice stops me when I'm three steps away.

"What the fuck were you doing in my house?" Max Harris. I'm in Max Harris's golf course mansion.

I freeze where I stand, rotating toward the sound with my hands raised in surrender, brain working to come up with some sort of explanation. Checking the doghouse. Needed the restroom. No way he's going to buy any of that. I absently wonder where Katy, the dog, is. Probably tied up out back. Probably has been for days. Poor thing.

I complete my turn. There's no one behind me.

A dull thud and a crash resound through the high-ceilinged corridor. A groan follows, then another thud, louder, like a body hitting the floor. "I asked you a question, bitch. What were you two doing in here?" The voice emanates from the room on my right, the door ajar. "I'll have you for breaking and entering, or better yet, I can just kill you. This is Florida. You've invaded my home."

A squeak of fear responds to his threat. I know that squeak. Genesis.

Bits of memory creep through my skull, sending prickling sensations crawling across my scalp. The plan. Chris and Gen headed to Harris's place to find evidence. He wasn't supposed to be home, must have come in and surprised them. But that was hours ago, before dark. And how did I—

Gen screams. I ignore everything else and charge for the door to the room across the hall.

A glowing figure appears directly in front of me, sending me skidding on the tile to a screeching halt. Kat holds up both hands as I'd done just moments before, indicating I should wait.

I could go through her, maybe, but given what happened the last time the two of us intersected, I think that isn't the best idea. "What do you want?" I hiss through clenched teeth.

Gen's sobbing carries from the room beyond. I don't have time for this.

"You'll be smarter if you go through the kitchen and around the other way," Kat says, far more coherent than I've heard her since her death. "You'll come in behind him. The bastard won't detect you." The bastard, her ex-husband, the man who arranged her death.

I tilt my head and study her. She's more solid, the edges sharper, more defined. She isn't dripping anymore, either. Her clothes are different from the ones she had on last time—the ones she drowned in. The straight-line black skirt hugs her hips and thighs; the red blouse has several buttons open, revealing the top of a lacy red matching bra. She doesn't look like a corpse. Except for the faint glow at the edges, she looks alive.

"I'm sorry," she says. "I wanted to come home to you. I loved you."

I shake my head once, hard, and make for the swinging doors at the end of the hall. She falls into step behind me. Uncanny the way her kitten heels click on the floor when I know she isn't really here. "You never loved me," I whisper over my shoulder without looking back. The swinging doors creak when I push through them. I hold my breath, but no one comes to check. I find myself standing in a cheerful kitchen with every modern, high-end appliance gleaming in chrome on the marble countertops. "You liked the thrill of being with me. The wrongness. The naughtiness. It made you feel edgy, just like getting arrested and flirting with every hot guy or gal we passed on the street. But you never loved me. If you'd come back, I would have told you to go to hell." Not sure how honest that statement is. It would be true now, but then…. Then, I might have accepted her with open arms. But she'll never hear that from me.

"I'm already in hell," she says, and the quiet of her voice forces me to look at her.

"You tried to kill me. You held me under the water."

She blinks, and I swear tears form in her luminous eyes. "I wasn't thinking clearly. I wanted you to get the charm, stop the deaths. I didn't want anyone else to end up like me, especially you."

So maybe she had felt something for me once. Or maybe she just realized how good she had it with me, compared to Max Harris.

She continues, "Communicating from one existence to the other, it's not easy. Easier now that we're on the same plane, so to speak."

"What do you mean by—"

A shriek from Gen interrupts my next question, and I'm done waiting. I burst through another door, sending metal bits of the now broken lock across the flooring, into a den or library, the walls stocked with hardbound books, a bar covered in expensive-looking bottles and glassware off to the side.

I spot Chris first, lying across a throw rug shaped like a bearskin. (God, I hope that wasn't a real polar bear.) Dark red stains the corner beneath his head, a gash across his temple bleeding profusely. I know head wounds bleed a lot; I've seen quite a few accidental ones at the construction site. He's conscious, but that looks pretty bad.

Gen is across the room, on the floor by an armchair, half sprawled like someone knocked her down. Her bruised face and angry red scratches along both arms start rage curling through my belly. Rips and tears in her skirt and blouse reveal further cuts, some still bleeding. Max has had them in there for a while.

Gen's eyes fly wide at the sight of my arrival, Kat right behind me and crowding me in the doorway. Kat's body presses against mine—I feel it, and smell her too familiar perfume, and it kind of freaks me out. I nudge her back a bit with my shoulder, and she's solid, at least to me.

Harris whirls toward the open door, aiming a gun straight at me.

Yeah, I guess I should've planned this better.

Chapter 54
Now You See Me

I DUCK as the gun goes off. The bullet misses me, passing straight through Kat and ricocheting off a couple of appliances in the kitchen before embedding itself in a wall. So fucking weird. Kat's body flares where it pierces her, but she shows no signs of damage. She flashes me a wicked grin.

"What the hell?" Harris stares at the shattered door, now hanging by one hinge, bits of broken wood littering the floor.

From where I crouch, I raise my hands in the air. Not doing anyone any good if I get myself shot, but I might trick him into moving close enough for me to try something. "Okay," I say, making my tone gentle. "Let's all calm down here."

Max storms toward me, gun still pointed into the kitchen. Good. Maybe he thinks I have backup. If he keeps the weapon trained away from me....

He walks right past where I crouch.

A cold chill replaces the rage.

"Whoever you are, come on out. If I find you myself, I'll shoot you." He stomps back and forth across the kitchen tile, opens the pantry, peers into the hall I came through. Nothing. Kat leans off to the side, arms crossed over her ample chest, watching his every move.

"Flynn," Genesis hisses.

"Not now," I hiss back. I put together the pieces, and I don't like what I'm building.

"Flynn?" Chris groans, blinking rapidly like he can't quite focus. Considering the head wound, he probably can't. "Where?"

But he should see me, even if I'm nothing more than a blur to him.

And he doesn't.

Oh. Shit.

Trembling takes up residence in my arms and legs, but it doesn't prevent me from sticking my foot out as Max returns to the library.

He walks right through my outstretched limb.

I think I'm going to throw up.

Gen opens her mouth to say something else, but I shake my head hard, and she clamps it shut. No use giving me away if I can find some way not to be completely useless here.

Sudden pain flares in the side of my neck, and I grab at the spot, gasping. It forces me onto my side, where I curl into a ball of agony. While Harris launches a kick at Chris's ribs, I spend the next minute catching my breath. I cringe when a cracking sound comes from Chris's chest.

"What's wrong with you?" Kat demands of me from the doorway. "Do something."

The neck pain eases, and I lever myself up, first to my knees, then to my feet. The glare I give her could melt steel. It's the one I always used when she pissed me off, and the familiarity of our interaction rocks me back a step.

"Why don't *you*?" I say, recovering my senses at least a little, knowing Max won't hear me any better than he heard Kat, which is to say, not at all.

"I can't," she says, pouting, hands on her hips. "But you—"

"What did you do to the door?" Max shouts into Gen's face. He must assume she used some sort of magic to burst it open. A ghost... or rather, ghosts, as I'm coming to realize... don't occur to him.

Of all the stupid times for me to die.

I don't know how it happened. I guess there's a connection with the pain in my neck, now almost unnoticeable, but I bet it will be back. If Gen can see me, and Chris and Max can't, then that's the only explanation I can come up with.

Dammit, Gen, I'm so sorry.

I stagger to the bar, leaning on it while I come to grips with my current state. Who am I kidding? I'm not coming to grips with this anytime soon.

When Genesis fails to answer him, Harris draws back the gun and slams it across her face. She screams, falling to the side, hand cupping her cheek as blood pours from her mouth. Chris pushes himself up on his elbows but falls with a groan.

My teeth grind together. I grab the closest bottle of some brownish whiskey and hurl it with all my strength at Max's back.

When it actually flies toward him, impacts, and shatters, I'm speechless.

I interacted with the bottle. I interacted with the kitchen and library doors and the knob on the closet.

I can touch things in the living world. Not people, but things.

And the people can't touch me.

Oh hell yeah.

Max flops forward across the armchair as I seize two more bottles, one in each hand, and let fly. One hits. The other misses its mark and slams into the bookcases behind the chair. Pain lances through my left shoulder, and I suck in a sharp breath, exhaling slowly. Even if I pulled something, it's too much pain just from throwing a bottle. Way too much. Max spins, grabbing at his skull, blood running over his fingers. His wild eyes search the space behind him.

Of course, he sees nothing.

Behind me, Kat laughs and cheers. I risk a glance back. She waves her hands like little pompoms, and she's no longer alone. A second ghost, another woman, has joined her in the kitchen doorway. Gorgeous woman: perfect figure, long, dark hair, large breasts, trim waist. Max's second wife. I don't know how I know that, but I'm certain. She nods at me, both acknowledging and encouraging.

"Teach that bastard a lesson," she tells me… no, begs. She's begging me to put an end to all this.

Movement draws my attention back to Max. He punches Genesis in the chest, doubling her over. She mewls like a wounded kitten while he screams down at her, "Stop it. Stop it now."

Shit. This isn't what I want to happen. I need to make this fast.

No more bottles out on the bar, and the cabinet beneath has a lock. I take three steps toward the bookcases, my right leg buckling on the fourth. Crashing down on one knee, I grab heavy hardback tomes from the lower shelves and hurl them, one after another, at Max's face. He brings up his arms to block them, then wrenches Genesis to her feet and holds her before him like a shield.

I manage to deflect my aim on the last book, barely missing hitting Gen in her already bruised cheek.

"Enough," Max growls. "You won't stop, I'll stop you." He places the barrel of the gun in contact with Genesis's temple.

I stop throwing things.

"Tell me where the other dyke bitch is," he says.

So that's why he hasn't killed Chris and Gen yet. He thinks I'm here with them, and he wants me. He wants me dead.

Oh, the irony.

"She's here somewhere, isn't she?"

Gen shakes her head, wincing as the gun barrel scrapes along her scalp. Tears pour down her face. Max cocks the old-fashioned revolver. Her eyes meet mine.

We'll be together, but I don't want it this way.

The pain courses up and down my leg, but I clench my jaw and ignore it, forcing myself upright. I step over Chris and lean so my hands are within grasping reach of a heavy ottoman, but I can't pick it up or throw it without risking the gun going off.

"Kick him," I say, knowing she and the other ghosts are the only ones who can hear me.

Her eyes go so wide I can see the whites all the way around.

"It's your only chance."

Genesis swings her foot back, nailing Max in the shin. At the same moment, she drives her elbow hard into his chest. I heave up the ottoman and drop it down on him. The gun fires. The bullet burrows into the furniture's thick cushion. I reach out and wrest the revolver from his fingers. Gen ducks under my upraised arms and throws herself across Chris to protect him from further harm. He protests from beneath her, but she isn't budging.

Max, stunned but still conscious, stares wildly around the room, focuses on the gun, which to him must look like it floats in midair, then makes a break for the door on the opposite side from the kitchen, leading back into the entry hall. I fire off a shot, nailing him in the upper leg. He stumbles but keeps going. Then he's out the door.

The dead wives cheer and high-five one another.

I gather my strength to go after him, working my way across the room by leaning on one piece of furniture after another.

"Flynn, wait!" Gen's voice stops me in my tracks. "Things aren't what they seem to be."

Chapter 55
Second Chances

"I'M DEAD," I say, going back and kneeling beside her and Chris, whom she's finally let sit up and lean against her. My heart aches. Saying the words out loud is harder than just knowing. Tears prickle behind my eyes, but I hold them in. Crying will make things worse, and tonight's fight hasn't ended.

God, this sucks. We can talk like this, maybe sort of be together, but how long can I have in this in-between state? And besides, it isn't fair of me to linger. She'll need to move on, find someone else, though that thought starts the rage roiling inside me again. I glance around, half expecting to see a white light, but nothing in the library changes. Maybe Gen can help me cross over, find peace, so she can have some too.

I take a deep breath, looking down at this representation of myself, marveling at the way my chest moves in and out. I'm exactly as I envision my body, what I expect to see if I look in a mirror: hair in a ponytail, favorite jeans, my Pink concert tee, work boots, and I wonder if people's minds create the ghostly images they want others to experience. A glance at the well-dressed, well-groomed ex-wives seems to confirm my theory.

Closing my eyes, I make the decision to begin the separation now. Twinges in my neck, shoulder, and leg encourage that thought. My condition is deteriorating even as I sit here.

"He's getting away," I tell her, wanting to touch her cheek, her hair, but knowing I can't. "I have to go. I'm assuming you two didn't have time to find evidence."

Her gaze drops, telling me I'm right.

My fist clenches around the revolver. "Then I need to stop him."

"You need to listen, Flynn," she says, surprising me by placing her palm against my face. It doesn't pass through. Instead, the warmth of her skin banishes some of my chills.

"You can touch me."

Gen shrugs. "I have a way with spirits."

"Flynn's here?" Chris asks, staring about like a blind man. His gaze lands on me but darts away. He can't see me. I move the gun a bit, not pointing it at them, just getting his attention. He nods, and his lips curl up in that infectious grin. "No wonder he got his ass kicked." The grin fades. "Wait. She isn't—?"

Gen shakes her head, then winces at the pain it causes her. "No, she isn't."

"Gen…." Denial is one thing, but she's completely delusional. I open my mouth to tell her so.

"She's a walker."

My jaw snaps shut.

"A what?" Chris asks. Good. I'm glad I'm not the only one in the dark, here.

"A walker. The strongest one I've ever seen, maybe the strongest the Registry has seen, if she can interact with the physical world the way she just did. I should have figured it out sooner. Her talent is the push. She can push with her spirit. It gives her an affinity for them. That's why she can see ghosts, at least sometimes. It's not because she has the Sight. She's out of her body, Chris," Gen says, speaking to her brother but staring right at me, "but she's very much alive."

"Like I tried to tell you," Kat says from the doorway as I slump on the floor in shock. "But you never listened to me, even when we were together."

Somehow I manage to give her the finger.

"You need to tell me what happened, Flynn," Gen says, recapturing my attention. "You're untrained. Trauma drives you to push. How did you get here?"

"I don't know." My voice comes out small and weak. I'm alive. Holy shit, I'm alive.

Gen's shoulders rise and fall with a weary sigh. She leans forward, placing her lips against my forehead. Tingling sensations work their way beneath my skin. Magic. "Talk to me," she mumbles, maintaining the contact. "You were with Leo, heading out to the lake to dive for the charm."

And just like that, the memories snap into place.

I jerk upright, away from her, every muscle stiffening. "Snakes," I force out, my breathing quickening and my free hand flying to my neck. "There were snakes. Water moccasins. Leo tried to fight them off... used some kind of green flash. He killed three, but the others...." I have to pause, the hyperventilating threatening to make me black out. I close my eyes and count to ten, striving for deep, even inhalations.

"Did you say green? A flash, not a beam?"

I open my eyes at her tone. Pure hatred like I've never heard from her before. And she's wearier now, the shadows around her eyes deeper. Sparking my memory cost her. I nod once.

"He tried to kill you. That was a redirection spell. He purposely turned the remaining snakes from himself to you. He could have sent them away or destroyed them with another spell, but instead…."

Instead he tried to get rid of me, remembered he would still have Genesis to deal with, and decided to pull me out of the lake.

Gen once described me as an opportunist. The real opportunist in all this is Leo.

"What happened then?" Gen urges, holding my empty hand between hers.

I shudder with the memory. "They bit me. We already had the charm, we were on our way out, and—"

The blood drains from her complexion, the bruises stark against her white skin. The fingers wrapped around mine tremble. "Where? How many times were you bitten?"

"Three." I point at my leg, shoulder, and neck. All of them ache in sympathy. "Leo got me to push some of the venom out. I remember that, then… nothing. I must have fainted." I smile a bit sheepishly. "Woke up in the broom closet out in the hall." I go on, telling her about Arielle, the useless phone, no ambulances. When I finish my brief recounting, she stands, pulling both me and Chris up beside her. Chris leans heavily on his sister's shoulders. He isn't doing well. I'm a lot steadier on my feet.

"We've got to get to the lake. Now," she affirms when I open my mouth to protest. Letting me go, she helps Chris toward the door leading to the hall.

I shake my head. The room spins, and I clutch the back of an armchair for support. "Not until I finish with Harris." I stare at the revolver in my hand. "Once I'm... back together... I won't be able to do it." At least not and get away with it. For what he's done to Genesis and Chris, not to mention Kat, his second wife, and all the other victims of the pond, yes, I can kill him. I prefer not to go to prison for it. "I won't have a better chance than this."

Spirits don't leave fingerprints. And I have no idea if I will be able to do this walking thing again and consciously find him.

"Let it go," Gen says. "He could be anywhere by now." We've made it to the hall and the front door. "We don't know how much time you have. You have to be whole when I heal you."

Chris shoots her a concerned look. I just stare.

"You can do that?" I ask.

"I can do a lot of things."

Leo told me Gen has many skills she doesn't advertise. Skills the predominantly null world can't handle knowing about. Looks like I'm going to be the beneficiary of some of them.

"Get to the lake," I tell her. "Ask Arielle to take Chris to a hospital. Max has a bullet in his leg. He can't have gone far. I have to end this. I'll join you as soon as I can."

I lean down and brush a kiss over Gen's lips, gentle since the lower one is split and bleeding.

"Be careful. And hurry," she says, tears falling again. "You're not dead, but I think you're dying."

I nod. There's nothing else to say.

Behind us, Kat and the other ghost follow us into the hall. They offer a wave. They have their arms around one another, and I wonder if…. Nah. They're just united against a common enemy. Even as I speculate, they fade from my view.

Chapter 56
Shadowed Pursuit

I SKID across the front porch, past the wicker couch and chairs, and stumble onto the lawn. It's full-on dark now. I have no idea what time it is. My spirit-walking self doesn't carry a cell phone or wear a watch. Go figure.

No sign of Max Harris in either direction, and the surrounding yards lie empty and still. Far down the street, a man walks a small dog on a leash, but otherwise nothing moves.

My ears register the persistent barking as I head around back. Katy comes into view, pulling at her tether, stretching it out to its limit in the direction of the golf course behind the mansion. Security lamps on the home's exterior have the backyard well lit, and the big husky mix stands bathed in a circle of yellow light.

I trudge toward her, gun extended before me, imagining how ridiculous it would look to a passerby—the revolver floating in midair across the grass. When I get closer, the dog turns in my direction, sniffing the air and whining, then lowering her body to lie flat on the ground, her head between her paws. I don't think she sees or hears me, but she's aware of my presence. Or maybe it's the floating gun effect.

"Hey there," I say, just in case.

Her ears flatten against her skull. So she hears something. Dogs' ears pick up higher ranges of sound than humans'. I wonder if walkers speak at different pitches.

She continues to cower as I get closer, her head swiveling from side to side. I check her over as I pass by. Water bowl empty again. Matted fur and muddy paws from digging up the petunias, no doubt. She looks thinner, too, and I worry she hasn't been fed since I built her house. At least that's sturdy, providing her shelter from rain and too much sun. If I survive this, I swear I'm adopting this dog.

Katy whines again. I scare her. Not my intention. I back off a bit and stare across the gentle rolling mounds of the golf course.

"Yes, he went that way. You'd better hurry if you want to catch him."

I whirl back toward the mansion, where one of the shadows detaches itself from the structure and steps into the light—an old man, gray-bearded and shabbily dressed, stains marking torn jeans and several buttons missing from a short-sleeved checkerboard shirt. I think I've seen him around the Festivity Starbucks a few times, but not often. Festivity's residents don't tolerate loitering vagrants for long. We've never spoken, yet the voice tickles my memory.

Katy leaps to her paws and growls, but the man waves a hand and she subsides, then ducks inside her doghouse.

It takes another second or two before I realize he isn't another ghost, and he can see me.

"Who are you?" I say, not quite pointing the gun at him. He wants me to catch Harris, so he's probably not my enemy. Doesn't make him my friend.

"No one of consequence," he says. "Harris is escaping."

I turn to look where he points. In the distance, I make out a figure, a shadow against the shadows, moving slowly away from the houses lining the manicured greens. On the far side of the course lies Festivity Health—the closest hospital. If he manages to reach it, and I doubt it considering how he stumbles and staggers, I can't imagine what he intends to tell the emergency room staff. He's nowhere close to anyone who can act as a Good Samaritan. I have a little time.

"I know you," I say, staring at the old man again. Taking a step closer, I peer past the beard and dirty clothes. "The pawn shop. That's it."

His head tilts to the side, lips curling upward in a grin. "You give her the ring yet?"

One more task left undone, one more regret if I don't survive. She'll never know how deeply I love her. My free hand clenches into a fist at my side. "None of your damn business. What are you doing here, and why are you helping me?" And how can he see me? He sent the dog away with a gesture. He's some kind of magic user, like Leo and Genesis, and I don't trust him. Not one bit.

"Let's just say I've taken a personal interest in you. Now get going. I'll attend to the mess you all made inside." He fixes me with a hard stare. "You have less time than you think." And with that, he returns to the shadows, blending in until he vanishes.

Okay, then.

I hadn't really thought about the blood and prints Gen and Chris would have scattered all over the mansion. Whatever sort of magic the old man has, I hope it's good enough to keep them out of legal trouble.

I head for the golf course, passing the doghouse and the property line designated by pink-and-purple petunias. As I suspected, Katy took out her loneliness and frustration on a good number of the plants. Several lay torn and strewn across the grass, others uprooted in their entirety and cast aside.

She's dug a deep hole in the dirt, and one of the spotlights from the house picks out the shiny black plastic of a garbage bag buried within.

I don't need to be psychic to guess what it contains.

"Well, we've got our evidence," I mutter, continuing on. "Now to get the killer."

He's pretty far out on the course, down between a couple of sand traps and a water hazard. But his pronounced limp slows him, and he falls even as I watch.

I waste a good minute with my eyes closed, concentrating on teleporting my out-of-body self from my location to Max's, but when I open them, I haven't moved an inch. So much for that idea. Gen says I need training. As much as I'm opposed to encouraging all this magic shit, she might have a point.

My leg aches when I break into a jog, forcing me to stop and start a few times, but I'm still faster than my quarry. In ten minutes I'm on him, the gun aimed at his retreating figure, him unaware of my presence in the dark and mist rising off the water nearby.

I have him right where I want him, and yet I hesitate. He hurt and killed so many people, but shooting an unarmed man in the back doesn't sit well with my conscience.

"Do it," Kat says, flickering into existence on my right and making me yelp and jump.

"If I could hold the gun, I'd do it myself," the second wife says, appearing on my left. I jerk away from her.

"Will you two knock it off?"

Kat smirks at me.

All the jumping around, rustling the grass and some low bushes, catches Max's attention. He spins to face me, staggering on the wounded leg. Blood soaks his expensive tailored trousers. His skin is pasty white. Plenty of moonlight out here. It glints off the revolver's metal surface. His eyes go wide at the sight of it. He searches around for whoever controls the weapon and finds no one. If he still thinks it's Genesis, that thought disappears fast. There's nothing out here for her to hide behind. Nope, it's just me, and he can't see me.

He takes a different guess. "Kat, honey, if that's you, it was all Leopold's fault. I just wanted you to have a little bad luck, for leaving me and all. He's the one who got you killed." His voice wavers; his lips tremble.

"Oh, fuck you, Max," Kat says, even though he can't hear her. She turns to me. "He always did think I was stupid."

"He thinks all women are stupid," the other wife confirms. "And how do you explain *my* death, you asshole? Leo didn't sneak up behind me and break my fucking neck. That was all you."

I wince at her shouting and her revelation. A broken neck must be a horrible way to go.

And then, for an instant, she lets me see what that looks like. Her spirit morphs, her complexion paling. Her neck twists to an impossible angle, the crushed bones pushing her skin outward in sickening bulges. Beside her, Kat grows bloated, her skin blue, her eyes sunken in their sockets.

I gag and swallow bile.

Determination reasserts itself, and I aim the gun at Max's chest.

Instead of raising his hands or running again, he grabs for the revolver. We struggle for the weapon, my shoulder and neck screaming in pain as he pulls with his superior strength. The gun goes off, the flash blinding me, the shot echoing across the open golf course.

Chapter 57
Halfway Home

WHEN MY senses return, I'm sprawled on the grass, the gun lying between me and Max Harris's corpse. His sightless eyes stare at the stars overhead. I'd close them, but my fingers would pass right through.

Or maybe not. If his spirit left him, then he's a thing, like the books in his library, or the ottoman, or the gun.

I grab his hand, still warm, and close it around the revolver's grip. The story forms in my head. The dog uncovers the second wife's body. Faced again with what he's done, he loses it, takes off across the golf course, and shoots himself, once in the leg, once in the chest, a victim of his own guilt.

Yeah, I wouldn't believe it either, but that's probably what the cops will come up with, or something along those lines.

I'm alone out here, the night air cool and fragrant, the crickets chirping. No sign of the ghosts, and I remember what Gen told me about spirits crossing over once their earthly problems are resolved.

Despite the hurt she caused me, despite her breaking my heart, I hope Kat finds peace. Kat has her closure, and I have mine. And with that closure and forgiveness, any last reservations I might have about making things permanent with Genesis fall away.

Assuming I can survive long enough to propose.

The walk back to the mansion seems twice as long
as the trip out. My limbs feel leaden, my breath coming in ragged gasps, even though I know I'm not really
breathing.

Or maybe I am. Are my increasing signs of weakness a reflection of my physical body back beside the
lake?

I have a sinking feeling I just hit the nail on the
head. Hah. Construction worker humor. My laughter
borders on hysteria. I'm really losing it.

Katy doesn't emerge when I pass her house this
time, but I glance inside to see her curled up, asleep,
and I take further pleasure in knowing Harris can't mis-
treat her anymore.

In the front yard, I encounter a new problem. I
have no way of getting from here to the lake. It isn't far.
Maybe a mile and a half. Festivity isn't a large town.
But I'm not capable of walking it. Not by a long shot.
Still, I have to try.

I get a couple of blocks before the first car passes
me. It's one of those NEV's, the electric vehicles that
move at a snail's pace. Despite the fairly late hour,
it's headed downtown, in the general direction I need
to go.

While I'm in considerable phantom pain from the
snake bites (ugh, phantom, now I'm really punchy),
I doubt I can be damaged further in this form. I'm a
freaking spirit.

Without any further thought, I leap for the side of the NEV and grab on to its frame, rocking the whole thing sideways with my impact. The couple inside glances back, then at each other, and shrugs it off.

Three transfers later, I make it to the Festivity sign traffic light, jump off the back of the pickup I hitched a ride with, and stumble through the gap in the sign left by Arielle's ill-fated car.

Gen is there, kneeling beside the lake, and Leo standing off to the side. No sign of the rental car or Arielle, so I guess Gen did what I told her to and had the waitress take Chris to the hospital. They've laid out some flashlights in addition to the glow cast from the spots.

I try to call out to them, but I can't get a good enough breath for shouting. Instead, I place one foot in front of the other, limping around the pond, coming up behind them and looking down at… myself.

Chapter 58
Life and Death and Life

I LOOK almost dead. That's an understatement. My eyes are closed, my chest rising and falling irregularly. Yellowish fluid, at least that's how it appears in the spotlights, drips from the punctures on my swollen neck. My mouth gapes open, air wheezing in and out of my straining lungs. The skin on my shoulder is blackened around the bite there, like necrosis has set in. Seems too fast for something like that to happen, but with the snakes magically enchanted by the charm, I suppose anything is possible. The leg wound appears a little better, the swelling not quite as severe, and I remember succeeding in pushing some of that venom out before I "walked."

Gen holds one of my hands in a bone-crushing grip, tiny sparks traveling from her body to mine, but the pinpoints of light flicker and fade, the stream weakening as her strength falters.

"Gen…," I whisper, dropping to the ground beside her, my legs giving out completely.

She gives a soft cry, releasing my physical form to grab my spiritual one. "God, Flynn," she gasps, holding me up by the shoulders, staring into my face.

I'm struck by her exhaustion, the bruising deeper than before, the dried blood on her cheeks, the pinched lines around her mouth and eyes. She looks as bad as I feel.

"It's done," I tell her.

Gen blinks, then nods once, though I catch the flicker of fear in her eyes. Of me? *For* me? Then it's gone. "Not important right now."

I glance around the lake, toward the street beyond the Festivity sign. "No ambulance, huh?" Leo has his reasons for not involving the authorities, but I didn't think Gen would hold to that with my life at stake.

"The wounds are cursed like the snakes that made them. No doctor can help you. Not until I do. You need to rejoin with yourself. I've kept you going. I can't do more without you together."

I turn from her to my body, barely clinging to life. "I, um, don't know how."

"Genesis?" Leo joins us, crouching near my head but leaving distance between himself and his ex.

"I thought I told you to stay away from her," Gen snaps, but there's no force in it. She's spent.

"Flynn's here?" He glances around, and I realize his insufficient power prevents him from seeing me in my current form.

"Yes, she's here. Now shut up." Gen squeezes my shoulders. "Just reach out and touch your face. The connection should pull you back in."

I start to do it, my hand inches from my body. Then I stop. "Gen, I need to tell you how much—"

She rises on her knees and kisses me, hard. It has to hurt her, but she keeps kissing me until she's breathless. "I know. Now go."

The second my fingertips brush my forehead, I'm yanked forward, wrenched through space like a fish on a hook. Gone is Gen's warm touch, replaced by overwhelming pain. My eyes snap open, my physical ones, and my back arches as I convulse. My head slams against the hard ground, a rock digging into my shoulder blade right where the glass from Leo's cabinet cut me—minor compared to everything else.

"Flynn!" She holds me down, but I buck and heave beneath her palms, unable to be still, unable to control my body at all.

"Please…." It comes out as a rasp. It hurts so much.

Gen drives her power into me, but even through my haze, I can sense it won't be enough. Each time one pain eases, another erupts like a volcano pouring lava along my veins. Swellings increase, then lessen, skin dies and regenerates, and all the while, the poison seeks my heart and brain.

She falters, her body rocking above mine, her eyes closed, breath fast and sharp as my own. I'm scared for her. She's so tired, so weak. The cooling sensation she produces starts coming in bursts rather than a steady stream. A moan of pain escapes her lips.

"Let her go," Leo says from somewhere behind my head. "She'll take you with her."

"Isn't that what you want?" Gen bites out, voice hoarse. "She told me what you did with the redirection spell. You're responsible. You're responsible for everything. All the deaths." She waves one hand over her shoulder in the direction of the lake while she pauses in her fight, gasping, wavering, searching for reserves she obviously doesn't have. "If Flynn dies, I owe you nothing."

The grass rustles by my ear as Leo stands, then paces in and out of my field of vision. He mutters to himself, arms crossed over his chest, still wearing the wetsuit he went diving in. He wanders down to the edge of the lake and stares out across its moonlit surface.

Gen takes a shuddering breath, places both hands on my chest. Sweat pours down her face, sweat and tears. I see failure etched in her shadowed features.

"It's not fair," she whispers. "Not after all this." She tries again, the magic trickling into me, but something goes wrong, some sort of feedback, and she jerks away with a sharp cry.

When she places her palms back on my chest, I use what remaining strength I have to reach out and cover them. "Stop," I say softly, not that I can manage anything louder. "He's right. Let me go."

I hate leaving her, but I want relief. I guess I'm a coward after all.

"No!" Her scream of rage at Leo, at fate, tears at my heart. I'm ripping her to pieces.

"Gen…."

Behind her something moves fast—Leo. Moonlight reflects off the knife in his hand, the same one he used to drive off that first snake. Guess he's changed his mind about doing his own dirty work.

"Gen!" It isn't much of a warning shout, but it's enough.

She turns, flinging one arm toward him in instinctive self-defense. Green energy cracks between them, the flash so bright I'm temporarily blinded, the *boom* like the space shuttle returning to Earth, breaking the sound barrier. Leo cries out, then groans, and something heavy impacts the ground at my side.

I blink furiously, willing away the sparkles obscuring my vision. Gen swims into focus, red hair flying out in all directions crackling with static electricity, eyes glowing a brilliant and terrifying emerald. She stares down at Leo lying beside me, curled in the fetal position, clutching at his chest with clawlike fingers, the other hand stretching for the knife that's fallen just out of his reach on the sand.

"You don't want to do this. I have ways of getting even," he snarls. "Even if I have to haunt you to do it."

I know the moment she makes her decision, the way her mouth sets in a thin, hard line, and I have no strength left to stop her. When she moves, the air around her hands literally sizzles. She touches Leo's forehead with her fingertips, gently, almost reverently. The other goes to the space in the center of my rib cage, palm flat on my skin.

The connection is made.

Life-saving energy suffuses me, setting my skin aglow in one gigantic rush of cooling, tingling, pain-easing power. I sigh with the first real relief I've had since I was bitten, even as Leo shrieks and writhes. She's killing him.

She's saving me.

She's committing murder.

I killed Max Harris.

That was self-defense.

So is this.

One thing to use a gun, a mundane weapon with bullets. Quite another to lash out with a power few have and fewer can control. I don't know whether to be horrified or relieved, but this is Genesis, and I trust her. I love her. I don't fear her. I won't.

Venom pours from the punctures, a steady stream. I draw a lung-filling breath through an unobstructed throat as Leo gasps his last.

My muscles relax and I go limp, not even aware I'd been rigid before. Gen blinks away the green lighting her gaze. Her hair settles in soft waves across her shoulders. The scent of ozone fades on the breeze. She reaches to touch my cheek.

I flinch from her.

Shit.

"Are you afraid of me, Flynn?" she asks, a faint echo in her voice the last reminder she just performed the impossible.

"I... don't know." Honesty. Not always the best response. And not entirely accurate. I *am* afraid of her, my lover, my Genesis. The hurt in her face cuts to the bone, but I can't take the words back. "He's dead?" I turn my head toward Leo, more of a loll. Tired, so tired.

"Heart attack," she says.

"You—"

"He was diving and he had a heart attack, Flynn. You got bitten trying to save him. I found you both." Her tone leaves no room for argument.

"Right."

I lie back and watch the stars overhead, watch her gather the knife and toss it into the center of the lake, getting rid of the evidence of his attack. With a touch to her face, she removes all traces of bruising, all the visible cuts and scrapes. Moving gingerly, favoring her ribs, which must still hurt, she collects the scuba gear strewn around and dumps it into the McLaren.

She sends a jolt of blue energy into Leo's phone, nods with satisfaction at whatever comes up on the screen, and calls for an ambulance.

I drift into unconsciousness just as it wails its arrival.

Chapter 59
Aftermath

I FLOAT in and out of consciousness, flashes of order-lies, white walls, doctors, bright lights, and at long last, a bed not on wheels swimming in my sporadic vision. Bandages swath my leg, neck, and shoulder, restricting my movement, but I don't have energy to do more than shift a bit on the mattress.

Somewhere along the journey I acquire an awk-wardly ventilated white gown and an IV, the needle causing the vein at the crook of my left arm to throb and ache, the drip cold each time it seeps beneath my skin. Whatever is in it makes me sleepier than I already am, but I'm painfully aware of Gen's absence in the otherwise empty, dim private room.

Private and expensive, I have no doubt. I also don't doubt Gen's picking up the tab, dammit.

I've never stayed overnight in a hospital. Well, ac-tually I think it's close to dawn. Some daylight peeks through a crack in the thick, drawn curtains. But regard-less of the hour, I'm a little uneasy. Beeping equipment, antiseptic smells, murmured voices from the hallway outside sometimes rising in brief alarm and then quieting again. All of it alien and unfamiliar.

A nurse arrives to change the IV bag—a tall, stern-looking woman with broad shoulders and a severe bun pinned to the top of her head. I'm not easily intimidated, but she intimidates me, especially since I'm already off-balance. Nevertheless, I ask about Genesis.

"Family only," she says, focusing all her attention on the bag.

"She's my—" I almost say girlfriend, instead, to my surprise, finishing with "—partner."

The nurse purses her lips like she just sucked a lime. "Immediate family only after five p.m..... No boyfriends, no *girlfriends.* She can see you during regular visiting hours." Then as an addendum, "This is a *Seventh Day Adventist* hospital."

Ah. Got it.

She hurries to finish her task, not bothering to retuck the blanket around me that she pulled aside.

"Gay isn't contagious," I call to her retreating back as she lets the door swing shut behind her.

Bitch.

Most of the day I spend sleeping, though I eat a couple of bland meals, Hawaiian Punch and Jell-O the highlights of both. I also visit my private bathroom, experiencing the challenge of unavoidable bodily functions, all while trying not to rip the IV out of my arm. Between the residual effects of the venom and the painkillers I must be on, I'm not steady on my feet, and I consider pulling the nurse call cord for assistance on the return trip, but embarrassment and pigheadedness beat risk and pain. When I wrangle my way back to bed, a doctor, much friendlier than the nurse, comes in to check the bandages and examine the healing skin around the bites.

"You're a very lucky woman," he tells me, blue eyes crinkling at the corners with his smile. "At least two of the snakes must have been old or bitten prey recently. Three full doses would have killed you."

No one, not the nurse, the doctor, nor an orderly who brings me another blanket says anything about Leo. I wonder if it's because they think I don't know, or if they just don't want to upset me further than I should already be over the loss of my "diving buddy."

Thinking about him proves to be a mistake. My next nap fills with nightmares, beginning with me shooting Max. Yes, he went for the gun, but he couldn't have hurt me with it. He couldn't even see me. Deserved or not, it wasn't quite self-defense.

I killed him. I'm not upset because I did it. I'm upset because I don't feel guilty about it. Not sure what that says about me. Not sure I want to find out.

Then come the worse dreams: Gen's eyes black as midnight when she attempted to drive Kat's spirit from my body, then glowing with green fire as she sucked Leo's life away and fed it to me to save mine.

I wake sweating and screaming. The doctor proscribes stronger sedatives.

I love Gen. I will deal with this fear.

I sleep.

Something shifts in the shadows of the hospital room. I fight my way through the drug haze and blink away the blurriness. Chris, seated in the single armchair, swims into focus.

"How'd you get in here?" Slurred speech. Terrific. I sound like a drunken sailor.

He gestures at his own lovely hospital-issue paja-
mas: drawstring pants, paper slippers, and a loose-fit-
ting top. (And how come he gets real nightclothes and
I end up with the extra-air-conditioning-in-the-back
version?) Bandages wrap his left bicep and peek from
where the shirt doesn't quite meet the waistband of the
bottoms. "I'm just another patient, taking a short stroll.
My room's right above yours. Guess I got lost." His
grin fades. "Gen's up there now. No 'family' issues visiting me, regardless of the hour."

"Couldn't she just, I don't know, whammy the
nurses and sneak right past them?"

"Yeah, she could." He stands so he towers over me.
"She doesn't show her extended skill set on a whim."

No. She uses it to kill someone and feed me his
life force.

My gut clenches in a tight knot. I swallow a mouthful of bile.

"And then there's that," Chris says, voice soft.
"The restrictions on visitors were only for the first couple of days. You're going to have to deal with the fear,
and fast, or you'll lose her."

Shit. He noticed.

"She knows you're scared of her. She doesn't want
to frighten you more by coming down here."

I take a deep breath, stalling so I can organize what
I'm about to say. Stalling so I can figure myself out.

I can't hold my breath that long.

"I'm not scared of… her," I clarify, fingers picking
at the blanket so I don't have to look at him. It's the
truth. I don't believe Gen would ever hurt me inten-
tionally. "Just what she did. I didn't know she had the
power to kill a person." Or the drive, though I don't
mention that.

A loud thud draws my gaze sharply to Chris, who rubs his hand after punching the back of the recliner. "She shouldn't have done it." Furious. He's furious at Genesis for saving me.

I raise my eyebrows, and he calms a little.

"I don't begrudge you your life, Flynn, and from what Gen tells me, he deserved it, and she had no other choice, but...."

But? I think about it. Gen had been near to collapse when she pulled that energy from Leo. She looked better afterward, but maybe after I passed out it caught up with her. "She's okay, isn't she?"

"Physically, yes." He won't meet my eyes.

Damn, I hate hedging. "What does that mean?"

"It means she needs you now more than ever, and the rest is for her to explain."

I let that sit a bit. Secrets and more secrets. There shouldn't be so many between people who love each other. But he doesn't seem inclined to share.

Chris rises from his seat, heading for the door, but I have one more urgent question.

"The charm, Chris. What happened to the charm? Is it still in my scuba belt?" Is it, even now, cursing every lesbian patient in this hospital?

"I slipped in here while you were unconscious and took it. Gen disposed of it properly," he tells me. I open my mouth to ask what that means, but he holds up a hand to stop me. "Don't worry about that. It's taken care of. Worry about you. And Genesis." The door closes behind him.

I slam my right palm hard against the mattress, the soft thunk not nearly close to satisfying enough.

Chapter 60
Tying Knots in Loose Ends

WITH THE pain managed and the drugs reduced, I can think enough to get information and take care of some things.

I spend the next hospital day alone, watching local, then national news, surprised the murder/suicide of Max Harris makes it to the country-wide stage. But Festivity advertises itself as the "perfect quiet small town your grandparents remember," and all the latest activity has made it anything but.

The good news is no one suspects Chris or Gen of anything. The old guy from the pawn shop must have done a good job cleaning up evidence. Sooner or later, I'll need to talk to Gen about him, but I hold off on it. We've had enough magic for now.

Leo's fate hits the front page of the town paper—one more (and hopefully last) victim of Dead Woman's Pond. There's a bit on me, too, with a reminder about watching out for poisonous snakes.

Fuck yeah.

Steve and Allie drop by after working the day at Kissimmee Lanes. They bring flowers and pizza, and though the conversation between me and Allie starts off awkward, we're soon back to our old selves. Glad she doesn't hold a grudge. I wonder if Gen said something to her, explained why I acted the way I did. Then again, I can't imagine how that discussion would have gone.

They also have positives for me. The bowling alley and the state decided not to press charges against me when two things happened: they found out I was Festivity's local hero, and several female customers protested that women have a right to defend themselves if attacked. I'm welcome to return to the lanes whenever I want.

The way my shoulder and neck hurt, I doubt I'll be bowling anytime soon.

My boss, Tom, also stops in with a message that the OSHA issues cleared up, that despite my mishap, our record otherwise is so clean we aren't in major trouble, and we're all going back to work in a week or so to finish the new apartment complex.

The doc lets me go on the fourth day, and I almost faint at the sight of the final bill, but a copy has already been sent to Gen's address.

Even with the promise of steadier construction work, I will never, ever be able to pay her back.

Chris picks me up out front and lets me off in the parking lot behind the pub. I'm glad to see he had his window repaired, from when I broke it. Before he leaves, though, I have one request.

"How do you feel about dogs?"

He quirks an eyebrow at me. "Fine, I guess."

"This place allow them?" I wave my hand at the building.

"Yes…." Wary. I don't blame him.

"I need you to do something for me."

I TUG the black vest into place over the long-sleeved, satiny dark blue shirt and study my reflection. Black jeans and black faux suede boots complete the look, and it isn't a bad one on me. Gen was right. I wear vests and satin pretty well. The double layer rests a bit heavily on my sore shoulder, but it's been over a week since I got out of the hospital, and I'm almost back to normal. Well, as normal as a "walker" with the "push" can be.

I tie a thin black ribbon around my ponytail and I'm good to go.

Almost.

My palms sweat as I head for the rear of Gen's closet, and I scrub them on my jeans before picking up the abandoned shoe and dumping the ring box into my hand. I spend a long minute staring at it before removing the engagement ring (since the box would make an obvious bulge) and tucking it into a vest pocket, leaving the wedding band inside.

Deep breaths, Flynn. You can do this.

You *need* to do this.

Chris was right. I'm losing her.

We haven't slept together since I got home. She insists on using the couch, sure she'll roll over and bump one of my healing injuries. But it's an excuse and we both know it. We talk, we share meals, we laugh, but every moment in each other's company feels hollow.

I do everything I can think of to prove I'm not afraid of her.

This is the one thing I haven't tried.

Chris waits for me at the pub's kitchen entrance. His gaze travels over my attire. "You look hot. And you should see Genesis. She looks—"

"Amazing," I say with a smile. She always looks amazing to me.

"Sexy," he corrects me. "Sexy as hell. I'd go into more detail, but I am her brother."

Sexy, huh? I swallow hard. I asked her to meet me for drinks at the pub, like that first date we had over a year ago. Told her I'd dress up and everything. She'd given me a smile that seemed a little sad, but she'd agreed to it. I wasn't sure she would.

"You okay?" Chris asks, throwing an arm around my shoulders and pulling me inside. "You're kinda pale."

I'm kinda nauseated, but I don't tell him. "You get it all set up?" I ask, ignoring his question.

"Yep. The place is packed. Your friends Allie and Steve are here, Arielle, too, most of your work crew from the construction company and their spouses, along with a bunch of Gen's regional psychic friends and some trusted, long-term client friends of hers. I've got them scattered around inside and out so it's not too obvious, but they'll be in the bar right at ten when you want them. DJ's prepped and ready to go."

"Good," I say, checking the hour on my phone for the fifth time since I headed down here. Nine thirty. I slide it into my pocket and clear my throat to hide my nerves. We pass through the kitchen, where the cooks and servers bustle about in a frenzied rush. From beyond the doors to the dining area and bar, a country song with a not-too-bad karaoke singer shakes the dishes in the cabinets.

Friday night is karaoke night. The busiest night of the week.

I have to be out of my mind.

At the doorway, I freeze up, my feet refusing to take another step.

"You'll be fine, Flynn." He gives me a little shove and I'm inside the bar, searching the packed, dimly lit space for—

Genesis.

Oh my God.

My heart does a little flip when I spot her. Must be a hundred people in the bar, but my gaze goes straight to her, standing by one of the barstools, her hand resting lightly on the polished wood surface, one high-heeled shoe up on the lower metal rung of the seat. My eyes trail their way up her bent leg to the thigh-length black dress she wears, draping her curves in tiers, accentuating all the right places. The scoop neck reveals the tops of her breasts. The spaghetti straps leave her arms bare. She's let her hair down, and it falls in soft red waves across her shoulders.

She's chatting up the bartender when I arrive but turns toward me as if she senses my eyes on her. Her eyebrows rise a little at the sight of me; then her lips curve upward in a smile, making me blush. Green eyes sparkle (not glow, sparkle), and she offers a wave.

I forget how to walk.

When I don't move, she takes pity on me and meets me by the kitchen. Her fingers reach out and brush my cheek, then cup my chin and close my mouth for me. I hadn't realized it was open.

She runs her hands down my arms, the satin of my shirt sending all sorts of pleasurable sensations to the skin beneath. "I like this," she says, and I swear her voice is huskier than normal. "You look fantastic."

I should say something, compliment her in return, but my mouth goes dry. She seems to grasp my dilemma because she laughs, the first real laugh I've heard from her since I got home.

"The way you're looking at me tells me all I need to know, Flynn. And thank you."

"You're welcome," I manage, following her back to the bar.

I'd told her I wanted to have a drink and then maybe grab a bite to eat. Really, I just need to kill thirty minutes.

The leg still bothers me, and I limp a bit, so she insists on giving me the empty stool. Then she turns and stands between my jean-clad knees, leaning back against my chest, my arms clasping around her waist. I rest my chin on the top of her head, breathing in rose-scented shampoo and just a touch of perfume.

This. This is what I want, now and always.

We order drinks. Gen sticks with a soda, but I order a rum and Coke, heavy on the rum—a double. She shoots me a look that's a mixture of curiosity and concern (beer is usually the hardest thing I drink), but I wave it off. The Yankees clock above the liquor shelves reads nine forty-five. I down half the drink in one go.

A couple more karaoke singers of varying ability do their numbers, and then, all too soon, the host clears the small number of dancers from the temporary floor in the center of the room. In my peripheral vision, the patio doors open to admit the people I had Chris invite for me. More of them drift in from the dining area. Chris takes up a spot right by the dance floor, where he'll have an unobstructed view.

"Huh," Gen says, not turning around, "I wonder what's going on."

If she turns she'll know, because I'm certain all the blood has drained from my face. I reach over and set my glass on the bar, clattering it with my trembling hand. Luckily she can't hear it with the ambient noise.

"We have a special request," the DJ says, a wide grin spreading across his youthful features. Dan's the karaoke host. We've known each other for months— Gen and I often hang out on Fridays and watch the singers. He's careful not to look right at me, but I can tell he's enjoying this.

Wish I was.

"One of our regular patrons asked permission to say a few words tonight. She's never sung karaoke. I doubt she's ever touched a microphone or spoken in front of a crowd before, and I'm betting she's just a tad nervous, so let's all give her some support. Flynn, come on out here." He points right at me and starts a round of applause that picks up in volume as people turn in my direction.

Here and there I pick up mutterings of "hero" and "the lake," and the applause increases tenfold.

I nudge Gen aside with my knee and slide off the stool, grateful my legs don't buckle. Gen stares at me, wide-eyed, but somehow I keep walking until I stand next to Dan. From across the floor, Chris gives me a wink.

Right. Now or never.

I reach out and take the microphone in my white-knuckled grip. Dan fades back behind his karaoke equipment, leaving the floor to me.

Chapter 61
The Problem With PDAs

I TAP the end of the microphone, making sure it's on and feeling stupid for checking. Of course it's on. Dan was just speaking into the damn thing.

A hush falls over the bar, even the uninvolved patrons waiting in expectation. Everyone smiles except Genesis, who looks utterly, hopelessly confused. That concerns me a little. She should have some sort of clue by now. But I shrug it off. Not like I can stop at this point.

I hold out my free hand to her, and she crosses to me and takes it, mouthing, "What are you doing?"

I fix a smile on my face that threatens to break it and keep going. "You know I have issues with public displays of affection. They embarrass the hell out of me."

Laughter from the crowd. Silence from Genesis.

"They also scare me more than anything or *anyone*," I say, meeting her eyes, "so you have to know I'm serious about what I'm about to say." I drop to one knee. I fish the ring out of my vest pocket and hold it out to her between thumb and forefinger. You could have heard a pin drop in the bar.

Gen's hand flies to her mouth, covering it. Tears well up in her eyes.

God, I hope those are tears of happiness, but I'm not so sure.

"Gen," I say, my voice faltering a little. I have to be careful how I word this. "Gen, I trust you with my heart and my life. Will you marry me?"

Hoots and hollers from the guys in my crew, along with some whistling and more applause.

I expect a cry of joy, maybe her flinging her arms around my neck. I don't expect the look of pure panic she gives first to me, then her brother, whose ever-present grin fades as they make eye contact.

No. Oh, please no. Gen, don't do this to me. Not here. Not now.

A collective gasp goes up from the crowd as she shakes her head and runs from the dance floor, pushing her way between the onlookers. She collides with someone, because glass shatters right before the kitchen door swings shut.

And that, Flynn, is why you don't do PDAs.

For a long moment I remain on my knee, head bowed, staring at the floor, at nothing. Eventually, I push myself to my feet, ignoring the murmurs of sympathy from all around me. My movements jerk as I tuck the ring back in my pocket and pass off the microphone to Dan, then head for the front entrance. Tears blur my vision. I swipe them on the back of my hand, but they keep coming. Just as well. They prevent me from seeing anyone's face.

Besides, I can't possibly humiliate myself more than I have already tonight.

I'm out the door and on the sidewalk before I register the voice calling my name.

"Flynn. Flynn, stop."

Chris. I don't want to talk to him. I don't want to talk to anyone. "Shouldn't you be off consoling your sister?" I growl, still walking. If I'm mean enough, maybe he'll leave me alone so I can find a hole to crawl into.

"Can't fix her. Only you can do that. So I've gotta fix you first." His hand rises in my peripheral vision like he's going to rest it on my shoulder, but I stiffen and he drops it to his side. "Can you be taught, Flynn?"

The words stop me. Don't know where I'm going, anyway. I stand outside the pub, at the corner not far from the outdoor bar and patio, knowing my friends watch through the front windows. The music hasn't started up again. I'm the best show in Festivity.

I push them from my mind. They don't matter. Nothing matters anymore.

Can I be taught? Chris's words—from what, a couple of weeks ago?—swirl around my head like annoying gnats. What, exactly, am I supposed to learn here?

Don't propose in public seems to be the lesson of the evening. Not when you don't know the answer.

Except I did know. I was absolutely, positively sure of Gen's love for me.

I still am. Despite her refusal. So what the hell happened?

Chris says nothing else, standing beside me, not touching me or coming into my line of sight. Just waiting for me to work things through.

Can I be taught?

I fix my gaze on the broken sidewalk, tracking the path of a line of ants from one square to another.

I ran away. Like I do every time I face confrontation with someone I love. After Kat left, I ran from the world. When Gen and I fought, I ran for the door. That wasn't Kat's spirit remnant controlling me. Not then. It was just me. All me.

I'm not running anymore.

"Where is she?"

Chris points to the back stairs.

Chapter 62
Do-over

GEN HAS left the apartment door unlocked. Wishful thinking, hoping I'll come after her? Or was she simply too distraught to remember to lock it?

No lights on in the living room, but she's easy to spot, huddled on the floor by the open window curtains, the streetlights casting shadows around her but making her glow. She's sobbing. It carries from across the room—heart-wrenching, tear-a-person-apart sobs, the kind that make her whole body convulse with each outpouring of emotion.

And hiccups. Of course she has hiccups.

I trip over one of her discarded high heels, kicking the shoe across the entry tile so it clatters against a wall. Her head comes up, but she doesn't turn around, just stares out the window at the street below. She sucks in a shuddering breath, chokes on a few more sobs, then gets some control over herself.

"I thought you'd be long gone," she says so soft I barely hear her.

"Almost was," I admit, taking a seat on the big couch. Nowhere near her. I rest my elbows on my knees, my chin in my hands. "Your brother thinks you need fixing."

She barks a harsh laugh at that. "Like something at your construction site?" Gen faces me now, her expression unreadable since I haven't turned on the lights.

I shrug. "I just want to know why." I pause and swallow hard, the embarrassment of the last half hour pouring back in a mad rush. It's all I can do to maintain my even tone. I want to yell. I want to punch something. But I'm scared that something might be her, so I tamp it down. "If it's the fear thing, I'm not afraid of you, Gen. The worst you can do is break my heart, and you've already done that a couple of times."

She winces at my words, jerking on the floor like I slapped her. "I know. I'm sorry. I never meant… that's not it."

"Then what?" My patience shreds. "Dammit, Genesis! Do you have any idea how hard that was for me?" I kick the coffee table hard, rattling the little knickknacks on it. "All these months you've told me to let go, not worry so much, be a free spirit, and you… you…." The tears press at the backs of my eyes, but I blink them away. I will not cry now. Later, when I'm alone, probably in yet another hotel room, but not now.

She crawls over to where I sit, not quite within my reach, but closer. "I never expected you to do that," she whispers. "Not in a million years. You caught me off guard. I wasn't ready for it."

"I thought you loved me."

"I do love you. But I couldn't say yes." Now she does come close enough to touch, her hand reaching tentatively to rest on my knee. I consider shaking her off, but I don't. If the contact lets her get out what she has to say, then so be it. "I couldn't take that ring without you knowing what you're getting into."

I sigh. This again. "Magic, scary stuff, psychic shit. Got it. I'm one too. Can't escape what's part of me."

"You're not an addict."

I peer at her, trying to penetrate the darkness, find some meaning in her face. "What are you talking about?"

She pauses, biting her lower lip, then seems to come to some decision. "When I was a teenager, not long after my parents died, Chris was in a car accident."

My muscles tense and I go very still on the couch. She's never said anything about this. Neither has Chris.

"He would have died. I was young, untrained. I didn't have the power to save him. So I stole it."

"From where?" Gen has told me her gifts come from within and the world around her, nature. It's there for the taking. She doesn't have to steal anything.

Her voice breaks. "I didn't know where it came from. I just grabbed what was there, taunting me from the fringes, dangling like a lure. Chris lived. A stranger died." Her whole body shakes. I can't help it. I slide off the couch to sit beside her on the floor, place my arm around her, and pull her close, let her cry it out.

"You didn't know," I say when she quiets. It's not quite a question, not quite an assumption, but she shakes her head vigorously.

"I didn't. I swear." She looks up at me, eyes pleading with me to understand, very much like the young girl she must have been when it happened. I tuck a strand of hair behind her ear and mentally shake my head.

I'm so lost to her.

"But the damage was done, Flynn. I'd tasted dark magic, and I was hooked. I've got an… affinity for it. It likes me." She spits the words. "It's easy. And it feels good. So good." Her eyes drift shut, her lips curling in a blissful smile.

I know that smile. It's the one she wears when I make love to her. That does scare me.

Maybe there's something to this addict stuff. I never understood it, the ability to get hooked on alcohol or drugs, anything mind-altering. But this… she certainly sounds like a junkie.

And a little voice inside me wonders if I can handle this. I tell it to shut up.

"It took months for the wanting to ease. Years before I could trust myself to tap any power at all. I slowly built back my skills, learned control, made my career. And then you came along."

It isn't an accusation, but it hurts just the same.

Me. Me with my risky lifestyle, my dangerous career, and then Dead Woman's Pond.

"That's how you killed Leo," I say.

"And it started the cycle all over again. I'm hooked, Flynn. I'm hooked and I'm scared. If the Registry finds out, I'll be punished. I can't ask you to—"

"Stop. Just stop." I cover her mouth gently with my hand. "You didn't ask me. I asked you." And oh, how wonderfully well *that* went.

"You didn't have all the facts." The words are muffled by my palm, but I understand them. Under other circumstances, it would be funny.

"Don't need them. I'm with you. I'll get you through this. If the Registry comes after you, they'll have to come through me."

"They will," she says.

My grin is fierce. "They can try. Doesn't matter. We'll get through it together."

Gen pulls my hand away, forcing my gaze to meet hers. "I will *never* be through it. It will always be there. Always."

"Well then," I say, cupping her chin and leaning in close, "I guess you're stuck with me." I press my lips to hers, pouring all my love, my strength, and my determination into the kiss.

She resists at first; then her body melts into mine, her lips parting, letting me in to deepen the kiss further. Her arms go around my neck, pulling me so tightly against her we're like one person. When we part, we're both breathless, and I wipe away the tears I've held in since I got up here.

"The question is, will you let me make things official?" I pull out the ring, fingers trembling, just as nervous this second time around as I was the first, if not more so. No one is watching. Doesn't matter. Once bitten, twice shy.

"God, I love you." Gen takes the ring and slips it on her finger. "And you are absolutely, positively insane."

PULLING ME by the wrist, Gen drags me back downstairs. I haven't seen a mirror, but I can imagine what I look like: tearstained cheeks, red eyes. Gen is shoeless, her dress wrinkled from sitting on the floor.

We reach the edge of the pub's dance floor and stop, waiting. No one left. I still see our friends all around the bar. Chris must have asked them to stay a bit, see what happened. Some smile at us, more whisper to one another, speculating.

Whatever.

Gen said yes. That's all that matters to me. I'm practically ready to take flight with it.

When the current karaoke singer, one of the older ladies, spots us, she stops, just stops, halfway through her rendition of "Crazy" by Patsy Cline. She isn't one of the friends I had Chris invite, just an acquaintance, a karaoke regular who does the same song week after week, a permanent fixture of the place. Dan turns off the music, and she holds the microphone out to Gen, saying, "I think you need this more than I need to torture these folks with my singing."

Cautious laughter from the crowd. Nervous.

Gen takes the mic and pulls me with her to the center of the floor. I never, ever want to stand there again, but I will follow wherever she leads.

"Well," she says with a little laugh, "one more rumor for Festivity to spread. We should start our own reality show."

The chuckles from the audience sound more genuine this time. Chris steps out from behind the bar. I would swear there are tears in his eyes too.

Gen straightens her shoulders, sobering. Everyone falls silent. "I've always been the extrovert in this relationship. What Flynn did earlier, well, anyone who knows her knows it would have taken a miracle, and yet she did it, because she loves me. She's the kindest, bravest, most loyal and caring partner I could ask for. And I ran because I didn't think I deserved her."

Not quite the truth, but close enough. My cheeks flame, but I can't take my eyes from hers. She's radiant—running mascara, rumpled dress, and all.

"Fortunately for me, Flynn's also very persistent."

"You mean she's a stubborn ass," my boss, Tom, hollers from somewhere behind me. The crew guys shout their agreement. I guess they've all had a few... on the house, knowing Chris.

"Yes," Gen says, "but she's *my* stubborn ass." She holds up her free hand, its back to the assembled on-lookers, the ring gleaming on her finger.

The applause and screaming, whistling and cheering, threaten to deafen us all.

Yeah, I can be taught.

Lesson learned.

"CAN WE get out of here?" We danced, we kissed (in public, repeatedly, but for tonight I rolled my eyes and went with it), we drank too much beer. Gen sang a couple of karaoke numbers, off-key, including my favorite Pink song, "Sober," which she was far from. I even got up there with the construction crew for a ridiculous rendition of "YMCA" complete with hats they produced from somewhere, though I kept to the rear of the group despite their efforts to push me forward. I have a half-way decent singing voice, but Gen is the only person who gets to hear it, and then only in the car and the shower.

"Definitely," she says, swaying with me to Chris butchering "You've Lost That Loving Feeling." I think she'd be swaying, regardless. I'm the one thing standing between her and the floor.

I do a double take at the glint in her eyes, the I'm-going-to-rip-your-clothes-off look. Not sure she'll stay conscious that long, but hey, I'm game to try. Since the "adventures on the picnic table" episode, we haven't made love, and that plus her recent insistence on avoiding physical contact with me has built a lot of sexual frustration.

We slip out the back door. I scoop Gen into my arms under the pretense of protecting her feet from the asphalt. Her shoes are still in the apartment entry hall. Really, I'm making sure she doesn't fall down the stairs. I've had quite a few myself, but I'm bigger than she is, and I handle alcohol pretty well.

The whole way, she works on the buttons of my vest, then my shirt. Mild panic has me scanning the parking lot and the upstairs landing, but it's after two in the morning. No one around to see my girlfriend stripping me as we head home. I'm glad she doesn't drop the clothes she gets off me. I like this outfit.

In the entry hall, I set her on her feet, keeping one arm at her waist in case she falls. She tosses my shirt and vest into the living room, missing the couch, but who cares? I have to kick the front door shut because she's all over me, planting hot kisses across the tops of my breasts, hidden by my black sports bra. Her lips travel up to my shoulder blade, extra gentle around the snake bite scarring, then along the tendons in my neck. That's as far as she can reach, and she pouts prettily up at me, encouraging me to lean down to her.

I have something else in mind.

Taking a firmer hold on her waist, I lift her. I press her back against the nearest wall while she wraps her legs around me. Now she can reach my mouth just fine, and she takes full advantage of it, leaving me panting in the wake of her next kiss. I'm no slouch of a kisser, either, and she rocks her hips against me, a slow, steady rhythm that sends heat radiating through my bare arms, abdomen, and lower.

A shift of position brings one leg up between hers, making a sort of seat for her, my knee pressed hard into the wall, keeping her lifted. Pain jolts faintly up my extended right leg, a reminder that I'm not completely healed, but I lock the joint and keep it braced.

"So strong…," she breathes, running her hands over the taut muscles in my upper arms, then reaching around to massage my ass through my jeans. Here, her words don't embarrass me. They drive me harder to please her. She pauses to adjust the lower portion of her dress so it falls to either side of my upraised leg, then leans in to accept my next passionate kiss.

I press one palm against the wall to maintain my balance. The other slips between us, under her dress, and down into the waistband of her panties. When I find her center of pleasure, she moans against my mouth, writhing with no rhythm or coherence, pressing down on my leg and fingers as hard as she can manage.

This won't take long.

I try to draw it out as much as I can, but before I know it, she loses herself to my touch, head thrown back against the wall, lips parted, gasping my name, eyes closed.

When she opens them, they glow green.

I freeze a moment, then grab her with both hands, my grip tight on her waist. "Gen…."

"I can make you feel as fantastic as you just made me." It's her voice but not, a strange echoey, distant quality to it that ices the blood in my veins.

"That's… okay," I tell her. "I'm good."

"Yes. Yes, you are."

Something arcs between us, a jolt of energy spiking right to my core, and I groan with it. As aroused as I already am, it's almost unbearable, the wanting.

Tingling vibrations work their way inside me, and I groan again, louder this time.

But despite the pleasure, there's pain, too, and a building weakness, a lethargy in my limbs, a heaviness to my eyelids. I get the vibe she's pulling energy from me to feed it back to me in a different form—something I suspect ends up hazardous to my health.

"Stop it, Gen," I say between clenched teeth. "You don't need dark magic to make me do this. I just want you." Reaching deep, I *push* the feeling from me. It evaporates, leaving me aching in its wake.

She blinks, shakes her head, then focuses on me, the glow gone from her eyes. I ease her to the floor and wrap my arms around myself, trembling with frustration and need, trying to hide my desperation and failing. It took an act of sheer will not to accept what she was offering. Holy hell, if what I just experienced is how she feels when she uses the dark magic, it's no wonder she's hooked.

"Sorry," she whispers.

I pull her in close. "It's okay," I say with much more surety than I believe. "I never thought this would be easy. Now, let's do this without help." I take her firmly by the hand and lead her into our bedroom.

Chapter 63
A Woman's Home
Is Her Castle

I LIVE in a dead man's house with my girlfriend and a different dead man's dog.

Every time I think my life can't get any weirder....

The attorney for Leopold's estate showed up at our apartment about a month after his "heart attack." Everything he owned: the house, the orange McLaren, a bank account with a couple million dollars in it, he left to "whoever was with him at the time of his death."

Apparently Leo had no family and very few friends. Go figure.

After much investigation, the lawyers determined Gen and I were the beneficiaries of his estate—a circumstance that left her uneasy as hell and me holy fucking rich.

Chris and I had the place cleared out before Gen and I moved in. No sense risking exposure to another evil artifact like the charm or the crystal in the cabinet. We bought all new furnishings, set up a nice little tarot-reading space for her in the front sitting room and a fully-equipped gym/workshop for me where Leo's seance table used to be.

I like the castle-house, but I'm not sure about having Genesis live here.

Despite his dying threats, she says Leo's spirit can't touch this place, and by living on the property, she can make certain it stays that way with something she refers to as "wards" against his return. Using good magic will "cleanse the house," according to her. Despite her guilt over spending the money of a man she killed, she wants to do this.

So I'll keep an eye on her, and we'll take it one day at a time.

Katy, Max's former rescue dog, loves it. She got a cozy bed right next to ours, a slew of toys fit for twelve dogs, and the constant affection from all Gen's clients. Chris misses Katy, but he can visit whenever he wants. He kept her for me, pulling her out of another shelter where the cops investigating Max's death dropped her off. But he knew it was a temporary situation until I could finalize things with Genesis and talk her into looking at a bigger place. Never expected a mansion, but I'm flexible.

Even as I think about it all, lifting leg weights in the home gym to rebuild my muscle strength, Katy follows Genesis into the room. My first days back at the work site haven't gone well. I tire easily and come home wiped. It worries me, but I don't let on. Gen needs to focus on her own needs, not mine.

She has the mail in her hand, a bunch of letters and, oh God, is that a *Modern Bride* magazine? The thought of a big wedding with lots of people in attendance starts my stomach swirling, but I guess I should have seen this coming.

Then I raise my eyes to her face, which is much too pale.

I clank the weights down and stand, wiping sweat from my brow on a hand towel. "What's wrong?"

She holds out one of the envelopes, an ornate affair in ivory with a red wax seal on the back and calligraphied handwriting. It's been opened, so she already knows what it says. "From the Psychic Registry." Her voice wavers.

I swallow hard against the sudden tightening of my throat. If they found out about what she did to Leo, that she used dark magic again…. "Are you in trouble?" Somehow, I'll find a way to protect her. We can sell off Leo's house and car, liquidate everything, take off for some island in the Pacific.

I make contingency plans even as she says, "No. It's for you."

My brow furrows as I take the envelope from her chilled fingers, remove the card inside, and read:

> *Dear Ms. Dalton,*
> *It has come to our attention*
> *that you are in possession of a great*
> *talent, one the Registry would like*
> *to assess, document, and train. If*
> *you would please accompany Ms.*
> *McTalish to the Registry's annual*
> *convention the last weekend in Oc-*
> *tober, we will see to your proper au-*
> *thorization and establishment within*
> *the psychic community.*
> *Sincerely,*

Linda Argyle
Board President

Why do I get the feeling this isn't an invitation so much as a command performance?

The End
(to be continued in Book 2—Dead Woman's Revenge)

Keep Reading for an
Exclusive Excerpt from
Dead Woman's Revenge

By Elle E. Ire
Nearly Departed: Book Two

Coming Spring 2022 to
DSP PUBLICATIONS
www.dsppublications.com

Chapter 1
Heroes

EVERY TOWN has its heroes. Festivity, Florida, has three.

Their names are engraved on a concrete wall encircling a large tree at the center of town. The first is Simon, a teenager who dedicated the last years of his short, cancer-ridden life to funding and building a veterans' memorial in one of Festivity's many parks. I never met him, but I'm glad he has a memorial of his own.

The second name on the wall belongs to Charlie, the eighty-three-year-old crossing guard who threw himself at a kindergartner, knocking the child from the path of a speeding van and taking the fatal hit himself. Didn't know him either.

And the newest addition, is me, Flynn Dalton, immortalized with a bronze plaque for diving into Dead Woman's Pond at the edge of town and pulling a woman from her wrecked, sinking car. I did a lot more than that, actually, including a later scuba dive to the lake's bottom to retrieve a cursed charm that was drawing in all the vehicles in the first place. Town Hall doesn't know about that part. Regular folks, or nulls, as my girlfriend, Genesis, calls them, don't know about a lot of things, and we need to keep it that way.

I'm the only one of the three to be honored while still alive—a dubious distinction, I've come to believe.

Six weeks ago, when all this first happened, I would have declined the honor. Saving a life is what anyone would have done. Who would watch a woman drown and do nothing? Now, as I stand in the heat of a late August evening, looking down at the names, I accept hero status with a numbness that's become almost second nature to me.

Shit. I don't need a plaque, or free meals at the Festivity restaurants, or a ten percent discount at the kitschy little gift shops.

Not that I wouldn't have appreciated the complimentary food a couple of months ago, when I could barely make my pay-by-the-week hotel room rent. But now….

I rub the spot on my left shoulder where a water moccasin bit me during my scuba excursion—one of three bites, actually, all engineered by the evil asshole who made the charm and spelled the snakes, good old Leopold VanDean. Dead now, officially and incorrectly ruled natural causes—heart attack trying to save me from the same water moccasin bites. Good riddance.

My right leg twinges in sympathy with the shoulder. The one bite that healed completely is on my neck. Genesis took care of that, but she had to use dark magic to do it, and she killed Leo in the process. In her own way, she's as scarred as I am.

So yeah, I paid the price for my heroics, and I'm still paying. Gen doesn't know it, and I don't intend to tell her. I can hide pain pretty well. But my limp is getting worse, and my left arm's range of motion is deteriorating.

And every few nights, Gen awakens me with her sobbing.

I don't want a plaque or meals or discounts. I want our fucking lives back.

GENESIS TOSSED and turned, her afternoon nap disrupted by the nightmares. She helplessly gave in to their grasp, once again startled by the clarity, the detail, which made her wonder if these weren't mere dreams, but something else… punishment.

"How old is his sister?"

Genesis frowned, standing beside her brother's hospital bed, watching the artificially-induced rise and fall of his chest. The equipment noises and the thin partition curtain didn't drown out the voices beyond the plastic divider.

"Seventeen."

"Damn."

A social worker, and the hospital representative who'd called her.

"She's a senior in high school. They run a business together; parents left it to them, along with a lot of money."

"She can't run it by herself."

"No."

A choked sob escaped Gen's throat.

No, she couldn't run the Village Pub alone. (Would a minor even be allowed to try?) But she wasn't going to have to do that. Chris would recover. He had to.

"Not sure what we're going to do with her, or what she'll want to do with herself."

The two women stopped talking as more footsteps echoed on the tile floor. Visitors for the room's other occupant, an elderly woman who'd fallen down a staircase. She spent much of the previous night moaning and begging for God to take her. Gen listened from the room's easy chair, to that stranger on the other side of the curtain, wishing someone could ease the woman's pain, take away the sorrow of her family.

Someone other than Genesis. Because she had nothing to spare.

The hospital rep and social worker murmured a few comforting words to the other woman's relatives and left without pushing aside the partition to see Gen. Just as well. She would have told them to get out.

No, she would have told them to go to hell.

If she were stronger, trained, Gen could have done something. As it was, she'd poured all her magical energies into keeping Chris alive. Sudden Florida downpour, slippery asphalt, car accident. No one's fault.

Brain damage.

He could survive the broken leg, the cracked pelvis, the fractured collarbone. But he'd slipped into a coma and despite all the doctors' efforts, he hadn't come out of it. Too risky to operate with him in this state, and he needed that operation. They gave him one day, maybe two, before the rest of his body shut down.

They'd just lost their parents. She couldn't lose him, too.

Genesis sank into this side of the room's only chair. It crunched around her, brown faux leather with a foot panel that swung out if she pulled a lever. She could sleep in the chair. She had slept in it.

On the other side of the curtain, someone started crying—a child or a young woman. Grief was universal.

"I love you, Grandma."

Gen swallowed hard.

The grandmother didn't answer. She'd been in and out of consciousness since her arrival.

Afternoon wore into evening and evening into night. Gen sat beside the bed, holding Chris's hand, feeding him her energy to the brink of her own collapse. If she fainted, the staff would take her from his side, break the connection, end him.

She stood between her brother and death, and death was winning.

No more sleep. She even feared running to the restroom, certain the machines would scream their alarms if she went to relieve herself.

Like they were screaming now.

Gen jolted from her doze, sitting straight up, then standing while the heart monitor blared a steady, ominous note. Weak, dizzy, what good could she do? The respirators kept pumping, but his heart had stopped.

Chris's hand had slipped from her grasp while she slept, and she scrambled for it, pulling the cold flesh between her equally chilled palms in frantic desperation.

The door slammed open, doctors and nurses bursting through the narrow space, pushing a crash cart ahead of them. An orderly dragged her from Chris's side.

"No!" It came out as a squeak, a feeble protest unheard by the trauma staff. "You don't understand."

Sobs she'd kept in since the accident broke free, crippling and contorting her. Before the medical personnel could spare a moment to remove her from the room, she ducked into the attached bath and curled into a ball on the floor behind the cracked open door.

The doctors worked with fierce determination, injecting her brother with needles, administering shocks to his chest that made his frail body bounce on the mattress, then settle to complete stillness. After a long while, they shut off the alarms, the monitors, the breather which forced one last lungful of air into Chris with a dying hiss.

They packed their equipment, the wheels of the cart squeaking as they rolled it out the door.

"What happened to the girl?" a nurse asked.

"Ran off, I think,," an orderly responded. "She was very upset. I'll radio the other orderlies to keep an eye out for her."

Gen barely heard the words as they all left the room and the door shut. Above Chris's body, a glow formed, taking on a vaguely human shape, Chris's shape, separating itself from its corporeal shell.

"Get. Back. In. There," Genesis snarled, pushing herself up and stalking from the restroom to the bedside.

Other than the old woman beyond the curtain in the bed nearest the door, they were alone.

Chris's spirit hovered, still in contact with his physical form, but pulling away. Not solid enough for a conversation, but it had flickered when Gen issued her command, so on some level, it heard her. It understood.

It just couldn't obey.

If he couldn't go back into his body, she'd pull him back. Not knowing what she was doing, acting on instinct, Gen plunged her hands into the swirling glow. They vanished to her sight, hidden by the ephemeral form, her arms seeming to end at the wrists.

Genesis sucked in a sharp breath as emotions suffused her: anguish, regret, and a love so deep, so great, tears streamed down her face from the sheer force of it. Love for her. And the brother-sister bond they shared pulled taut, tethering the three of them: Genesis, the ghost, and the corpse.

"No!" she screamed, this time throwing all her self, all her remaining strength into reuniting Chris's body with his spirit.

Not enough.

Her heart pounded, racing, straining. Her breath hissed between her teeth as pain wracked her.

She sought other sources: the gardens outside, the approaching thunderstorms, all the good, the light, the energy Mother Nature kept in its reserve, but these were too far from her reach, and the ones she could tap, still not enough.

Her magic touched the electrical energy buzzing in the equipment all around her, filling the rooms of the ICU, the very walls themselves, but it felt wrong, did nothing, not natural. Perhaps if she'd been trained, she'd know how to make use of it, convert it, but the Registry had invited her for training and she'd declined—too soon after her parents' deaths, too desperate to be with Chris, to be near family, to help him reorganize and keep the bar and restaurant going, to finish high school with her classmates and maintain some degree of normalcy.

At the edges of her awareness, power nudged, teased, tingled. Strong power.

Green.

To her other sight, the green glow taunted, and she resisted. Green, she knew, meant bad, sickly, tainted. She didn't know how she knew; she just did. When she touched it, just a taste, it felt… corrosive.

Chris's spirit pulled farther from her, floating toward the ceiling, almost beyond the limits of her fingertips.

With a final moan of despair, Genesis thrust one hand behind her, out of Chris, toward the power source, and forced a conduit between them.

The energy passed through her, no longer sickly but invigorating, orgasmic in its pleasurable intensity. Her knees went weak.

The alarms blared once more, beeping and screeching, and she searched the room for the source. Not Chris. The doctors unplugged his equipment before they left.

The old woman.

Gen grabbed at the curtain with her already outstretched hand, throwing it aside with a zing of metal rungs across the metal bar. In the bed beyond, the grandmother thrashed weathered, wrinkled hands, her chest rising and falling irregularly while a pebbly wheeze issued from her gaping mouth.

Beside her, Chris gasped. His eyelids fluttered. His spirit sank back into his body.

And in that moment, Genesis realized what she'd done.

Like a recurring nightmare, the door burst open once more, the same trauma team swarming the room, moving her quickly and firmly to the far side of Chris's divider curtain and closing it to perform their life-saving—no, life-extending—methods on the elderly woman. But Genesis knew in her aching heart they'd be too late.

She peered around the curtain's edge at the woman's sunken facial muscles, devoid of animation, the filmy, blue eyes staring at the ceiling, focused on nothing.

Her ghost detached itself from her body, much more rapidly than Chris's, solidifying into a recognizable and stunningly beautiful, younger woman. She floated past the doctors and nurses still pumping, shocking, injecting, passed through the curtain, and settled into a regal pose before Genesis, one hand on a curvaceous hip.

The ghost flipped long, brown hair over a bare shoulder, her strapless evening gown in a style from a much earlier era flowing around her long, shapely legs. Jewelry sparkled on her wrists and about her neck, catching the overhead lights with an otherworldly brilliance.

"Two in one night. Cursed room," a large male orderly muttered from the curtain's far side. He wasn't far off the mark.

When Gen wished someone would ease the grandmother's pain, she hadn't intended this.

"This isn't what I wanted," Gen whispered. Behind her, cases clicked shut as the trauma team repacked their gear.

"It's what I wanted," the woman said, in a melodious voice incongruous with the cigarette-damaged rasp she'd used with her visitors. "I'm ready. Don't punish yourself." With a grateful smile, she disappeared.

Chris groaned, catching a doctor's attention—a resurgence of life, transferred from the old woman into Chris.

"My God," a nurse cried.

Orderlies shooed Genesis into the hallway while they reconnected the equipment. Shortly after they permitted her to return, Chris opened his eyes and focused on Gen, a slight grin curving his lips, which faded at her stricken expression.

She took his hand in hers, reassuring him while she swallowed bile.

Not a miracle. Not by a long shot.

The scene shifted, as scenes in dreams often did, to… the bedroom Genesis now shared with her girlfriend, Flynn, formerly Leo VanDean's bedroom. And how twisted was that?

He'd left the house and all of his assets to those with him at the time of his death, perhaps not considering that the beneficiaries might be the people who caused his death.

They'd cleared out the old furnishings: four-poster bed in dark cherry wood, elaborately carved armoire, dressing table (what straight guy owned a dressing table?), and antique full-length standing mirror. In their stead stood light maple furniture, flowered comforters, an easy chair in pastels, lace curtains. Gen had done the decorating; Flynn let her run with it.

The new looks helped disperse the lingering sense of Leo's presence.

Genesis rolled from the bed where she'd lain down for a quick nap—she hadn't been sleeping well since their struggles at Dead Man's Pond, though Flynn insisted on calling it Dead Woman's Pond—a more accurate name. A glance at the bedside clock got her moving faster. Flynn would be home from work soon, should have been home already.

She needed to make herself presentable before Flynn saw her. Matted hair, tear stains, and red-rimmed eyes weren't what she wanted Flynn to see.

Gen went to the mirror, picked up the hairbrush from the side table, and froze.

"Hello, Gen," Leo said, staring out at her from the glass, designer shirt and slacks perfectly pressed, smile wicked. "You pretended to be so good, clinging to your righteous indignation whenever I spoke of the dark powers. I always knew we were two of a kind."

GEN'S OWN sobs woke her. She sat up in the bed, staring across the room at a mirror that only reflected herself. Her heart raced, her breath coming in quick gasps. Third nightmare this week and becoming more intense.

She needed a break, before it broke her.

Her limbs trembled as she stood and moved to the window. No sign of Flynn's car—Leo's formerly orange McLaren that Flynn had immediately taken to be painted a more sedate metallic blue.

With the setting of the sun came concern. Flynn had come home later and later since she started back to work at the construction site a couple of weeks prior. Was Flynn avoiding her? Was she afraid of her? Flynn swore she wasn't, but….

She pulled her cell phone from the charger by the bed and dialed her brother.

"Yo, Gen!"

"Chris." Clinking dishware and loud conversation interspersed with cheering carried from the background. "Let me guess, game night?"

"Yankees vs. Red Sox. You're messing with fate, here."

Like many other rabid fans, Chris believed if he didn't watch every second of every inning on the huge flatscreens at the Village Pub, the Yankees would lose.

"Don't worry," Gen said, putting on her fake, cliche psychic voice, low and breathy, "they'll make a comeback in the ninth. You got Flynn down there?"

Flynn loved her seat at the corner of the patio bar, sipping her favorite Breckenridge Vanilla Porter and annoying Chris by rooting for whomever the Yankees played against.

"Hang on, Sis." Footsteps followed, then the creaking of a swinging door and a slam. The ambient noise faded with its closing. "Nope, not here. I'm out back. No sign of her car, either." A bit of a snicker on the last statement. Flynn loved the idea of a sports car, but the reality, and the attention that came with it, intimidated her. She'd be more comfortable behind the wheel of her old, now junked, pick-up truck. Chris's tone sobered. "You okay? You sound a little off."

Leave it to her brother to sense whatever she wanted hidden. Genesis sighed. "I'm fine, but she's not home, yet. I'm not her keeper, but I am a little worried."

Chris laughed. "Of course you're her keeper. You're engaged. Flynn just hasn't figured out her role in it, yet. I'll keep an eye out. Don't stress. I'm sure she'll be home soon, probably with a pizza and an apology."

Genesis hoped so. But she'd learned not to ignore her impulses.

Her impulses were screaming. Something bad was coming. Maybe not now, but soon.

ELLE E. IRE resides in Celebration, Florida, where she writes science fiction and urban fantasy novels featuring kickass women who fall in love with each other. She has won many local and national writing competitions, including the Royal Palm Literary Award, the Pyr and Dragons essay contest judged by the editors at Pyr Publishing, the Do It Write competition judged by a senior editor at Tor publishing, and she is a winner of the Backspace scholarship awarded by multiple literary agents. She and her spouse run several writing groups and attend and present at many local, state, and national writing conferences.

When she isn't teaching writing to middle school students, Elle enjoys getting into her characters' minds by taking shooting lessons, participating in interactive theatrical experiences, paying to be kidnapped "just for the fun and feel of it," and attempting numerous escape rooms. Her first novel, Vicious Circle, was released by Torquere Press in November 2015, and was re-released in January 2020 by DSP Publications. Threadbare, the first in the Storm Fronts series was released in August 2019 by DSP Publications, followed by its sequels--Patchwork and Woven, in 2020. To learn what her tagline "Deadly Women, Dangerous Romance" is really all about, visit her website: http://www.elleire.com. She can also be found on Twitter at @ElleEIre and Facebook at www.facebook.com/ElleE.IreAuthor.

Elle is represented by Naomi Davis at BookEnds Literary Agency.

ELLE
E.IRE

*Deadly Women,
Dangerous Romance.*

VICIOUS
CIRCLE

Assassin meets innocent.

Kicked out of the Assassins Guild for breach of contract, hunted by its members for kill-ing the Guild Leader, and half hooked on illegal narcotics, Cor San-dros could use a break. Down to her last few credits, Cor is offered a freelance job to eliminate a perverse political powerhouse. Always a sucker for helping the helpless, she accepts.

The plan doesn't include Cor falling in love with her employer, sweet and attractive Kila, but as the pair struggles to reach the target's home world, pursued by assassins from the Guild, Cor finds the inexplicable at-traction growing stronger. There's a job to do, and inti-mate in-volvement is an unwelcome distraction. Then again, so is sexual frustration.

www.dsppublications.com

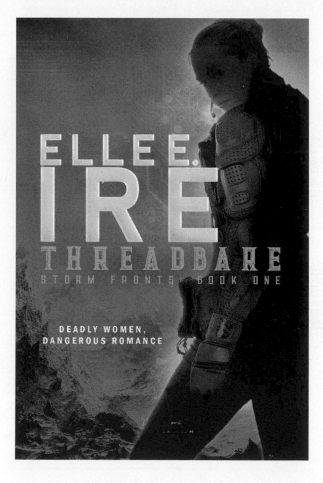

ELLE E. IRE

THREADBARE

STORM FRONTS: BOOK ONE

**DEADLY WOMEN,
DANGEROUS ROMANCE**

Storm Fronts: Book One

All cybernetic soldier Vick Corren wanted was to be human again. Now all she wants is Kelly. But machines can't love. Can they?

With the computerized implants that replaced most of her brain, Vick views herself as more machine than human. She's lost her memory, but worse, can no longer control her emo-tions, though with the help of empath Kelly LaSalle, she's holding the threads of her fraying sanity together.

Vick is smarter, faster, impervious to pain... the best mercenary in the Fighting Storm, until odd flashbacks show Vick a life she can't remember and a romantic relationship with Kelly that Vick never knew existed. But investigating that must wait until Vick and her team rescue the Storm's kidnapped leader.

Someone from within the organization is working against them, threatening Kelly's free-dom. To save her, Vick will have to sacrifice what she values most: the last of her humanity. Before the mission is over, either Vick or Kelly will forfeit the life she once knew.

www.dsppublications.com

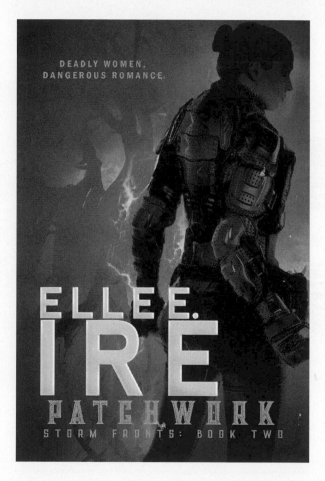

DEADLY WOMEN.
DANGEROUS ROMANCE.

ELLE E.
IRE

PATCHWORK
STORM FRONTS: BOOK TWO

Storm Fronts: Book Two

Empath Kelly LaSalle means everything to cybernetic soldier Vick Corren—and Kelly deserves a partner who can love her in a romantic way.

For the first time since receiving her robotic enhancements and an AI that makes her faster and stronger than the average merc, Vick thinks she can be that person.

Vick wants Kelly for life, and she'll do whatever it takes to be worthy. A holiday on a tropical planet seems the perfect time for Vick to demonstrate her commitment.

And she has big plans.

But the best intentions unravel when they're pursued by a rival mercenary company that wants Vick's technology—with or without her cooperation. A competitor for Kelly's affection is determined to tear them apart, and a lover from Vick's past has depraved plans of her own. Vick might not be able to save their lives without giving herself over to the machine she's trying so hard to transcend.

www.dsppublications.com

DEADLY WOMEN,
DANGEROUS ROMANCE

ELLE E. IRE

WOVEN

STORM FRONTS: BOOK THREE

Storm Fronts: Book Three

What if the mirror does reflect what's inside?

Mercenary Vick Corren is steadfast in her love for empath Kelly LaSalle. When it comes to her love of herself, not so much.

After an acidic-lake dunking on a distant moon shows Vick what's really beneath her synthetic skin, it doesn't matter that she heals. All she can see is the metallic shell of the soldier she once was. It's a cruel reminder that she's a cyborg. An AI. Less than human.

And that's not Vick's biggest problem. Her clone, the sadistic VC2, is on the loose and on the hunt. Her mission? Eliminate Vick and make Kelly her own.

Can Vick resolve her crippling identity crisis in time to defeat VC2—a terrifying version of herself that she might have been if not for Kelly's love?

www.dsppublications.com

For more
great fiction
from

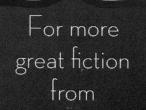

DSP PUBLICATIONS

visit us online.

WWW.DSPPUBLICATIONS.COM